*Medical instruments line the back wall of the tent: a canister of oxygen, a diagnostic cart, stacks of paramedic's bags, trays of cutting and injecting implements, and a trash barrel overflowing with drained ampoules and plasma bags. In the corner, a skeleton sits in a folding chair wearing the rags of a spattered white smock. A surgical mask hangs around the neck bones, and a head wrap still clings to the skull. An injector rests in its bony lap.*

*Beckert looks in the trash barrel and selects one of the empty ampoules.*

Morphine.

*Every glass phial reads the same. He tosses the one he holds back to the barrel where it clatters noisily, and he stares at the seated surgeon.*

*"Guess you saved the last for yourself."*

*Beckert leaves the tent, confronting death on a scale he cannot comprehend. From the platform looking out, almost all of the skeletons are slumped in the same direction, facing him. Their thin bones reach over one another as though the dying were dragging themselves across the dead, all to reach the medical tent for a painless release from life...*

# BLACK HAWKS FROM A
# BLUE SUN

# BLACK HAWKS FROM A
# BLUE SUN

# F. ALLEN FARNHAM

CADRE ONE PUBLISHING
SALEM, MA 2010

CADRE ONE PUBLISHING, LLC.
(WWW.CADREONEPUBLISHING.COM)

COPYRIGHT © 2010 BY F. ALLEN FARNHAM
ALL RIGHTS RESERVED.

LIBRARY OF CONGRESS CONTROL NUMBER: 2010905462

SOFTCOVER ISBN : 978-0-982-71160-6

**This book was produced *entirely* in the United States of America.**

Cadre One Hawk and Angry Ghost Image by Bob Cram, Jr.
(www.bobcram.com)

Photograph of Earth obtained from National Aeronautics and Space Administration (NASA), Image ID AS11-44-6692, "Close-up of Earth and Terminator", Apollo 11. Used with permission.

B&W image *Argo, Beckert, and Thompson* by Marek Okon
(www.okonart.com)

# CONTENTS

*To Mike L, Tom W, Cam C and Toby N for the honesty only true friends provide*

*And especially to my parents, David and Carole Farnham, for the immeasurable support*

# THE ORIGINS OF *CADRE ONE*

The facility was small, almost insignificantly so. Not that a mining camp needed to be large. This wasn't a sprawling Colony like New Bangalore, or New Dresden. There were no crops to grow, no cattle to graze. Here, there was only metric tonnage to be scraped up and hauled off. And when you're 8.6 Light Years away from home, efficiency is to be admired.

Soshiba Varicorp (SoVar) prospectors had sifted the system decades earlier, marking a crater on an otherwise unremarkable asteroid as an Economically Viable Strike. The description was comically understated, of course. Once mining crews arrived, they found a crater saturated with Platinum, Rhenium, Iridium, and Rhodium. Economically viable, indeed.

Skilled men and women of *SoVar Mineral Extraction* got right to work. They bored through the crater walls, surveying, analyzing, and reinforcing along the way. Ore yields were high—too high, in fact, to comfortably enjoy their success. Pirates were as real in the Black as they were on the seventeenth century Barbary Coast, and just a whiff of a strike this rich would draw them in, gunning.

Working fast was their best means of coping with that fear, so they erected enormous solar collectors at the asteroid's edge to keep the smashers and smelters running around the clock. SoVar promised well-armed contractors were en route and, when they finally arrived, gave mining crews their first real breaks in years.

Low gravity made it easier to sling ore around, but thick,

clunky mining suits were cumbersome. Getting in and out of them was no picnic, either, as miners had to ride a tether up to the freighter or its tender at the end of every shift, get sprayed off one at a time, then slog to maintenance and turn the suit in for recharge. The process could take hours.

Miners begged, cajoled, and eventually demanded shelters on the ground so they could suit up and walk right out to the job site. Where the strike had already delivered quota-plus yields with unknown resources still waiting to be found—and a work stoppage was out of the question—bosses acquiesced. The ring-shaped mining tunnels would be finished and pressurized then modern conveniences installed for daily living.

With most building materials available locally, basic structures were complete in a couple of weeks. Food and life support equipment was transferred from the tender on station, since it would remain as long as the mining crew remained. The rest arrived in the next freighter along with technicians to install them: hydraulics, cabling, computers, medical equipment, and a few extra luxuries to make the years away from home worthwhile. Once all the seals were tight and the machines were calibrated, miners took occupancy.

Then the easy money dried up. Beneath the crater's ore-rich surface was only hard gray stone. So they looked out across deep seas of frozen methane and water on the asteroid's perpetual night side. Prospecting tools mapped out trace metals, extending from the crater like rays, but not in sufficient quantities to be worth clearing the ice first. So they went back to their tunnels and drilled four evenly spaced exploratory shafts.

After 150 meters of vertical descent, all they had to show were broken drill bits and hard gray rock, proving that all of the good ore had smashed into this place via meteorite. There was nothing left to find. There was no more reason to stay.

Packing up and hauling out the machines they had just installed would have been more costly than leaving them in place. So the Project Manager made a strict line item decision on the balance sheet and shuttered the new construction, entirely. Workers packed up the final ore shipment and rode home on the last freighter.

The facility remained abandoned for decades. After all, who cared about a tiny place so far from home with nothing of value around it? Why bother with a place no one knew about but the crews who worked it, a place in a sterile and hostile environment so far away from shipping lanes? It remained invisible but not forgotten. For when SoVar was approached for a project that required the *ultimate* in secrecy—a place where civilian oversight must be *completely* avoided—they saw cause to re-open that distant facility.

The Covert Accelerated Defense Research (CADRe) Project never appeared on any Defense budget, and funding was enormous. There was no bid process—the award silently fell to the only company large enough to manage an operation of this scale: Soshiba Varicorp. Materiel could always be diverted discreetly, but the kind of research military brass wanted could not be accomplished by machines. The most talented researchers would have to participate willingly. And anyone who *refused* an offer could not be trusted to keep that secret.

To ensure fidelity, SoVar executives psychologically profiled their candidates, assessing who would be most likely to accept the conditions required. Armed with accurate profiles, stupendous compensation packages, and threat of liquidation for refusal, SoVar executives assembled exactly the team they wanted with a minimum of breakage.

Great care was taken to ensure the facility remained hidden. Regular supply trains could draw unwelcome attention, so the station was updated with state of the art life support and recycling machines. Transmissions of any kind from the site were expressly forbidden. A permanent garrison was installed, and the exploratory shafts—drilled in search of valuable ore—were fitted with potent weapons should any unwelcome visitor come calling. Such devotion to obscurity became the enclave's saving grace.

As an alien foe burned its way through the colonies to Earth, enclave researchers listened to transmissions from ships fleeing the destruction. Calls were desperate, overlapping, frantic, terrified. They ended one by one, as if a row of circuit breakers were being flipped, until they ceased altogether. For months after, researchers scoured the channels but found only garbled alien noise and static. Earth and her colonies were gone.

Researchers turned to one another, grappling with the enormity of being the last of their kind. There would be no more transports. Local resources could carry them for a while; but food, air, and water systems required constant maintenance. Spare parts would have to be fabricated on site. So the survivors set about renovating their limited spaces to accommodate anticipated needs. Building replacements from scratch proved harder than anyone imagined, and work schedules grew long under the load.

For months they labored, enhancing their meager (and now permanent) accommodations. When they believed they had the toughest problems solved, however, the worst one of all revealed itself—out of the full staff and garrison of eighty, only six were female. Relationships strained under wanted and unwanted attentions. Touches and gropes escalated to a brutal personal assault. In the absence of God or government, jealousy had turned murderous.

All assembled to view the body and to witness the crime of passion bludgeoned into it. A shockwave passed through them as they confronted the violence of her death and the chilling possibility that they, the last survivors of humanity, might drive themselves to extinction. The enclave's only law was formed at that moment as a warning to any who would repeat such a barbaric act: "Anyone who harms, or allows to be harmed, another human is a threat and must leave." The murderer was banished from the outpost in a small container to die alone in deep space.

With no way to resolve the imbalance of gender, such passions remained a clear and present danger. Many feared it was only a matter of time before it happened again. So CADRe researchers returned to their performance enhancement experiments and crafted a pharmaceutical to blunt libidinal drives.

Libidinal inhibitors had an unexpected, yet welcome, side effect of diminishing emotion, as well. Users of the drug felt less bound by depression, loss, anxiety, and fear. Without such distracting thoughts, the surviving enclave was better able to focus on what was practical. The formula was added to food synthesizers. Productivity soared.

For a time, resources held out. Life support systems were well made and kept a high efficiency. For the inevitable losses in recycling, a sea of ice surrounded them—rich with water and the organic building blocks for nutrients. Limitations of reproduction were clear, however. With so much health risk to the few women, and their inability for strenuous work during pregnancy, natural childbirth was no longer an option.

Animal vivisection labs had long ago fallen to disuse. (A sad truth at the end of civilization is that people will do almost anything for scarce luxuries; and, given that animals taste better than what you can coax out of a synthesizer, it wasn't long before all of the untainted breeding pairs had been eaten.) The lab was also one of the most secure locations in the facility, due to the fact that viral products of their research were *extremely* dangerous. Thus, it was decided the lab would be repurposed as a human incubation chamber for future generations. With focus and determination, a retrofit was made.

Despite good planning and diligence, however, batch after batch of mutated embryos had to be culled from each crop. A shallow gene pool, aggravated by chromosome breakage from the blue-white star's radiation, produced rampant defects in every embryo. If there was any hope of humanity continuing, they needed to offset the mutations faster than they occurred. With the same dispassionate determination, they applied their genetic enhancement experiments to their own children.

The new breed benefited from enhanced musculature, acute senses, sharp intellects, lightning reflexes. But in blundering through the genome, researchers decanted many who were crazed, autistic, or psychopathic. These individuals were lobotomized to recover, at the least, their labor potential. With additional experimentation, the enclave learned how to integrate small chipsets into the lobotomized brains, which could be programmed with menial tasks. These "reconstitutes" become the lowest echelon in a newly stratifying society.

Free from any kind of oversight or moral restriction, the enclave expanded on the syntheses of man and machine. After years of experimentation, they were ready to attempt integrations with healthy brains—the progenitors of Cadre Geeks.

Art, music, and literature were left aside in the pragmatic march of daily life. New machines required new programs to operate, cramping the already-stuffed storage racks. Data on life outside the enclave became unaffordable indulgence, even data on their home world, Earth. With storage space so limited and the scale of their new designs so large, data not immediately required for survival was crowded from the system. Efforts were made to preserve Earth's memory by verbal tradition, but each generation inherited a greater workload from the previous. Less class time was devoted to the verbal passage of memory in favor of more practical instruction.

The senior officer of the enclave watched the effect on his people, saw how (despite the emotional leveling of inhibitors) they were losing themselves in longing for Earth and its reminders of a better life. He decided such distractions were ultimately counter-productive, and he ordered any remaining data on Earth and the colonies destroyed. "There is no more Earth," he explained. "No reason it should still be getting in our way." After an extended period of grieving for what all understood could never be, productivity increased.

The senior officer maintained a basic file for himself and for future leaders of the CADRe facility that, should the opportunity arise, they might someday return. Over time the file was repeatedly lost to system errors or failures, and had to be rebuilt from human memory. Each time, details became abstracts; facts became approximations. Soon there was no point to maintaining any file at all, and the knowledge became a verbal tradition, passed from one leader to the next: *We come from a place called, 'Earth', and if the opportunity comes, it is our duty to return.*

For generations, the outpost endured by enhancing their recycling processes and by scraping resources from the rocky asteroid. Yet it was clear the supply would not last forever. Eventually, someone would have to leave the enclave and collect more.

But how? From where?

The enclave's telescopes turned toward deep space and searched. Every time they found an object of interest, the enemy was near, and the frustrated people argued at length over what should be done.

Gradually, they realized alien ships were the best targets of all, abundant with machinery, fuel, life support, nutrients. Driven by the specter of starvation, production turned toward the new goal of capturing and collecting an alien vessel. The project was vast, requiring solutions to myriad problems: how to detect a fast-moving target, transport to the target and intercept, how to get inside the ship quickly, how to overwhelm the crew and take control, how to pilot the ship home, and how to do all of this without the enemy getting word out that humans still exist.

Capturing an enemy ship meant risking lives, and there was no misunderstanding that discovery by the aliens meant extinction. So the enclave planned carefully, anticipated every contingency they could conceive, designed a non-reflective transport, devised tactics, trained the best of their genetically-enhanced offspring, and equipped those soldiers with overwhelming firepower.

At long last, a team of three highly specialized soldiers (designated Gun, Geek, and Brick) was dispatched to wait along a deep-space lane of travel. The Geek (an advanced synthesis of human brain and computer) was the software expert, able to link into networks and program them at the speed of thought. The Brick, with a hulking frame and brutal strength, was the remover of obstacles, demolitions expert, medic, and repair technician. The Gun, tall and commanding, was the weapons and tactics specialist, leading the team with unquestioned authority.

When a bulk freighter passed within range, the soldiers awoke from cryogenic suspension and pursued in their non-reflective craft. They studied the freighter exhaustively, listening for transmissions, pinpointing the source of broadcast, seeking a penetration point, and watching for enemy activity in the vicinity. Once all was set, they activated a broad-spectrum interference generator, bored through the hull, eliminated the crew, and piloted their quarry home.

Enriched by supplies from the captured ship, the enclave was sated. In time, however, these resources ran low, and it became necessary to collect again.

The enclave had grown.

CADRE ONE

# PART THREE

# SUOVETAURILIA

A gentle tone cycles from low to high.

Thompson's eyes roam behind their lids until the lids part
like tearing tissue paper. He blinks hard, driving the haze from
his vision, and takes in numerous control panels surrounding him.
Screens, interfaces, and consoles are illuminated in soothing green.
Disorientation is fleeting, and memory rushes back to him.

*The mission...Earth...we must be close*, he thinks.

A hint of frost covers Thompson's armor, and he watches it
sublimate in a line down his torso then out to his limbs. Fingers and
toes tingle with restored sensation. He braces for the surge of fire
that always follows but it does not come. A brief shudder passes
his length and little else. There is no searing of nerve endings, no
partially thawed arm to fix, no period of bewilderment.

*Something's wrong*, he thinks. *I feel...good.*

He holds his breath with eyes shut, still waiting for that brutal
shock, until he can hold it no longer. The cabin's cold dry air makes
him cough.

"Good morning, Major," says a voice to his left.

Thompson rubs his face and looks at a young man in the pilot
seat. Light absorbing armor covers him up to his neck. A large
headset rides on his crown, ending just above his ears. Goggles
cover his eyes and they flash with scrolling code.

"Morning, Geek." Thompson flexes his arms and yawns, still

marveling at how good he feels.

A *clang* to Thompson's right draws his attention, and he sees Argo leaned forward in his recliner, big hands clamped around the rails. The Brick's eyes are crushed shut and his teeth are bared in anticipation of agony.

Amused, Thompson watches Argo's hard-set expression dissolve into confusion. The Brick releases the recliner rails and stares into his hands, flexing them over and over. He clears his lungs and looks at his comrades.

"What the…?"

"Better than usual?" Thompson asks.

Argo blinks at the phenomenal understatement. "Yeah. Usually, waking from cryo's like being electrocuted in molten iron. This was...*pleasant*."

The Gun runs hands down the recliner rails in appreciation. "Finally found something the Colonists are good at."

"Morning, Lieutenant," Beckert calls from across the cabin.

Argo nods back. "Sergeant."

Thompson reaches to his console and enters a code. Multiple holographic windows project above it. "How long've you been awake, Geek?"

"Twenty-two hours, fifty-three minutes."

"Why so long?"

"Reconnaissance, sir. None of our planned landing sites are accessible, so the ship woke me early."

"*None* are accessible? Reason?"

"Colonist maps are, uh, *inaccurate*."

Thompson pulls up an external view on his console and a three-dimensional globe renders above it. Green and brown landforms float amid vast blue expanses. Cyclonic smears of white wrap the globe from pole to pole. He squints.

"What's different about it?" the Gun asks.

"Landmasses are smaller," Beckert reports, "and oddly shaped. Looks like they sank. Or the oceans rose. One or the other."

"Oceans..." Thompson's mind staggers at the thought. *Cadre*

*One has stores of one million liters, carefully conserved via
recycling and collection, but the combined volume of Earth's oceans
is over a* trillion billion *liters...we'd never run out...*

He sweeps the thought aside and pulls up a second globe in an
adjacent holowindow. On it, he projects the Colonist map of Earth
then slides it onto the live view, aligning them so the continents
overlap. The merged globes prove what Beckert described: the
coastlines have all retreated.

Thompson keys his console, plotting sites of interest marked
for investigation. Hundreds of red dots appear along the edges of
continents, almost all of them now offshore and under meters of
water. He sits back in his recliner, dismayed.

"Major, I'm also tracking eight-hundred forty-seven objects in
orbit." The Geek sends data to Thompson's console, and hundreds
of indigo points populate around the holographic globe. "Most are
only a few meters long. Satellites, probably. But we've got a cluster
of larger vessels. One is nearly two kilometers long. Seems to be
the focus of activity."

"Show me," Thompson orders.

Beckert highlights a dense cluster of blue dots above the globe
and magnifies them. At the center is an oblong vessel with a blunt,
squared-off bow. It thickens toward the middle then tapers slightly
before flaring to its widest at the stern. Long bulges press out from
the hull, close together yet not overlapping, giving the entire vessel
a muscular appearance.

Thompson fixates on the enormous vessel, admiring its
polished curves. "That one's almost twice the size of the *Europa*."
Then his eyes fall on the ring of companion ships around it. Though
over six hundred meters long themselves, they seem dwarfed by
comparison.

"What are these ships around the big one? Are they in our
catalog?"

Argo studies configurations in his console, comparing and
contrasting against what he sees in Thompson's screen. "Looks
like a variant of a heavy cruiser class, but the silhouette is different.

These have long struts at the bow and broader sterns. Must be a new model."

Thompson rubs his chin. "Keep up your analysis. See what you can find out."

"Aye, sir."

"Geek, do we have a landing site?"

Beckert turns, looking at the Gun through streams of code in his goggles. "I'd welcome suggestions, sir."

Thompson contemplates the large ship with its escorts. Hundreds of tiny vessels swarm around them, ferrying back and forth between other large ships in the area and the planet below. The target-rich environment intrigues him, but, with all the military hardware present, he knows it would be a short-lived visit.

"What do you think's going on?" Argo asks. "Mineral collection? Military mobilization?"

"No idea," Thompson admits, still gazing at the screen. "But it's something big."

The Gun shifts focus to the continent below the orbiting vessels. It is by far the largest of all the planet's landmasses, stretching from daybreak to dusk on the planet's sunlit side. Red dots are scattered generously across the interior, particularly to the extreme west and east; but Thompson scowls.

*No way we'll be able to approach these without getting spotted...*

He spins the globe and studies landmasses on its far side. A large northern continent extends from ice-shrouded islands near the pole, through broad plains and north-south mountain ranges, to a narrow isthmus near the equator. Below, another large continent quickly widens from the isthmus then tapers toward the southern pole, narrowing to a curved horn at its tip. Few red dots mark the edge of the southern continent.

With the flick of a finger, Thompson rotates the globe back to the northern continent.

"Geek, you've been up almost a full day. Did you capture data on the planet's far side?"

"Aye, Major," Beckert answers. "Sending to your console now."

Before the Gun's eyes, the globe updates and coastlines shrink inward. The southern continent retains its same basic shape, but the northern continent changes dramatically. Peninsulas, river deltas, lowlands and islands recede or disappear entirely. A large section of the western coastline disappears at a geologic fault. And a long promontory of land at the southeastern corner is completely submerged. Even so, red dots pepper the interior of the landmass, leaving a wide assortment from which to choose.

"Do we have data on enemy settlements?"

"Affirmative," Beckert answers, and hundreds of new points on the globe appear in white. They form a thick band in the tropics of the planet, every settlement located on the present shorelines.

"So *many*...they really dug in." Thompson's eyes drift over the globe as he spins it back and forth. "Seems they prefer low latitudes...warm, wet environments. Interesting..."

"Sir," Beckert calls, "once we hit atmo, we'll be visible and any course corrections will give us away. If we hope to simulate a random meteor, we need to select a landing site right away."

Thompson stares hard into the globe, rotating it pole to pole, magnifying and minimizing areas in his search. Then he opens an adjacent window and instructs his console to remove any location currently underwater. Nearly all of the red dots disappear. Next, he instructs his console to delete any point of interest that is within ten kilometers of an enemy settlement. Of the few red dots remaining, most disappear. Last, he directs his console to prioritize remaining sites by terrain with natural cover and proximity to mission-essential objectives.

One red dot glimmers on the coast of the northern continent, roughly half way up the eastern seaboard. A line extends from it to a secondary window where matched criteria are listed: government center, complex infrastructure, dense population center, multiple military installations, and numerous cultural sites. The nearest enemy settlement is over thirty kilometers to the south.

He enlarges the area and finds a mountain range with multiple folds and valleys less than a hundred kilometers northwest. Thick vegetation blankets the ridged terrain.

"Geek, set co-ordinates forty degrees north latitude, seventy-eight degrees west longitude. Bring us down into one of the valleys. Should find some good cover there."

"Copy that, Major." Beckert's goggles pulse and the craft thrusts to its new trajectory.

As he waits, Thompson switches his rendered globe to real time view. A swirling orb, bright with yellow sunlight, hangs magnificent and inviting. Though the planet is distant, sudden urgency puts him off balance.

*Our ancestral home—lost for centuries, forgotten as an unattainable dream. It's right here, right in front of me...*

His analytical mind can easily dissect the forces at work in the cyclonic weather systems, yet there is something greater than the sum of the planetary constituents. If anyone asked, he would be at a loss to describe the unusual sensation, except to say it is familiar. Like when the Counselor tried to explain the concept of art during the *Europa*'s long voyage to Cadre One...

*For hours, Thompson watched the Counselor display image after image of flawed, low-resolution depictions. Some were humans dressed in bizarre outfits, engaged in pointless unproductive activities. Other images were of buildings, or earthly landscapes, old sea vessels and the like. True, there was some appreciable skill in rendering such images by hand, but why bother? A photo was millions of times more accurate and required only milliseconds to produce.*

*The Counselor shook his head again and again, frustrated. He pushed back from the console and chewed his lower lip, studying his obstinate pupil. Suddenly, he leaned forward and summoned an image as if to punish his student.*

*"Let's see what you think of this one!"*

*The Counselor pulled up a black and white image titled, "*Ascending and Descending*" by M. C. Escher. Atop a square building, a staircase connected at all four corners with several pedestrians climbing and descending. Thompson folded his arms and scoffed until he noticed the stairway continued infinitely up or down, depending on direction of travel.*

*"But...that's impossible."*

*He leaned forward and stared at the visual paradox. Lines of perspective on each leg of the staircase were correct. Even the support structure of the building below was accurate.*

*"This can't be!"*

*"Well, there it is, Thompson. What do you think of that?"*

*"I... I don't know what to think."*

*"But you* feel *something, don't you?"*

*Thompson tried to blank his expression, yet the perplexed fascination was still there.*

*The Counselor's shoulders rounded as if a great weight was removed. "That,* my friend, is the *purpose* of art.*"*

Thompson smiles at the memory. It proved a gateway to appreciating form without function, the acknowledgment of beauty. As deep a revelation as it was, it was not nearly so profound as this vibrant planet growing ever nearer.

"Gun," Argo calls, "I need you and Geek to lie back in your recliners a moment."

Thompson stirs from his recollections. "Sure."

Beckert sits back into his recliner, as well, and Argo runs comprehensive diagnostics on them both. All the while, the image of Earth grows larger in Thompson's screen.

"All right," Argo announces, "looks good."

Thompson turns to the young Geek. "Any contacts in our flight path?"

"Already accounted for, Major. We'll approach over the northern polar region and hit atmosphere over land. That'll put the fewest enemy eyes on us during descent."

The Gun stares at the globe compulsively. "Brick, are you saving data?"

"Affirmative," the big man replies. His large hands dance over his console, pouring data streams into his docked labset: topography, magnetic field, atmospheric aerosols and gaseous composition, gravity, density, temperature, every bit of information the craft's sensors can convey.

"Final course correction and deceleration on my mark…" Beckert's goggles pulse with instruction. "Three…two…one… *Mark*."

The cabin buzzes and small blue sparks pop at console edges as inertial damping envelops them. More than just weightless, Thompson feels *insubstantial* like a cloud of molecules in an electrically charged hologram. He ponders what would happen if he moved—if he might drift apart like smoke—then applies his full concentration toward remaining still.

Beckert triggers the final braking maneuver, slowing the craft from seventy-five thousand kilometers per second to fifteen. Such radical deceleration should have smashed them to quarks, Thompson knows; but there is no tactile indication anything has happened, other than the projected globe over his console grows less quickly than before.

Inertial damping dissipates, normal feeling returns, and the Gun lets out a held breath. Shaking his head, he says, "I'm never gonna get used to that."

"Popping orbital relay. Jettisoning main drive," Beckert advises. The craft jolts with a muffled *boom*. "Course set. Atmospheric interface in ten seconds."

The planet now fills Thompson's holowindow, save a curve of horizon at the top. Enormous islands slide gracefully below. On larger islands, rivers thread like veins across white and brown landscapes.

"Nine...eight...seven..."

On the flattening horizon a vast inland bay appears, extending over a thousand kilometers in all directions.

"Six...five...four..."

Thompson looks over at Argo, but the Brick continues his work, too busy to appreciate the magnificent view.

"Three...two...one...*Interface*."

Thompson braces for another jolt. Instead, there is only eerie calm and a slight pinkish-orange glow surrounding his holowindow like an aura.

"Hull temp crossing six-hundred degrees," Beckert announces.

Thompson remains glued to the screen as the glow intensifies. The image crackles, nearly breaking up before restoring itself.

"Eight-hundred degrees..."

Argo moves with speed, saving last bits of data on the system's yellow sun before they dip to the planet's night side.

"One thousand degrees..."

Buffets of wind rock the craft.

"Trim angle of attack holding...TPS tiles intact. Hull temp thirteen hundred degrees..."

A gentle *whoosh* of air grows louder and buffeting sways the men in their recliners.

"Sixteen hundred..." Beckert states with raised voice.

Out of habit, Thompson punches up the basic indicators of ship systems. From stem to stern, everything is green bars. When he goes back to real time view, all he gets is static. Punching keys only yields the same result.

He looks over at Argo and sees the Brick sitting patiently in his recliner, fingers interlaced across his torso. His labset is no longer docked on the console.

"Argo, why can't I get video?"

"We're surrounded by plasma," the big man explains. "It's affecting our sensors. We should be out of it in a few minutes, but..."

"But, what?"

Argo grimaces. "We're visible to anyone looking. Might as well be sending out a *beacon*."

"Z-minus five minutes," Beckert calls over the roaring wind.

"Roger that." Thompson closes his video screen and opens a new one. The computer renders an image of their craft, which resembles a teardrop cut in half with three bulges on the flat side. From a sidebar he selects, *Initiate and prime crash systems*.

The image rotates to the flat side of the craft, highlights three bulges in yellow, and queries, *Arm crash pod ejection system?*

*Confirm*, he selects, and the three pods flash from yellow to red.

Thompson leans back in his recliner and tightens his harness. "Lock in!"

Argo checks his equipment one last time then clicks into his restraints. Beckert does the same.

Buffeting becomes severe, and Thompson shouts over it, "Sealing crash pods. Switch to helmet mic and confirm hard seal."

From both sides, thick walls of his pod rise to the low ceiling and latch tight with a *hiss*. The Gun swallows to equalize pressure in his ears.

"*Hard seal confirmed*," Argo radios.

"*Hard seal confirmed*," Beckert echoes.

"Close faceplates and stand by."

Thompson slides his face mask down then rocks gently in his recliner, contemplating his destination.

*Beyond this pod is our ancient home, an entire planet where we once numbered in the billions...a place where people breathed without life support, ate and drank what the land produced for them. Incomparable surplus of an easy life...*

*The things we could build here...once we clear out the intruders.*

"*Z-minus one minute*," Beckert warns.

Thompson shakes himself, amazed how quickly the minutes passed. "Maintain radio silence after ejection. Once you're on the ground, police up your gear and vaporize your pod, then converge on me."

*"Aye, sir."*

*"Aye, sir."*

Thompson's mind focuses and he draws slow, deep breaths to prepare for the imminent g-forces of ejection. Centered and ready, he sways in his recliner.

*"Three...two...one...MARK."*

Explosive *clangs* ram from below and Thompson is crushed back into his recliner. Violent, roaring wind surrounds him as the pod tumbles end over end. It shifts and wobbles in its race toward the ground, spinning the Gun in his gimbaled restraints. Hydraulics whine in the cramped space, pushing out long-finned air brakes, and the pod abruptly halts its tumbling. Thompson spins once more in his gimbals before settling, choking down bitter fluid at the top of his throat.

"Just like simulation," he mutters.

The Gun taps at keys of his console, occasionally missing in the buffeting of free fall. Holo-screens display an image of his egg-shaped pod with an altimeter racing down past ten thousand meters. The bottom third of the pod highlights with a caption that queries, *Ballast Purge?*

Thompson smacks a flashing red button and another staccato *clang* echoes through the pod. The entire bottom of the egg, containing heavy life support and cryogenic machinery, drops away. His pod lurches with deceleration and curves into steeper descent. Then he feels a sharp *thump* against the hull, confirming the ballast has detonated as intended.

Three narrow booster nozzles highlight at the bottom edge of his pod diagram. Thompson cycles a switch on the left of his console and nozzles flash from yellow to red. *Landing Thrusters Armed*, the caption reads.

Wind shrieks outside as the altimeter ticks below one thousand meters. He draws a breath through gritted teeth and mashes the button.

Thrusters ignite, slamming the Gun into his recliner, flattening his chest, and stretching the skin of his face. The pod shudders with phenomenal intensity, then, just as suddenly, the thrust ends. Hydraulics bray again as air brakes retract into the pod, but the altimeter reads, *50 meters.*

*Thrusters worked too well...I'm too high!*

Thompson gasps as the pod drops and drags him down with it. *This is gonna hurt...*

Hands clamp recliner rails. Breathing quickens.

The pod punches through forest canopy, slams sideways into a rocky outcropping, and ricochets down a forested slope. Young trees snap at the trunk but old trees shrug the pod aside, brutalizing its occupant. Seams in the outer shell rip, spraying the interior with dirt. There is a harsh jolt from below as if launched from a ramp, and the egg is falling again. With a deafening *crack*, one side collapses inward and the recliner breaks loose. The pod rolls over once more and comes to rest. Water sloshes in from below.

Thompson's eyes dance in their sockets. Delayed bolts of pain explode through his head as he struggles to catch his breath.

A lightning-blue spark surges at the bottom of the pod, and the few functioning lights whiff out. In darkness, a single silvery beam penetrates the egg through a split seam overhead. Seen through his auto-compensating lenses, the ray shines like gleaming metal, casting an ethereal glow around it. For a moment he lies in the wreck of his pod, listening to the hiss of steam and watching smoke swirl in that brilliant shaft of light.

*Alive...I'm on the surface!*

He clears restraints and pushes out of his recliner, feet plunging into shin-deep water.

*Find Weapon...Kit...and Team...*

He stretches out in search of his rifle, grazing submerged boxes and pod fragments, until he finds a familiar shape still snapped into its broken wall cradle. When he lifts it from the water and checks it over, his sturdy weapon is unbent.

Thompson rips the wreckage away from his trusted companion, obsessing over the rifle's actions and optics. Satisfied, he pulls a battery from his waist, slaps it into the slot, and primes it. Internal coils sing with power flow then silence at full charge.

A quick scan around the interior shows no sign of the escape hatch, only a thin split in the hull. His eyes lower to the now knee-deep water. Crouching low, Thompson feels for the hatch and finds it directly beneath him.

*Naturally*.

The Gun stands and slides an armored hand into the split above, feeling the gap. The hull is thin beyond the split, its impact-diffusing layers having frayed and peeled away in sheets. Thompson looks for something to widen the split, but all he finds are bent braces, sections of broken console and composite layers. With nothing else of use, he shoves the butt of his rifle into the gap and pries. Alternating metal and carbon fiber layers groan in protest then snap and split wider, offering a view to the outside world.

Stark moonlight streams between leafy branches, shining directly onto the pod's exterior. Gentle breeze whispers through the leaves with an eerie soughing that immediately reminds him of a faulty air lock. And wisps of vapor rise past the gap, catching moonlight in ethereal glow.

Taking hold of the pod's interior, Thompson peels through layers until he makes a hole large enough to squeeze through. Then, he searches for a piece of reflective metal. Once found, he shakes water from it and juts it through the gap, turning it like a periscope. In his improvised mirror, the Gun finds himself in the middle of a shallow black water pond. Steam rises on all sides, and, with moonlight diffusing brightly, his line of sight is only four to five meters, at best.

Thompson drops the mirror and activates the scope of his rifle, setting it to link wirelessly with his visor. A small translucent window opens in the bottom left of his view.

With both hands, he thrusts the weapon up through the gap and levels it. The infrared scope peers through the fog easily, revealing a landscape of rocks, trees, moss, and torn up soil. Tiny heat sources flit through distant branches, keeping a wary distance.

He retracts his rifle and rests it on the remains of his broken recliner.

*Get your gear and get outta here.*

Rummaging through water and debris, the Gun collects his back rack and pulls each case from it. One by one, he hurls them out of the gap, and they land at the pond's edge with dull *thuds*. After another quick sweep through his riflescope he hauls himself up through the hole.

The pod shifts beneath him as he tries to stand on it, and when he leaps, the spongy exterior flexes. His launch ends well short of the pond's edge and he sinks knee-deep into black muck.

*Quick, now! Blueskins will have eyes on you.*

Rifle held high, Thompson slogs the rest of the way to dry land. Head swiveling in search of the enemy, he collects his gear and snaps each case to his back rack. Once reassembled, he lifts the rack overhead and guides it onto rails in his back armor. The rack slides neatly into place and locks tight.

Rifle in one hand, the Gun runs up his trail of destruction, policing fragments from the pod, until the trail ends at a circle of flattened young trees. He looks up and sees a rocky outcropping forty meters above. Broken saplings dangle over the edge.

*Must've bounced of that... The second drop... No wonder I hit so hard.*

Thompson lugs his fragments back to the pod and tosses them into the steaming pond then palms a bulb-shaped device from his waist. He rotates the cylindrical neck, and a red display clicks up to *5:00*. A matching timer appears in his visor.

With a deep breath, he grips the neck, mashes the end with his thumb three times, and lobs the device inside the split open pod.

His muddy boots dig deep into soil as he bolts up the slope, using thinner trees like handles. Nearly atop the ridge, the counter in his visor reaches zero and a brilliant flash turns night to day. Thompson dives to the ground and covers his head.

A vicious *thump* telegraphs through the bedrock, followed by a thunderous *crack*. Limbs and leaves are blasted from trees. Boughs crash over and around him as stout trunks sway then straighten. Booming echoes fade as they roll down the valley.

Thompson shrugs his way from beneath snapped branches, knocks off the dirt, and completes his climb.

Trees end at a crest of native gray stone, and, once atop it, Thompson looks out across nighttime terrain. A plume of black and white rises from a charred scar in the trees where his pod used to be, illuminated from beneath by smoldering orange flame and from above by a nearly full moon. Peering through his riflescope, he scans the burning crater and finds no trace of his battered egg, just an oval field of felled and carbonized trees. With a nod, he lowers his weapon and looks out across a valley that is dreamlike and surreal—a scene so spacious and unconfined, so cluttered with competing textures, that it seems a deliberate effort to overwhelm and confuse.

A bright flash behind him makes him crouch and pull his weapon close. The ground *thumps* under his boots again and a sharp *crack* rushes past with its entourage of echoes.

Thompson hustles to the far side of the ridge crest and looks into the adjacent valley. Roughly halfway up the far side, a brilliant fireball balloons and dulls to deep red as it rises in the clear air.

*That's either Beckert or Argo.*

Breaking his own order, he dials his radio transmitter down to its lowest output and transmits, "Team Forestall, respond with location."

His radio crackles with static, then, "*Brick, here. Top of ridge, directly above crash site.*"

Thompson raises his riflescope and traces a line from the burning crater to the ridge crest. At first he sees nothing. Then, he finds a thick tree arching to one side. The Gun magnifies the bent tree and sees a black mass squatting on the listing trunk. It flashes a lamp on its head.

Thompson sets his rifle output to "signal" and triggers rapidly, coding a message in light.

*Stay put. Keep watch*, Thompson codes. *Coming to you.*

The dark mass extends a large fist and gives a "thumbs up" signal.

Thompson hops down the steep grade, letting gravity pull him as fast as possible. His strong legs absorb the shock of each landing and launch him again, covering large stretches of slope in every bounce. By degrees, the terrain levels and he sprints through vines and creepers to the valley floor.

Near the bottom, he hears a noise like static, only deeper. His pace slows and just beyond the thinning trees ahead is a frothing stream of white water, undulating and spitting. With a cautious glance to the sky above, he steps toward the stream, studying its curves and motions. A variety of different solutions cross his mind, but urgency hastens his decision.

The Gun straps his rifle securely to himself and sprints at the white water. At the stream's edge, he hurls himself into the air and straightens out like a missile, plunging into the powerful currents. Immediately, he is dragged to the bottom and slammed into the rock bed. Currents drag and grind him against immovable stones downstream. No longer sure of up or down, he reaches out with his arms. One hand grazes a patch of gravel and it is the clue he needs to orient himself. Flailing and paddling, he points his legs downstream and pushes hard off of the next boulder he contacts.

Moonlight streams through his visor as he explodes past the chaotic surface. Pulling with all his strength, he drags himself to the shallows then slogs from the stream to the cover of trees. At the tree line, he looks over his shoulder with dismay.

"Never do that again..." he tells himself.

Working the stiffness from his back and arms, he takes his rifle in hand then dashes through underbrush to rendezvous with Argo.

# LIVING LIFE SUPPORT

Thompson crests the mountain ridge and crouches at the edge of a broad clearing. In pre-dawn light, trees stand straight and true at the far edge, save one listing heavily to the side. Argo perches atop the arching trunk like a colossal vulture with his massive cannon across his lap.

Argo turns his gaze from the sky, notices Thompson in the weeds, and raises a hand in greeting. Thompson sprints over and clambers into the branches of an adjacent tree.

The Brick points straight out over the valley, and Thompson follows his outstretched arm. Just beyond the horizon, a thick column of sooty smoke and dust billows into the air.

"Our ship's crash site?" Thompson asks, his voice electronic and clipped through his helmet speaker.

Argo nods. With voice equally modulated, he adds, "Now look closer."

Thompson raises his riflescope and magnifies the distant cloud. Fires below the horizon tinge the underside of the cloud in dull orange and feed the sooty fumes above. He is about to lower his rifle when a tiny speck moves from behind the dense smoke, just high enough to reflect early morning light. It orbits the column slowly.

"*Already?*" Thompson nearly shouts.

"Showed up twenty minutes ago." The Brick searches the brightening sky above. "Probably imaging this whole place from orbit."

"Any sign of Beckert?"

Argo swivels and points far down the next valley. A scar in the trees cuts all the way to a turbulent race of thrashing water at the bottom.

Thompson pulls his rifle tight and squints through the scope, searching downstream. He finds occasional black fragments of Beckert's pod against the light river stones but no sign of the Geek.

"Move out!"

Thompson leaps from the tree. Argo drops beside him with a heavy *thud*, and the leaning tree snaps back, launching branches and leaves like a catapult. The Operators dash down slope, vines and brambles snatching at them in vain, catching in their joints or under overlapped plates, but not slowing them in the least.

As Gun and Brick near the valley floor they hear thrashing of another river ahead. They creep forward then halt at the tree line, contemplating a raging torrent of free-flowing water. Gun and Brick glance at each other, imagining such quantity funneling directly into Cadre One's stores, then look across to the opposite slope. Midway down, a long line of broken foliage leads to a trail of plowed gravel and runs straight into the frothing river. Thompson considers crossing, recalls his previous attempt, and thinks better of it.

Argo sets off downstream but Thompson grabs his shoulder and pulls him back under tree cover.

"Hang on…"

The Brick goes still and the men wait in silence. Turning toward his leader, the big man shrugs. Then a low, fast craft streaks past overhead. Its supersonic boom arrives an instant later, jarring the men where they stand. Crackling echoes bounce up and down the valleys.

"On me!"

Thompson keeps inside the tree line and sprints downstream. Argo follows, carving great divots of earth with every stride.

\*\*\*\*\*

The men run for kilometers without a sign of their missing comrade until Thompson abruptly halts in his tracks. Argo nearly bowls him over.

The Brick waits for an order. When it does not come, he asks, "What's up?"

The Gun stares into the river, imagining Beckert trapped in his pod under churning waters, pinned by rock or debris.

"Could we have run by him?"

Argo looks into the white water, pondering the possibility, until he notices a new sound—heavy and constant like the noise of the river but deeper, coming from farther downstream.

"You hear that?" the Brick asks.

Thompson listens. "Yeah. What is it?"

Argo jogs ahead. The terrain takes a steeper grade and the river fans out over a broad area of sloping rock. Shallow water splashes and sprays over slick stone.

Glinting metal grabs Thompson's eye. He speeds without caution across matted green rocks, slipping through the shallows, and snatches up the metal.

Turning it over, the Gun announces, "Color and composition matches. This is interior pod cladding."

Argo shifts his stance. "Okay. Means Beckert's pod rolled through and it's split open."

"So where is he?" Thompson turns and searches over the watery slope. Near the middle, an angular rock divides the stream. Fresh scrapes mar one side of it. Just past the rock, the stream dives out of sight with a deep roar far below.

Thompson hops nimbly to the scuffed rock, and he skids to a stop at the edge of a thirty-meter cliff. Below is a great kidney-shaped bowl, suggesting what once must have been a reservoir. The eastern wall bears a deep notch where it failed. Now, only the floor of the reservoir still holds water, overflow draining through the failed eastern wall.

He kneels and looks over the cliff edge, watching river water cascade in swirling mists. Morning sun peeks over mountain ridges to the east and shines directly on the falls, refracting in arcs of prismatic color.

The mists part and Thompson sees a pool at the waterfall's base with a faint glint of metal at the deep bottom. Without another thought, he cradles his rifle and leaps off the cliff.

Argo watches his friend drop from sight, and he hustles down the slick rocks in full alarm.

"*Thompson!*"

Bracing himself on the angular rock, the big man leans over the edge and peers through the mists. In the pool below, circular waves spread from Thompson's splashdown.

Hugging his cannon to his chest and muttering, Argo steps to the edge and propels himself off the cliff. Time seems to slow as fat drops of water hang lazily in the air around him.

With a tremendous crash, he plunges into the pool and sinks to the bottom. Beckert's pod lies directly ahead of him, bashed in on all sides. Thompson is at an edge, pulling at a large fracture. Argo surges through aerated currents and takes hold of the split seam. Wedging his foot on the lower edge, he grips the upper edge and strains. Adrenaline pours into his bloodstream as he roars with effort. Reluctantly, the seam flexes then unzips one heavy gauge bolt at a time.

Thompson dives inside and finds Beckert pinned beneath his recliner, his console, and the pod's interior bracing. The Gun switches on his helmet lights and shines them at Beckert's goggles. The young Geek's eyes open in surprise.

Thompson tears at the crushing pile, hauling aside the heaviest obstructions, and Beckert slips free. Before the young Operator can collect his kit, Thompson wraps an arm around the Geek's chest and drags him from his would-be tomb.

Argo releases the seam once his teammates are clear and the pod frame snaps together like toothless jaws. All three slosh from the water then rush through the mists to the cover of trees. Argo leans on Beckert, pressing the Geek firmly to the ground and holding him down while he scans the sky overhead.

"I'm okay, I'm okay!" Beckert protests.

"Lie still," Argo orders. He reaches behind himself, pulls a large case from his back rack, and plunks it down beside him. With a touch, the case opens and spreads like a flower. Medical tools extend in all directions.

"I'm getting his kit," Thompson announces. He props his rifle, dashes back to the pool, and dives into the clear water.

Beckert tries to sit up, but Argo puts his large hand on his chest.

"I said, lie *still*!" The Brick looks sternly at his patient then notices one of Beckert's eyes is blotched red. He pulls a small light from his kit and shines it from eye to eye, noting how the pupils constrict.

"Your left eye is damaged. Can you see through it?"

Beckert blinks, unaware. "Works fine."

"Do you remember what happened?"

The Geek thinks for a moment. "Don't remember hitting the ground. Just a lot of rolling and bashing…"

Argo gently pushes Beckert's face to one side. Deep scrapes mark the side of his helmet. "Are you dizzy? Nauseous at all?"

"A little, but I'll be fine."

Argo leans back. "Go ahead and sit up."

The Geek sits up and drags a foot under him. He pitches to the side, just catching himself.

"Whoa…"

Argo rushes to steady him, but Beckert puts his hand up. "I got it. I'll be fine."

"Sit down and take a moment."

Beckert settles onto the soil, crossing his legs. Water trickles from overlapping plates of his armor.

"Increase your O2 mixture one percent for the next thirty minutes."

"Yes, sir." Beckert's goggles pulse once in compliance.

Argo packs up his medkit and swaps it for his labset. While they wait for Thompson, Beckert meditates. Argo runs tests on air quality.

Minutes later, Thompson emerges from the pool, dragging a fully assembled rack with one hand and clutching Beckert's pistols with the other. He hustles to his comrades and sets the rack down. Taking up his rifle, he looks to the sky.

"Any contacts?" the Gun asks.

"None," Argo answers.

"Good. Gear up. We're leaving."

Beckert grabs his pistols and checks the actions. Satisfied, he twirls them around his fingers, clips them onto his lower back. When he rises, the Geek tips to one side, steadies himself with hands out to each side, then collects his rack and slides it onto his back.

Thompson leans close to Argo. "How is he?"

"Knock to the head. Concussed, I think."

The Gun looks past Argo's shoulder. "Sergeant, can you run?"

"Aye, Major."

"Good."

Thompson opens multiple locks on his rifle, partially dismantling it and shaking water from it.

"Clear your weapons," he orders. "Then we run southeast for six hours. When the shadows are long enough, we'll risk some high-ground recon. Copy?"

"Yes, *sir*!" Beckert and Argo reply in unison. Beckert pulls a bulb-shaped device from his belt and arms it. He cocks his arm to throw it into the pool.

"Hold," Thompson counters.

Beckert lowers his arm, confused.

"Enemy's too close," the Gun explains. "They'll swoop right in."

Beckert nods and repeatedly mashes the bulb end to disarm it. He hooks the device to his belt and pulls a case from his back rack. Inside is a stack of caseless ammunition, which he clips to each thigh. The last two mags, he slaps into the grips of his pistols and racks the actions.

"Argo, you ready?"

Argo latches the last catch on his cannon. "Aye."

"Maiella, are you ready?"

"*Sir?*"

Thompson whirls on the Geek. "*Are you ready, Sergeant?*"

Beckert straightens nervously. "Aye, Major!"

"All right. On me." Thompson bounds off into the brush.

Beckert looks at Argo, bewildered, and the Brick reassures him silently with a terse head shake. Shrugging, Beckert runs after his leader. Argo rolls his head in a wide circle, adjusts grip on his cannon, and follows with frequent glances to the rear.

\*\*\*\*\*

Thompson lopes to a halt near a natural clearing. Late afternoon sun shines in long angles past green leaves tinged with yellow, orange, and red.

"We'll take a short break here," he says, leaning against the white bark of a broadleaf tree. Beckert props himself with one arm and bows his head as he pants. Argo slings his cannon and takes out his labset.

Thompson watches Argo fiddle with the device. "Got results yet?"

"I do," the big man replies without looking up. "Air quality is good. Microbial content is high… but I can do something about that." His thumbs trigger a sequence and the labset fills a ported phial. The Brick removes the phial and presses it into a port in his neck armor. The fluid is sucked in with a hiss.

"This'll boost our immune systems for a few hours." He repeats the process for Thompson and Beckert, plugging the phial into each of their necks. "But give it a moment to circulate."

As the Geek and Gun catch their breath, they stand straighter. With some anxiety, they reach for the release lever on their faceplates.

"It's okay," Argo advises. "Go ahead."

Thompson zips the lever open. Warm dryness sweeps over his sweaty face and he takes a tentative sniff. Rich, unprocessed air flows into his nostrils, full of arboreal aromas. He fills his lungs again and again.

Beckert retracts his mask to the top of his helmet, leaving his goggles in place. His eyes bulge with the new sensations of raw, planetary atmosphere. He grins at the wonder of it, enjoying the smells and smacking his lips at the subtle taste.

Argo raises his mask, scarcely marking any difference, and continues thumbing his labset.

"Nutrition interval," Thompson declares. He takes a box from his rack and opens it, distributing the contents with a wrist snap. Argo catches his with one hand, still working on his portable lab. Beckert catches his portion between pistols and rips the plasticine package with his teeth. Argo finally stows his labset, and all three take a knee as they masticate the doughy, bland, protein.

"It's amazing…" Argo states to no one in particular. "The scale of this environment…and no processors to regulate it. Completely self-sustaining, continually renewed. A perfect machine."

He takes a big bite.

"Makes the old air-regs at Cadre One seem…*paltry*."

"You think this was all engineered?" Beckert asks through a mouthful.

Argo takes a long look up, brow cinching together, lower lip jutting. "I don't know... Possibly."

A heat source appears in Beckert's goggles. The Geek's pistol flashes out instantly, aiming deep into the woods. When his head catches up to his hand, he locks gazes with terrified wide-set brown eyes. A shiny, black nose quivers at the end of an elongated, slender face. Short brown fur covers the creature from its long receiver-like ears down to its four narrow legs, and on its head are planted sharp branches of bone.

The creature spins around and dashes away, its white tail bouncing along until it disappears into the woods.

Thompson's rifle is poised and ready. Argo hefts his cannon to the rear, protein bar crammed in his mouth. The Brick's nostrils are flared; his eyes are sharp and intense, ready to kill.

"*Contact?*" Thompson whispers urgently.

Beckert clips his pistol. "Sorry, Major, false alarm. Indigenous life form."

Thompson lowers his rifle and gives Argo an all-clear hand signal. The big man snorts, resets the safety on his weapon, and bites off another chunk of protein.

"That should remind us to keep moving." Thompson claps Beckert on the shoulder. "Good eyes."

The Gun picks up the ration box and collects the wrappers. Argo takes the box and, when Thompson turns, he snaps the box onto his leader's rack.

"Let's go," Thompson orders. "Geek, take rear."

Thompson and Argo jog into the brush, but Beckert lingers. He looks out where the animal stood, thinking about every feature. He saw one in the Colonist archives before, but...*this one was alive and it was looking right at him*. A pleased smile crosses the young man's face, and he dashes after his team.

# THE DEAD PLACE

Thompson crouches on a high outcropping of rock, looking
west over the wide plain his team has crossed. Dusky shadows
blend his charcoal armor with stone still damp from late-day rain.
And as the sun dips below distant mountain ridges, long rays of
rosy light shine up at wispy clouds overhead.

He struggles to comprehend the arching sky as it shimmers
with ribbons of neon green, blue, and violet. Behind the ribbons,
millions of stars twinkle. The Gun is no stranger to stars, having
lived and traveled among them his whole life. But here, with
no ship or ceiling, the context is all wrong. For a moment, he
feels adrift and reeling as though he might fall upwards into the
bottomless expanse.

Squelching the bizarre sensation, he returns his gaze to the
western horizon where hundreds of reflective specks hover and
swarm.

"Hey."

Thompson turns to see Argo behind him.

The big man squats, hands over a canteen, and asks, "What do
you make of it?"

"They're clustered tight." Thompson takes a long draught
of water and passes the canteen back. "Means they've found
something."

Argo squints into the distance. "Beckert's pod?"

"Fair guess." At mention of Beckert, Thompson glances at the
young Geek stashed beneath a jutting boulder. "How is he?"

"He's definitely concussed but won't admit it. Doesn't seem to have affected his HDI or synaptic bridges. Still..."

"Can he function?"

Argo looks away thoughtfully. "He *can*, but he *shouldn't*. What he needs is rest."

"You know we can't—"

"I *know*, Thompson."

The two men stare in silence at the horizon.

"Can you do anything for him?" Thompson asks.

"I'm watching his brain chemistry and blood flow. This kind of injury, it... It takes time."

Thompson nods with reluctant acceptance then looks up at the shimmering ribbons above. "What's wrong with the sky?"

Argo cranes his neck as far as his thick collar armor allows. "Colonists call them, 'Aurora.' Charged particles from the local star get channeled along magnetic lines of force. When they hit atmosphere, it glows." The Brick's face wrinkles. "Only supposed to happen near the poles, though."

"Why's that?"

"A planet like this should have a strong magnetic field. That field would deflect those particles far to the north or south. For whatever reason, the magnetic field is erratic and weak. It's letting that radiation through."

"Are we in danger?"

"No, no. We get a lot worse at Cadre One." The Brick's eyebrow lifts. "If anything, all that interference might make us harder to spot from space."

"Finally, some good news," Thompson snorts. "So what's wrong with the planet. Is it broken?"

"Might have been caused by the attack... But then, a spinning, liquid metal core can reverse its poles, sometimes. Could be going through an inversion."

Thompson's interest dissolves and his eyes return to the horizon. Squinting, he sees a tight cluster amid the swarm with multiple bright lights aiming down. Resting his rifle on his raised knee, he zooms in on the cluster. Argo takes Thompson's non-verbal cue and pulls his cannon into his lap.

"What do you see?"

"Movement…standby."

Argo hunches while Thompson zooms to maximum. In the scope, six platform-like vessels hover with undersides wavering from hot thrust. Brilliant lights at their corners stream down into the rocks and trees below. Slowly, the platforms rise.

Thompson's eyes dart back and forth, searching for detail in the over magnified image, as ascending platforms clear the trees. Dangling beneath, silhouetted by white steam, is Beckert's battered pod.

"That's it. We're leaving." Thompson slides back from the outcropping. Argo follows closely.

"Can Beckert run?" Thompson asks.

"He's medicated, so—"

"Carry him," Thompson orders. He pauses long enough for Argo to lift the Geek over his shoulder then rushes off through the undergrowth.

\*\*\*\*\*

Steep slopes and tangled thickets hamper movement, making the Operators work for every step. Thompson extends the bayonet on his rifle and slashes through foliage. Though sharp, the blade requires a wide swing, and hours of the repetitive motion make his shoulders ache.

A loud *buzz* halts Thompson in his tracks. Looking down, he finds a rope-like creature coiled and staring with elliptical pupils. A forked tongue slides past its pitted snout and waves over its head. Chevrons of brown and black run its length to a furiously vibrating rattle on its tail.

The creature uncoils and noses toward the brush. Before it can escape, Thompson grabs it by the middle. The snake strikes repeatedly at the Gun's armored hand and wrist. He holds it out toward Argo.

"Have a look. *Angry* little thing, isn't it?"

Argo watches the snake chew on the rubber pad of Thompson's index finger.

"I don't expect it likes being caught any more than we would." Argo inspects the alternating chevrons as the creature writhes. "Looks like a Timber Rattler from the Colonist Archive. If that bit you, it could kill you. But they're docile if you leave them alone."

Thompson hurries to set the snake down, suddenly concerned he might be hurting it. The snake threads its way beneath a fallen tree and disappears.

Embedded in the rubberized pad at the end of his finger is a short, needle-thin fang. Thompson pulls it loose and spins it between his thumb and forefinger. *Delicate and deadly*, he thinks in admiration. Swinging his arms in alternating circles, he limbers up to start cutting again.

"Ready?"

Argo swaps Beckert from his left shoulder to his right. "Ready."

\*\*\*\*\*

Thompson crests another ridge and discovers a reprieve in the mountainous terrain. From his vantage, he surveys a broad, forested plain to the east, gently illuminated by pre-dawn sky. Directly ahead a river meanders north to south, some sections turned white with rapids. Nowhere does he see a good place to cross.

He swings his scope further south and discovers a black scar in the forest over ten kilometers wide. The river flows directly to it.

Argo sets his burden down with a groan and leans against a stout trunk. He unscrews the cap on his canteen and takes a long slug. Argo offers the canteen, but Thompson ignores it, still focusing on the charred gap in the forest.

"Spot something?" Argo asks, stowing his canteen.

"Due south, thirty clicks out."

Thompson hands over his rifle. While the Brick gazes through the scope Thompson scrambles up a tree and scans the sky. Overhead, an object gleams from low orbit—a ship presumably— so large the Gun can see its elongated shape with his naked eye. At first it appears solitary then he resolves a faint constellation of smaller reflections surrounding it.

To the west, he spies hundreds of tiny specks, hovering above and circling a spot beyond the horizon on plumes of pale blue thrust.

"That should be Frederick," Argo announces, lowering the scope from his eye and staring off at the blighted spot.

Thompson swings down from the branches and *thuds* onto the dirt.

"Who?"

"Not who. *Where*. Frederick was a city, according to the colonist maps. Small military base. Over sixty thousand residents." Argo passes the rifle over as the realization sinks in. "Sixty *thousand*."

"I couldn't see a bit of it left." Thompson takes his rifle back. "Looks like the sun reached out and touched it."

Argo nods. "How do the skies look?"

"Crowded. And more flying up from the south. Best guess, they're converging at the failed reservoir and fanning out from there."

"No point staying here, then." Argo bends over to lift the still unconscious Geek. Thompson stops him.

"You've carried him long enough. I'll take him. You blaze a better trail, anyway." Thompson squats, raises one of Beckert's limp arms, and passes it behind his neck. When he stands, Beckert comes up with him. Holding the Geek at the waist, Thompson squats again and allows Beckert to drape over one shoulder. With both arms, the Gun supports his comrade and stands. He shrugs a couple of times to adjust his grip.

"We'll cut straight to the river and follow it south. Move out."

*****

Morning daylight fades into late afternoon. Birds chirp and sing throughout the Operators' marathon, periodically interrupted by the distant booms of aircraft streaking by. With the tight cover of multi-colored canopy overhead, and the speed at which the planes are racing past, there is little concern of being spotted.

Trusting Argo's vigilance on point, Thompson absorbs sights, sounds, and smells of his bizarre environment. At first, such incomprehensible variety is the screaming noise of sensory overload—a too-intense contrast from an erstwhile deprived and monochromatic experience. He squints and grimaces against the blare of colors, forms, textures, and scents, yet behind it all is a deep fascination that refuses to relent. While careful to keep sight of Argo and watch his sectors for threats, the Gun finds himself giving in to indomitable beauty pouring into him, so content in mindless exertion that he scarcely marks the passage of time.

When Argo lopes to a stop, Thompson hurtles back from his thoughts and notices how sparse the vegetation has become. Trees are stunted and gnarled with thick knots in the trunks and branches. Leaves are still vibrant red, yellow or orange, yet are curled and misshapen. Soil crunches beneath his boots, and when he looks down he sees the dirt is loaded with brittle black shards.

Argo turns to face his comrade, labset in his large hands. "This place is hot. We should seal up 'til we leave."

Both men open their mouths wide as their faceplates drop and lock with a hiss. After a couple of swallows, pressure in their ears equalizes and processed air circulates past their nostrils.

Argo's voice comes clipped and mechanical through his helmet speaker, "This whole place was glassed." He thumbs his labset, absorbing the data. "Heat and compression on a stellar scale."

"Isomer weapons?"

Argo shrugs. "Don't know…maybe." The Brick continues forward, following the trees as they become shorter and more gnarled, until they end at a circular field several kilometers across. The surface is homogenous black gravel, smooth and bowled slightly, with an occasional tree limb or animal bone. Farther out, dust devils twirl over shimmering mirages.

"There's nothing here," Argo says, shoulders drooped in disappointment. "This is a dead place."

"Then we keep going," Thompson states. "We'll find something."

The Gun waits for Argo to store his labset and passes Beckert over. As the Brick adjusts the unconscious Geek across his huge shoulders, Thompson takes his rifle in hand and casts a wary eye to the sky.

"We'll go around the edge, under tree cover," Thompson says, "then look for a river crossing on the far side."

Argo faces Thompson and nods with Beckert draped over his shoulders like an armor-plated stole.

"Right behind you, Gun."

\*\*\*\*\*

Kilometers pass under the regular cadence of their strides. Late afternoon yields to dusk. Black-winged creatures take to the sky in dense clouds. Croaks and peeps call through the forest from every direction. Far away, a lupine howl carries through cooling air.

Thompson slashes his way through thickets and creeper vines then freezes. His hand flies up in a sign to *halt* then *get down*. The two men crouch low in the bush, and Argo follows Thompson's pointing hand to a massive pale gray structure in a clearing far ahead. It seems to root directly in the ground and rises at a constant angle well above the forest canopy.

Thompson takes cover behind a thick tree trunk, aiming his rifle at the sloping construct. Argo sets Beckert down quietly and thumbs the safety of his cannon.

Thompson peers through his scope, tracing the dimensions of the edifice, and finds no entrance or window. Its surface is heavily pock marked, and everywhere the smooth surface has chipped away there are long trails of rust running down toward the base.

With a hand signal, he orders Argo to *wait*, and the Gun steps cautiously ahead.

Light colored chips and chunks surround the base of the construct. Thompson stoops to pick up a hand-sized piece and turns it over. Its hardness makes it seem like rock, but sandy whiteness gives it away as a kind of cement. When he squeezes the fragment it yields, crumbling into many sandier pieces. He drops the remains, dusts off his palm, and strides closer.

In deeper gouges, exposed metallic reinforcements are little more than rusty nubs. Plants and small trees root in enormous cracks running through the structure, wedging them farther apart.

Thompson grows bolder, moving to the base of the colossal construct and out from under the forest canopy overhead. His eyes follow the slope to its top where he finds an arching span extending all the way across the river valley. Jaw dropped in amazement, he signals Argo to *follow* and scrambles up the angled abutment.

Argo collects Beckert and pursues. The Brick's heavy steps gouge the rotten concrete, dislodging layers of loose scale and sand, making the huge warrior stagger and scuff his way up the steep slope.

Atop the abutment, Thompson crouches beside corroded railings and peers through his scope. To the east is an overgrown bridge deck, devoid of heat sources. To the west, a deep and narrow notch is cut into the valley's side, aligning with the approach of the massive span. Rock slides have buried the bottom of the notch, creating a boulder field where no trees can root, and far beyond the notch Thompson spies the distant swarm of hovering craft. Hours earlier, it clustered tightly over the failed reservoir. Now, the swarm has flattened and spread out over surrounding areas.

Thompson throws a leg over the decrepit railing and steps out onto the mossy bridge deck. It feels plush under his boots, and, as he marvels, it occurs to him that he is standing on something man-made—something constructed by his terrestrial forebears over a thousand years ago—and it still stands as a monument to their expertise. It is also potent reminder that those who built it were all murdered by a remorseless, blue-skinned enemy. The Gun's sinews tighten and he squats, raising his rifle scope again.

Argo crests the bridge's foundation and crouches beside Thompson. "What do you see?"

"Nothing." Thompson lowers his rifle, still looking out across the span. "If we cross here, it'll save us time."

Argo looks out across the suspended road of dilapidated concrete, asphalt, and weeds. Then he looks down to the river valley over a hundred meters below.

"Pretty far with no cover…"

Thompson looks over his shoulder at the swarm of search craft. Already, the cluster is wider than before.

"On me." Thompson springs up and runs out onto the flat top. Argo shrugs Beckert tighter to his neck and dashes after his leader.

Unburdened, Thompson easily pulls ahead. The farther he runs across the span, the less moss and soil mats the surface. Soon, he is running across loose chunks of grayed asphalt. Broad potholes— scooped from the surface by centuries of rain, wind, and frost— sprout hardy shrubs and grasses.

Approaching the span's apex, large sections of road sag where reinforced concrete has cracked into circular sectors. Some sags have dropped away completely, revealing severely eroded and cracked concrete beams beneath. Thompson skirts the ragged edges, casting a wary glance down at treetops and river far below, when a sudden gust shoves him close to the bridge's rail. Wary of being blown over the side, he veers toward the center divider.

Alarming at first, the strong wind is cool, evaporating sweat on his face. It streams through his nostrils, filling his lungs with damp night air, thick and satisfying. His heart beats stronger, his limbs feel refreshed, and his eyes are wide with wonder.

Never before have his senses been so thoroughly aroused. Even in the heightened intensity of an assault, attention was sharply focused on the mission. Here, his awareness spans a vast spectrum of new experiences: the smell of soil and pine, the taste of air loaded with humidity, the coolness on his sweating skin, the howling of free flowing wind, the shimmering ribbons of light across night sky, and the red moon rising full on the horizon. A sensual symphony overwhelms him, making him feel simultaneously small while connected to something truly huge.

An absurd idea washes over him:

*The rocks, the trees, the air and water, the creatures among them...possibly the entire planet...is it all one system? Is it* alive?

*With every breath...I'm connected to that living system. So are Argo and Beckert... This is where we are from...where we are meant to be...*

*But the Blueskins are NOT a part of this system. They're invaders. They don't belong. I don't know how I know this, and I don't care. This was a Human world, and it will be again.*

Thoughts of Beckert and Argo remind him to check on his comrades. When he looks back, he sees he has outrun them, so he jogs to a halt and crouches. While waiting, he drinks in his surroundings.

"Maiella has to see this."

More surprising than the sudden thought of Maiella is the realization he said her name aloud. And then he realizes how badly he let his guard down with inappropriate indulgences. The Gun chastises himself harshly and banishes his distraction. Returning to an austere state of mind, he watches Argo lumber up the fractured span.

Above and far behind the Brick, a bright light drifts between the walls of the mountain notch followed by a second. The lights cease their lateral drift and grow brighter.

Thompson raises his rifle. Peering through his scope, he dials in on the lead light source and shifts the wavelength to minimize washout. The scope resolves two small, streamlined aircraft, heading their way. Beneath them, a triangular pink beam oscillates.

"*Argo!*" Thompson shouts. "Move fast! They're *coming!*"

Argo pivots mid-stride to see the advancing lights. He whirls about and lowers his head, re-doubling his sprint, feet pounding the broken asphalt.

Thompson slings his rifle and rushes to join his comrade. Matching pace, he orders, "Give me your weapon!"

Argo passes the heavy cannon over then lifts the unconscious Geek across his shoulders like a yoke and holds him with both hands. Without the swinging cannon, his stride lengthens.

Thompson hefts the cannon with both arms, compensating for its mass. As the men crest the middle of the arching span, Thompson spots the end of the bridge. He sneaks a look over his shoulder and sees the lights are much closer.

"Move it, Brick! *Come on!*"

Argo's footfalls *thud* faster and he pants with effort.

High-pitched whine of turbines pours through the valley cut. Thompson looks again and the lights are almost to the notch.

*Argo isn't going to make it.*

He curses through clenched teeth.

"Run ahead, take cover where you can!" Thompson shouts. Argo acknowledges with an exaggerated grunt as he thuds by.

As the aircraft pass the notch their noses lift and they slow then level out. Each craft takes a side of the wide bridge, and their oscillating pink beams sweep the top, overlapping at the center divider. Hover jet thrust shakes the entire span. Chunks of asphalt roll and dance.

Thompson ducks to the outer railing and crouches low, thumbing the cannon's output higher. Adrenaline and neurostims flow into his blood. His leg twitches with anticipation, his mind collapses to bloody intent, and he aims at the nearest craft.

*Cracks* like pistol shots behind him. The bridge lurches and sways. Eyes wide, Thompson spins and watches the edge of a massive concrete slab snap free, teeter on its crossbeam, and plunge out of sight. Clouds of dust belch skyward, and seconds later a violent crash of smashed timber rises from below.

"*Argo!*" Thompson yells. He jumps to his feet, trying to balance on the still swaying surface. Thick dust rolls over him.

The aircraft thrust forward, shining their lights ahead into the dust cloud, but the beams scatter in a diffuse glow. Obscured within the cloud, Thompson searches the edges of the broken slab, frantic for a sign of his comrades.

*Nothing.*

Already, night breezes are clearing the column of rising dust. Thompson rounds the gaping hole in the bridge and sprints for the safety of trees at the far end of the span.

One aircraft slides out to the side and drops level with the bridge deck, aiming intense spotlights at the fresh damage. Its pink beam re-orients, sweeping over the newly broken edges and then over the shattered slab fragments amid the trees. The companion craft roars with thrust and accelerates toward the far side of the bridge. Thompson dives beneath the corroded centerline guardrails as the craft streaks overhead then watches the craft brake hard and come about. Its oscillating pink beam widens to cover the span's full width and the aircraft slowly glides back over the span.

The Gun looks through the triangular beam at protective cover of thick forest just beyond. His head swivels back and forth, finding no escape, and he glances at the weapon in his grip. Argo's cannon is fully primed and charged, begging for release.

*These two would be easy kills*, he thinks, *just hovering, unsuspecting. But the rest of the swarm would be here in seconds...*

Brilliant lamps on the craft's stubby wings bathe a broad swath of bridge in white light, and the pink beam winds its way over the wide span, careful not to miss any nook or crevice.

*I'm out of time.*

Thompson scuttles under the center railing then glide-steps to the edge, keeping the cannon trained on the advancing craft. Peering over the rail, he discovers he is well past the deepest part of the valley but there is still a thirty-meter drop to the treetops below.

*Too far to fall.*

The bridge shimmies under the advancing craft's powerful jets. Small pieces of asphalt roll into the many sags and holes then tumble off the sloping edges. Pebble-sized pieces pelt him, driven by hot, dry exhaust. His finger slides inside the trigger guard. Then he imagines Beckert and Argo injured beneath the bridge as waves of Blueskin search craft come roaring in for the kill.

*Blast it!*

Thompson resets the cannon's safety and throws the strap over a shoulder. He leans against the railing, testing the resilience. Most of the fasteners have corroded away, giving the thick bar play. It flexes, but not easily.

He throws one leg over, then the other. Corrosion and dust make the rail difficult to grasp, and his palms become instantly damp inside his gauntlets. He crouches and lowers a leg down the side of the span, searching for foothold. The toe of his boot scrapes away layers of loose scale, sending sandy chips spinning and flipping to the ground.

The bracket in front of him breaks, initiating a chain reaction to the left and right. He hooks an arm and hangs on, feeling the pop of each bracket as it detaches. The railing drops several meters and jangles as though trying to shake him free before settling.

Thompson opens his eyes. Pointed conifers and spreading broadleafs sway in the breeze below his dangling feet. To each side, the railing has pulled loose from the bridge deck, creating a long and shallow dip. Where he hangs, the railing's corroded shell has fallen away, revealing a thickly braided cord of sturdy synthetic fiber. His eyes roll with relief and gratitude to the engineers.

Gusts blow him close enough to the bridge to catch one of the many cracks in its side. Still hooked on the thick cord, he shoves a flat hand into a crevice and arches his fingers like a wedge. The Gun transfers weight to the wedged hand and releases the railing. Dangling from the side of the crumbling bridge, he scrambles down the diagonal crack until he is standing on an arched rib of the spandrel wall.

The craft slides directly over the span above, its vibration releasing a hail of concrete chunks. Thompson hunches against the bombardment, barely able to maintain his hold. Heavy dust swirls around him, filling his eyes and mouth.

The Gun squeezes his eyes shut and coughs, blinks repeatedly, then peers through the haze at a curtain of dust and debris advancing directly below the craft. There is no sign of its oscillating pink beam penetrating the bridge deck.

When the curtain passes in front of the aircraft hovering off to the side, it catches the hovering craft's bright spotlights; and the curtain becomes dazzlingly bright. Thompson squints against the glare then spies two black lumps near a hollow of broken concrete beneath the main deck.

Like a circus performer, Argo hangs by his knees from an exposed girder. All around him is bright white of freshly detached concrete where a thick block has dropped away and left a pocket to hide inside. Held by the wrist, Beckert dangles like wet laundry, and Argo carefully reels him up into the hollow. The pink beam scans across the column many times from the opposite side but never touches them.

Whine of thrust grows louder, and the two aircraft ascend. With roaring crackles they jet over the valley to the east and disappear from sight.

Thompson exhales, unaware he had been holding his breath. He hooks his thumbs under the cannon's shoulder straps and squares up to a cross member beneath his teammates. Every centimeter is covered in sand and fragments, threatening to pitch him off to the river below, so he shuffles along, sweeping his path as he goes. And when the cross member drops with a strident *snap*, the Gun hustles over the treacherous remainder before it collapses.

On the opposite side, he shimmies and gropes along the spandrel wall until he stands beneath Argo's hollow. With feet planted and both arms raised, Thompson flips his hands toward himself. Argo releases Beckert, and the Geek drops into Thompson's ready grasp.

Argo flexes at the waist and pulls himself upright. Gingerly, the Brick climbs down, favoring his left arm.

"You okay?" Thompson asks.

Argo nods. "Tweaked my shoulder." He rotates the sore joint.

"I'll be fine. You?"

"Unharmed."

In the ensuing silence, treetops sway in the breeze below and the river splashes along its banks.

"*Okay*, Argo, you were right. We should've stayed under cover."

"Wasn't going to say anything."

Thompson looks up the support column then looks down the arching rib to the abutment at the far end. He passes Beckert over to Argo.

"On me. We'll rouse Beckert once we have cover."

"Understood."

The men carefully walk down the arched rib to the widened haunch where it joins the abutment on the eastern side. New stress fractures split the reinforced concrete. With a trace of sadness, Thompson understands the bridge will not stand much longer.

They hop off the haunch onto the sloping abutment and dash up the rough surface. Thompson checks the sky and scouts the deck before waving Argo out. Together, they sprint the last few meters to the cover of trees.

\*\*\*\*\*

Thompson charges on through the brush to an isolated line of hills and races up the slope. Argo follows closely, Thompson's swept-aside branches slapping against his weathered face. With a snort, he pulls his faceplate halfway down.

The Gun jogs to a stop on the southern peak, sets the cannon down, then jumps into the low branches of a tree and climbs. At the very extent of his vision, past low hills that flatten near the horizon, there is a faint glimmer. He pulls his rifle from his shoulder and sights through the scope at distant sparkles.

What appeared to be multiple objects is, in fact, a river that twists and bends on its way to a much larger body of water. Light from the rising moon reflects off the surface, glittering like diamond dust. Thompson lowers his rifle and gawks at the beauty of it.

Argo lays Beckert on the mossy soil and pulls out his labset. After thumbing in a formula of neurochems and glucose, the Brick detaches the phial and plugs it into Beckert's neck port.

Minutes later, Beckert stretches and yawns. He looks up at Argo's sweaty, grime-smeared face and grimaces.

"Did I miss something?"

Argo guffaws. "Yeah, you did. How do you feel?"

Beckert sits up and smacks his mouth a couple of times. "Not bad. Where are we?"

Argo points to the tree Thompson climbed. "Go see for yourself."

Beckert rises from the padded soil and climbs up beside his leader. Thompson is intently focused on a distant place, and the Geek follows his gaze.

"See something?" Beckert asks.

Thompson lowers his rifle and nods, still looking out toward the horizon. He passes the long weapon over and points.

Beckert lifts the scope to his eye and trains it just below the horizon. Among the tree-covered hills are numerous black scars. He kicks the magnification up a notch and searches the scars. To his surprise, there are ruined structures beyond the edges. The top floors are blasted away, leaving twisted frames like bony hands reaching for the sky.

"Washington?" Beckert asks.

Thompson nods.

"Washington."

# PROOF OF THE SLAUGHTER

While Thompson and Argo take well-earned rest, Beckert perches in a tree and watches the night sky. Displayed in his goggles are over a hundred channels of radio transmissions, all in heavy use. Most are open, un-coded, and the Geek passes through frequencies listening to the alien voices. They are melodic, interspersed with *clicks* and an occasional *cluck*, sometimes gruff, as if scolding.

A thick band on the upper end of the radio spectrum is encrypted. With little else to occupy the hours of watch, he sets his HDI to the task of decoding it; but the cipher is advanced and eludes his usual code-breaking heuristics.

Intrigued by the challenge, Beckert steps back mentally from the individual frequencies and monitors the radio band as a whole. With a grin, he discovers the transmissions are occurring in packets across multiple frequencies. There is redundancy in the packets, as well, and Beckert knows such a transmission would be hard to jam.

*Military, most likely*, he thinks.

There is also a network presence among the swarms of search craft, tenuous at this distance, yet available. He would like nothing more than to be hacking in were it not for Thompson's order of radio silence. Instead, Beckert sits and mulls over the frequencies, entertaining himself with the enigma of secure alien communications.

A far-off rumble draws the Geek's attention. He lifts his gaze to watch two fat bodied aircraft jet north and west into the mountains. Dual rows of portholes run along their streamlined fuselages.

*Hmm, personnel transports? Bringing in experts to study my pod? Or maybe ground troops to search. Maybe both. Should've left a booby trap...bomb, or something.*

*Whatever the case, Argo's big tracks will be easy to follow.*

Beckert glances down at his sleeping teammates, knowing they had a tough slog to get this far and need the rest. But if the Geek could carry them both he would, just to keep moving.

Timers in Argo's and Thompson's visors reach zero and a tone cycles in their ears. The men wake with a start, instantly clutching their weapons. Beckert looks down from his lofty perch and drops to the ground.

"Morning, Major, Lieutenant," he says with a salute.

The Brick and Gun stretch stiffly.

"Report," Thompson demands.

"Sir, enemy forces continue to mass at our crash sites, including multiple presumed personnel carriers. We should expect an intensified air and ground search."

Thompson checks over his rifle as he listens. "What else?"

"Lots of radio chatter, sir."

"What kind?"

"Sir?"

"Loud and excited? Calm and even?"

"Calm and even. But several frequencies are heavily encrypted. I wasn't able to listen in on those."

"Can you break it?" Argo asks.

"Working on it, Lieutenant."

"Good man." Thompson pats Beckert on the back. "How're you feeling?"

"Good, Major. Eager to get going."

"We will. Nutrition interval first. Then clear traps. Five minutes."

Argo distributes the rations and the team chews in silence.

Beckert collects the wrappers.

Thompson and Argo unlatch catches in their lower back plating and remove a thin, rectangular cup with a short tab on one side. Holding each cup by the tab, they turn it upside down and knock it against a convenient stone. Several grams of compressed, dark cake crumble out. The men puff away the remaining particles.

Beckert looks on with amused surprise. "That's some outdated gear, there." He reaches to a point on his lower spine and hooks a finger under a notch. He pulls on the notch and a short tray slides out, divided by multiple slats. A comb-like gate drops onto the slats and when Beckert pushes the tray back in, the crumbly debris is scraped out. He checks his pistols and stands patiently while Argo and Thompson latch up their armor.

"Hear that, Major?" Argo asks with a sideways glance. "The kid just called you old."

"If I'm old, Brick, you're *prehistoric*." The Gun grips his rifle and looks out toward the eastern horizon. "Right, let's move. Geek, take point."

"Aye, sir!" Beckert turns and dashes down hill into the brush. Thompson is about to follow when he feels Argo's hand grip his shoulder.

"Hold on," the big man says. Once he is sure Beckert is out of earshot, he continues. "Those planes at the bridge… They had us, but then they just left. It's been bothering me."

"We were lucky."

Argo shakes his head skeptically. "The *moment* we were in the open, they came running. Something spotted us, I know it."

"If they saw us, why'd they leave?"

"That's what's bothering me."

"Maybe they don't know what they're looking for." Thompson thinks for a moment. "For now, we stick with what we got. C'mon, time to go."

Argo nods and the Operators charge after Beckert into the brush.

In the trek east, gently rolling hills flatten into wetland marshes. A major east-flowing river to the south saturates the land, creating a sprawling terrain of irregular lakes and braided streams. Thick creeper vines form dense nets, which snag the Operators in their muddy trudge. Clouds of gnats swarm their faces, trying to pour into their eyes, mouths, and nostrils. Biting flies peck at their cheeks relentlessly.

Freed from carrying an unconscious teammate, Argo keeps his labset in hand, monitoring environmental conditions. The device detects higher-than-usual radiation, of a similar nature to the black scar they passed in Frederick. Though not alarming, the increase remains constant for several kilometers, telling him that beneath his feet, under meters of silted muck, is another chunk of blasted glass—Gaithersburg, most likely.

The terrain rises again, diverting the river and its floodplain to the south. Grateful for the respite, the team treks up onto firmer, drier ground.

Far to Beckert's left, a ledge protrudes from the gentle slope. He nearly dismisses it when the geometry of it makes him look again. Though rounded by weathering and mostly buried, the lines form a ninety-degree corner. He breaks from his path and heads straight to it.

Patches of moss cling to its sides along lengthy cracks. Sandy debris litters the ground around it, and rust stains pour out from circular cavities. Beckert's breath quickens. One hand reaches out and touches the surface to make sure it is no illusion. Cautiously, he traces a path to the other side of the corner, still marveling.

"What did you find, Sergeant?"

Beckert spins to see Thompson standing behind him. "Something man-made, I think!"

Argo back-steps toward the others, keeping guard behind them. His large head swivels for a quick glance. "Looks like a building's cornerstone. Should we check it out?"

Thompson looks up and down the slope. "No," he says at last. "Not enough left to warrant a search. Keep moving."

Beckert lingers, ensnared by fascination. Argo cuffs him with an open hand.

"Major said, *move*."

Beckert's cheeks redden with embarrassment, and he dashes ahead.

Daylight wanes, bringing longer shadows. A strong sea breeze carries a salty smell through the thinning trees and low scrub. Larger pieces of rubble are more common, protruding from dark, irradiated soil; and on Argo's recommendation, Thompson orders, "Seal up!"

Beckert and Argo groan with relief to be freed from biting pests, but getting a clean seal without closing them inside the facemask proves another challenge, entirely.

Atop the next hill, the tree line ends abruptly. All three crouch instinctively and survey a very different place from what they were expecting.

Colonist archives showed Washington, D.C. was many kilometers inland, built between the banks of the Potomac and Anacostia Rivers. The center of the city was oldest with numerous stone structures erected by primitive tools and hard labor. More modern buildings stood at the edge of the old city, forming rings of high-rise dwellings and office spaces. Super highways and rail systems threaded in from all directions, permitting the daily commute of millions from their suburban homes. This city was a living organism with a pulse and breath, driven by each of its inhabitants, daily.

Now it is a still and blighted place.

Suburban neighborhoods are little more than ash beneath the Operators' boots. Mighty skyscrapers are sheared off, toppled, or collapsed in jagged heaps. And the city's nucleus is a five-kilometer-wide crater filled with murky water.

The Chesapeake Bay has risen to meet the city, its surf gently scouring the southeastern sections. The Potomac River, slowing drastically upon meeting the Chesapeake, has silted in a narrow river delta, which buries the western areas of Foxhall, Palisades, and Burleith, along with most of Arlington and all of Potomac Heights. Despite the cleansing flows of water and wind, there is no living thing to be seen.

Clearing accumulated greenery from his armor, Thompson asks, "How's the radiation?"

Argo frets at the display on his labset. "*Bad*. This place must've taken numerous hits. It's glowing hot."

Thompson looks out at the rubble-strewn black desert. He had hoped to search some of the old government buildings in the city's heart and the Pentagon in particular. No trace of them remains. His search is not without possibilities, however. A line of structures built on the backside of a hill, sheltered from city center, stands with lower floors intact. Their metallic frames stick up and curve away from the blast zone—the skeletal 'hands' he saw through his riflescope.

"How long can we stay?"

Argo arches an eyebrow. "*Stay*? We can't stay here. We—"

"*How long*?"

Argo sighs and looks across the scorched landscape. "Four hours and we're pushing our rad limit. Anything past six hours…" Argo trails off.

"Six hours, *yes*?"

"Six is the *absolute* limit. You know I hate to do this, but as your medical superior, *that's an order*."

Thompson grimaces. "Fine. Six hours. No longer. Argo, you check out that row of wrecked buildings. Beckert, you get to that high flat top and find something intact if you can. I'm taking that far hill. Set your timers to rendezvous in four hours. That'll give us a buffer if something goes wrong or if we find something important. Radio silence unless emergency. Then rally here, at this point. Understood?"

"Yes, Sir!" Beckert chimes.

"Understood," Argo replies.

Thompson checks the cloudy sky for patrolling planes, finding none. "All right. Move out."

# Mud and Rubble

Argo trudges through small streams and silty mud before reaching the first building in his row. Though fractions of their former selves, the ruined structures tower over him, some leaning to the point of imminent collapse. Corroded girders extend from the upper floors like bones stripped of their concrete and glass flesh. On the sides, five floors up, the buildings are scorched in angled lines pointing up at the same point in the sky.

*Hmm, air burst for maximum blast effect.*

All of the surrounding buildings have fully crumbled, leaving a hilly terrain of weathered blocks and rust. The Brick climbs over them easily and stands at the row's southwest corner.

*Where to start?*

The ground floor is stuffed with the rubble of upper floors, so he jogs around the rear of the building in search of an entrance. As he runs, the Brick notices an occasional cross member, many floors up, connecting the buildings together.

*This was all one structure…*

Twisted girders make it clear the building was also tall, but just how much taller is a mystery.

*Must have been a phenomenal construct in its day.*

The northwestern corner has fared best, being most sheltered from the blast, and Argo spots a gap in ground-floor rubble. Warily, he steps in through a window, tiny bits of glass still clamped in the frames. The floor is a loose mud of powdered concrete and blown-in dust that slides greasily under his heel. Concrete ceiling sags between joists. Walls are little more than corroded beams, broken pipes, and decayed wires.

Conscious of his mass, he edges his way inside. To his right, heaps of rubble pile up through the next floor. To his left, all the way to the building's corner, the space is open. Wind whistles through the exploded windowpanes. Slow drips seep through cracks in the bottom of the sags, the *plip, plip, plip,* providing the only audible accompaniment to the whistling breeze.

Hairs on his neck and forearms stand on end. He whirls about, knowing there was no sight or sound of the enemy to alarm him; yet something reached out to him, subliminal and elusive. His eyes squint as they roam the ruined walls, finding nothing to justify the odd sensation.

*Am I hallucinating?*

With an annoyed grunt, he continues inside, slide-stepping through mud, searching with his toes for solid footing, testing each step before committing his bulk to it. Ceiling sags above appear ready to fall at the slightest disturbance so he takes care to stay beneath the ceiling joists, lest he find himself suddenly buried.

Late afternoon sun streams in through empty windowpanes. Where the rays end, however, the interior is dark as night. Sufficiently hidden from the outside, he risks his helmet lamps, letting his beams shine across frayed cords, naked wall supports, and broken masonry. Toward the middle of the building, there is a tight group of intact block walls. Intrigued, Argo shuffle-steps over to it.

He steps around the walls, discovering they form a narrow enclosure, and the mud thins at an open doorway on the far side. When he shines his lights through the doorway, he finds two staircases: one ascending, one descending.

*Good! Might find something in the lower levels.*

The Brick moves to the descending stairway, but enthusiasm dims when he sees murky, standing water only half a flight down. Velvety black mildew lines the walls.

*Up, then.*

He places one foot gingerly on the first step. Eyelids squeeze shut, teeth clench, breath holds, and hands clamp to his cannon. He shifts his weight onto the step.

It holds.

His breath rushes in a great exhale, and he brings his other foot up. Bouncing lightly, he tests the stairway and it feels solid. More confident in his progress, the Brick climbs to the next floor.

The second floor is barren. Wind flows through the empty space, creating eddies of dust behind the main support columns. Sunlight spills across sagging depressions in the floor where ceiling chunks from floors above have come to rest. Small puddles fill the shaded bottoms.

If the sags on the floor seem near to collapse, the low hanging ceilings of this floor are on the verge of bursting. Weathered cracks are wide enough that sunlight streams through. Only severely corroded internal reinforcements knit the gap.

Delicately, he steps away from the staircase and walks over the grid of floor joists. Absence of walls makes short work of his search, where only a single heavy door attracts his attention. Still in its frame, the door defiantly bars access to a room whose walls have long since blown away.

Argo moves freely toward the southern sections, able to pass between rubble piles on the narrow joists. A group of standing walls encloses another stairwell, but thoroughness forces him to complete his search before leaving the floor.

At this end of the building, Argo looks up and sees open patches of sky between twisted and decayed beams. Every floor above him has failed, debris cascading from one to the next until the ground floors were filled, and only the rigid bones of the building remain.

Lowering his gaze, he looks across a gap to the building's southern segments. The floors on those sections have likewise failed and all that remain are hollow frames.

He turns northwest, looking across terrain his team crossed on approach. Setting sunlight washes out his vision, and he shades his eyes with one hand. Tiny reflections hover above the lone ridge where they rested earlier.

In a panic, he realizes what a dark figure he cuts against the light concrete, sunlight full on him.

*Stupid! Stupid!*

He fades back into the middle of the building, watching for any sudden movement of the hovering reflections, heart thudding in his chest. No change.

His jaw muscles flex and he chides himself again for lack of caution. He peeks again at the distant reflections. They remain in place.

With a healthy dose of head shaking and muttering, Argo climbs the staircase to the third floor. The Brick glides north along the joists, looking down through wide holes to his left and right. Nearly back to intact flooring, he spies strange hardware dangling above one of the open floor pits. He picks his way toward the oddity, hugging the support beams and stepping around them. Shape of the hardware suggests it was once square, as though something was securely installed here then was wrenched free.

At the big man's feet the floor is broken away completely between girders, but the next floor down has a square hole punched through it. He looks again at the mount on the ceiling and guesses the dimensions to be very close.

*Something heavy and solid was installed here*, he reasons, *and fell through to the floors below. It'd have to be massive and durable to punch through reinforced concrete. Strong enough to still be intact?*

Argo sets his cannon down and lays himself like a plank across the girder. He extends outward, hoping to see the bottom. The best he can manage, however, is an angled view of the first floor.

Determined, he gets his feet beneath him, collects his cannon, and hurries to the southern section of stairs. Delicately, he tests the steps and descends.

The square hole is easy to find, so Argo sets down his cannon and lays prone again, using his toes and palms to nudge himself toward the edge. He peers through into a dark pit with velvety black walls. Mirror-like water at the bottom reflects his helmet lights. Just beneath the surface there is the faintest outline of something rectangular.

*What is that?*

A sharp *crack* at his feet makes his eyes go wide, and the floor slab bends away beneath him. He snatches at exposed lengths of rebar, but they break like dry twigs in his hands, and the Brick tumbles into a pit.

The slab tumbles after him, exploding dust and sandy chunks.

Argo crashes feet first into the murky water, sinks swiftly to the bottom, and mires waist deep in cloying muck. The slab slams flatly onto the water above him. He raises his arms in time, diverting the slab to one side, but the weight of it drives him to his armpits in loose silt.

He strains his powerful limbs. Dark sediments only draw him deeper, and the Brick freezes in place, helmet lamps barely penetrating the churning, opaque currents.

Teeth grinding, he mutters, "Should've seen *that* coming."

# A More Fitting Icon

Thompson scurries over and around great mounds of ash-loaded glass. Like all of the rock formations he passed before, long fractures run through the rounded heaps. But these have razor-sharp edges that slice the wind with brittle, crystalline moans. Each mound offers its own tone, depending on the lengths and widths of cleavage—some strike dissonant chords with the breezes, others eerily harmonious.

Sun dips below the mountains to the west, and in twilight his armor makes him a shadow among shadows. He sprints uphill to a high point of land, feinting around massive blocks of pale, blasted stone. At the hill's apex, he takes shelter behind the root of what must have been a tremendous wall of the same pale stone and crouches. Looking back the way he came, he sees glinting specks of reflected sunlight drifting above the horizon.

Turning forward, he peeks over the failed wall at total devastation to the southeast. What he mistook for one large crater is in fact five, closely overlapped and filled with murky water. Surrounding terrain is uniformly smooth and black.

*Such firepower...*

His visor shows plumes of heat below the surface of the unnatural lake, feeding billowy columns of steam that drift with the prevailing breeze. He raises his rifle and looks through the scope, magnifying spots of boiling and bubbling deep underwater. Whatever the source of all that heat, it is well-hidden in murky depths. So he lowers his weapon, unsure what the hotspots mean.

Turning west, he looks over a shallow valley, where its far side is swept clear all the way to the new river delta. On the near side, there is an unusually tall heap of rubble. Returning the riflescope to his eye, he zooms in and discovers the heap is propped up by a standing ruin behind it. The ruin's long foundation points directly at the cluster of craters, and Thompson understands the blasts must have been absorbed by the building's front three quarters, leaving the back quarter intact. In a sweeping arc from northeast to south to west, no other building stands. Choice made, he runs downhill past the mounds of sighing glass and weathered stone blocks.

Away from the central craters, the terrain is rugged with crumbled structures. Thompson's long legs propel him gracefully over the shifting slabs and jagged fragments until he can see the building's standing walls. Rifle ready, he takes cover behind a toppled pillar and studies outlines of the structure.

A long front section has utterly collapsed and the debris has spread out into an enormous pancake of hard-packed material. From the midsection back, the building rises one intact floor at a time in a concave ramp up to the standing rear section. Most of the brick façade has dropped away and melted into red clay at the foundation. Leading away from the foundation and down into the valley beyond, a swath of fine red sediment stains the dark soil. Wide, empty windows permit sea breezes to pass with a low howl.

After a couple of quick breaths, he bursts from his hiding place and sprints toward the building with Olympian speed then short-steps to a halt beside a ground floor window. Peeking through the crooked frame, he sees the space inside is hollow in its lower levels, where all but the upper-most floors have dropped to the ground in thick layers. Horizontal bands encircle the interior walls at regular intervals, marking the former placement of each collapsed floor. Only the most rugged supports and load bearing columns remain in place and even these are fractured beyond belief, leaning visibly toward the valley. His eyes trace the weakened support columns up seven floors to a heavily cracked and bowed ceiling.

*No way I'm climbing those.*

He moves to the front of the building where the long ramp of destruction piles against the standing ruin. Time has reduced the mixture to coarse cement, making the ramp remarkably compact.

He follows the easy slope to an open floor. From all appearances, the flooring should have fallen away decades ago—fractures and cracks crisscross every bit of the decking, walls, and ceiling. With one foot planted on the ramp, he jabs at the broken flooring with his other. Sandy dust kicks free but nothing else. He puts some weight on it, ready to leap away. The floor holds.

Thompson eases his way off the ramp and onto the cracked floor. Loose chunks crunch and shift beneath his boots and there is the slightest bounce with each step, making the Gun stare at his feet with confusion. Where the cracks end, the bouncing sensation ends as well, so he thinks no more about it.

The space inside is open. All of the interior walls are down, leaving only the support columns to interrupt his view. Though better preserved than the ragged entryway, the interior is severely dilapidated. Not one of the windows maintains its square corners. All of the internal braces and supports lean. The entire building has shifted, giving nature a billion cracks to wedge apart with ice and time, yet it has not fallen. It is as if the building wills itself to stand out of spite for gravity.

With his rifle held tight to his shoulder, Thompson speeds across the floor, searching every corner, beam, and niche, finding nothing of interest.

*Next floor, then...*

The Gun stands beneath a gap in the ceiling and leaps. His strong hands grip the edge, and he pulls himself up. Half through and propped on his elbows, he looks around. It is a very similar scene to the one below: crooked windows, crumbled supports, fractured flooring.

He lowers his head to push himself all the way up and sees what looks like a transparent fabric at the edge of the gap with threads so fine he has difficulty focusing on them.

Thompson lifts his hanging legs through the gap and kneels at the edge. After a quick glance around, he clicks his helmet lights on low and puts his face to the floor.

A gossamer of reflective strands wraps the edge of the gap. He recoils from the oddity, sitting up. As his lights shine out into the open, he finds reflective strands everywhere. All around him, between the support columns and crisscrossing every surface, netting glints in his helmet lights.

The Gun looks down at himself and sees fine silks have gathered in the joints of his armor, the ends flying weightlessly in flowing air. He lifts the gathered strands from the crook of his arm and rolls them into a cord. Tugging the cord between his hands, he notices significant resistance before it snaps. Individually, the strands are insubstantial—he never noticed them walking through— but combined, the tensile strength is amazing.

Having risked light long enough, the Gun clicks off his lamps. The strands disappear, to his great disappointment, leaving the space with its original dilapidated appearance.

As Thompson moves toward the middle of the space, he notices the ceiling is woven with a thicker mesh of the translucent strands. Dead center of the floor are multiple balls of white spun fibers. Thrilled for something to investigate, he hurries to the curiosities.

Capsules of silken bundles, all half a meter or less, lie casually on the floor. Above the pile is a large, round hole in the ceiling. Webbing is thickly spun around the opening, forming a wide tube that rises and diverts to one side.

Thompson returns his attention to the silken bundles. He extends his bayonet with a *shick* and carves into the nearest one. The fibers cut reluctantly, clinging to the flat of his blade. With care, he bisects the ball, freeing a compressed lump of off-white feathers and hollow bones. The desiccated carcass spills out, its downy feathers flying in the breeze before catching in numerous invisible strands.

Thompson looks again at the fibrous tube above him, when caution urges him to step away. Keeping careful watch of the tube, he searches the rest of the floor. Nothing else draws his interest, so he hops up through another gap in the ceiling.

Propping himself on elbows again, he surveys the new environment before pulling himself through. Silken veils connect support columns, ceiling, and floor like ghosts of walls that once stood. Spun fibers cover every surface in white mats.

He presses all the way up through the gap and crouches near the hole. Veils scarcely move in the breeze, giving them a very taut appearance. Narrow tubes feed in from other areas, connecting the various chambers in a labyrinthine fashion.

*What made this?*

His grip tightens on his rifle, but the lack of movement or heat sources in his visor suggest whatever did this is long gone.

With his rifle pulled tight, he duck-walks stealthily toward one of the veiled walls. More silken bundles cluster in the chamber beyond, attached to the ceiling and floor. Some dangle between on thin cords of spun silk.

Thompson presses the tip of his bayonet into the veil and draws a vertical slit. As he steps through, the strands snag him, requiring effort to break free.

Patrol of the area inside shows it remarkably intact, held together by the micro-fine threads. He sets his attention on the silk-wrapped bundles and, like an exploratory surgeon, dissects them. Fresher victims fall from the cases, almost all of them types of birds, causing him to second guess his assumption that this place is uninhabited.

Slinging his rifle, he takes one of the larger birds in hand. Its black plumage contrasts starkly with the white wrapping. A naked head with empty eye sockets elongates into a hooked beak. Scaly legs attach at the mid section and end with sharp-taloned toes. The Gun takes a wing in each hand and extends them, surprised by the one and a half meter wingspan and the cluster of white feathers at the wingtips.

Thompson contemplates the creature, its head slumping loosely at its chest. He lays the bird down on the silk wrapped floor.

Sticky threads cling to the wings, holding them out. The bird's head flops up and lands facing right.

A lightning bolt of recognition strikes. The Gun looks down at the subtly emblazoned emblem on his rifle then back at the bird. There, stretched out on the floor, is the likeness of Cadre One's icon.

Thompson realizes he is staring. He takes a step and nearly stumbles, his right foot oddly rooted to the floor. Surprised, he looks down and finds a black, bulbous creature busily knitting his ankle with long, spindly legs.

He tries to shoo the creature with his rifle. Despite only being the size of Argo's boot, the creature is strong and it refuses to budge. Thompson plunges his bayonet through the creature's body, pinning it to the floor. Completely impaled, the creature continues to weave.

Astounded at its mission focus, the Gun lifts the spitted creature, holding it upside down before him. He looks into a row of eight shiny black dots. The mouth is little more than a red maw with two articulated, dagger-like teeth. Thrashing legs bear subtle bands of brown, and the pierced abdomen is marked with two nearly parallel zig-zagging lines. With a flick, he hurls the creature across the chamber. It rights itself and staggers away.

When he bends to cut the webbing at his ankle, a tension on the back of his helmet stops him. He looks up into the belly of another creature that is attaching his helmet with long lines to the ceiling. Annoyed, he slashes the lines and spikes the creature before tossing it aside.

At his ankle, a smaller creature has already resumed the work of the first and is netting him up to the knee. Another approaches his left foot, spins around, and starts weaving. Eyes gaping, the Gun shifts his stance and punts the new arrival into the veiled wall. In the same motion, he pivots and stomps the creature knitting his knee. The eight-legged thing merely slumps, its carapace barely flexing under his heel.

Behind it, a scuttling carpet of fist-sized and larger creatures pours through multiple connecting tubes. The slice he made in the veil is already sewn shut, notably thickened. He is being hemmed in.

Thompson slashes at the webs around his leg and tears free. Outnumbered, he dashes away from the advancing horde and cuts through the thinner interior veils. He hacks and carves a path through each chamber, gaining a little ground, powering his way past the clinging strands, searching for a way out.

Two creatures with bodies the size of Argo's torso, launch from tubes to his left and right. Javelin-like legs skitter over his armor, hooking in the overlaps and wrapping strand after strand around him. Sickle-shaped fangs seek for his throat, probing for a weakness.

Thompson struggles with his long weapon, the butt of it catching in the close webs, and he finally jabs the bayonet up into one of his attackers. It refuses to release. He pulls the blade out and rakes it down the creature's side, amputating all four legs at once. The creature drops and scuttles awkwardly away, its severed legs still hooked in his armor.

Thompson wrestles with the other, using his bayonet and brute strength to break its winding threads. With a frustrated roar, he frees his right arm and takes hold of one leg at a time, ripping it from the body. The creature's grip slackens and Thompson punches it in the underbelly. The hit catapults the creature across the chamber, where it lands and struggles to stand on its remaining legs before limping away.

The Gun frantically clears himself of the tangled threads and staggers toward the next chamber. He makes a circular slice in the dividing veil, dives through into a much larger chamber, rolls to his feet with long strands from the floor coming up with him, and looks into the face of a creature over two meters long. Fangs like sabers protrude from its flat head. He shrinks back, leveling his rifle at its plate-like eyes. It does not move.

The Gun gasps with anxious breath, staring at the slumped behemoth. Its massive carapace is dented, almost deflated. Three-meter legs sprawl in all directions, and what he first mistook for hair are thousands of younger creatures slurping fluids from the joints.

Once past his initial shock, he detaches his gaze from the monster and scans the entire chamber. More spheres of spun fiber adorn the upper corners, most with small holes in them.

Thompson's eyes bounce from the massive body to the hair-like young, to the meter-wide egg sacks, making the connections.

*An incubation chamber...*

*And this one gave its life to nourish the young...*

Grateful not to deal with the monster in life, he backs away.

Behind him, a horde chews and clambers through the tangles of his passage. Close by, Thompson spots a wide tube that bends toward the floor. With a quick slash, he drops through and lands on a spongy pile of silken bundles below.

The bulbous creatures swarm from the hole above him and hang upside down from the ceiling. Larger ones form a perimeter while smaller ones spin thick strands across the opening. In moments, the tube is completely sealed, leaving just the perimeter of larger guards. They watch Thompson as closely as he watches them, front legs raised, open red maws flanked by menacing black fangs.

"Okay, I get it. I'm leaving."

The creatures maintain their angry posture, letting the Gun retreat. Freed from attack, Thompson pauses and contemplates his would-be devourers.

*Such cohesion, focus, will, and sacrifice... Our ancestors must have had reasons for choosing the icon they did... But if they wanted to identify with something, this armored eight-legged life form would have been a better choice.*

Conscious that he has intruded, the Gun distills his impressions into a mental snapshot and hustles out the way he came.

# THE FIRST OF US...

Beckert makes long, graceful strides over crystalline black ground, boots crunching on the brittle soil. He vaults obstructions and dodges protruding beams with the ease of a porpoise at sea despite the constant throbbing ache behind his eyes.

A flat-topped hill looms before him, and he rushes up the slope to a square, open field. In the late afternoon sunlight, weak mirages shimmer over irradiated black gravel.

To the northeast, stunted trees cling to low hills, adding the only real color. To the south, the Potomac delta drains into the edge of the Chesapeake Bay. Everywhere between is devastation. Vast rubble fields extend from Chevy Chase in the north through Cleveland Park, McLean Gardens in the south, and Tenleytown in the southwest. Dust clouds roll across blasted, blighted landscape.

Beckert crouches and scans the ruins. Even with his goggles' magnification, there seems little worth investigating. These once-proud buildings are knocked down to their foundations, and materials of their construction are so weathered and corroded they have fused into sterile, radioactive pavement.

*What about sub-floors? Could lower levels be intact? Might be astounding numbers of artifacts buried under there...*

*Without heavy excavators and plenty of time I'll never know.*

He glances up to the sky, watching black birds with enormous wingspans patrol in wide circles. Then he lowers his gaze and looks across the wasteland, zooming in on the eastern hills. Lumpy, curving tree trunks jut from compacted soil with sparse and sickly foliage. He follows the line of hills south, searching over mounds of scorched concrete, and stops when he spots a cylindrical tower to the southeast. The main structure surrounding it has collapsed to a fortified foundation, yet the tower stands straight and true, less than two kilometers away. Beckert hops to his feet and rushes down from his vantage.

Intervening terrain proves a difficult course of jutting beams, shifting cinderblocks, and ledges of wreckage. Despite his agility, it takes the better part of an hour to close the distance, and Beckert pulls himself over the last tall pile to find the tower standing just ahead. Its lower levels are buried in the wreckage of the main building. Armored skin covers the cylinder all the way to its flat roof, interrupted only by a ring of heavy shutters near the top.

He steps closer with reverent awe, feet automatically negotiating the sandy approach. At the tower's base, sand yields to chunks of eroded cement, singed metal, and shattered glass. Nowhere does he see an entrance.

Climbing atop the rubble, Beckert walks the tower's perimeter. Numerous beams and brackets extend into mid-air where the tower once connected to the main structure. Two floors up on the far side there is a short ledge jutting from the tower. Just above the ledge is a door.

Restraining a shout of excitement, Beckert clips his pistols to his back. He maps out the sturdiest handholds then climbs, swings, and flips himself up the side. Atop the ledge, he perches like a gargoyle and surveys the collapsed complex. It is much larger than he realized, where the foundation continues over the hill and part way down the far side. Circular foundations at corners suggest there were other towers attached to the outside of the building, but are broken off at the base.

*Weren't armored like this one, I guess.*

Turning about, the Geek studies what seems to be a standard security door, much like ones at Cadre One. The access panel is utterly destroyed, however, jutting brittle fiber optics through a smashed touch pad.

His hands skim over the door's smooth surface then trace the jams. Its whole frame is warped, most likely from when the main building was ripped away; and the door has shifted in its tracks, leaving a slim gap at the bottom left side.

Beckert reaches to his back rack and retrieves a pry tool. Wedging the flat end into the gap, he draws a deep breath before a mighty pull. The door scoots with a deafening *screech*. Beckert nearly drops the tool in alarm as echoes return the screech again and again. Wincing and cursing, he resets the pry tool. Small, regular tugs nudge the door millimeters at a time with slight chirps. Soon, the door halts and refuses to slide no matter how hard he pulls.

Beckert sizes the gap. Eager to get through it, he removes his pack and pistols, placing them inside. Turning sideways, he slides himself between the door and frame. No matter how he turns, his helmet will not pass. With so little time to search, he cracks the seal on his helmet and lifts it from his head. Hot, dry air evaporates the sweat between silver terminals embedded in his scalp.

He detaches his HDI and goggles from the helmet, setting them just inside the doorway. The too-wide helmet he leaves on the outer ledge, obscuring it with convenient chunks of concrete and dust, then slides through the gap into darkness.

In orderly fashion, Beckert snaps the HDI over silver contact terminals on his head, clicks his goggles firmly in place, slides his rack onto his back, and takes a pistol in each hand. Goggles automatically compensate for low light, revealing the interior space in dim red monochrome. Fixed consoles and tall scanning equipment flank the entrance, beyond which is an open floor. Fine dust blankets everything and even his tentative steps are enough to make it airborne. He tries to stifle a sneeze without success.

Despite irritating dryness coating his throat and sinuses, possibility of the floor collapsing beneath him is a greater concern. Beckert feels the surface with his toes, tapping gently before committing his weight. Despite ravages of centuries, it feels solid, so he moves into the room's center. Like the exterior of the tower, the room is circular, but it feels much smaller than it should be.

*Either the walls are triple thick, or there's something I'm missing...*

He looks back at the entrance, seeing his own tracks. In each boot print, the dust has been smudged away, exposing polished ceramic tiles. Beckert looks down at his feet, and slides the dust aside. The letters *G-I-L-A* gleam up at him. He kneels and sweeps away more of the dust, uncovering more letters and part of an image. On hands and knees, he works faster, coughing and sputtering amid whorls of choking particles until the image is revealed. He stands to see its entirety.

A four-meter-wide hawk—head turned right, wings spread, talons empty—adorns the floor. Below it, inscribed into a curving banner, are the words *VIGILANTIA, SERVITIUM, VIRTUS, INVICTUS.*

Stunned to immobility, he stares for long minutes, breathing the dusty air, goggles clicking photo after photo and stitching them into a hi-res mosaic. Then he drops to his knees and caresses the image.

*The Cadre was here. This PROVES it.*

Hundreds of questions form in the Geek's mind, all demanding immediate answers. His eyes lift to the circular ceiling that hides upper levels of the tower. It appears to be a single sheet of metal without fixtures or seams. Neither does he see any doorways in the walls. He squints skeptically.

*There must be a way...*

Beckert returns to the entryway and walks the room's perimeter, tapping the smooth walls with a pistol. Halfway around, he hears a faint, hollow echo. To confirm, he pounds the panel with his armored fist and the echo returns a bit louder.

Beckert clips his pistol and pulls out the pry bar. With a confident stab, he wedges the flat end through the panel's seam and yanks. Metallic veneer shoots away with little resistance, revealing a stone gray subsurface. Four bright fasteners secure a smaller, rectangular panel. The heads of the fasteners are irregular, requiring a very specialized tool to remove. He grins, having exactly that tool in his kit, and backs out the shiny bolts.

Beneath the secondary panel is a flat black rectangle. Ribbon cables attach at the lower edge and run into the wall. The configuration is familiar, as Cadre One has many of these sensor pads embedded in the walls near critical access points. Power is a problem, however, as lines route through each pad to ensure the door remains locked during outages. Beckert knows the pad also requires sequential pulses of exact voltages to prevent someone bypassing it. Too much voltage, or too little, will keep the lock shut. Only the correct magnetic key code will send the right voltages to the locks and release them.

Beckert cradles his chin, considering the power problem.

*Assuming draw is the same as Cadre One's, my HDI could supply it. Maybe...*

With more delicate tools from his kit, the Geek taps lines onto the ribbon cable and fashions a wire harness for the open ends. He snips the incoming power lead and plugs the recharge lanyard of his HDI into the main bus. With a thought, he flows power into the magnetic sensor pad. A tiny green diode on the pad's corner illuminates.

Goggles scroll with code as his HDI connects with the sensor pad. To his amazement, the pad recognizes him as an authorized user automatically, permitting him into the diagnostic/admin functions and displaying available commands.

*MAINTAIN PASS CODES?* the pad offers.

*Too easy*, Beckert thinks with a smirk. He instructs the pad to list valid codes and copies them. Closing the admin functions, he runs all six pass codes in succession and six individual clunks sound from the wall to his left. A perfectly concealed door recesses with a hiss.

The Geek disconnects, retracts his lanyards, and packs up his tools. Pistol in hand, he steps to the recessed portal. Apprehension and excitement vie inside him as he hauls the door aside. It slides stiffly, requiring constant pressure due to the non-functioning motor assist, and he trains his weapon past the door's edge.

Darkness beyond defies the light gathering of his goggles, giving the space an indefinite dimension. He takes a tentative step in. The floor beneath him drops a millimeter and *clicks*.

Beckert leaps back and rolls to the side. He crouches beside the open portal, breathing fast. Dust flies from his sudden movement, tickling his sinuses with each rapid inhale. Stifling another sneeze, he waits.

No sound.

Beckert pulls a box from his pack frame and dumps the empty food wrappers. He lobs the box into the open doorway and aims his pistols, fingers on triggers. Seconds pass. He listens.

Nothing happens.

Gathering his nerve, he slides his goggles up to his forehead, flips them inside out, and thinks a bright white onto the lenses. With his improvised headlamps he can just make out a black-painted stairwell so steep it might as well be a ladder. Light sconces are embedded in the walls but are dark and functionless.

He searches around the doorway for more booby traps. Not finding any, he collects the box and cautiously strides over the floor plate to the stairs. Every step is welded in place, yielding not so much as a creak under his ascent.

The staircase switches back and at the top of the flight is a wide-open security door. Pistols trained on the open doorway, Beckert creeps up the remaining stairs and steps through. Inside is a windowless, circular room with curved rows of workstations that face a low dais at room's center. The dais is equipped with its own terminal and a high-backed chair. Flat screens cover the walls in all directions, extending all the way up to a five-meter ceiling.

As Beckert moves through the rows, he cannot understand why all of the terminals have been physically damaged. Some are smashed, others have foreign objects embedded in them. Most show some amount of burning. He stops at one terminal and removes a fire axe from a network junction box. After wrenching it free, he stares at it, bewildered, then sets it down.

*Why would anyone do this?*

With nothing else to see besides wrecked consoles, he returns to the stairwell and ascends.

A high security pressure door bars access to the room on the next floor. Thick, motor-driven pistons seal the portal from all sides. He thumps his hand against the door, feeling its substantial strength.

*Need Argo for this one.*

Beckert ascends again and arrives at a spartan chamber, furnished only with simple concrete benches around the perimeter. At center is a circular basin three meters across and devoid of water. Mummified fish lie at the crusted bottom like bony strips of leather with gaping mouths and empty eye sockets.

Six evenly spaced viewports are cut into the walls, filled with solid blocks of glass and covered by armored shutters. Timeworn gaps in the shutters allow thin beams of sunlight to pass. To the east, some of the shutters have dropped away, and Beckert moves to an unblocked viewport for a glimpse. Radiant orange and red clouds soar over a phenomenal expanse of glittering water. His head tilts with the majesty of it and he puts his hands up to the thick, pitted glass. Overwhelmed, he slumps onto one of the concrete benches.

*Such beauty...*

The Geek stares at the bright clouds until blue spots burn onto his retinas. Blinking, he rises from the bench, returns to the stairwell, and climbs the last flight.

Stairs end at a short landing. Barring further progress is a simple, windowless bulkhead with a horizontal lever mid-height, right side. Beside it, there is something else, something raised above the surface that he cannot quite make out by touch. With eyes finally adjusting to the dark, he leans close to it. The meager light from his inverted goggles shine upon the familiar Cadre Hawk, clutching twin globes in its talons. A pentagonal cluster of gold stars is centered above it.

Beckert straightens to attention, routine and protocol so ingrained that even here he cannot force himself to barge into a General's chamber. The Geek clears his throat and raps his knuckles against the bulkhead three times.

"General, if you *do not* want me to enter your quarters, please say so."

Predictably, there is no answer.

"Sir, I take your lack of objection as permission."

The Geek grips the lever and thrusts it down. Metal scrapes harshly against metal, and the door screeches as it swings. Aiming his pistol straight ahead, Beckert follows it into the room.

The air has a musty harshness more severe than the entryway and leaves a bitter taste on his tongue. Nearly gagging, Beckert covers his mouth and breathes only through his nose.

Thin rays from a shuttered skylight offset the darkness, illuminating the front edge of a desk and two deep chairs placed opposite. At Beckert's approach, black dust—fine as smoke—swirls in the light. It loiters in the air, coating his sinuses, and he wishes for his helmet.

Bright rays of natural light shrink his pupils, making the rest of the room difficult to see, so he flips his goggles over and lowers them over his eyes. Compensating for contrasts of bright and dim, his goggles reveal the room in all its dimensions.

Circular walls enclose a large office space. Two couches sag against the wall to the right, with a low rectangular table dividing them. To the left, a sculpted hawk stares at him with piercing eyes. Matching gazes, Beckert strides to the wall-mounted sculpture.

Every feather of the spread wings is carved in life-like detail, frozen mid-swoop, legs thrust forward. Taloned feet clasp two spheres: one yellowish-white, one slightly smaller and bluish-white. Fine dust covers the top surfaces, yet the hawk's eyes are unmarred. He would not be surprised if the statue shook itself off and flew away.

Turning from the hawk, Beckert spots four transparent cases on the wall behind an off-center desk. Curious, the young Operator moves toward them then freezes, not breathing. Slumped over the desk is a desiccated corpse.

Black dust blankets the corpse, camouflaging it with the

desktop. Paper-thin scraps of skin and wisps of hair cling to an eyeless skull. Shoulder and arm bones rest flat on the desk, leading to hands held together by brittle tendons. On the floor around the wheeled chair is a lumpy ring of dust with protruding ribs, vertebrae, and leg bones. A pelvis, wearing the shreds of trousers, remains seated.

The Geek looks closer and finds a tattered collar still encircling the neck bones. Pinned to it is a cluster of pentagonal stars in untarnished gold.

*The General!*

From the five-star cluster, Beckert's eyes move to the skull, turned on its side. He peers at it, amazed at its smallness—this person could not have been taller than one and a half meters.

*How could one so stunted be general of the Cadre?*

He scrutinizes the skull and notices a hole in the temple. The Geek's eyes move to the bony hand. It still holds something.

Beckert leans in and puffs away powdery dust between the fingers. A stifling cloud billows from the desktop, and he recoils, fanning it away. There, beneath withered metacarpals, an ivory handle reflects the fading light.

Beckert gently lifts the General's hand. Tendons snap, and dry bones fall to the desk. He grimaces as if in pain.

"Sorry, Sir."

Damage done, he takes the item from the desk and rubs it. Much of the tarnish falls away, revealing intricate engravings in silvery metal. An elongated barrel extends from a rotating, six-chambered cylinder. Beneath the cylinder hangs a thin trigger, enclosed by a ring-like guard too small for Beckert's armored finger. The overlapping letters *G-S-P* are carved into the grip, and on the other side is a detailed carving of a perched eagle with wings spread. Again, he is confused.

*Clearly, this is some sort of pistol, with grip, trigger, barrel... but such a small caliber...delicate mechanics...the images engraved into it... What good could it have possibly been in combat?*

He looks at the barrel, letting his goggles measure its bore.

Then he looks back at the skull and its temporal perforation. A match.

There are no signs of struggle around the room, and a sickening revelation takes hold. Beckert drops the pistol to the desk where it clatters noisily.

*Did you self-terminate?*

Pushing through his confusion, the Geek takes photographs in hope that Thompson or Argo might be able to explain.

Turning from moldered bones, Beckert faces the first in a row of plexi-steel wall cases. Black dust clings to them and he sweeps it away, finding plush red fabric inside. Propped above the bunched cloth is an elongated D-shaped item. Its top and bottom curve to points, which are connected by a taut cord. The tips are bright white and carved in exquisite detail with many rows of soldiers in overlapping plates of armor. Along the curvature of the object are alternating sections of cord wrappings and unintelligible inscriptions. Just below the midpoint is a narrowed grip.

The polish, the craft, the careful preservation all suggest the item is extremely valuable. Aside from its intricate appearance, however, he sees no utility and dubious worth.

*Strange that anyone would keep such a thing...*

Determined to solve at least one mystery, Beckert inspects the rest of the case. At the back, he finds a painting of a man, very round in the middle, sitting in a wheeled cart. Long hair is tied up on his head, and he is draped in loose plates, possibly a primitive form of armor. The man is attended by others, similarly attired, who sit astride tall, four-legged creatures with long heads. Many of the creatures appear impatient with a single hoof raised. One man holds patterned flags aloft.

The group gazes down at a distant field where thousands of men plunge long poles and metal into one another. Many ride creatures in full gallop, looking backward from their saddles and drawing on the cords of these D-shaped devices. Barbed shafts lie across the drawn bows.

In a fit of disbelief, Beckert exclaims, "They're *killing* each other?"

The Geek scours the painting for some sign of the blue-skinned enemy, but vivid slashes and trails of red confirm human on human violence.

Mind reeling and stomach turning, he forces himself to take it in, to document and store it in his HDI. As he is about to move on, he notices the corner of an untarnished brass plaque on the wall above. He clears the dust with a thumb and reads.

*"Subutai, most renowned of Ghenghis Khan's Dogs of War.*

*"This bow was discovered in the tomb of Subutai, wrapped in silk and placed atop the General's body. It is unlikely the bow was ever used in combat, as Subutai was not a physical leader. Yet it was clearly treasured, as he carried it at all times.*

*"Such craftsmanship was rare in his era, and only someone of extravagant means could afford such work. This simple fact, along with the following translated inscription, suggests this bow was a gift from the Khan himself:*

*"My General, My Friend."*

Many words in the plaque are unfamiliar to the young Operator. The context is clear, however: this was the personal weapon of a general—a general who slaughtered his own kind—and it was bestowed out of *appreciation*. Beckert grips his aching temples and squeezes.

*This makes no sense at all.*

The next case is the same width, though less tall, and when he sweeps the dust aside he finds more of the bunched red cloth. Cradled above it is a bright, curved blade, over a meter long. Only the outer edge is sharpened, and the inner edge bears an indented channel down most of its length. A perpendicular metal disc separates the grip from the blade and is carved with a scene of rocks, water, sunlight, and gnarled trees. An inlay of a black bone, traced in white, runs the handle's length to a golden pommel with twin silk tassels.

Beckert gazes longingly at such elegance. His eyes trace the polished metal, and he notices subtle patterns cut into the blade. Even these cuts are polished, giving them the appearance of hovering above the mirrored finish.

On the cradle's lower rung rests a scabbard. Black lacquer coats its length from the silk cords at the top to the gold inlay disc at its base. A circle is stamped into the center of the disc with rays streaming out in all directions.

*Finally, something sensible*, Beckert thinks. *A good bladed weapon for close quarters...*

Like the previous case, there is a painting of a man inside. Unlike the chaos and barbarism of Subutai's image, however, this image depicts a large man sitting peacefully. Angular black robes exaggerate his shoulders, secured with a sash at his waist. His hair is neatly tied and bundled at the back of his head. Wispy facial hairs adorn his mouth and chin.

The Geek looks closer and recognizes the weapon's grip at the man's waist with the scabbard tucked through the sashes. He finds the plaque above the case, rubs away obscuring dust, and reads.

*"Minamoto-no-Yoritomo: Japan's first Shogun.*

*"The term Shogun is an abbreviation of Sei-i Taishogun, meaning 'Great General who has subdued the Eastern Barbarians.' Under Yoritomo, the term quickly came to mean 'de-facto ruler.' After seizing power, he marginalized the aristocracy, reduced the Emperor to a figurehead, and made Samurai the ruling class."*

Beckert looks back at the tranquil figure. Most of the words in the plaque elude his understanding, but this was clearly a man of action.

*Interesting that he should look so relaxed...*

The next case is both shorter and wider than the last, appointed with the same red cloth. The object inside bears numerous scars, nicks, scrapes, and dents. The metal is dingy, unpolished, yellowed. At one end, a sharp point widens into a long, double-sided blade. The blade is broadest at the midpoint then quickly rounds into a cylindrical sleeve. Several rivets are driven through the sleeve.

Beckert shrinks back at such crudeness. It enjoys the same plush accommodations as the others, suggesting this battered, ugly thing is equally valued. He nearly passes by, when curiosity compels him to learn why such base metal should be worth preserving.

The image inside the case is of a mosaic, large sections of which are missing. On the left of the image, a young man with free brown hair, large eyes and nose, drives a long-headed animal into a formation of soldiers on the right. Soft armor covers the man's chest, adorned with a fretting face. With one hand, the man holds a long spear, which impales an opposing soldier.

The image is no help at all, so he clears the plaque and reads.

*"Alexander the Great.*

*"Arguably the most successful military commander in history, Alexander of Macedon waged his campaign all the way from Greece to the banks of the Beas River in India.*

*"Already famous for his undoing of the Gordian Knot, Alexander achieved his greatest fame at Gaugamela. There, his army of 47,000 faced approximately 1,000,000 Persian soldiers. Outnumbered over twenty to one and meeting on a battlefield prepared by the Persian Commander, Darius, Alexander charged at the head of his own forces and broke Darius's lines. Fearing for his life, Darius fled the battle,*

*leaving his troops disorganized, where Alexander was able
to crush them.*

*"This spearhead was Alexander's personal weapon,
and its marks attest to the many times he put himself in
harm's way. His boldness was tempered by practicality; and
he insisted on keeping and maintaining this reliable weapon,
rather than trade for something untested in battle, no matter
its appeal."*

When Beckert looks again at the spearhead, he understands its
latent worth. His own pistols are battered, scarred, and extensively
repaired. He trusts them implicitly, knowing they will function
when he needs them. It is a wisdom he instantly identifies with, an
insight possibly into Alexander's success.

The last case on the wall is open, its red fabric tattered and
grungy. In the center is an empty cradle. At the back of the case is
a well-preserved black and white photograph, however, depicting
a stern-faced man in polished metal helmet and knee-high black
boots. His heavy, plain coat hangs to mid-thigh, with a gun belt
strapped around it. A bright white pistol grip juts from the holster.
The man's eyes have a fearsome intensity.

Beckert clears the adjacent plaque and reads.

*"General George S. Patton*

*"Brash and supremely confident, Patton believed
he was the re-incarnation of valiant warriors, including
a Roman Legionnaire, an officer under Napoleon, even
Hannibal, himself. A devoted and professional soldier,
Patton consumed any news, report, or publication about
his enemy to better understand him. By understanding his
enemy, he reasoned, he would know how to defeat him.*

*"In World War II, General Patton turned the Germans'*

*blitzkrieg tactics against them, and his 3rd Army was continually on the move, scoring victory after victory. His style was absolute, with no objective but total defeat of his opponent. While the Germans had many allied generals to contend with, Patton was the only one they truly feared.*

*"'May God have mercy on my enemies, because I won't.'"*

Beckert lingers at the vacant case, staring at the image of the drably-clad man. There is the same intensity he sees in General O'Kai, the same intensity of every general displayed at the Cadre memorial. The recognition resonates, building a familial link to this long-dead soldier. He breaks off mid-thought, his jaw dropping.

*He must have been the first of us.*

Never before has Beckert desired to possess something as intensely as this photo. His hands work of their own volition, detaching the simple frame from its mounting and storing it in a pack compartment.

His tour of the cases complete, he reflects upon each of them. There must be a special insight from each weapon into the success of its owner. One is obvious: the mended yet sturdy spearhead shows Alexander's pragmatism. He did not care for ornate or flashy things. The others did, however. Even Patton, in his drab clothing, carried an ostentatious sidearm.

*But how could that be useful? Was it distracting to an enemy?*

*Maybe the Major and Lieutenant can make something out of this.*

Beckert strolls through the room, stopping briefly at the couches. Synthetic fabric sags over metal frames, the cushions crumbled to a pile underneath. Neither the couches nor the table dividing them offer anything of interest. Above the table, fastened to the wall, is another dust-covered plaque. He slides himself between the furniture to clear the inscribed brass plate.

*"You are the wife of a German officer; so you will take what I have to tell you upright and unflinching. You shall know the truth. This is the grimmest of struggles in a hopeless situation. Misery, hunger, cold, renunciation, doubt, despair, and horrible death.*

*"I cannot deny my share of personal guilt in all of this. I tell myself that, by giving my life, I have paid my debt.*

*"Augusta, you will sense when the hour has come for you to be strong. Don't be embittered and don't suffer too much from my absence. I am not cowardly, only sad that I can't give greater proof of my courage than to die for this useless cause.*

*"Don't forget me too quickly.*

*"--Anonymous German soldier's last letter home from Stalingrad (Volgograd), 1943."*

A smaller brass plate is mounted below the main plate.

*"In few words, the horrors of war are made plain. It is a potent and poignant reminder that unrestrained hostility does not just end lives. For those left behind, it ruins them. Remember these words, graduates, and let them steer your conscience during your careers as professional soldiers.*

*"–Maj. Gen. Walston Booker, Commandant, National War College"*

Beckert's goggles scan the plaque and save the image in his HDI along with the others.

The Geek investigates the deep chairs opposite the desk. Like the couches, they offer nothing of note. So he walks behind the desk again, drumming his fingers on the top.

*There's a drawer...*

With the same unease he felt at the entrance, he hesitates then slides it open. A short glass, an empty bottle, some loose pistol cartridges, and a picture frame reside within. He lifts the frame and turns it over, seeing a woman and three small children in brightly colored clothes, laughing. On a table before them is a rectangular item, planted with fifty burning sticks along its edges. Within the framing of tiny flames are the words, *Happy Birthday, Daddy* in rough script. The image is scanned and recorded, then returned to the drawer.

Raking his toe through the dusty ring around the chair, Beckert drags several gold adornments into the light. He kneels and picks through the dust with a finger, pulling out various medallions, rings, buttons, and insignias. There is a surprising quantity.

He scoops the golden assortment and lays it out on the desk top, reading each piece. *For uncommon Valor...Courage... Service...Duty...Achievement...Loyalty...* The awards describe a man of impressive accomplishments.

Beckert nudges the awards around the desk, grouping like ones together, when he grazes an irregularity in the desk's surface. His finger traces a wide, rectangular seam.

*A monitor?*

In an instant, he has pry tool in hand, and he levers the seam. The action is gritty and resistant, but the top of a large viewscreen edges into view.

*A workstation!*

Beckert moves to the right side of the desk and locates an access panel. Inside, the workstation is crowded with copper-plated circuit boards, all turned green with corrosion. Black trails run down from the seam in the desktop, forming dried rivulets on the compartment's inner walls. A large battery backup is completely discharged, bristling with crystals where the fluids pooled.

Such poor condition tempers his excitement, but he fires up his HDI anyway and jacks into the maintenance port.

Code scrolls by in his goggles while he attempts to explore the circuits. As expected, nothing works. He shuts his HDI down and sits back.

*Maybe there's something in there I can salvage...*

The Geek pulls several boxes from his rack and opens them with a touch. Tools both delicate and sturdy spread from the opened boxes. Pliers in hand, he clamps the end of a circuit board and pulls along its rails. The brittle board snaps where he gripped it, leaving a pliers-shaped notch.

*This is gonna take forever.*

The Geek takes a full breath and looks into the guts of his electronic/photonic patient. Returning pliers to the box, he selects long tweezers and a scraping tool. With surgeon's care, each connection and rail is stripped, cleared, and loosened. Slowly, gently, he slides the board from its place. Every bit of it is rotten.

Beckert sets the board on the desktop and moves on, working through all of the network interfaces, communication interfaces, graphics processors, even the bulky power supply and battery backup. All of them are corroded beyond recovery.

He wipes sweat from his sparse eyebrows then focuses on a fist-sized box deep within the machine. It sits on the rugged motherboard in a square socket. Bundles of fiber optics and raised bus rails feed in from all directions.

*Let's see if you remember anything.*

With another deep breath, he reaches in. The moment his tools touch the box, it collapses. Inside is a silvery, translucent crystal with symmetrical branches in 45 degree and 90 degree angles.

Beckert grins at the glimmering jewel. He takes his time tweezing away debris, removing the restraints, and he eases it up from the socket. There is a slight *pop*. His heart skips a beat, and he stares, frozen. Then terror turns to joy when he realizes the crystal is intact and free of the mount, undamaged. With a great exhale of relief, he reaches in and collects the crystalline memory core.

The Geek turns the core over and over, letting his HDI analyze it for cracks or imperfections. The crystal's thick branches sparkle with microscopic interior facets but there are no defects.

Treating it like a freshly decanted neonate, Beckert rests the crystalline core on the desktop and removes his back rack. Laying the rack flat, he pulls more boxes free and unpacks them. Beside the memory core, he lays out an assortment of his own circuit boards, wires, harnesses, and a battery. Moving down the row, he assembles the parts and seats the memory core in his improvised machine.

Lines of code scroll in his goggles as his HDI powers up. He pulls a lanyard to the assembly and connects it with a *click*. Perceptions buzz as they cross over into the virtual domain of his HDI, giving Beckert the sensation of weightlessness in infinite space. Lines of code scroll faster and soon he is swimming in a digital sea of strings and pathways. Wasting no time, he goes right for the general's archives.

"*ENTER PASSKEY*," demands the crystal.

Beckert initiates his usual strings of hacks. A surge of feedback hits his HDI like a maul.

*Good security*, he thinks, wincing.

The Geek pulls back and studies the virtual construct floating before him. He orbits it and passes through it, admiring the complexity. Regardless of the intricacy it is a familiar system, and once he has the correct string the access point unfolds into a galaxy of directories.

His HDI automatically categorizes by date stamp and selects the most recent entry, dated nearly one thousand years earlier. The file is labeled, *Resignation*.

Beckert executes the file and video plays in his goggles of a man at a metal desk, wearing a charcoal gray dress uniform with choker collar. Bright medals and ribbons adorn his chest, shoulders, and sleeves. Unlike the crisp perfection of the uniform, however, the man is pale and emaciated. Hands clasped on the desk before him, he speaks in a deep baritone.

"To President MacFarlane, Prime Minister Mehta, Chairman Zukhov, General Secretary Choi, and Chancellor Wilhelm, may this message find you alive and well."

The man grits his teeth, making the corners of his jaw bulge. "Our fleet is annihilated. We…"

He interrupts himself, looking away before resuming.

"We need to prepare for a total ground assault. I have promoted Major General Noromi to Full General, and have given him command of Regional Earth Forces. He is a supreme tactician, far better at urban combat than I, and he will provide our people their strongest defense.

"I have evacuated my staff via the D.C. tunnel to our Arlington Command Bunker, where they will continue the fight. I must recommend you evacuate your civilian populations into shelter and fortify them with supplies for several years. The enemy is coming in overwhelming force, and, if the massacres at our colonies are the example, they will kill everyone they find…"

He pauses, reaching out to something off screen. When he looks back, his eyes are watered, and his voice falters.

"I could not halt our enemy's advance through the colonies and I have failed to defend our home. I therefore resign as Supreme Commander of United Armed Forces. General Noromi has my endorsement as successor. He is dogged and relentless, and… well…" The general nods to himself, jutting his lower lip slightly. "He's a tough soldier.

"Regarding research stations Cadre One and Cadre Two, their secrecy may be their saving grace. There have been no shipments to or from them since this war began, and I have broadwaved a message to maintain perfect silence. We may not know for some time whether or not they survived, but I pray they do."

The official demeanor drops, and the general picks up a short glass. He drains the last of a brown liquid, savors it, and swallows.

"My love and prayers to you and yours."

He sets the glass down and lifts a white-handled revolver from a desk drawer.

"I'm going to be with mine and beg their forgiveness."

*RECORDING END.*

Beckert flees from the memory core and lifts his goggles,

hyperventilating. Black dust rolls deep into his lungs, launching a fit of coughing.

Once settled, he looks again at the general's skeleton, then at the tarnished pistol, which killed him. He re-opens the drawer to look at the framed photograph of the woman and children.

Utter defeat was engraved in the general's drawn cheeks, sunken eyes, and wrinkled chin. Beckert expected a commanding presence with determined brow, broad shoulders, radiant confidence…anything but this desolate shell of a man.

His mind leaps to General O'Kai. No matter how he tries, Beckert cannot imagine his own general in such a state.

*O'Kai is the most stalwart, ingenious, and capable person I've known. No way would he give up, not ever. But what if this man was once like O'Kai? Could the enemy be that powerful?*

Mystery heaps upon mystery. Determined to find some answers, Beckert lowers his goggles, returns to the virtual world of the memory core, and watches the video a second time.

He studies the general's demeanor more than what he says. There is a determination within those tired eyes, now that he is looking for it, and…

"CADRE *TWO*?"

Beckert slaps his hands to either side of his head, not believing he missed it the first time. He halts the video.

*Cadre Two…* he thinks again, the hugeness of the revelation scarcely fitting in his mind. His eyes roam the office, stopping on the hawk statue. He stares at the bluish-white orb, at last understanding why it looks so familiar.

"That's *our* star…"

He yanks the lanyard of his HDI free and hurries to the statue, not caring about the swirls of dust. His goggles scan the orb for exact color and dimension.

The Geek's attention shifts to the Yellowish-White orb, and he scans it just as thoroughly.

*Could you be to scale?*

The relative size and color suggest an F class star, late in its main sequence and becoming a red giant. If the bluish orb represents Cadre One, the comparative size and color temperature alone could rule out over ninety percent of known stars in the galaxy. And considering the fact it would likely be a comparable distance from Earth, his search narrows to a handful of candidates.

Realization leaps from thrilling discovery to deadly panic.

*If the Blueskins find this…*

Beckert takes a pistol by the muzzle and smashes the butt against the outstretched talons. The legs break off and the orbs shatter on the solid floor plates. He kneels and pulverizes the fragments.

Rising to his feet, Beckert looks down at the mess he has made. He sweeps his feet through the powdered porcelain to ensure no identifying fragments remain. Beside him the winged statue seems accusing in its glare, giving him a twinge of regret for smashing something so beautiful.

*1:00 until rendezvous*, his goggles display. The timer minimizes and slides to the upper left corner where it continues the countdown.

*Three hours already?*

The Geek surveys the office, but the office lighting looks exactly the same. He lifts his goggles and realizes late day sunlight has been replaced by silvery moonlight—his goggles compensated so gradually, he never noticed the change.

Beckert strides to the desk and disassembles his improvised machine, returning each part to its proper container. The memory core receives special accommodation in the empty food container, packed and padded alongside the dead general's golden adornments. He gives the sealed box a shake, ensuring the contents are secure and rattle-free before snapping it onto his rack.

With all of his equipment packed, Beckert takes a final look before departing. He faces the exit but turns once more toward the display cases. Bright metal of the curved blade will not let him leave. It seems to call to him, as if begging not to be left behind.

Beckert hurries to the case. Pry tool in hand, he pops the

latches. The vacuum-sealed case inhales dusty air with a *whoosh*.

The Geek reaches for the blade's handle and lifts it from the cradle. It is lighter than he expected. His other hand grabs the shiny scabbard, and he slides the blade home with a subtle *click* then wedges the sheathed blade between his rack and armor.

On his way out, Beckert turns and puts his heels together. He snaps a respectful salute to the slumped general, spins, and hurries down the stairs.

At the entry floor, he takes a step toward the foyer and hesitates. Behind him, the staircase continues down into unexplored areas.

*Being late to a rendezvous is bad, but missing something vital could be worse.*

After a moment of silent debate, the young Operator returns to the staircase and slides down the handrails for faster progress.

The stairway switches back over and over until Beckert is certain he is several meters underground. Still, the staircase descends. Total darkness forces him to invert his goggles again for their meager light. Not a single portal or doorway opens from the deepening shaft.

The next flight lands him up to his waist in water. Spreading waves crash against the close walls and slosh up, collapsing and meeting in the middle before settling.

*Without my helmet, this trip is over.*

He looks into the depths, finding only blackness. On the wall beside him, however, is a bright yellow arrow pointing down the stairwell. The words, *DC Tunnel* are stenciled inside it.

The Geek flashes back to the general's resignation, and he remembers something about the staff being evacuated through a "DC Tunnel."

Giddy with excitement, Beckert climbs the long flights back to the surface. Collecting his helmet at the tower's entrance, he latches it securely before dashing across darkened landscape to rendezvous with his comrades.

# Aschimothusia

Alone at the rendezvous point, Beckert hunkers down and watches two patrol craft sweeping Washington's northern outskirts. The counter in his goggles reads *+00:15* in bright red, but Argo and Thompson are nowhere in sight. The Geek shifts uneasily in his crouch.

Unable to wait another second, he leaps from his spot and heads toward the nearest cluster of standing structures. Bright moonlight provides ample illumination, and he picks up Argo's deep tracks in drying mud.

The tracks lead to a relatively intact section of building then proceed inside through a ground floor window. Beckert runs on his toes, careful to step only in Argo's steps, and he breezes through the open floor plan. Tracks continue up to the second floor then end at a section of freshly broken concrete.

"Hammer Fall," challenges an electronically clipped voice behind him.

"Killed them all," Beckert replies automatically. The Geek turns and sees Thompson crouched near the outer wall several meters away, face plate raised. The Gun lowers his rifle and resumes his gaze out the window.

Beckert hustles to his leader and kneels.

"Sir, I couldn't wait at the rendezvous, there are—"

"I know," Thompson interrupts. His gray eyes follow a slow-moving search craft at the city's eastern edge. "I was about to collect you when I saw you approach."

Beckert looks his leader over, noticing he is covered in mud. He is about to ask but the Gun speaks first.

"Did you find anything?"

Beckert's eyes light up. "Yes, Sir! A standing tower in the next valley." The Geek points and gesticulates. "Such things inside, Major!" Beckert becomes lost in his recollections. "But they don't make sense. They—"

A roaring crackle to the west silences him. Both men raise weapons and take cover behind support beams. Peering around the beams, they see a pair of search craft decelerating half a kilometer from the rendezvous spot. Triangular pink rays fan out beneath the craft.

Thompson's lip twitches. He points to a thin rope leading into the pit.

"Get down there and help Brick pack up. We're leaving."

"Sir!" Beckert acknowledges. He looks over the edge of the deep pit and sees a large, rectangular object at the bottom. A broken slab of concrete leans against it, half submerged in the surrounding water. In the top of the rectangular object, an Argo-sized hole is cut. Dim light flickers from within.

The Geek takes hold of the carbon-fiber braid and rappels expertly. He drops onto the object and peeks through the hole into a vault of some kind. Numerous racks are tossed, their contents spilled across the floor.

"Ah, Sergeant," Argo greets from inside, labset in hand. Muddy residue covers the big Operator head to foot. "I'm glad you're here. Hurry!"

Beckert pours himself through the hole head first, catches the edge with his fingertips, flips upright, and drops to his feet. Piles of square plastic crunch beneath him.

"Gah! Careful!" Argo chides. "Those are media records!"

Beckert freezes, eyes searching for a clear place to stand. When he steps away, there is a long string of *snaps* and *cracks*.

"Here," Argo states, tossing over a small electronic device. "See what you can do with this." The Brick resumes his study of the vault's corner.

Beckert looks down at the flimsy device. *Too delicate to be Cadre made*, he reckons. A glass lens is nested at one end with a viewfinder on the opposite side. He flips out a side display and finds a narrow slot, occupied by one of the plastic records.

"It's a media recorder."

"I figured that out," Argo says with a smirk. "Can you fix it?"

"Yeah, sure. But Major says we're moving out."

Argo spins around, eyes wide. He looks over the scattered records as though in pain. Grimacing, he reaches into a compartment of his rack and pulls out two thick sacks. One he holds out to Beckert.

"Bag what you can. Move fast!" The Brick's hand shovels loose plastics into the wide-mouthed bag. Beckert stashes the small video recorder then drags the open bag through the piles like a fishing net.

With both sacks stuffed to capacity, the soldiers look at what they must leave behind—another ten bags at least. Argo pulls his drawstring tight and passes the sack to his comrade.

"Take this."

Beckert zips his own drawstring tight and takes the cavernous bag from Argo. Argo collects his weapon and crouches beneath the entrance hole. Lifting the bulky cannon over his head, he leaps up and catches the opening's rim, pressing himself the rest of the way through. His round helmet pokes down from the hole.

"Pass me the bags."

Beckert lofts each bag up to his comrade. While Argo splices the drawstrings into a harness, the Geek looks into the corner where Argo was working. Propped inside a bent cabinet are two small skulls. He steps over to them, noting the marks of Argo's handling. Below is a mixed heap of brittle bone and synthetic fabrics. Arm bones reach from one skeleton to the other.

Beckert takes the skulls and places them with the rest of the bones, having to guess which belongs to whom. When he steps back a terrible feeling washes over him. Unlike the swift death of the General, these people had to wait for their end. Awareness of mortality must have consumed them. Huddled close and locked in darkness, their embracing arms offered the only comfort.

Pushing through the heaviness in his chest, the Geek notices an intact brown bag beside one of the skeletons. The cover flap is thrown back, and the mud-streaked interior proves Argo was rummaging through it.

Unable to restrain his curiosity, the young Operator delves into the contents: personal electronics smashed to oblivion, small notebooks, short pencils in vibrant colors, dried out waxy sticks in shades of deep red, a cracked leather binder stuffed with numbered cards and IDs, a brown plastic bottle with a white cap, and a ring with three times as many baubles as key fobs.

A small zippered pouch hides near the mouth of the bag, and Beckert excitedly opens it. Inside are eight more of the media records.

"*Sergeant!*"

Beckert's spine straightens with something like terror. He spins to see Argo's scowling face poking through the roof.

"Gun said, *Move out!*"

"*Y-yes, sir*," the Geek stammers. He thrusts his hand into the small pouch and retrieves the extra records. Hustling to the exit hole, he stuffs them into a box from his rack.

Crouching low, he leaps up through the hole, scarcely needing any effort from his arms to press himself through. He looks Argo in the eye.

"Sorry, sir, I…"

Argo's fist thumps into the Geek's chest. Beckert looks down at the clenched gauntlet and takes the carbon braid from it. Argo spins the Geek around and loops the sack harness across his chest.

"*Today*, Geek."

Beckert nods submissively and pulls himself hand over hand up the rope. When he crests the broken concrete edge, Thompson is crouched, waiting.

"Was my order unclear?"

"NO, Sir!" the young Operator states as he gets to his feet.

Thompson looks hard to make sure the message is received. "Take the northwest corner and watch for a pattern in enemy movement."

"Understood!" Beckert draws his pistols and runs stealthily to his position.

When Argo's big arm slaps flat on the concrete, Thompson takes the Brick's hand and helps him over the edge. The Gun gives his friend a questioning glance.

"I don't know what's wrong with him," the big man shrugs. "But I'll find out, and I'll fix it."

Thompson nods, satisfied. "Won't be long before the whole planet shows up. Take the southwest corner and look for gaps in enemy coverage."

"Roger that." Argo takes a half step away when he faces his friend again. "Thanks for getting me out of there. I thought that muck had swallowed me for good."

Thompson nods modestly and slaps his friend on the shoulder, partly for reassurance, mostly to get him moving.

With his north and south lookouts in place, Thompson dashes to the western face of the building. Hunkering behind the frame of a window, he looks out at a row of lights racing in from the distance. Through his riflescope, he zooms in on the formation and spots two heavy transports plus twenty search-craft flanking them.

The Gun clenches his jaw and turns to the two search-craft nearby. They hover over the rendezvous spot, turbines whistling forcefully. He lowers his rifle and runs to the eastern face, keeping hidden behind support columns. Under bright moonlight, four search-craft make a lazy orbit at the far edge of the city. Between him and the search-craft is an expansive wasteland. Grays and blacks of the irradiated concrete remind him of the cratered surface of home.

Thompson checks his six-hour counter, noting only one hour forty left. He runs to Argo's position and kneels beside him.

"What do you see?"

Argo points a flat hand at lights approaching from the southwest. "Another three coming in."

Thompson spots the trio and watches them slowly drift to the East.

"Looks like they're taking orbit behind the others," Argo says.

"Looks like," Thompson echoes.

The big man points down into the broad river delta. "If we can make it into the valley, we could get into the river and walk out, submerged."

"Pretty slow going...You said we have to be out of here by six hours."

"The water is flowing in from outside the radiation zone so we'd be okay. Plus, it'd give us some cover."

Thompson thinks a moment. "Assuming the bottom isn't total muck..."

He looks Argo over, recalling the effort it took to free him from the cloying silt. "It's an option, but let's keep looking. C'mon."

The men rise and pad swiftly to Beckert's lookout. Argo keeps watch while Thompson crouches beside the Geek.

"Tell me something good, Sergeant."

"Enemy's keeping outside the radiation zone, for now. But since we can't stay, time is on their side. I think they'll soon have us surrounded."

"Agreed. Suggestions?"

"It's rough terrain, sir. Anywhere we go, it's gonna take a while." The Geek looks past the high flat field he crossed and bites his lip. The taste of bitter dust hits his tongue again.

"The tower I found has a substructure. It was flooded, but seemed intact. And the General mentioned a tunnel, which—"

"The *General*?"

"Yes, sir! The top of the tower is a General's office, and—"

"You spoke to a *General*?" Thompson interrupts again.

"I saw a video, from before. And I found this." Beckert slides the sheathed sword from between his armor and rack. Thompson marvels at the elegant weapon. His hand instinctively finds the release catch, and he slides the blade partway from the scabbard. Ghostly characters catch the moonlight, seeming to hover above the metal.

"GUN!"

Thompson and Beckert both whirl at the sound of Argo's alarm. The Brick flicks his head toward the rendezvous spot. Both search craft have turned toward the building. Their noses dip as they thrust forward.

Thompson slaps the blade home and jams it between Beckert's armor and rack.

"To the tower. You lead. *GO!*"

Beckert springs from his second-floor perch and slams down onto the drying ground. Argo sails out behind him, thumping hard and sprinting after his young teammate. Thompson takes a last look at the approaching craft and leaps to the ground. His feet carve deep tracks in the damp earth.

Argo and Thompson labor to keep up with the gazelle-like movement of their younger comrade. The Geek's path leads them over leaning frames, hanging ledges, and sprawling rubble fields. There is no time to second-guess whether the damaged structures will support them; and they blindly trust their guide as they jump, climb, and sprint after him.

Turbine engines whine louder behind them. Searchlight beams spill through gaps in the concrete.

"*DOWN AND COVER!*" Thompson commands.

All three slide to a stop and wedge themselves under whatever cover they can find. The ground rumbles and vibrates, shaking loose sand over them. Both search craft roar by, pink beams missing Argo by centimeters.

Thompson pushes free of his cramped niche and rushes up a mound of rubble. Ahead, one of the craft banks gently and peels away. Hot thrust from the rear of each craft blurs their outlines.

"GO!" the Gun orders, tracking the turning craft with his riflescope.

First Beckert races by, then Argo, and Thompson follows. Adrenaline tightens his sinews, giving his stride great spring. Pleasure centers of his brain fire with the influx of stress. Chemical triggers amplify aggression, boost his metabolism, sharpen his awareness, suppress complex thoughts. The sensations, long absent since his assault on the *Europa*, remind him what it means to be alive. How he missed them…

Beckert leads them up to the high, square field and skirts the edge, keeping close to the cover of collapsed buildings. Thompson pauses and looks back. Two thick transports, with six hovering escorts, have landed at the city's western edge.

He kneels and supports his rifle with a knee. Through the scope, he watches a suited team of blueskins run from each transport. Bulky packs ride on their backs. Full-face helmets cover their heads. Gloved hands carry long tubes and rods with circular halos.

Thompson rises and tears off after his comrades only to find them crouching at the far side of the open field. They stare at a single search craft loitering above the tower.

"How did they know to look there?" Beckert asks.

Thompson zooms in on the tower, studying it through his scope. "Did you leave traces?"

"No, Major."

"It's still standing," Argo states matter-of-factly. "Made it interesting to you, didn't it?"

Beckert pops his eyebrows and nods.

Thompson lifts his view to the hovering search craft. "*You're in my way*," he growls at the craft. "Brick, take position north of the tower. I'll take west. Geek, you draw it between us. On my signal we concentrate fire at the focus of that pink beam."

"Once we clip this thing, they'll be on us fast," Argo advises.

"Agreed." Thompson lowers his weapon and surveys the surrounding terrain, watching the search craft at the eastern edge of the city as they turn in. With eerie calm he gives the order, "Move."

Beckert leads the team across charred terrain, jinking around loose slopes of decayed brick, working a path closer to the tower. The roar of turbines is everywhere, and soon, the sound grows loud enough to be felt. Beckert climbs a pile of rubble for a look. Through a gap, he spies the lone craft still loitering at the tower. Its pink beam sweeps up and down the metallic surfaces.

The Geek scurries down the slope and leans close to his comrades, having to yell to be heard.

*"It's just over this hill, Major, 'bout a hundred meters. There's a clear path all the way."*

Thompson punches Argo in the arm.

*"Go!"*

Argo nods and glides into the darkness. Thompson grabs Beckert by the head and speaks directly into the Geek's helmet microphone.

*"Stay here and wait for a double ping on your radio, then draw the craft up the open path. When we bring it down, haul ass to the tower!"*

Beckert nods, *"Aye, Sir!"*

Thompson stalks away into the night.

Beckert climbs the rubble again with a watchful eye in all directions. Search craft pore over the DC ruins in coordinated patterns, concentrated in the northwest. Bright lights crest the high, flat field behind him. Beckert instinctively shrinks into the rubble around him as his goggles filter the glare and dial in on two large-bodied vessels approaching, much wider than the transports he spied earlier. The vessels slow and spin about, then plunk down atop the elevated field on massive landing struts. Wide hatches, covering the back ends of each craft, open and lower to the ground.

The Geek turns toward the tower and watches the hovering search-craft turn slow circles around it. Its brilliant searchlights never leave the cylindrical walls, and its scanning pink beam pores over every detail.

Enemy radio chatter is constant and heavy, covering hundreds of channels simultaneously. Despite the crushing enemy presence around him, Beckert waits patiently for Thompson's signal.

*Ping, ping.*

Beckert reaches for the sword at his back. Gauging the position of the moon, he draws the blade and angles the mirror-bright metal toward the hovering craft.

Immediately, the turbine pitch rises and the ground rumbles with powerful thrust. The craft noses sharply down, charging Beckert like a bull. The Geek slides the blade home.

"*FIRE!*" Thompson shouts via radio, and two devastating blasts impact the craft from each side. The midsection explodes and breaks apart, dropping the cockpit like a stone. The back half rears up and slides sideways out of sight, crashing with a jarring *thump*. A bright fireball rises behind the tower, illuminating clouds of lofted dust.

Drawing both pistols, Beckert launches over the top of the hill and sprints down into the roiling dust. Hail of concrete and machine parts clatter over him as he sways and dodges around bulky obstacles. He hops down from a flat slab of concrete onto the open path and finds himself directly beside a smashed and bent cockpit. The alien pilot is pinned inside, its legs crushed by the collapsed frame. A cup shaped mask hangs loosely from one side of its helmet and saffron eyes roll in a daze. Beckert aims his pistols at the creature's head.

The pilot turns its stiff neck in surprise and sees the weapons in Beckert's hands. Its pale blue skin becomes paler, and it trembles. An aching moan issues from its split lips as it awaits the killing shots.

Beckert stares, watching rivulets of blue blood roll down the creature's long snout. He sees the terrible wounds, the mortal fear, the helplessness. Looking the sad creature in the eye, his fingers tighten around the triggers but will not squeeze.

*This isn't the monster I was trained to kill.*

Roar of incoming craft reminds the Geek to get moving. Beckert lowers his weapons and streaks up the path.

At the base of the tower, a heavy door falls out of the hazy air and crashes beside him. The young Operator looks up to see Argo yelling down at him from the tower entrance.

"*LET'S GO GEEK!*"

Flashes in the haze show Thompson crouched on a protruding metal beam beside the elevated tower entrance. His long rifle aims toward the distant field, sniping rapidly. Heavy return fire sizzles into the armored tower, showering him in sparks.

Beckert clips his pistols and throws himself up the tower's side.

"*Get in there!*" Thompson yells, and his aim rises to a cluster of incoming missiles. His shots explode three in mid-air, shifting the rest off course around the tower. Beckert is barely over the ledge when the missiles streak past, hit the ground, and explode, shaking the structure violently.

Argo levels his cannon at a formation of approaching craft. A violet glow coalesces around him and he triggers twice. The lead ship rocks and smokes, losing altitude.

"*You, too, Brick!*" Thompson bellows.

Argo nods and follows Beckert into the tower.

Thompson triggers furiously, desperate to suppress the threats rocketing in. He grits his teeth with concentration, trying to shrug off the small arms fire scoring and chinking his armor. In frenzy he swings his rifle from threat to threat with lethal precision, neutralizing them one by one.

Movement of something large draws his attention. Between shots, he glances at the distant, high field. There, heavy transports have disgorged gargantuan tracked vehicles. Wide, flat turrets ride atop the vehicles with long barrels. As the tanks motor away from the ramps, the turrets rotate toward the tower.

Thompson's eyes bulge, and he jumps up from his crouch.

"INCOMING!" he yells as he throws himself through the open portal. Beckert and Argo are waiting at the stairway.

"GO, GO, *GO!*" the Gun roars, as shells slam through the tower walls. The building lurches, tossing Thompson to the floor. Beckert and Argo rattle in the close confines of the stairwell, falling down to the next flight and landing in a crumpled heap.

Thompson picks himself up, looking eye to eye with the cracked hawk mosaic in the floor. With no time to appreciate the scenery, he scrambles toward the stairwell and dives down it.

The tower shudders again and again as the team leaps down entire flights of stairs, swaying, until a phenomenal *CRACK* tears through the upper sections of the building. *Screech* of tortured metal carries throughout, and the stairwell undulates beneath them. Another concussive blast rams through the structure above, much closer than before, stunning Beckert and Thompson.

Fighting through double-vision, Argo grabs his slumped teammates and drags them deeper down the stairwell. Slamming above intensifies, yet the shocks become less forceful as he descends. A horrible groan—pierced with metallic pops—yields to a thunderous *crunch*, and the shelling subsides.

Argo slows his pace, unaware how rapidly he was breathing. He calms his mind, listening to the fading reverberations and small fragments bouncing down the stairs from above. With care, he sets his teammates down and clicks his helmet lights on, surprised at the quantity of dust rolling by.

Beckert and Thompson startle themselves awake and hasten to their feet. Still clutching their weapons, the men spin in search of the enemy. Argo calms them.

"Whoa, *whoa*, we're all right."

Thompson shakes his head, trying in vain to clear the ringing in his ears. He flexes his jaw over and over, at last getting the pressure behind his eardrums to equalize.

"What happened?"

"Sounded like the tower came down," Argo explains.

Thompson looks up at the barrier between him and his pursuers. "Then let's make sure this stairway goes somewhere." His gray eyes fall sternly on Beckert.

"This way!" Beckert says as he slides past Argo and runs down the switch back stairs.

Thompson flicks his head for the big man to follow. With one more flex of his jaw and a heavy blink, the Gun runs after.

The flights pass swiftly until Beckert unexpectedly halts. His helmet lights fixate on a large yellow arrow pointing down the stairwell. The words *DC Tunnel* are stenciled inside it.

"Why'd you stop?" Thompson asks.

"I'm sure there was water here before…"

At waist height along the wall, there is a line of scum. The arrow points directly to it. Beckert looks down the stairwell, and the lower surfaces glisten with moisture.

"If water is getting out, it's a good sign," Argo volunteers.

"Then why are we standing here?" Thompson demands.

Beckert takes the major's unsubtle prompt and speeds into the undiscovered depths. He slips on the slick steps, just catching himself.

"Careful," he warns, "slippery."

Beckert rounds the next flight and standing water reflects his helmet lights. He treads to the water's edge and watches as vibrations telegraphed from the structure above send gentle ripples across the surface.

"One side, Geek." Argo brushes past and wades into the water. Looking over his shoulder, the big man adds, "Confirm your hard seal."

Beckert blinks at an icon in his goggles. Air pressure rises momentarily in his suit then resumes normal. *Hard seal confirmed,* displays in his goggles.

The Geek steps cautiously after his submerged comrade, Thompson close behind. Argo's passage churns the water with fine sediments, and the two follow the mottled glow of the big man's helmet lights.

After two more switchbacks, the stairway ends, and the Operators step into a thin layer of soft sediment. Ahead, the glow expands dramatically.

Beckert extends his pistols at the end of each arm. Neither touches wall. As if passing through a veil, he steps into clear water and his lights stream into a broad, fully submerged chamber with three-meter ceilings. Argo's cloudy trail diverts to the right, where it ends at the middle of a wall. Argo stands facing the wall, sediments swirling around his movements like a semi-translucent aura.

Thompson presses past Beckert, intrigued by a clean spot at the room's center. The Gun stops at the edge and watches the kicked up sediment being sucked through a small, corroded grate.

*Not even Beckert could fit through there*, he thinks.

A bright spark from the right draws the Gun's attention. Within the swirling cloud around Argo is a brilliant gem of blue flame. Copious bubbles rise from it and spread across the high ceiling.

While Argo cuts and Thompson waits, Beckert walks the room's perimeter. At the wall opposite the stairs he finds a subtle outline, camouflaged by clinging sediments. The young Operator clips his pistols and rubs his hands over the door. Translucent crustaceans, visible only in motion, flee from his scrubbing. At the middle of the portal, he feels raised characters and bright gold reflects in the wake of his cleansing. With a final swipe, he uncovers a pentagonal cluster of gold stars above the Cadre Hawk icon.

Beckert steps back and studies what he assumes is an escape hatch or personal lift for the General. If there was a matching door in the office upstairs, he completely missed it.

The bright blue light dims and Beckert turns from the hatch to watch his teammates shove a heavy bulkhead aside. The door slides into its pocket with a solid *clunk*.

Thompson's helmet lights swing toward the Geek like a lighthouse in a fog. He gives the hand signal to follow.

Beckert pushes off the wall and surges toward the open door, the sacks on his back dragging like parachutes, and feels his way into a wide corridor.

The glow from his teammates halts a few meters ahead, and the water takes on a rusty color. Then the glow lurches forward, followed by another heavy *clunk*.

Beckert moves to his right, tracing a hand along the wall. His left hand reaches straight ahead like a blind man's as he strides through rusty water, following the dimming glow. His hand catches the edge of a doorway, and his toes jam into something solid.

He stumbles forward in slow motion onto a severely corroded bulkhead. Its bars and locking mechanisms are rusted into a solid mass. Apparently, Thompson and Argo ripped it right from its hinges.

The Geek presses himself up from the bulkhead and steps carefully forward into open space. The rusty color clears and his lights shine into an arched pedestrian tunnel, roughly three meters high and flooded to the ceiling. White tiles of the arch make the tunnel appear bright as day.

Argo and Thompson are far ahead, and the young Operator struggles to catch up. Media sacks tug against him, making his boot treads slip on the tiled floor as if he were in a frustrating dream. He hooks his thumbs into the harness cords, cinching them tight, and powers onward.

The tunnel opens up to a concrete platform, and its roof rises several meters higher. Where the platform ends is a larger tunnel, running perpendicular. Argo and Thompson stand at opposite ends of the platform, shining their lights down each tunnel opening.

Beckert strides to the edge of the platform and looks down onto a set of rails running down the middle of the tunnel, until the tunnel turns out of sight in each direction. Pale, worm-like creatures undulate in the gently flowing currents.

Thompson and Argo turn from their reconnoitering and join Beckert at the edge of the platform. Thompson pulls his team into a close huddle and presses their helmets together. Using the conduction of the solid armor plating, he shouts to his comrades.

"This is good. Excellent work, Sergeant!"

Beckert grins behind his faceplate.

"Did the General say where this tunnel goes?" Thompson shouts.

Beckert's mouth moves, but cannot be heard.

"*What?*"

Beckert takes a deep breath and yells. "*He said it went to an Arlington Command Center, but that's all.*"

Argo hooks a thumb over his shoulder. "Arlington would be

that way."

"Then that's our path," Thompson declares. "Follow me, stay alert." The Gun releases his comrades and jumps off the platform. His mass pulls him quickly to the bottom where he lands with a puff of sediment. Rifle in hand, he hooks the toe of his boot on the ties crossing each rail and leans forward as though climbing a horizontal staircase.

Argo urges Beckert ahead then drops down behind him, and they stride after their leader.

The tunnel bends left and merges into a much larger tunnel. Thompson's lights fade into the expansive water, making the cavern appear infinite, and he halts. Risking extra intensity of his lamps, he shines beams over multiple parallel rails along the floor that continue out of sight in each direction.

Thompson strides across the flooded expanse, crossing six sets of parallel magnetic rails before finally reaching concrete wall. The wall rises from nearly upright then leans over into a high arch, propped up by massive ribs and cross beams. Plastic and glass light sconces run its length, all of which are dark and corroded. Several meters above them, however, he spots a catwalk.

Crouching low, the Gun raises his arms and launches like a missile, needing only a single flap of his arms at the end of his flight. His strong hands grip the catwalk's edge and he hauls himself onto it. When he stands, his helmet breaks the water's surface.

Unhindered, his lamps shine up to an arched ceiling. Pipes and wires slump from detached brackets, dripping liquid in thin streams. The concrete arch of the tunnel, however, is in remarkable condition and bears no obvious sign of stress.

The tall soldier lifts his rifle above the chest-high water and shakes it vigorously. Keeping it raised, he peers through the scope. Though he cannot see to the end, he can see that the tunnel rises several hundred meters ahead.

He turns around and scans the opposite direction. A tiny red speck glimmers in the distance then is lost. He hunts for the reflection to no avail.

*Droplet on the lens, probably.*

Lights shine up at him from below, and the Gun leans his visor into the calm water. At the floor of the cavernous tunnel, Argo and Beckert wait patiently. Thompson signals them to proceed with a hand gesture, and the Operators forge on through the flooded tunnel.

# Hunger is Universal

Tedious slogging leaves Thompson's legs weak and burning. Nutrition interval passed long ago. Hypoglycemia makes every step a chore. And having sampled the planet's rich atmosphere, his lungs protest the stale dampness of recycled breath.

*Argo and Beckert have it worse*, he reminds himself. *They're completely submerged.*

He plunks his face into the water to check on his comrades. Their lamps glimmer weakly, far behind.

With a sighing exhale, Thompson halts his trudge and leans on the catwalk's rail. A cramp seizes his quadriceps.

"ACH!" he shouts, grabbing his thigh with one hand, but armor plates resist all attempts at massage.

He grips behind his knee and lifts, whole leg rising like a plank. Boot wedged against the railing he bends the knee joint and leans in, forcefully lengthening clenched muscle. Pain mixes with relief in equal measure, and he punches his thigh, splashing the waist deep water.

*Gettin' old.*

When he looks back at Argo and Beckert, their helmet lamps are flashing on and off. Alerted, he wraps the rifle strap around his forearm and leans over the rail for a better look. His movement sends ripples across the surface making it harder to see, so he dunks his face directly into the water and stares into a pinkish-white maw.

Water explodes around him and long jaws *snap* across his torso. The creature curls over, ripping the Gun from his perch, and dives. Driven by a powerful tail, it speeds away from Argo's and Beckert's fading lamps.

Thompson presses against conical brown teeth and scaly white skin, seeking some leverage against the shockingly powerful jaws. He thrashes, kicks, and punches, straining to get free. In response, the beast spins then smashes him again and again into the solid floor. Each hit kicks breath from his lungs and his eyes cross before he goes limp. Water rushes around him as the beast resumes its serpentine swim.

He feels tugging on one of his arms. As sense returns to him, Thompson realizes it is his rifle, dangling from the strap coiled around his forearm. The Gun reels his weapon in and extends the bayonet.

He moves carefully, not wanting to provoke another pummeling, then stabs the blade into scaly hide. The beast bites down harder, rolls, and slams him like a toy, every hit bursting through his brain with flashes of bright light.

Thompson slumps from the cudgeling, arms and legs draping. The rush of water surrounds him again, flailing his limbs in the currents. A searing pain crawls up his back that twists and grinds savagely, alternately hot and cold.

Consolidating his scattered thoughts and strength, he draws what breath he can. The Gun tucks his head forward to strike again when his helmet lamps shine into a small red orb that reflects like a mirror.

He aims and stabs his bayonet through the beast's eye. The crushing vice on his body releases and a thick tail slaps him like a steel girder. He sinks in the shallow water, coming to rest in a heap of animal skulls, antlers, and rib cages.

Thompson stomps through loose bones in search of solid footing, gasping his first full breaths in minutes. The bones, fuzzy with white fungus, vomit clouds of silt and rotten flesh. He staggers over shifting piles, thrusting with his heels, rifle held in a death grip as he swings it back and forth through the chummed water.

Breaking the water's surface, he drags himself up the grade

onto greasy flooring. Jittery and weakened, he falls onto his backside, staring wild-eyed across the roiled water, watching for the beast to come at him again. He pushes up with one hand and gets to his feet. A guttural roar behind him shakes the ground.

Thompson spins into a crouch. He levels his rifle and squeezes the trigger. A blue spark sizzles internally with a jet of steam. The weapon does not fire.

A three-meter tail smashes the Operator into a cartwheel, and sends him careening into the concrete wall. He bounces and falls forward onto his visor.

Thompson's hands scrape through slime and excrement, seeking his weapon. Unable to see through his muck-smeared visor, he pushes up weakly, drags a hand across the eyepieces, and finds his rifle close by. The battered Gun snatches it from the muck and rises to his feet, swaying in his stance, but the creature is gone. Gentle waves lap up on the water's edge with a v-shaped wake headed back toward Argo and Beckert.

"No, no, no, you don't," he says drunkenly. "We're not finished."

The Gun staggers into the water and collapses, face first.

\*\*\*\*\*

Thompson's eyes flick open. He finds himself lying face down on his belly, looking through an open visor at a slime-covered floor. Rank stench of decay pours unfiltered into his nostrils. He slides his elbows below his chest and pushes up.

"Hold it," Argo chides.

Thompson freezes, aware of cool air on his back. Beside his spine, just below his ribs, he feels the prodding of surgical tools under his skin.

"Wha…What's going on?" Thompson tries to press up fully, but Argo's hand plants between his shoulder blades and drops him to the deck.

"*Lie still*, Gun. That means *don't move*." Argo readjusts his grip on his tools. "Big fella got a tooth in you somehow. Lined up with a seam under your thoracic plates."

A dart of pain shoots through Thompson's right side, and he inhales sharply through clenched teeth.

"Is it bad?"

"Easy, Major. It tore you up pretty good, got your kidney." Argo places a curved lance into his med-kit and selects a pencil-shaped device. "Just relax and let me fix you."

Thompson props his chin on his overlapped hands while Argo works. From the inside out, Argo clamps flesh together and draws the pencil-shaped device across each tear, leaving a thin bead of glue. The glue bonds instantly, and Argo tugs gently on each repair to test it. Thompson twitches with each tug.

"You'll have some blood in your urine, but I'm more concerned about septicemia." Argo pinches the Gun's thick back skin together and glues it. "That thing's mouth was teeming with bacteria."

"*Was?*"

"Yeah. Geek and I took it down."

The moment Thompson feels Argo's hand lift he turns to look at his surgeon.

"Where is it now?"

Argo points with his glue pen, and Thompson follows it to a scaly beast over six meters long, tangled in black cord, slumped half in, half out of the foul water. Stubby legs sprawl from a wide, pale body. A crooked smile runs the length of the flat head, jutting an occasional tooth. At the base of the skull, Beckert's sword is driven to the hilt.

Beckert sits on the animal's back, scraping and welding Thompson's back armor plates. He looks up at the major, waves, and resumes his repair.

"When I saw it coming toward us, figured it had swallowed you," Argo explains. "Thought we'd have to cut you out."

"Almost did," Thompson adds warily. "How'd you catch it?"

"Geek got up onto the catwalk and snagged it with some rope

as it passed. It yanked him in and rolled so many times, he got lashed to the thing." Argo chuckles to himself.

"And then?"

"I caught the loose end of the rope, and it towed us all over the place. Nearly tore my arm off with all its thrashing. It finally got tired and swam back this way. Once it came up out of the water, Beckert drew his blade and finished it."

Thompson gets to his feet with a wobble. Argo rushes to steady his patient, but Thompson stiff-arms him.

"I got it, I got it." The Gun raises his arms and stretches, testing the closure of his wound. "Did a good job, Argo. Feels good."

Argo nods and cleans his tools before stowing them in his med-kit.

Thompson steps to the reptilian carcass, feet squishing inside his boots. He sits down on it next to Beckert and removes his boots one at a time, draining the bloody water.

"There," Beckert announces, holding up Thompson's armor plates. "That should do it."

The Gun takes the armor from Beckert and inspects the repairs. All are well done.

"Give me a hand with this?" the Gun asks, passing the armor back to his junior comrade.

Beckert receives the plating and hangs the top of it on Thompson's shoulder frame. He zips the mesh inner layers to the rest of the suit then locks the external fasteners.

"All set, Major."

"Appreciate it." Thompson spins in place, searching. "Got my rack?"

"Not much left of it, sir." Beckert reaches behind the dead creature and produces a twisted rail with two crushed boxes attached. "Bite strength of this thing was incredible. Lucky it didn't snap you in two."

Thompson takes the rail and opens the bent boxes. Foul water pours from them. He reaches in and pulls out punctured water skins from one, soggy and mashed protein bars from the other. He drops the trash to the floor and looks out into the expanse of water. Spare rifle cells and replacement optics, tools, first aid kit, extra food and water are somewhere out there, scattered and fouled in rotten sediment.

"Who's got a protein bar? I could eat my own hand."

Beckert produces a compartment from his rack and opens it, offering the contents. Thompson takes three bars and holds one out for Beckert.

"No, thank you, sir. Already had mine."

Thompson turns to Argo, who is still cleaning his medical instruments. Argo looks at the black wrappers as if they were the answer to a prayer.

"Yeah, I'll take two."

Thompson tosses the bars to his comrade. They bite through the wrappers like famished wolves and chew in silence.

Beckert snaps the box back into his rack. While the others eat, he searches out the loose end of the carbon fiber rope and starts winding it around his elbow. With a great deal of lifting and grunting, he untangles the rope from the creature's legs, body, and tail.

Once his rope is coiled, Beckert crouches and looks into the beast's half-closed eye. True, it was fearsome in life, but in death, there is no thrill of victory. He studies the five-toed front feet, like webbed hands with sharp claws. He runs his own hand along the thick, knobby hide of its face, admiring the complexity.

*Such a beautiful design.*

A fist closes around his heart and squeezes.

"I'm sorry I killed you," he whispers.

"What's that, Sergeant?"

Beckert looks up at Thompson in surprise. "It's too bad, sir, is all." He stands and looks down at the still animal. "It was a remarkable life form."

"It tried to eat me."

"Hunger is universal. We're no different."

Thompson struggles to swallow the last bit of protein in his mouth. "You're right, but...don't over think it. We're alive and in good health. You did it right."

"Yes, sir," Beckert replies. He leans over the creature's neck and withdraws the bright blade.

"Mind if I look at that?" Thompson asks, changing the subject.

"Of course." Beckert grips the blade at the tip and passes it hilt-first. Thompson takes it delicately and cradles the sword in his palms.

"I understand why you couldn't leave this behind." The Gun takes the blade by the grip and slashes the air suddenly, as though striking an invisible opponent. He steps back from his lunge and passes the blade back to the Geek. "It has excellent balance. From the General's office, you say?"

Beckert's eyes light up. "Yes, Major. *Amazing* things there."

"And you took photographs?"

"Aye, sir! In fact..." The Geek reaches into a compartment and retrieves the black and white image of the old general in the steel helmet. He passes it to Thompson eagerly.

Thompson grins. "This is the General you saw in the video?"

"Uh, no, sir." Beckert presses two fingers into his temple, still confused by what he found. "This one is older...I think he was our first."

"Our *progenitor*?"

"I believe so, sir."

Thompson holds the picture in awe, already imagining its place at the head of the Cadre Memorial. He offers it back to the Geek.

"This is important. Keep it safe."

"Aye, sir!" Beckert replies. He tucks it away securely. "There's more..." Beckert's mouth falls open mid-sentence, as though stuck. Thompson's brow lifts in anticipation.

"Spit it out, Sergeant."

Beckert shuts his mouth and lifts his eyes. "The General mentioned Cadre One and Cadre *Two*..."

Argo sits straight up, nearly dropping the tool he is cleaning. Thompson's eyes widen. His head turns to the side, yet his eyes remain fixed on the Geek.

"Cadre *Two*?" the Gun repeats.

"Yes, Major, I'm *sure* of it. Watched it twice."

Thompson squares his shoulders with the young Operator. "I'll want your full report when we find a safe place to stop."

Beckert smiles, showing his even, white teeth. "Affirmative, sir!"

"Carry on, Sergeant."

Beckert salutes and wipes the curved sword before slipping it into its scabbard. Thompson strides over to Argo.

"Did I hear that right?" the big man asks.

Thompson nods seriously. Argo looks down at the ground, exhaling.

"Cadre *Two*…" The big man shakes his head and finishes packing up his MedKit. "That adds some color to things." He clicks the kit onto his back rack and smirks. "Huh. It's obvious, actually… there'd be no need to call it Cadre *One* unless there were others." He pulls his cannon into his lap. "So what was Geek going on about, before that?"

"First-kill anxiety," Thompson explains dismissively. "How are you doing?"

Argo stands. "Was glad for the break, but I'm packed and ready." The Brick hefts his cannon in emphasis.

Thompson looks for his rifle and finds it in Beckert's hands. The Geek is rubbing it clean with a small cloth.

"That's good, Sergeant," he calls out. "Ready?"

Beckert lifts the twin sacks of media records and tromps over to his teammates. "Ready, sir." He slips an arm through the harness.

"I'll take it," Thompson insists. "My load's a little light."

Beckert hands off the sacks, water still draining from the dense fabric. Thompson slides his arms through the harness and cinches it tight across his chest.

Beckert hands over the rifle. Thompson checks it out of habit.

"There was water in the optics, Major, but I got it all out. Polished the focus, as well. It's a hundred percent."

"All right, thank you, Geek." Thompson looks at his team. "On me."

The three spread out and run into the long darkness, minds ablaze over a lonely outpost called, *Cadre Two*.

# Beckert's Entourage

Grateful to be on dry ground, Thompson sets a swift pace down the parallel rails.

Mesh inner layers of his armor wick away perspiration and dry his waterlogged feet. He knows the suit's recapture filters will purify the fluids before filling his canteen, but the thought of drinking the bloodied chum water from his boots is unsettling.

Dark light fixtures pass by in endless succession as the Operators run, marking off distance like a silent metronome. Smaller tunnels feed in and merge with the larger tunnel, but Thompson ignores them, opting for the spacious and clear path straight ahead.

The tunnel's slight upward grade turns downward and leads to more water. At its deepest the level only rises to Thompson's waist, yet all three seal up anyway, in case the floor drops out or if they should stumble.

Once the grade rises they return to drier footing and lift faceplates. Acrid stench of ammonia wafts from far ahead, stinging their sinuses. Thompson covers his mouth with a gauntleted hand and raises his helmet lamps to maximum. At the limit of vision he sees dark, oily mounds covering the parallel rails.

Argo pulls up beside him, his eyes watered. "Smells like the waste tank on that passenger liner we collected."

Thompson recalls that long-ago mission. While inventorying their capture, they opened an access hatch and discovered the main tank of a massive septic system. It must have been a long flight before they intercepted.

"Yeah," the Gun snorts, "it does."

The team forges on, and as their boots sink into the greasy, crumbly piles, they recoil from plumes of released ammonia. Gagging in their tracks, they look down and see millions of insects scuttling over and through the fetid mounds.

Argo arches his back, and his helmet lamps illuminate a shifting brown carpet of creatures clinging to the high ceiling. High-pitched squeaks, almost beyond hearing, voice collective protest at the light.

Thompson trudges to the side of the tunnel, where piles are shallower, yet every step through the thin crust belches noxious vapors. Flat beetles teem from the perforations and swarm over his boots. Nausea overwhelms him, he seals his mask, and breaks into a run.

Beckert follows too closely and gets a face full of kicked up guano before he can drop his face mask. Sputtering and retching, he emerges from the piles behind Thompson, flips open his faceplate, and hunches over.

Argo stamps through the last of the heaps. Beckert looks up at the Brick with reddened eyes and a long line of saliva hanging from his bottom lip. The big man laughs behind his airtight mask and gives the Geek a hearty slap on the shoulder.

Beckert opens his mouth to protest then faces the floor and spits out salty saliva.

"Keep it down," Thompson warns.

With an affirmative nod, Argo opens his visor and falls in line behind Beckert.

Once past the fetid heaps, the tunnel turns right, and rays of dim light shine around the corner. Patches of green root where the light strikes.

Thompson clicks off his helmet lamps and moves to the wall. Beckert and Argo take their cue, following closely. Then the Gun's hand thrusts up suddenly, and the team freezes mid-step. Argo and Beckert hold their breath, waiting for Thompson's next signal.

The Gun pulls his rifle to his shoulder and glide steps ahead, pausing at the bend in the tunnel. He kneels, keeping his weapon level, sweeps the area, and beckons his team forward.

Brick and Geek hustle quietly then drop to a crouch behind their leader. Without looking back, Thompson hand signals Argo and Beckert, *forward*. Both men spring ahead, weapons ready.

Rounding the bend, they split to opposite sides of the tunnel, staying in shadows. Immediately, they see what had alarmed Thompson: far down the tunnel, beyond tall grasses and shrubs, something big lies across the rails. Argo crouches and aims his cannon at the massive object.

On Beckert's side, the tunnel roof is open, letting in early morning sun like a skylight. Vegetation is more dense and the Geek stalks like a panther through ferns and hanging vines. Once near enough he hunkers down in the shaded plants, and his goggles magnify the oddity crossing the rails. Individual riveted plates form a smooth skin over the object's length. Curls of paint hang from corroded surfaces.

When Beckert crouches, Argo moves up. His massive frame twists through the sparser plant life until a flash of movement springs nearby. Long faced brown quadrupeds, the kind Beckert spied in the forest, leap from their rest en masse and flee past. Argo's nostrils flare until he calms and releases his cannon's half-pulled trigger.

The herd moves like liquid over green plants then curves around Thompson as if he were a rock in the stream. The Gun aims cautiously at the flowing herd and watches bouncing white tails disappear into the darkness.

*Little point to a stealth approach, now*, Thompson thinks. He rises and rushes forward. Argo and Beckert pop up from their spots as the Gun runs by, and they take flanking positions to each side.

The tall soldier runs straight up the middle, rifle ready.

"Brick, swing left. Geek, take right."

Argo tromps to the left side of the object and pauses. He peeks around the edge and finds a pleated collar ringing the end of it. A heavily rusted hitch protrudes mid height, and a horizontal doorway allows access inside.

Looking in, Argo finds rows of seats bolted to the left wall and it occurs to him this is some kind of transport lying on its side. All of the upholstery is decayed to the frame, dangling scraps of synthetic fabric. Above, a continuous row of shattered windows runs the length. At the far end, Beckert peeks in through the opposite door.

The Brick steps around the rusted hitch and investigates the toppled train car's underside. Large circular magnets form even rows down the length. Cast aluminum mounts for each magnet are thick with white crystals.

Nearby, dozens more train cars pile against one another haphazardly, some still hitched together. While contemplating the wreckage, Argo feels Thompson's hand on his shoulder.

"Kneel down," the Gun says.

Argo takes a knee and Thompson springs off his back, lands delicately atop the sideways rail car, crouches, then peers over the derailed trains. The pileup is far larger than he realized, resembling an overgrown colony of bacteria under a microscope.

Bright shafts of sunlight constrict his pupils in the dark tunnel, hiding the way ahead, so he peers through his riflescope. In augmented view, hundreds of meters ahead, he spies a sloping wall of dark earth, concrete blocks, and stone filling the tunnel. Crashed train cars rise partway up the slope as if washed upon it. Chagrinned, he lowers his rifle.

"See anything?" Argo asks.

"Tunnel's collapsed. Filled in to the roof."

"Hmm." Argo looks into the maze of trains then looks up again at his leader. "Orders?"

Thompson strokes the bristly stubble on his chin and glances at thick vines and twisting roots spilling in through the open ceiling. Water traces the runners, drips from the ends, and splashes across the chaotic pileup. Briefly, he entertains the idea of climbing out by the hanging vines. But the longer he stares, the more certain he is he can hear aircraft turbines beyond the skylight.

"Continue searching," the Gun orders. "Let me know if you find anything in these wrecks."

"Understood," Argo replies.

Beckert steps out from behind his end of the train car. "Copy, Major."

Argo and Beckert weave between wrecks. Thompson crosses over top of them, peeking down into each as he goes, finding only oxidized alloys, shattered windows, and a hardpan of sediment.

Soon, the jam is so dense there is no more room between compacted cars. Beckert and Argo join Thompson atop the wreckage and the Operators hop car to car until they reach the sloping cave-in. Argo swivels his head in all directions, and grimaces.

"I don't see a—"

"Hear that?" Thompson interrupts.

Beckert and Argo look up. Though faint, the whistle of aircraft turbines filters down through the skylight.

"Not good," Argo observes, "but expected."

"I'm surprised they aren't already here." Thompson cranes his neck at the opening, trying to gauge if there is any cover around the opening. "Well. We can't wait for them to smarten up."

Thompson starts up the slope when Argo catches his leader by the arm.

"I don't know that popping out in full daylight is our best option, Gun."

Thompson looks down at the large hand gripping him. Argo, suddenly aware he has laid hands on a superior, releases.

The Gun pivots to Beckert. "Sergeant, give us a moment."

Beckert ducks out of sight and hurries toward the edge of the man-made cavern. Argo and Thompson make effort to keep the volume down, but snarls in their voices carry, so the Geek feigns interest in a fern here, a sprig of grass there. Feigned interest turns genuine when he spots a set of tiny, hand-like prints in a patch of mud.

Beckert sweeps foliage aside, eager to see something new, and he follows the prints to a large, flat stone wedged against the tunnel wall. There is a narrow gap between stone and wall with overlapping tracks leading in and out.

*Either there are a bunch of them, or one is really busy...*

Beckert sizes up the stone and takes hold of it. Putting one foot against the wall, he pulls with his whole body. The stone is deeply mired but shifts in the damp dirt.

He exhales fully and takes another deep breath. Hands set again, he pulls the stone completely free, lets it slump to one side, then blinks in surprise at a larger triangular gap behind it. Beckert drops to hands and knees and peers through. Whatever caused the roof collapse folded a long section of the wall in and over itself, leaving a narrow channel that runs as far as he can see.

Vehement chattering berates him from the channel. Beckert clicks on his helmet lights and several pairs of green eyes reflect back at him. Their chattering abates as the animals turn their ringed tails and scamper away.

"Thanks for showing me the way you guys," he says with a grin, and the young Operator shimmies into the corridor. It is a tight squeeze, forcing him to elbows and knees. Multiple scrapes run parallel down the folded walls. A thin layer of damp earth covers the floor, clear of blocks or debris but covered in paw prints.

"Did someone clear this out?" he wonders aloud. Curiosity draws him farther. Along the way he sees more parallel scrapes on the folded walls, especially where it narrows, and after several minutes, Beckert reaches the end. It flares toward the exit, giving him more room to move, and he is amazed to find metallic braces propping it open. He gets a foot beneath himself and draws his pistols.

Past the opening, the tunnel continues and Beckert's lamps fade into spacious darkness. He considers turning back and informing his comrades.

*No point telling them if this is a dead end...*

Duck-walking the rest of the way, Beckert emerges beside

the toe of a rusted load lifter. Yellow paint still clings in random patches. His eyes rise up the squatting legs to a vacant pilot cage. Perched atop the cage, and supported by both arms, is a gigantic section of concrete wall.

Beckert marvels at the size of the slab directly above him. More incredible is that the loader still holds it aloft.

Careful not to touch, he moves closer and inspects the rust-scaled machine. Every plastic button and every rubber grip surface has been gnawed away by tiny teeth, wires spilling from the chewed-apart consoles. Padded cushions for a human driver are gone, with only a few synthetic threads tracing former outlines. But the hydraulic lines, armored against accidental cutting, remain intact. Thus stands the ancient lifter, like Atlas carrying a flat Earth.

Behind the lifter an excavator is parked on rusted treads, bucket still holding its final load. Several lumps of gray brown fur huddle in the remains of the driver's seat. Reflective green eyes watch him carefully.

He shines his lights around the area, illuminating sandy floors and arching tunnel walls. Thick cracks in the masonry beside him are filled with some kind of gray bonding chemical, and all rubble around the opening is shored up by substantial bracing.

*This must have been a rescue…*

Beckert steps farther into the tunnel then turns back toward the tunnel cave-in. The front end of a train car sticks out at an angle from the crushing pile, its back half mashed flat like a tube of paste. Overhead, a gigantic shaft intrudes at an angle through the roof, over half the tunnel's width. Its mottled surface reflects almost no light.

He hops up the steep slope for a better view. Close enough to touch the intruding object, he shines his helmet lamps over pitted and scorched plating. Long streaks are gouged in, extending the entire length. His jaw drops.

*This is a space ship.*

Beckert steps back, still shining his lights on the crashed vessel. Wonder mixes with sorrow as the whole scene comes into view: this ship fell from the sky and plunged through meters of dirt and stone, collapsing the tunnel onto speeding trains, and the following cars piled up like falling ropes. But there was a rescue.

*The survivors were taken somewhere...*

Beckert's lights swing into the yawning blackness ahead.

*Now I should get the others.*

The young Operator hops down the slope of blocks and boulders, ducks under the huge slab, and scrambles through the slim corridor. When he emerges, he looks right into Thompson's rifle.

"*Gah*, kid! I almost *killed* you!" Thompson lifts the barrel away.

Beckert rises nervously. "Major, Lieutenant! Good news! I found a way through."

"We saw your tracks leading over here." Argo rises from the plants, thumbing the safety on his cannon. "Not sure I'm gonna fit through there, Sergeant."

"It gets wider past the mid-point. If we could get you that far, the rest would be easy."

Argo looks skeptically at the narrow entrance. He shakes his head, but sets his cannon down and removes his back rack. Next, he removes his helmet and unlatches his thick breastplate.

Beckert moves to assist, taking components from Argo as they are removed. The Brick strips to his under-suit from the waist up, still wearing a skeptical expression.

"Let's try it."

The big man sits down and extends his legs into the corridor. He raises his arms overhead and scoots his butt forward. His chest just passes if he holds his breath out, but no matter which way he turns, his shoulders will not fit.

"Thought so," he grumbles. "You'll have to do it, Gun."

"Do what?" Beckert asks.

"Dislocate," Thompson answers. He slings his rifle and helps Argo out of the corridor.

"Geek, leave the rope and take Brick's equipment through. Arrange it on the other side for fast assembly. After that, scout ahead. If you encounter resistance *do not engage*. Return and report, is that clear?"

"*Very* clear, Major."

Argo takes the coils of carbon fiber from Beckert and ties one end around his waist. The rest he gives to Thompson who wraps the Brick's torso, cinching tight with each winding.

Beckert takes Argo's rack and test fits it in the corridor. *Too wide*. He grabs the breastplate and lays it outside the corridor like a giant bowl. Compartment by compartment, he breaks the rack down and piles it neatly in the bowl with the Brick's armored arm components on top.

The Geek shoves the breastplate into the corridor. Weighed down by the equipment, it scrapes harshly.

"*Ach*!" Argo grouses. "What are you doin' to my kit?"

Thompson smirks. "He knows how to fix it. On your way, Geek."

Beckert nods and grips the breastplate underhanded, trying to lift with each shove. It makes little difference.

At the end of the corridor, Beckert lifts the bowl and carries it from under the concrete slab. The armor, he arranges in order of assembly. Argo's rack and storage compartments, he rebuilds into a single unit.

With some anxiety, Beckert turns over the breastplate. All of the carbon doping is rubbed from the center chest area, leaving an abraded patch of native gray. He quickly flips the plate over and grimaces, letting it wobble on its curved surface, then scurries through the corridor. Near the end, he announces himself and steps out.

Argo is lying on his back, wound with rope up to his armpits. His constricted chest rises and falls in short, panting breaths.

"How's my…armor…Sergeant?"

"Uh, fine, Lieutenant, just fine." Beckert hastily diverts to the Brick's helmet, back plating, and cannon. As he did with the breastplate, Beckert loads the back plate like a sledge and skids it through the tunnel.

When he reaches the end, the ring-tailed creatures are climbing over Argo's back rack, sniffing it. One tunnels into the Brick's forearm armor, back legs and tail sticking out.

"*Hey*!"

The creatures look at him defiantly through black masks and continue rummaging.

Beckert hurries through his grinding shuffle and runs at the would-be thieves with his arms raised.

"*Get*! Get outta there!"

Ringtails race for the darkness save the one waist deep in Argo's forearm armor. Its back legs kick frantically, driving the piece out of the neat arrangement and away into the tunnel.

"No! *No*! NO!" Beckert shouts as he chases the escaping armor. The creature twists and bonks away from the rubble, leading Beckert to clear tunnel flooring. Without the sand and concrete filling in the magnetic tracks, the armor falls between a set of rails and wedges.

Beckert dives for the armor and catches it with both hands. He sits up, and the creature comes up with it.

"Oh, come on, let go!"

He jostles the armor piece, trying to free its occupant. Skinny black feet kick and scurry in mid air.

"Outta there!" he says, shaking vigorously.

A rapid series of angry chirps sounds from the top of the tube. The Geek lowers the armor and looks down the open end. A terrified face chirrups back at him, whiskers quivering.

When Beckert looks closer, he sees claws at the ends of tiny paws are hooked into the inner mesh.

"Oh, you're stuck. Okay, hang on."

Cradling the creature's back end with one arm, he reaches in and gently lifts the small black paws away from the mesh. The creature snarls and bares teeth, but does not bite. When the last claw is freed, the animal drops out of the armor and scampers back toward the excavator, chortling.

Beckert watches with amusement until he realizes how far he

is into the tunnel. He stands and jogs back, only to find the furry animals crawling over Argo's equipment again. They retreat at his approach but do not flee.

"Not afraid anymore, huh?"

Some stand on their back legs and sniff the air. Though wary, their attention is riveted on the young sergeant. Inquisitive chirps pass one to the other.

Up close, Beckert notices most are similar in size, save one, which is significantly larger than the rest and keeps the most distance. Its chirps sound gruff, scolding, but are mostly ignored. The smaller ones venture closer.

"Look, I can't have you damaging the Lieutenant's gear." Crouching down, Beckert reaches to his back rack and pulls a compartment from it. His audience moves closer, shiny black noses twitching. He opens the box and removes a bar of protein.

"Major'd probably shoot me for this…"

He tears the wrapper and pinches off a corner. Twitching noses draw closer, shrink back anxiously, and return. Each time they get nearer until one is bold enough to take the protein from Beckert's hand. It bounds away with its treasure, siblings in hot pursuit. The larger one remains, however, studying him.

"You hungry, too?"

The larger animal watches Beckert until growls and thrashing come from the shadows. The Geek breaks off an end of the bar and tosses it.

"Here, go feed your team."

The large one snatches the protein and hurries into the shadows. Beckert rolls the wrapper over his remainder and stows it in his rack, warm with satisfaction.

While the furred creatures tussle, the Geek opens his repair kit and fills in the scuffs on Argo's armor. When finished, he assembles the armor into two sets. First set is built from hip plating, legs, and boots, standing upright on the broad waist with heels in the air. The other comprises arms, gauntlets, and helmet locked onto the standing torso, faceplate sealed. It looks like Argo buried up to his navel.

*That'll keep 'em out*, he thinks.

The Geek scrambles one more time through the corridor. As before, he announces himself at the end and steps through. Daylight streams in at a steeper angle, shining directly upon the jam of trains.

Argo lies near the entrance, torso mummified in black rope. Thompson grips one of the Brick's arms by the wrist with a boot planted on his chest.

"Remember…down and…forward," the Brick says between pants. With his free hand, the Brick stuffs a wad of cloth into his mouth.

"Major, I'm ready to scout ahead. Is there anything else that needs to be taken through?"

Thompson takes his boot from Argo's chest.

"Sure." He lifts the harness over his head and passes the sacks of media records to the Geek. "Take these. That'll be all, Sergeant."

Beckert takes the damp sacks into the corridor. To keep them from bunching up, he turns backwards and tows them between his legs. Part way through, he hears Thompson's voice counting down and a sickening *clunk*. The muted roars are unquestionably Argo's.

The Geek's stomach turns with sympathetic pain, and he looks over his shoulder, hoping he can make it to the end before he hears Argo's other shoulder dislocating. He almost makes it.

Upon his return, the ring-tailed animals welcome him expectantly. He smiles at them.

"No, that's all." Beckert scoots from beneath the suspended slab, leaving the sacks with the rest of Argo's gear. The creatures follow at his feet, cooing and reaching up to him. He steps carefully around them, but they follow, begging with insisting chirps.

Beckert looks into the tunnel depths, and sighs.

"Sorry, I gotta go."

The young Operator draws a pistol and jogs into the darkness, his new entourage hurrying after him.

# ARLINGTON CEMETERY

Running through the tunnel is monotonous, yet soothing. Smooth walls with gentle turns offer clear sightlines ahead and behind—surprise or ambush is unlikely. So Beckert lets his mind wander back to the tower and its office full of oddities. No matter how he tries to put that puzzle together, the pieces just will not fit.

A long bend steers him north, beyond which the grade rises. Moisture glistens between the rails, flowing down to a tunnel-wide grate at the bottom. Dozens of tiny heat sources mill about the grate then dive into it at his approach.

The Geek lopes to a halt and crouches for a better look. His lamps shine past corroded bars into a shallow trough where beady red eyes glare at him. With shrill squeaks, the creatures flee down drainpipes, dragging hairless tails behind.

Out of habit, Beckert checks over his shoulder. Far off, reflective green eyes bounce along in pursuit. As they get closer, he can hear their chortling. He shakes his head at their persistence.

"Glad you find me so interesting."

Before his entourage can surround him again he takes a step up the grade but slips, just keeping his balance.

"What the...?"

The Geek aims his lamps at the floor, noting that where he slipped, a rusty-colored slime has been scraped away. He peers at it curiously, then steps up onto a dry, raised rail and ascends. Young ringtails start up the rails after him until the large one issues a scolding hiss. It races at the pack, growling and cuffing until the smaller ones skulk back into darkness. Beckert halts and watches them retreat.

*You know something about this place?*

He faces the long incline ahead and grips his pistols firmly.

*One foot in front of the other*, he thinks.

Halfway up, his nose wrinkles at a sulfurous odor. It grows more pungent toward the top of the incline, and once the tunnel levels out Beckert hears the *plip, plip, plip* of liquid ahead. He steps cautiously toward the sound then halts when his lamps shine upon glistening tendrils, dangling from the high ceiling. Round pools lie beneath each tendril, and fat drops *plop* to the pools like lazy rain. Fascinated, he creeps forward and shines his lamps across an inverted forest of phlegm-like hangers. One breaks, and the lower half falls to the pool with a *splat*.

Staring at the ceiling, he slips off the rail; and his boots crunch on slimy ground. Beckert looks down in disgust at tread-deep muck and the fleshless skeleton of some small animal crushed under his heel.

The Geek steps back onto the rail and crouches for a better look. The skull is only a few centimeters long with oversized, curving incisors. A hunched spine carries a thin ribcage and a narrow pelvis before ending in a thick tail. Clumps of matted fur surround the bones.

Beckert pans his helmet lights over the area. Hundreds more skeletons are mired in the slime. Miniscule insects hover and buzz around them.

*I see why the ringtails don't come up here.*

He closes his faceplate and walks under the dripping tendrils. Drops splash over his goggles, smearing them with fine strands. After swiping the strands away, he hunches to keep his eye wear clear of the cloudy rain.

Ahead, individual pools merge into a singular pond. Train rails here are heavily corroded beneath languid drops and disappear completely at the pond's edge. Beckert picks his way around the shallow, rust-colored water, boots slurping with every step.

Beside him the wall ripples as a thin film of water cascades over bacterial mats. Gnats and midges swarm at his approach, surrounding him with the nasal scream of tiny wings.

*Glad I sealed up. I'd be inhaling these things.*

The dripping tendrils end at the pond's far edge. Beckert steps through, grateful to get past the revolting area, then looks back at the bizarre ecosystem.

On this end, he sees a network of ceiling cracks, through which water seeps. From that source, whatever nutrient the water carries flows down the slight slope, feeding the hanging tendrils. Some drips to the floor from phlegm-like tendrils, and the rest clings through surface tension, nourishing microbial colonies down the walls.

*What a strange world... Insects feed on the microbes, presumably. Do the small animals feed on the insects? And what feeds on them?*

Finding no answers, he turns about then notices beads of water on his pistols. He gives the weapons a shake, but the beads remain. He looks closer and rubs them with the heel of his gauntlet, discovering what he thought were beads of water are rings etched into the metal.

"Acid!"

Frantically, he gets down on all fours and shakes like a dog, flinging corrosive drops from his armor and rack. Getting to his feet, he looks back at the big pond.

"What if I had walked through that?"

Realizing he is talking to himself, Beckert gives himself another full body shake, lifts his faceplate, and runs ahead into the dry tunnel.

With no more signs of life and no branches to either side, the lengthy tunnel feels desolate, and Beckert starts to miss his ring-tailed friends. A narrowing of the tunnel ahead takes his mind off other distractions, however, and the Geek approaches stealthily.

Train rails merge from six to four, then the tunnel shrinks

again around the narrowed railway, and his lights shine into a dense group of rail cars packed into the bottleneck. The Geek runs on his toes and slips along the tunnel wall.

Reaching the nearest train car, he crouches, clicks off his lights, and listens. Silence is so perfect his racing heart sounds like a drum in his chest. For long moments he waits in darkness, hearing only his pulse and breath, unnerved by the totality of sensory deprivation.

Beckert clips pistols to his back and reaches out with his hands. They glance over granular flooring, bumping the rails. He stands up and waits, listening, with one hand on the train car. No sound.

The Geek slides forward, finds the end of the train car, and slips around the corner, halted by the joined hitch of the rail car ahead. Feeling its shape, he progresses to the rear of the next car, discovers the outline of a deck and railing, takes hold, and climbs silently onto it.

The deck is not flat and lists to the right. Arms out to each side, he keeps his balance, stands, and listens.

No sound.

Reaching up, he feels for the roof of the car. Like a cat, he hops up on the deck railing then springs up on top of the car, crouches in darkness, and waits.

Silence.

The Geek creeps forward on toes and fingertips. The train car's smooth roof plates flex beneath him with mild creaks that seem deafening in the quiet. Beckert continues, spider-like, until the roof plates round off and end at the car's front. He pauses at the edge.

Still, no sound.

Beckert clicks his lamps on low. At his feet is an accordion-like collar joining his car to the one ahead. Rips in the pleats allow him to see metal planking below, bridging the two cars. Overhead, the ceiling of the narrowed tunnel is much closer than he realized. No longer the vaulted arch of the main tunnel, it has closed to a couple of meters above the train. Behind him, boot prints mark his progress in thick dust. Ahead, columns of train cars slump in their tracks. The lines are so close in the narrowed tunnel, many of the cars lean against one another.

Beckert hops easily from one to the next, each small jump carrying him closer to some unknown place.

*A popular spot, from the number of trains packing in...*

The low tunnel bends left then opens into a much wider space. Beckert brightens his helmet lamps and stares into a vast, semi-circular rail station. More tunnels feed in to the left and right, likewise jammed with slumping trains. Colossal pillars prop up a flat ceiling, and long piers run between tracks like spokes in a great wheel, leading to a broad platform at the hub.

Excited, Beckert grabs his pistols and jumps down to the nearest pier, but his boots *crunch* through dust-covered heaps. The Geek looks down and gasps in horror, up to his knees in brittle human skeletons.

Nearly panicking, he leaps back to the train roof and stares down at the human wreckage. Skulls, rib cages, arms, legs, pelvises and spines cover the full run of the pier, draping over every edge. Dusty veils blanket them and billow softly when disturbed.

The Geek turns away and hops to an adjacent train. Anxiously, he peers over the edge and finds a pier also covered in dried, overlapping bones. He leaps over the pier to the next train, but that pier is littered with bones, as well. Everywhere he looks, the ancient dead pile upon one another: between the trains, inside the cars, on the piers and platform, even at the sides of the tunnels leading into the station.

*All of these people...so many... So MANY!*

Beckert kneels on dusty roof plates, overwhelmed. The dead seem to whisper voiceless terror from every direction, all of them crowding, surrounding, blaming for the injustice of their end. He closes his eyes and concentrates, focusing and centering his unbalanced mind. Breathing slows; heart rate calms. Reason returns, banishing the restless spirits of his imagination, and he opens his eyes.

*I'm in control.*

The Geek strides toward the front of his train, all the way to the circular hub, and he surveys the wide platform. Vague trails meander through the remains, marked by crushed bone and dark stains. Against the wall of the station hub, skeletons pile atop one another in a more orderly fashion as if deliberately stacked there. And beside them is an intact fabric tent covered in dust and dark splotches, emblem of a red cross on the closed flap.

Aiming for the makeshift trail through the bones, the Geek drops from his perch and picks his way to the tent. Cautiously, he throws the synthetic fabric aside, thrusting his pistol in at the same time.

Inside is a stainless steel table, upon which rests its final patient. The body lies on its back, scraps of a square-cut v-neck shirt draping a collapsed rib cage. Ragged drawstring pants clothe the lower pelvis and leg bones. Only the pant cuffs are free from stains, retaining their original sky blue.

Perched on the table's edge is a white porcelain bowl, speckled with dark brown dots. Desiccated fly husks crowd the bowl, resting on their wings with curled legs in the air. As Beckert looks around he finds them everywhere, littering floor and surfaces.

Medical instruments line the back wall of the tent: a canister of oxygen, a diagnostic cart, stacks of paramedic's bags, trays of cutting and injecting implements, and a trash barrel overflowing with drained ampoules and plasma bags. In the corner, a skeleton sits in a folding chair wearing the rags of a spattered white smock. A surgical mask hangs around the neck bones, and a head wrap still clings to the skull. An injector rests in its bony lap.

Beckert looks in the trash barrel and selects one of the empty ampoules.

*Morphine.*

Every glass phial reads the same. He tosses the one he holds back to the barrel where it clatters noisily, and he stares at the seated surgeon.

"Guess you saved the last for yourself."

Beckert leaves the tent, confronting death on a scale he cannot comprehend. From the platform looking out, almost all of the skeletons are slumped in the same direction, facing him. Their thin bones reach over one another as though the dying were dragging themselves across the dead, all to reach the medical tent for a painless release from life.

For the first time in his life, Beckert slumps to his knees and weeps.

# WORTHY SHELTER

Thompson sits on his rump, legs straddling a narrow corridor. A massive slab of concrete hangs overhead, suspended by the arms and shoulders of a rusty load lifter. Between the Gun's knees extends a taut rope of carbon fiber. He hauls on it with all of his strength, and Argo, mummified in the black rope, scrapes through the corridor another centimeter.

Perspiration rolls from Thompson's eyebrows, soaking into the mesh cushions at his cheeks. He scoots forward, sets his back, and hauls again.

Argo exhales just before each pull to make himself as slim as possible. He knows he must remain as relaxed as possible, to not tense up and flex, and in so doing, make himself wider. But the corridor is at its choke point and the Brick is wedged in tight. With both shoulders dislocated, unable to draw breath, and Thompson straining him through too narrow a gap, the big man huffs in agony.

"Brick, try shifting side to side...maybe scuff your shoulders through a bit," Thompson says. As the Gun hauls on the rope, Argo's head swings back and forth in the corridor. The Brick's dislocated shoulders scrape forward millimeter by millimeter.

"Gun Thompson, sir."

Thompson drops the rope and whirls, snatching up his rifle. The wild look on his face drains when he sees Beckert kneeling at attention and saluting.

"You *are* stealthy," he says, laying his rifle beside him. The Gun picks up the black fiber rope and hands the free end to Beckert.

"Brick's jammed up. Here, help me pull."

"Aye, sir."

The men take position and set their postures.

"Brick," Thompson says into the corridor, "like before." Thompson looks over his shoulder. "On three. One…two…*three*!"

Both men haul on the rope. The added strain, with Argo's head rocking, pops the big man through the bottleneck like a cork. Geek and Gun stumble backward then march away from the corridor, towing Argo into the open. The Brick's face is deep red and dripping with sweat. The rope binding him is frayed into fine wool like a puffy sweater.

"Get it off!" The Brick demands between rapid, shallow breaths.

Thompson cuts the knotted rigging with his bayonet. Beckert spools the freed cord around his arm. The rope is heavy with perspiration.

Argo's glassy eyes shut tight, and his jaw clenches as he waits for the constricting rope to uncoil. Beckert, sensing his comrade's pain, moves with speed.

Argo's undershirt is soaked, and dark purple bruises show through the transparent fabric. His shoulders and upper arms are rubbed skinless, seeping a thin mixture of blood and sweat.

"*C'mon*," the Brick begs. Finally, the compressing rope slackens enough for Argo to take a full breath. His huge chest rises and falls. The redness drains from his face, but the discomfort is still there.

"Thompson, my shoulders. Put 'em in. *Put 'em in.*"

Thompson kneels beside his friend and grips a beefy arm. Gently, he raises the arm and pulls firmly at the wrist while rotating. The bone reseats into the socket with a *clunk*.

"*Gah*! Okay, okay," Argo rushes between quick breaths, "do the other one!"

Thompson hops to Argo's other side and repeats the process, rotating the opposite direction. There is another *clunk*, and Argo exhales in a rush. The Brick sits up and crosses his arms, massaging his aching shoulders.

"Geek. MedKit."

Beckert jumps to Argo's equipment and retrieves the kit. He sets it beside the Brick and opens it for him.

Argo reaches toward the tools and winces. Grimacing through the pain, he reaches again and selects his injector. After setting a deep needle depth, he loads a phial, primes it, presses the injector against his shoulder, and triggers a dose. Swapping hands, he presses the injector against his other shoulder and triggers. Relief smooths the creases on his weathered face. He wipes his brow and replaces the tool in the kit.

"That was interesting," he mutters and rotates his huge arms slowly, working the medicine into inflamed tissues.

"How do they feel?" Thompson asks.

"They still work." Argo looks up at his comrade. "Did a good job. Thanks."

Thompson extends a hand and helps the big man to his feet.

"Gear up. We're mov…" Thompson breaks off mid-sentence, cocking his head. The crackle of thrust, then the whistle of hovering turbines grows louder through the narrow corridor. All three freeze in place, waiting for the sound to fade, but it holds steady.

Argo runs to his armor and starts dressing.

"Sergeant!" Thompson calls urgently. "Does this tunnel lead anywhere?"

"Yes, Major. Big complex. I couldn't get in, but I'm sure the Lieutenant could—"

Thompson strides to the lifter before Beckert finishes his thought. He spins his rifle around and smashes its hydraulic fittings with the butt. Centuries-old fluid jets from the broken hoses, and the lifter's arms descend. The concrete slab grates against the tunnel wall as it lowers then slips from the top of the lifter's pilot cage. The movement flops the lifter onto its back and the slab crashes down in front of the corridor, blocking all but a tiny gap.

The Gun runs to the sacks of media records and climbs inside the harness. Argo is fully dressed, sliding his equipment rack into the rails of his armor. The rack sets with a *click* and he hefts his cannon. Thompson looks him over.

"Can't believe we got you through."

"Yeah," Argo says, shrugging his aching shoulders. "Let's go a *different* way next time."

Thompson turns to Beckert, who is squatting down with a brood of black-masked animals. The Geek tosses something into a corner and the animals go skittering after it.

"Sergeant, on point."

"Aye, sir. This way!" Beckert dashes into darkness, pistols drawn, and his teammates run after.

The young Geek leads the team down kilometers of dark tunnel, up the slick rise, past acidic tendrils, through narrowing tunnels, and onto gridlocked trains. Argo's bulk compresses the train roofs noisily, and the din echoes in the close tunnel. Eager for an end to the metallic groans and *pings* of popping rivets, Argo lowers himself into a three-limbed scoot and follows the Geek down to the circular platform at the station. Thompson hops down beside him, crunching though web- and dust-covered heaps of brittle bones. Brick and Gun both stare, stunned at the scale of death around them.

"Was there a battle?" Argo asks.

"I don't see any blast marks," Thompson counters. "What do you make of it, Geek?"

"I think these people were already dying, sir." The Geek points at the tent with the red cross. "A MedTech was retiring them."

Labset in hand, Argo taps his thumbs against the screen. He strides to the stacks of bones along the wall and sweeps the labset over them.

"I'm not finding isotopes in the remains. But there is a radiation source nearby." The Brick pivots until he is facing the station hub. "Inside the complex, I'd say."

Thompson brightens his lamps for a better look, and the bones sparkle as though in a frost. Everywhere his light falls, reflections shine from within the heaps of dead.

He crouches and digs through dusty piles, retrieving a scrap of cloth with something glinting in the middle of it. He flips the cloth over and finds the gold bar of a second lieutenant's rank insignia.

His hand plunges in again, retrieving a gold insignia with seven leaves in the shape of a star, stem down—his own rank of major.

Beckert searches the piles at his feet, coming up with lieutenants, captains, and a lieutenant colonel.

"They're all officers..."

Thompson nods heavily and continues digging. Toward the bottom of his pile, he finds laminated ID cards, crusted with thick dust. He rubs one of them clear.

"Lieutenant James Dunbar," he reads.

Thompson studies the man's face. The skin is light and even, free of burns or scars. The hair is receded to the top of the man's head and is close-cropped with patches of gray at the temples. The smile shows white, even teeth.

Passing the ID to Argo, the Gun adds, "Check it out. He made Lieutenant, barely a mark on him."

Argo takes the ID card, studying it intensely, before passing it back. "He must've been a *remarkable* Operator."

Flipping Dunbar's ID to the back of the short stack, Thompson clears the front of the next card. The woman pictured has skin of the deepest brown, and her dark hair curls tightly against her head. Her jaw line is angled and delicate, her lips full. Penetrating eyes stare out from the photograph.

"Major Naresa Embiko."

Like Dunbar, the woman is free of scars. Thompson mentally conjures Major Chusan and Major Ralla, both of whom bear a visual testament to the trials they have survived—Chusan, especially, with a face that is mostly skin grafts.

*Reaching Lieutenant unmarked is a feat. Reaching Major unscathed? Unheard of...*

Thompson clears the remaining two cards and fans them like

a short poker hand. With their ethnic variety and even complexions, the soldiers in the photos look more like colonists than cadre. And not one of them carries the grim intensity of an Operator. Not one.

He tosses the cards back at the skeletons, wondering if these faces represent the future of a blended colonist/cadre population. The thought of new generations inheriting colonist frailty is taxing. But the bones remind him these faces belonged to living people, and he shames himself for judging them.

"Major, have a look at this."

Thompson looks up to see Beckert standing at the entrance to the main archway, staring straight ahead.

The Gun strides over and glances into a four-meter-tall hallway. About ten meters in, a floor-to-ceiling gate blocks entry with stout bars. At the base of the gate a pile of bone stands two and a half meters high like a frozen wave.

Squinting, Thompson steps into the hallway, looking down at the gravel of crushed bone underfoot. Dark stains cover the floor. More dark streaks and spatter stain the bare concrete walls.

From the bone pile's density, he guesses—in life—the bodies must have reached the ceiling. Testing his theory, he shines his lights to the top of the gate. Dark stains smear the arch and uppermost bars.

"Looks like they trampled one another, trying to get in," Thompson announces.

Beckert peers down the grim hallway. "Why weren't they let through?"

Thompson wades deeper into the pile. Brittle bones snap and collapse at his touch, wafting clouds of dust, and he lowers his faceplate. When the pile rises to his chest, the Gun uses his rifle butt like a spade to clear a path. Underfoot, he feels the floor is uneven, as if something has been compacted from trampling. And he stops cold when he realizes it is the pulverized remains of those crushed by a panicked mob.

*That soldiers could do this… Officers, no less…*

Standing at the bars, Thompson looks through to a wider

chamber with sentry posts on each side. Bone fragments have spilled through the bars, littering most of the chamber floor. Bullet holes and dark spatters mar the wall of the left sentry post. Streaks from the wall lead down to a slumped skeleton wearing a flak vest, an open-faced helmet, and boots. A small handgun lies beside the remains.

Beyond the sentry posts, an arched hallway continues many meters before ending at a vault-like door. A large eagle, wings spread, is emblazoned on the door with a vertically striped shield over its body. Above its head is a circular field with stars arranged in a six-pointed pattern. One leg grasps a branch with leaves and berries, the other grasps a cluster of arrows. The eagle's beak holds a flying banner, reading, "E. PLURIBUS UNUM", and beneath the eagle is the number "1775" printed boldly.

Thompson studies the emblem, observing the recurrence of the number thirteen: the stripes on the shield, the stars in the circular field, the number of leaves and berries on the branch, the number of arrow heads, the number of letters in E PLURIBUS UNUM. The significance eludes him, however.

His eyes fall to the stout bars of the gate. Time seems to have had little effect. He grasps with one hand and pulls, but the gate is firmly rooted. Bright metal shines in the spot his hand rubbed clear of dust.

Thompson wades back toward Beckert, crunching and snapping through the dusty bones.

"Get Brick."

"Aye, sir." The Geek runs back to the platform, where the medical tent glows with internal light. Beckert runs up and throws back the tent flap. Argo stands facing the surgeon's skeleton, examining the injector.

"It's just as you said," Argo says, turning to face his comrade. "He was retiring them... *All* of them."

"Lieutenant, the Major needs you."

Argo's eyebrows lift, and he tosses the injector into the dead surgeon's lap. The skeleton collapses.

"Let's go, then."

Beckert leads the Brick into the arched hallway. Thompson waves to the big man, beckoning him toward the gate.

"There's a barricade we need to get past," Thompson states.

"Okay. What are we looking at?"

"Solid bar, steel alloy. Nickel based, most likely."

The Brick sets his cannon down and strides up the path Thompson made through the bones, enlarging it. He leans close, inspecting the bars Thompson rubbed clean.

"Oh, yeah, this is good stuff," the big man confirms. "Sturdy welds, too." He grabs the bars with both hands and rattles violently. "Don't typically see it used outside of engines and reactors."

"Why's that?" the Gun asks.

Argo faces his friend. "Thermal tolerances are high. My torch won't cut it." He turns back to the rugged bars. "Gonna take a while to grind through."

"Can't you blast it?"

"Might bring the roof down." Argo juts his lower lip. "And this gate would probably still be standing."

Thompson grimaces. "Get started. I'll keep watch."

"Understood." Argo steps from the pile and removes his back rack. He pulls a rugged power tool from a compartment and fishes for a drill bit.

Thompson crooks a finger at Beckert, indicating he should follow, and leads the young Operator out onto the platform.

"Start scouting the other tunnels. Move fast, do not engage. When you return, challenge word is *redline*. The reply is *blueshift*. Understood?"

"Aye, sir. Redline, blueshift."

"On your way."

Beckert salutes. He leaps up to the nearest train roof and fades quietly into the darkness.

"Should be ten to fifteen minutes per bar," the Brick yells from the hallway, "provided the grinder holds out."

Thompson nods. "Sooner is better, Argo."

"Roger, that." Argo's grinder shrieks to action. He lays into the rounded bars, sweeping the cutting edge up and down with a storm of sparks.

Thompson leaps up to a nearby train roof and walks out into the open station. Once he has a good view of the adjacent tunnels, he takes a knee and clicks his lights off. One tunnel glows with light, dimming quickly as Beckert progresses deeper into it.

Metallic screech from Argo's cutting would drown out anything softer than a rocket launch, so the Gun lifts his riflescope and sweeps like a turret. No heat sources are visible other than fading light from Beckert's tunnel, and the fountain of sparks at the alloy gate. With so little to draw his attention he is suddenly reminded of the multitude lying dead all around him.

Thoughts of these people shambling and crowding in search of safety, the panic and terror which drove them to trample one another, the sentry who witnessed a human flood breaking against his gate but would not or could not let them in. He shivers and tightens grip on his rifle.

Thoughts turn to the enemy, the ones responsible for the chaos and destruction, the ones responsible for humanity's annihilation and the Cadre's desolate life among the stars. Do they know where he and his team are? Are they waiting above for them?

He looks straight into the tunnel that brought them out of Washington. Sparks from Argo's grinding provide just enough light for night vision, and Thompson traces the dented train roofs back.

*If the enemy gets through that cave-in, we left an easy trail.*

Operator instincts urge him to keep moving, to reconnoiter another tunnel, to do anything but loiter here. It feels like madness to stay.

He looks over his shoulder at the gate. From what Beckert described of the general's video, a military command center might lie beyond that portal with the promise of answers, technology, and information. It is precisely the objective he seeks, and the opportunity is too great to pass.

A sour *clang* precedes the winding down of Argo's grinder.

"Blast it!" the Brick curses.

"You all right?" Thompson calls out.

"Broken bit," the big man yells back. After a moment, the grinder spins up again. Argo leans into the obstinate bars, showering himself and the dusty bones with sparks.

While the grinder roars on, Thompson maintains his rigid stance. His eyes scan one tunnel to the next and back. Steely arms keep his weapon level, ready for the slightest hint of the enemy.

His stomach growls, reminding him of the six hours since he and his team ate. Always, the need for an interval interrupts more vital priorities. The more he thinks about the idea of food, the mess, the waste, the more it seems a failure of design.

*With all they know about physiology, you'd think the MedTechs could give us a battery, or pill, or injectable...or something...*

The Gun's mind wanders in the low light, thinking about MedTechs, the Operator Corps, Cadre One, and how it came to be that his life of devoted service earned him and Argo a suicide mission into the heart of enemy strength.

*By gunning down your own kind*, he recalls bitterly. *Accident, or not, there's no difference. You were in charge. You're responsible. You're a criminal.*

Muscles of his jaw flex.

*There's no place in the Cadre for dishonored criminals. And the* Europa? *How could I live side by side with the colonists after I murdered seventeen of them?*

He purses his lips and shakes his head.

*It was a relief to be chosen for this mission*, he admits to himself. *At least I spared another Operator from this death-run and can end my days with a shred of honor. I owe the Counselor a debt for that...*

Thompson contemplates the white-coated man, wondering how he convinced General O'Kai to choose him and Argo for this mission. Even more, Thompson wonders how the Counselor convinced O'Kai to turn custody of Maiella over to him. Smart as the Counselor is, the thought of him supervising the rowdy woman makes him grin.

*She'll test you, Counselor, I have no doubt.*

His sharp eyes continue their vigil when it occurs to him that this planet is his home now. Not the *Europa*, not Cadre One, but this world—with its toothy predators, sweet air, and flowing waters—will be his permanent residence.

*For as long as we can survive...*

Dried-out skeletons below are proof enough that humanity once flourished here, but more than proof, he feels a belonging. Dormant parts of him awakened with his first breath of unfiltered planetary air. And now the idea of a simple berth or cabin seems intolerably confining.

*If I could return...would I?* He nods to himself. *To see Maiella again, yeah, I definitely would.*

*If she were here, instead of Beckert, we could transmit the mission data to the orbital relay and escape to the wilderness, maybe live for a while at least...*

*But she isn't. And my oath to O'Kai was sincere. We will send Beckert home, somehow. He'll need transport...that means direct confrontation with the enemy to get it. And if he's to have any chance of escape, Argo and I have to hold the enemy back long enough...*

Thompson looks up through the concrete ceiling.

*With all that firepower in orbit, Argo and I won't make it.*

The Gun sniffs hard, shoving the gloomy thoughts aside.

*It's a good death.*

He looks down at the skeletons, his face hardening.

*And the blueskins are gonna feel it.*

The grinder winds down unexpectedly.

"Gun, *contact!*"

Thompson spins in his crouch, rifle ready. Argo snatches his cannon and runs out of the hallway. He swings past the corner and takes a knee, aiming the big weapon toward the gate.

The Gun zooms the view in his scope. Four bars of the gate

are severed, telling him Argo was cutting for nearly an hour.

*I should've kept us moving*, Thompson curses. He zooms further, focusing on the door with the eagle emblem.

"Brick, lob smoke and kill your lights!"

Argo palms a grenade from his waist. He flings it past the bars and it skids to a stop just before the door. Copious white clouds belch from the hissing device, filling the end of the hallway and rolling back.

When the Brick's lamps click off, Thompson's visor shifts to infrared. Residual heat from Argo's cutting illuminates the nearby bars; and at the end of the hall, the hot smoke grenade spins and rolls, washing the door in rays of reflected heat.

Metallic *clunks* sound from the large door. It shifts with a rusty groan. Thompson leans forward in his crouch, thumbs his safety, and slides his finger against the trigger.

The door scrapes another few centimeters. Bright light filters past the edge, creating long beams through the shifting smoke. The door is shoved again and scrapes wider.

"*Redline*!" a familiar voice yells before succumbing to a coughing fit.

Thompson lets out his held breath and takes his finger from the trigger.

"*Blueshift*! Brick, move up!" The Gun pivots and resumes his watch of the tunnels.

Argo resets the safety on his cannon and strides up to the gate. Beckert emerges from the brightly lit smoke, holding his faceplate down. Once clear, he raises his faceplate and wisps of trapped smoke escape. He coughs harshly.

"Sergeant, good to see you," Argo greets. "Where is that light coming from?"

"Sunlight," Beckert replies hoarsely. "This facility is blown wide open."

Argo watches the smoke draining past the open door, imagines it becoming a vertical column in open sky.

"*Close that door!*"

Beckert runs back into the smoke and shoulders the heavy portal into its frame. Trapped, smoke rises slowly toward the ceiling and loiters. The Geek strides out of the swirling haze, carrying the deactivated smoke grenade.

"I don't think it'll be noticed, Lieutenant. There's a steady flow of steam from the complex that goes up a couple kilometers. Reeks of sulfur."

"Sulfur?"

"Yes, sir." Beckert tosses the smoke grenade back to his comrade.

Argo catches it absently and hooks it onto his belt, ponders what significance sulfur might imply, then yields to the more pressing issue. "Is there a release for this gate?"

"One moment." Beckert steps over the flak-vested skeleton into a niche on the left side of the chamber, disappearing from Argo's sight.

"I got a panel here...no power, *naturally*," Beckert gripes. "Standby."

Argo hears what sounds like a metal cover being pried. The thin metal breaks free and flutters on squeaky hinges.

"Yes!" the Geek cries. Sounds of hammering mingle with Beckert's grunts.

Argo's eyebrows knit. "What's going on?"

"Almost there, Lieutenant." The hammering ceases, replaced by the grinding of gears. The grinding stops and Beckert's head leans unexpectedly around the corner.

"May I borrow your torch, Lieutenant?"

Argo nods and tosses the cutting tool through the bars.

"Thanks." Beckert disappears again. A loud *pop* is followed by a flood of dazzling blue light and a deep *hiss*.

Argo turns from the brilliant light and looks far into the station. If Thompson is out there, he blends perfectly with the darkness. The Brick gives a "thumbs up" gesture, in case the Gun is watching.

The glare and hissing abate, punctuated by something heavy

and metallic falling onto concrete. Argo turns in time to see a bulky electric motor make its last tumble across the floor. Beckert grunts again, and lets his breath out in a huff.

"Lieutenant, would you mind shoving the gate to the left?"

"My left or your left?"

"Uh, your left."

Argo hooks his arm through the bars and hugs his neck against them. He digs his toes into the compacted bones and pushes hard.

Beckert grunts with unseen effort, and the gate scrapes noisily into the wall.

"That's good!" Thompson shouts.

Argo spins to see Thompson standing behind him.

"Get your gear, Brick."

Argo complies, packing up his tools and replacing the rack on his back. He collects his weapon then slides sideways through the open gate. Thompson steps through after him and takes hold of the bars.

"Let's close it up, Geek."

"Ok, sir, give it a push."

Thompson leans in with all of his strength. Loose bones fill the tracks, making the gate grind and catch. Argo steps in behind his comrade and puts his shoulder to the bars. Bones crunch and explode under the gate's progress until it finally rams shut.

Thompson releases his grip and points to the niche Beckert occupies.

"Brick, give me a motion sensing charge in this hollow with a three second delay."

"Aye, sir."

"Geek, come with me." Thompson strides toward the large door at the end of the hallway. Beckert notices the emblem for the first time.

"Huh. That's elaborate…"

"Sergeant, what are we looking at here?"

Beckert snaps out of his fascinated stare. "Circular complex, Major, five-hundred meters in diameter and about all of it ruined.

No roof. The core is blasted right out of it, and strangely, the deck plates are bent *up* at the edges."

"Hmm, internal explosion." Thompson pauses at the door. "Signs of the enemy?"

Beckert's eyes bulge. "Yes, sir! There's a lot of activity centered on the tower we escaped through. Big excavators working on it as we speak. Maybe a couple hundred search craft blanketing the outskirts. They're avoiding this place, though."

"Reason?"

"Unknown, sir."

Argo steps closer, labset clicking away in his hands. "Might have something to do with the radiation."

Thompson takes hold of the door. "Let's go."

Argo's hand lands on his shoulder. "Gun, wait."

Thompson turns with impatience.

"We've already taken a high dose," Argo reasons. "Whatever we do here, we need to be quick about it."

The Gun weighs the information, sensing in the angle of Argo's eyebrows he is referring to Beckert in particular. *No point to sending the kid home if he's too sick to survive the trip.*

"All right. We'll search fast. If Geek's right, we may not find much here, anyway. Seal up and follow me."

# Alpha Mode Failure

Thompson, Argo, and Beckert seal faceplates and stride through hanging smoke. Thompson finds the door's edge again and hauls on it. Stiff hinges groan in protest, and long beams of sunlight stream into the haze. Momentarily blinded, the Operators blink as their visors auto-adjust.

Beyond the door Thompson finds a short hallway with no ceiling but bright blue sky above. Holding up a hand to block the sun, he looks out across a circular chasm. Billows of thick, roiling steam rise from the center, and through curling vapors he catches a glimpse of the far side. As Beckert described, it is easily a half-kilometer away.

Poking his head through the threshold, the Gun looks up. The broken, dilapidated edge of what must have been a thick concrete dome still shelters the perimeter of the complex. Corroded girders jut from meters-thick concrete, bent skyward and coated in layers of white mineral. Structural cables and conduit hang from the shattered rim like dead vines.

Thompson steps out through the doorway and slides cautiously down the roofless corridor. At its end is a steep drop off down into multiple exploded sublevels. Each level is smaller than the one above, reminding him of terraced pit mines he saw in Colonist archives.

Fragments of concrete sprawl haphazardly from one level to the next, bridging them like ramps. More wires and cables drape across upturned floor joists at the inner edge of each level. Calcified deposits coat every surface, making the complex white as porcelain.

Dense steam occludes the bottom of the pit, however, feeding the enormous column rising skyward through the broken dome. Thompson follows the column up to a clear blue sky.

"How'd you get in here, Sergeant?"

"I'll show you."

Beckert slides past the Gun and strides into a dilapidated corridor on the left. He guides his teammates past many dark offices to one that is bright with natural light. Hard-packed sediment is spilled out from the open doorway, and the Geek points inside.

Thompson peers through the doorway and looks into a spacious room. Sediments slope up toward a wide gap in the ceiling. Sunlight shines through it.

Beckert ducks through the doorway and beckons the others to follow. "I found a sealed tunnel marked, 'Bypass under construction,'" the Geek continues. "The doors had simple mechanical locks, so I got through easy. All kinds of lifters and excavators in there." He stops at the open ceiling, pointing through it.

Thompson climbs the sloping sediments for a better view and follows the Geek's finger. High up in the crater wall, beyond a narrow split in the surrounding concrete dome, is a section of exposed concrete tunnel.

"I saw light and found the side of the tunnel was open," Beckert continues. "When I looked out, I saw a huge crater with this place at the bottom. Figured it must be the Arlington facility, so I ran down from there."

"*In the open*?" Argo nearly yells.

"No, sir!" Beckert replies. "I waited for the wind to blow the steam column in my direction, and I ran beneath it. I had cover."

"Okay," Thompson states, turning from the cracked ceiling. "We need to get searching. You two, start on this level and work your way around to the far side. Then find a way down and start searching the next level. Mark the floor where you descend and I'll follow."

"Aye, sir," Beckert and Argo reply in unison. They hurry through the doorway and head off to the right. Thompson follows them out and turns left.

The Gun follows a gently curving corridor along the rim of the complex. The outer wall seems to have held up well, retaining its shape and much of its surfacing. The inner wall, with all of its holes, buckles, and missing sections, is more like the suggestion of a wall. Warm sunlight diffuses in the column of steam, providing ample illumination through myriad gaps.

Thompson halts at every doorway and searches inside, finding decayed furniture and workstations, hanging light fixtures, empty cabinets, and fallen ceiling tiles, but not a thing of use or interest.

As he works his way toward the far side of the complex, he notices the concrete dome overhang is shorter, and the surfaces have more of a whitewashed appearance. Calcified deposits are thicker, some hanging in elongated fingers below railings and joists.

The Gun has nearly come full circle when he finds an arrow drawn on the sandy floor, pointing to a ragged hole in the deck plates. He erases the arrow with a boot and drops through, finding two sets of footprints leading in opposite directions. He follows the larger set.

Roughly a third of the way around, he finds another arrow and descends on well-marked handholds.

As fast as Thompson moves to catch up, his team remains ahead, and he descends through ten levels before his boots hit solid foundation. Warm steam fills the air, and the area is slick with moisture. Mineral deposits here are so thick, they form clay-like caricatures of the objects they encase. Green-tinged water stands in shallow pools.

The center of the complex roars in a single continuous exhalation. Layered beneath is also white noise of rushing water, like rivers back in the mountains. Thompson steps through the mists toward the sound. Argo's hand reaches through the fog and halts him.

"Easy, there, Gun. Long way down."

The mists part and Thompson looks past his toes at a steep drop of well over a hundred meters. Culvert-sized pipes are broken off at the walls, draining water into the cylindrical well. Hoping to glimpse a bit farther, the Gun shifts his visor to infrared. The bottom is a complete washout of thermal energy, so he steps back from the edge.

"Alpha Mode Failure," Argo explains, tapping his labset.

"What's that?" Thompson asks.

"Your worst case scenario in a fission reactor. Total meltdown of nuclear fuel. Loss of cooling leads to a runaway thermal event and overpressure of containment. In a water-cooled core—which I'm assuming this was—could be steam, or hydrogen, or both."

"Overpressure?" Thompson surveys the levels above with their up-bent floor plates. "You mean explosion?"

"Aye. Enough to blow the roof off, as well as whatever rock and dirt were covering it."

The Gun turns his attention back to the steaming pit. "And the core? Where'd that go?"

"In theory, it could melt its way down to magma...unless it hit something that could dissipate all that heat."

"Like ground water?"

"Sure, if there was enough of it."

"So it could still be down there, boiling away?"

Beckert emerges from the steam, breathless with excitement. "Sirs, I found a vault!"

"Anything inside?" Thompson asks.

"Still sealed! Need your help getting in."

"Lead on, Sergeant."

Beckert weaves through webs of mineral-encrusted cables to a vault door, two meters square. At center is a section chipped free of calcified deposits, revealing stainless steel beneath. The same eagle and shield emblem is etched into the door with the words "COMMAND REFUGE" engraved beneath it.

Argo stows his labset and strides forward. While the door appears solid, the mount framing has jarred loose from the encasement of concrete. The Brick takes a pry tool from his rack and jabs it into the gap.

"Stand back."

The big man jumps to the side, using his momentum to help pull on the pry tool. The framing grinds from its mounting, and the door, with frame, tilts forward. Argo stabs the tool into the gap again and repeats the motion. The door leans farther forward, and gravity takes over. Hinges buried deep in the wall are torn out like tree stumps from hard-baked soil, and the vault door slams flat on the deck.

Thompson aims his rifle into the opening.

"Brick, get in there. We'll follow."

Argo stows his pry tool and grabs his cannon. Stepping over the fallen vault door, he ducks into a long, low corridor. Swirling mists follow him in, curling around his hunched shoulders.

Smooth, dark plates on the floor, walls, and ceiling have a like-new luster, but the corridor is dark as a mineshaft beyond his augmented vision.

At last, the corridor ends at a flat-black wall with branching corridors to left and right. Argo readies his cannon and peeks down each path. To the left, the corridor ends at a sturdy bulkhead with a wheel at center. Engraved above the wheel is the familiar eagle with shield. To the right, the corridor ends at a floor-to-ceiling hatch labeled, *ESCAPE.*

The Brick announces over his shoulder, "Clear!"

Thompson and Beckert fly down the corridor and halt behind Argo. Thompson orders, "Geek, take left. Brick, take right. I'll take watch." The Gun squats at the intersection and levels his rifle at the steam-filled entrance.

Argo moves to the escape hatch and peers through its round porthole. Through the window he finds a modest chamber with a circular tunnel cut through the opposing wall. Four cigar-shaped carts are suspended from the ceiling.

Beckert advances to the wheeled door. With a pistol clutched in one hand, he reaches out with the other and turns the wheel.

The wheel squeals, yet offers little resistance, and the door swings heavily on pristine hinges.

Beckert flicks his pistol straight out and follows it into a circular space with a high, domed ceiling roughly twenty meters across. Helmet lamps shine across tall screens dominating the left wall of the room. On the right, a high-backed chair sits atop a raised dais. Between are three semicircular rows of workstations on risers, facing the dais.

The Geek glides through the workstations, elation checked by tattered uniforms and old bones still occupying them. The closer he gets to the dais, the higher the rank of each desiccated corpse; and in the front row, every uniform has two or three stars on its collar.

Beckert climbs onto the raised dais. From there, he looks out at the wall screens and every seat of the twenty-four workstations.

*The entire room focuses to this spot.*

Reluctantly, he looks down into the large chair. A mummified occupant reclines against one side of the winged back, mandible dropped into its lap. Hollow eye sockets stare up toward the ventilator at the ceiling's apex. On the collar, a four star rank insignia is amended with an extra star pinned beside it.

The Geek looks down to the unbuttoned uniform jacket. Over the chest pocket is a simple black badge, engraved with the name, "Noromi," in white letters. Beckert turns away, recognizing the name from the haggard general's video resignation—the soldier praised as being "dogged and relentless."

*I guess that wasn't enough...*

On his right, opposite the entrance, Beckert notices three more doorways. He hops down from the platform to investigate when light shines in from the entrance, and Argo strides into the room.

The Brick halts, his lamps washing over rows of desiccated flag officers. "*Oof.*"

"Yeah," Beckert says. "I didn't think we'd find anyone alive, but finding more bodies is—"

"What've we got here, Sergeant?"

"A last stand, I think."

Argo strides up to the raised platform. "I mean, what have we *got*?" The big man pushes the winged chair aside, careless about the clatter of collapsing bones, and studies Noromi's terminal. "Hardware looks well-preserved. Let's see if we can find a way to restore power."

"Aye, sir," Beckert replies. He heads to the first of the three doors and shoves it aside. A long hallway extends before him with thirteen doors on the right and one marked "HEAD" on the left. He moves down the row, shining his lamps inside each room on the right. Two bunks occupy each room with an identical gray suitcase beside every bunk.

The last door is marked with five stars. When Beckert opens it, he looks into a spacious room with a single large bunk. Portraits of old soldiers in dress uniform, chests heaped with ribbons and medals, adorn the walls. An intricately patterned rug with end tassels covers most of the floor. A shower stall, vanity, and commode stand in a corner. Two suitcases lie open at the foot of the bunk, their contents laid out carefully.

Beckert steps through, leaving boot prints in a light coating of dust. Up close, he can see blankets on the bunk are still tucked in tight. The extra clothes are arranged exactly as they were left. Leather shoes are cracked from dryness and age, but the polish still shines.

*These bunks were never slept in.*

The Geek backs out of the room, carrying a heaviness in his chest he cannot understand, and retreats to the main chamber. There, he notices the top of Noromi's terminal is flipped open. Argo is not in sight, but both of the remaining doors are open and sounds of rummaging come from the farthest.

He follows the sounds to a room densely packed with pipes, wires, and machinery. Argo's lights bounce off the low ceiling behind a dusty water recycler. The Brick peeks over the recycler at Beckert's approach.

"Find anything?" the big man asks.

"Personal quarters. Doesn't look like they were ever used."

As Beckert works his way over, he takes in the mechanical marvels around him. "Looks like *you* found something."

"Yeah," Argo replies enthusiastically. He drops down and continues working. "I'm amazed this is intact."

Beckert stoops under thick conduits and straddles his way over a steam duct. "Amazed *what's* intact?" The Geek steps around the water recycler and finds Argo crouched at the end of a four-meter long cylinder. The end cap is pulled from the cylinder, exposing a centered axle and bearings.

"Generator."

Beckert grins. "That's great! Does it work?"

"We'll find out." The Brick takes out his labset and jacks into a service port on the generator. Its screen scrolls with streaming data. "Hmm. Thermal protect circuit tripped." Argo stoops down to his kit, removes a foil tube, and places the narrow spout at one of the bearings. With rapid squeezes, powdered lubricant puffs out. Once the bearing is fully covered, he works his way down the axle, dusting each point thoroughly.

Taking the generator's rotor in hand the Brick manually turns it. At first, the action is gritty. Then, as he rolls the rotor over and over, it loosens.

"Lieutenant," the Geek begins tentatively, "any possibility this could attract attention if we fire it up?"

The Brick shakes his head. "Already checked. The walls of this place are thick enough to keep all that radiation *out*, so it'll keep anything we're doing *in*. Besides…" The Brick points to a large diagram on the far wall. "…air, water, and power are all closed systems, no external exchange. We're good."

Beckert moves over to the diagram. Leaning close, he studies the looped cycles for each system, verifying Argo's assertion.

Argo closes the generator's end cap and moves to a manual breaker box attached to the long machine. "Let's see how it goes." He takes a breath and cycles the switch.

A clattering racket issues from the far end of the machine as a loose gear alternately catches and grinds. Before Argo can get to it, the gear engages and smooths into a rising hum. The Brick stares into his labset, monitoring start up procedures and clearing old fault warnings.

The machine screeches hideously, and Argo's eyes go wide. His hand reaches for the manual breaker when the screech ends and the smooth hum returns.

Argo and Beckert watch for long moments, waiting for the next sign of trouble. No smoke, no harsh noises, no sudden flashes of light interrupt the peaceful whirring; and Argo's labset shows all systems performing within tolerances. Slowly, Argo takes his hand from the manual breaker.

"Geek, check the power console, see if it's active."

Beckert opens his mouth to ask where when a glow of green diodes draws his eye. He steps past thick bundles of wires to a station at the back wall. An illuminated display finishes the last of its initialization routine and lists a numbered menu of options.

"I have a Start screen," he shouts over the hum.

"Good," Argo says, not taking his eyes from the generator. "Check the breakers."

Beckert taps the appropriate option.

"All breakers are open."

"Close the mains, only."

Beckert taps a key. Behind him, there is a blue flash and three small explosions. The breaker opens.

"*What was that?*" the Geek yells.

Argo runs from the generator to a bank of rack mounted batteries. Three of the cells smolder with viscous red fluid sprayed around them. He finds the manual breaker for the rack and opens the line.

"It's all right," the Brick states, "got some shorted cells in the battery backup. They're by-passed now. Let's try it again."

"Okay, here goes…" Beckert squints his eyes and closes the main breaker. To his relief, there are no more sounds of destruction, just an extra row of illuminated diodes on the console. The display confirms, MAIN BREAKERS CLOSED. He opens his eyes a little wider.

"How we doin', Geek?"

"Looks good, Lieutenant. Green bars."

Argo weaves his way to the power console beside Beckert. He reaches in front of the young Operator and calls up a list of breakers by name and system.

"Water, power, food, air…" Beckert reads aloud. "This place looks self-sufficient."

"It's a bunker within a bunker," Argo notes. He looks down at his labset and taps it with a thumb. The device clicks infrequently. "Surprised how good the rad shielding is." His eyes roam over the ceiling and walls as though looking through them. "Could be a good place to rest, if we can.

"Go back to the command room and keep watch as I close the breakers. We want power to the General's terminal most of all, and I want you right there if it shorts."

"Aye, sir!" Beckert hustles into the domed command chamber, climbs up to the general's console, and shines his helmet lights upon exposed circuit boards.

"Ready!" he shouts.

As Argo closes breakers, wall sconces near the floor flicker in a soft white light around the perimeter of the room. Pinpoint spotlights in the ceiling shine narrow beams onto each workstation below. A macabre audience illuminates before the young Geek, seated at or slumped across their stations. Beckert's skin crawls, and he averts his eyes from their infinite stare.

Tiny lights strobe in the array of circuit boards. As he watches, they twinkle like green and orange stars in a night sky.

"That's it!" the Geek shouts.

Terminals at each workstation flare to life. Screens at two stations *pop* loudly and go dark. The rest flicker with illumination.

Behind the curved rows of workstations, tall wall screens illuminate. Each flashes repeatedly, SEARCHING FOR SATELLITES.

Beckert eases the top of the general's terminal into place,

and the embedded screen displays a login prompt. He smiles as he draws a lanyard from his HDI and notices Thompson at the entrance, looking in at all of the activity.

"Major," Beckert greets.

"I didn't dare to hope…" The Gun looks back toward the corridor then looks directly at Beckert.

"Know what to look for?"

"Yes, sir! Search for military tech, details on Cadre Two, and anything that provides an exploitable advantage against the enemy."

"Exactly right." Thompson slides the double harness over his head and carries the sacks over to Beckert. He plops the fat bags down.

"Maybe we can condense these as well." He turns toward the sound of heavy machinery.

"Brick!"

There is a *clank* from deep within the mechanical room and the sound of a wrench dropping to the floor. Argo tromps to the doorway with his cannon.

"*Sir?*"

"It's all right, Brick, at ease. Sun's gonna set in a couple of hours, after which I'm going up for a look around. I want Geek plugged into that terminal sifting data. You'll have watch while I'm gone."

"Understood."

Thompson returns to his watch, peeks down the long corridor to make sure there are no threats, then returns to the entrance. "What have you figured out about this place?"

"Some kind of command bunker," Argo explains. "A little run down, but a worthy shelter."

"How's the air?"

"Clean. We can stay here long as we need to."

"Good to know." The Gun starts toward the exit. "You two, take an interval and clear your carbon traps." Thompson pauses at the door and stares straight ahead at the escape hatch. He turns suddenly.

"Brick, are you at a point you can stop in there?"

"Sure. What do you need?"

"I want to know if this escape tunnel goes anywhere."

"Will do, Gun."

Beckert flips a nutrient bar to Argo and the Brick catches it easily.

"Major?" offers the young Operator.

"I'll have it after." Thompson points at the entry bulkhead. "Keep this closed," he says, and pulls it shut.

Beckert places a hand at the release catch of his faceplate then looks at Argo with an unvoiced question

"Yeah, it's safe," Argo states. "Go ahead."

Argo and Beckert lift their faceplates. Air like a desert breeze wafts over their damp skin.

"*Whew*," Beckert says, "who left the heater on?"

"Yeah, real dry, too." Argo looks at the bar of protein in his hand. "I'm going to pack my tools and see where that escape tunnel leads. You need anything?"

"No sir," Beckert answers, pulling the sacks of media records close. "I'm good here."

Argo nods and walks quickly into the mechanical room, leaving Beckert at Noromi's terminal. Alone with their sparse meals, all trace of civility disappears and they bite through the plasticine wrappers like famished animals.

# How We Died

After respectfully moving Noromi's bones, Beckert seats himself in the general's chair, slides up to the console, and engages his HDI. Code strobes through the goggles, and his consciousness projects into the machine.

Free-falling into a virtual world, he breaks through security barriers with ease and glides into a vast system. Islands of information extend in all directions, crowding together in dense, shifting groups. They surface and submerge beneath one another in a torpid boil, constantly changing.

Beckert emits his preferences to the system space, and files flock to him from the islands. They line up by relevance, overlapping like a deck of spread cards, and extend out of his virtual sight to the right.

The Geek extends a virtual hand toward the top file, and there is a slight resistance to the hand moving forward, like an invisible membrane. It confuses him until he discovers it is his own reluctance reining him back—he knows what he is going to see, and it terrifies him.

Suppressing his fear, and shaming himself for hesitation, Beckert selects the first file and plays it in a window above the orderly row of files. Frantic voices yell amid chaotic flashes of combat. Screams, detonations, and horrible deaths fill the screen from hundreds of perspectives. The young Geek blinks then recoils, unprepared, at innumerable, unimaginable horrors streaming through his mind in vivid resolution.

Argo returns from scouting the escape tunnel, cycles the hatch, and pauses at the intersection where Thompson stands watch.

Thompson greets him with an open hand, noticing the Brick's armor is dripping with water. "Did you find an exit?"

"Didn't make it to the end," Argo answers. "The tunnel's flooded a few kilometers down, and I went as far as I could before time was up. There was a faint light ahead, though."

Thompson looks down the long corridor toward the steaming pit.

"Light's a good sign." He looks back at his comrade. "It'd be good to know for sure."

"Shall I go back?"

"No. I still need you to take watch when I head up. I'm ready to go, but check on Geek first. See how he's making out."

"Understood."

Argo steps past Thompson and passes through the Command Refuge bulkhead. Beckert is still in the general's chair, goggles flaring with code. But the young Geek props his head in his hands.

"What's wrong?" Argo asks.

Code halts in the Geek's goggles. Beckert slides the eyewear up and presses his fingers into his eyes.

"It's...it's *awful*..."

Argo steps in front of the console. "Sergeant, look at me. What is it?"

Beckert takes his fingers away and his eyes shift as though the painful images are still bouncing around inside them. He disconnects the lanyard and rises from Noromi's chair.

"I'm sorry, sir. I was streaming the latest combat logs, and I was overwhelmed. So much *death*..." Beckert takes a deep breath, regaining composure.

Argo looks down at the console, uneasy at the thought of what cold and incontrovertible truth it contains. "Show me."

Beckert regards his comrade with concern and nods. He makes a few keystrokes on the console, and the wall screens at the back of the room illuminate. Each large screen partitions into eight individual windows, for a total of twenty-four simultaneous feeds. With another few taps, each window fills with the first frame of a video. Earth, the moon, and deep space resolve in high detail. The last keystroke sets them all in motion.

A cacophony of shouted orders and screams erupts from the screens, underscored by deep rumbles and punctuated by powerful explosions. Argo's eyes go wide as he watches the final acts and transmissions of commanders in fiery combat. Outmatched in every regard, the commanders frantically maneuver and counter attack until the shrill end of transmission. Warships fracture and split as numerous missiles plunge through their armored skins; fields of troops scorch from coordinated air assaults; cities vaporize beneath indigo clouds; massive defense installations crumble and melt under atomic bombardments.

Argo's eyes flick from window to window. Millions die before him in seconds, desperate shrieks preceding every moment of one-sided devastation. Such loss of life gut-checks him, stunting his deep breaths, and his stalwart conditioning is overcome by a visceral rage.

"*ENOUGH*," he bellows.

Beckert halts the videos, and the wall displays go dark.

"And that's how we died..." Thompson says with eerie detachment.

Argo and Beckert both turn in surprise, spotting Thompson in the entryway. Even though the wall screens are blank, Thompson stares into them as if he can still see every detail.

"There's three days of video for each workstation," the Geek announces solemnly. "After that, it's a couple weeks of dead air."

Thompson breaks off his gaze and looks over the corpses in each seat. "Three days? They had to deal with this for *three days*?"

Beckert nods. "In real time." The Geek taps keys on the console. "There's a record of their commands and tactics, as well, although...we know the outcome."

"I want it all, Geek," Thompson declares. "Leadership Council can analyze it. By seeing what *didn't* work, they might figure out what *can*."

"Uh, we're talking *exabytes* of data, sir. If we left the uplink open for a *week*, we wouldn't get it all to the orbital relay, and with a sustained broadcast, the blueskins would intercept—"

"Then we transport it," the Gun says coolly.

"The memory core is cumbersome," Argo adds. "Over two hundred kilos and bigger than you. It's also well secured. Removal—"

"Not the core, Argo, just the data." Thompson turns to Beckert. "Didn't you say you found a smaller memory core in the tower?"

"Yes, sir."

"Most of the files were deleted, yes?"

"That's right, Major."

"We don't need full color audio and video. Can you vector map the individual units and store their movements in a compressed form?"

"Sure, that's easy enough."

"All we need are Xs and Os, Sergeant. Give me that, stats on each unit, their movements, commands executed, and results." Thompson thinks for a moment. "So long as there are transcripts, we can lose the audio as well. Probably make it easier to analyze if they don't have to see and hear people dying."

"Aye, sir."

"How long to compress and download to the smaller core?"

Beckert juts a lip, considering the job. "Two to three hours, best guess."

"All right. Get started. I'm going up." Thompson turns to Argo. "You ready to take watch?"

The Brick nods. "Yes, sir."

"Walk out with me."

Thompson leads his teammate to the intersection and pauses. "Seems like whatever was distracting Beckert is gone. Did you speak to him?"

"Aye. He resolved his issues."

"I agree. He took that battle archive well... Better than you did."

Argo's jaw flexes in embarrassment at his outburst. "You're right, Thompson, I—"

The Gun holds a hand up. "Plenty of things here'll distract us. I think I even called Beckert 'Maiella' once."

Argo smirks. "Yeah, you did."

"We have to watch out for each other, make sure we all keep focus. That we're in control, *always*. That goes doubly for me, understand?"

The Brick straightens his embarrassed hunch. "I do."

Thompson cracks a smile and slaps Argo on his armored shoulder. "See you in three hours."

The Gun bounces backwards, turns, and runs down the long corridor. Argo crouches at the corner and watches his comrade disappear into the darkening mist.

# The Censure of Genia Mendes

Beckert slumps in the general's wing-backed chair, nearly bored. Download from Noromi's terminal to his memory core is proceeding well. And he has several automated tools searching for hidden files on the Cadre projects. There is little for him to do.

Utterly unsatisfied with idle time, his eyes seek about the room for something of note. Something undiscovered, something worth his attention. Then he finds it: a level slot in the front edge of the general's terminal. He sits up suddenly and traces a finger over the dimension.

*About the same size as a media record... Could it be a reader?*

His eyes swing to the damp sacks at his feet. After untying the harness, he dunks his hand into the closest bag and pulls out a fist full of media records. Every one is wet and covered in fine silt. With an annoyed sigh, he tosses them back and ties the harness.

He thinks about the vault they came from and the rag-wrapped skeletons maintaining their eternal embrace...and the brown bag beside them, with its secret stash.

Beckert leans forward, pulls a compartment from his back rack, opens the air-tight box, and finds all eight media records pulled from that brown bag. They are pristine, untouched by water or mud.

Excited, he fans them out. Each record bears a hand-written label with date, so he lays them out chronologically and picks up the first. He is about to dunk it into the slot when his knotting stomach makes him hesitate.

*Is it just more death?*

*No, this'll be different, I'm sure of it.*

His stomach unknots, and he slides the record into the slot with a subtle *click*. The center wall screen illuminates with a crude counter, which ticks down to zero. A loud beep blurts through the audio system and the title, *DC News, 2472, July 17, Van der Beek interview (unaired, unedited)* fills the frame.

The screen blanks then fades up on a thin brunette. Her green eyes are offset by eyeliner, her slightly drawn cheeks are well-tanned. A sharp maroon business suit squares her shoulders, and gold-rimmed spectacles perch on the bridge of her nose. She sits in a stylish chair, legs crossed modestly.

"Good morning. This is Genia Mendes with the Financial Report." The woman adjusts her spectacles. "Today, I'm here with Chief Marketing Officer of Soshiba Varicorp, Doctor Manfred Van der Beek."

She gestures to a long-legged, balding man with a paunch and square jaw seated opposite her. His black silk suit is immaculate and tastefully accented. Leaning comfortably in his chair, he tugs at a sleeve and exposes a thick band of gold around his wrist.

Perched on the edge of her chair, the woman turns to her guest and smiles graciously.

"Thank you for taking the time, Doctor Van der Beek. We're glad you could join us."

"My pleasure, of course."

"There's hardly anyone in the world who hasn't heard of Soshiba Varicorp, as you are, by far, the world's largest employer, isn't that right?"

Van der Beek smiles. "That's correct. When you include all of the support and contracting companies on our payroll, we employ nearly a quarter of the world's working population."

Genia beams in admiration. "It would be impossible to discuss all of your company's products and services in the time we have, so let's focus on the largest and most fruitful of your endeavors. Could you tell us about that?"

"You mean our colony program?"

The woman nods affirmatively. "How did such a huge program ever get started?"

Van der Beek smooths his tie. "The energy and climate crisis of the late 21st century brought some of the worst economic devastation humanity had ever seen. It used to be that, in times of war, victorious powers participated in the reconstruction of the defeated. Not so in the *economic* wars of the time. Where wealth, water, and energy were super-concentrated in a few powerful nations, those without it withered, and entire nations turned refugee. Fundamentalism, banditry, piracy, and xenophobia grew as never before. Desperate, sad times."

The man leans forward.

"But our company's founders looked out and saw a vast, untapped labor potential. Only something truly *huge* could adequately utilize it. And they were thinking big."

"Even so," the woman counters, "going from idea to implementation is a big step."

Van der Beek nods. "That's right. It was a radical move forward in mankind's progress. Truly a multi-national effort, since this was before any form of effective global government, you see. Everything was accomplished via persuasion and incentive. A remarkable feat."

"Absolutely," Genia agrees, "especially when you take into account how long it took to turn a profit on initial investment."

"One hundred fifty years before the project was in the black, adjusted for inflation, of course."

"That day became a corporate holiday, I understand, and later became the *global* holiday we call, *Emancipation Day*. Is that right?"

"Indeed." The man laughs to himself. "Did you know the CEO at the time named it '*Black Thursday*?' No sparkle in that guy at all."

"One of your first acts as the new Chief Marketing Officer was to change that, wasn't it?"

"That's right. I mean, it was a liberating, historic event!" The man looks up in fond recollection, raising his hands up as if he were framing a banner. "*Emancipation Day*. That sums it up so much better."

"Ironic," the woman says subtly.

Van der Beek leans in. "Pardon?"

Mendes continues without missing a beat. "If your project was so cost intensive with such a long timeline to profitability, how did you attract investors?"

"Ah! Glad you asked. The project architects knew the original research and development would produce spin-offs in *all* sectors. If you think about it, it's so simple. A colony would need everything necessary to support human life: agriculture, pharmaceuticals, machinery, durable housing, transportation, administration, recycling systems, energy efficiency and production. I could go on and on…and they all had to be of the utmost efficiency, to boot. So every one of our products had application right *here* on Earth. Investment in the project assured access to that research."

"But there was little incentive to an *individual* investor," Genia adds.

"That's true. We thought of ways to arrange the debt structure and allow for the paying of annual dividends, but…the costs of administering such a program was unwieldy, especially when the company was getting the majority of funding from businesses and governments."

"The appeal to industry is clear, with all of the research you were providing, but what was the draw for government investment?"

Van der Beek shifts in his seat. "Well, it gets complicated when dealing with political structures, to be sure. A lot of tap dances and pony rides if you catch my meaning. But in every population, there are social issues. Chiefly, these problems stem from poverty and crime. And, as I mentioned earlier, crime and poverty were epidemic. SoVar's founders went to the most addicted, hopeless, disease-infested slums they could find: Rio, Kolkata,

Bangkok, Moscow, Los Angeles, Kinshasa, Mexico City, you name it, and they developed a plan that would solve those social problems for good. Nations *threw* money at us."

"Yes, could you tell us more about that?" she asks politely.

"Sure. SoVar established self-contained facilities on the outskirts of these failed urban centers—production centers complete with housing, cafeterias, schools, and hospitals. People moved from the slums into their new homes, received clean food and water, a secure environment."

"That sounds expensive. How did that benefit your company?"

"Well, the stipulation was that the social benefits would serve as the people's compensation, and they would work in the production centers."

Genia's eyes narrow. "Sounds like incarceration without trial."

"Yes," Van der Beek says, "I was afraid you'd see it that way, and I understand why you think '*Emancipation Day*' sounds ironic. But consider this: these nations were unable to cope with the scale of destitution. Here were large groups of people who, in their desperation, spawned criminals at a frightening rate. Disease and addiction were *catastrophic*. They drained government resources in police, fire, health, and social services, yet lacked the opportunity to contribute anything. And every year, the slums got more crowded."

The woman nods sympathetically while the man continues.

"Now we have these people secure in one of our facilities, and their basic needs are *finally* being met. Crime plummets, addiction plummets, spread of disease plummets, sanitation improves. Government services needed to manage the awful conditions are freed for more productive pursuits. Without the squatters, the city can be reclaimed and restored. New businesses supporting the production facility move into the reclaimed neighborhoods, encouraging people to move in from other areas. With crime smashed, and sanitation high, the city attracts new businesses and opportunities. More businesses and more residents mean more tax revenues. More tax revenues permit greater services, parks, facilities, which makes it even more desirable to live there. In short, a dead city is resurrected."

"So the company attains an inexpensive work force, and the governments have major social problems managed for them."

The man raises a long finger.

"Let's not forget about the people of the slums. Their living standard was *instantly* raised. They can wake up in security, knowing they have three meals a day. Injuries or sicknesses can be treated immediately and their wellness is remarkably improved. Even the addicts, we saved. And their rehabilitation was anything *but* inexpensive, Ms. Mendes. It was truly a humanitarian venture where everyone benefited."

Genia focuses on her interviewee sharply. "So the relocation was voluntary?"

The man's brow furrows as he tries to decide if the question is an indictment. "No. They were compelled."

"Did the people see it as a good thing for them?"

Van der Beek straightens his back and stares harshly. "Have you ever seen a child dying of cholera? Dysentery? Malaria? Have you seen the scars and infected wounds from rats gnawing on them at night? Gangs of eight year olds murdering for pay? Addicted mothers? Ten-year-old prostitutes?"

He pauses tersely.

"When you see someone who is desperately injured, you don't *ask* first, you *take* them to the hospital so they can be helped."

"People are allowed to leave a hospital, Doctor Van der Beek."

The man looks down. "I understand where you're coming from." He looks up suddenly. "But where would they go if we let them leave? Back to their old lives? Remember, anyone with the ability to escape that hell would have done so *long* before we arrived. These people had *nothing*. Now, I accept that such actions draw scrutiny, and the company has received a lot of negative attention as a result. But I believe *completely* that it was the right thing to do then, and it *continues* to be the right thing to do now."

Genia's expression softens, her gaze becomes warm and friendly. "I apologize if I offended you, Doctor. These are difficult moral dilemmas with no clear solution. We're obliged to discuss them."

"And I respect your position," Van der Beek says, his shoulders rounding. "We need these questions asked of us."

Genia nods. "I appreciate that. Let's move on to one of SoVar's greatest successes: the colonization of new worlds."

She gestures to a panel on the wall between them. The panel illuminates with the image of a shining glass and metal dome. A short, conical vent stands at the dome's apex.

Van der Beek turns in his seat and smiles in fond recognition. "Ah, New Bangalore."

"Well named, it seems, as the majority of its colonists came from the Bengaluru production facility."

"That's right. Only the best and brightest earn the opportunity to join a colony expedition. Bengaluru has regularly raised the top workers in each generation."

Genia watches her interviewee carefully. "Is it true that the colonists may be offered work *outside* of the production centers?"

Van der Beek swivels forward. "Yes, it is. After their term of service off world, they're free to work anywhere, in fact. Their commitment to hard work is well documented, and their governments are quite willing to have them back in society. But then, by the time a colony is up to full production, we find the colonists have developed extremely useful management skills and are quite diverse in their areas of expertise. We try hard to retain their services."

"How hard?"

The man grins mischievously and clasps his hands. "Our contracts are juicy."

Genia arches an eyebrow. "How juicy?"

"Why, Ms. Mendes, are you job hunting?"

She returns the mischievous smile. "Not yet." Her face resumes the serious expression. "So what about the families of these freed workers? The ones still in the production facilities?"

"Freed workers can visit their families any time they wish. We encourage it, in fact, because it provides a strong role model to the others and motivates them to succeed."

"Can the families leave with the freed workers?"

"Yes, but only so long as the freed employee has the means to support them. Remember, the governments want a guarantee that Soshiba Varicorp will hold up its end of the bargain. That's one of the reasons we offer such generous contracts."

"It could also be seen as leverage, using the family to keep the freed worker in the company."

Van der Beek shakes his head. "Again, I understand your perspective, though I assure you that *isn't* how we use it. If the free employee finds other lucrative contracts outside our company, he can pursue them and bring his family along."

"But honestly, who can compete with a firm employing one quarter of the world's working population?"

The man nods modestly. "It's true, we usually offer the top prize. But there's nothing wrong with that. We are a business, after all, and we want the best. We're not afraid to pay for it. The CFO constantly talks about our investment in 'human capital,' but I hate that term. We invest in *people*. And it's a sound investment."

Genia nods in acceptance and shifts her posture. "Let's skip forward to the present. Soshiba Varicorp has redefined our standards of living with the influx of wealth and materiel from its three functioning colonies. And I understand your fourth expedition is scheduled for launch?"

"That's right. This one is headed for a planet thirty times farther away than New Bangalore, so we had to redesign almost every part of the colony ship. We probably overbuilt this one, but you never know in space. No point putting sixty years worth of human endeavor into something if you can't be sure it'll get there."

Genia turns in her chair and looks off camera. "Do we have a photo? We do? Put it on."

The screen changes from the New Bangalore colony to a gleaming vessel, colossal in every regard. Van der Beek glows like a new father.

"There she is. The *Europa*."

Genia's mouth drops. She quickly draws herself together, but not before her guest notices.

"I saw the schematics and plans," Van der Beek explains, "but nothing equals a photograph. I must say...I had the same reaction first time I saw her."

"It's amazing," Genia recovers. "The web's awash in telescope photos of the ship in orbit...hazy, far off...I've just never seen her up close like this."

"Few people outside the company have. We're pretty tight on security, you understand."

"Of course. Does the *Europa* have a captain?"

"Oh, yes, the crew is fully assembled, though I know most folks' interest ends at the skipper." He chuckles to himself. "That used to irritate the hell out of my granddad."

"Why, was he second in command somewhere?"

"He was XO of the first permanent moon base. Base commander took all the interviews, leaving my granddad to run the show. No kidding. Then the base commander retires after six months and lands a media deal that doubled his life salary. So my granddad does all the work, ends up as base commander, but no one wants to talk to him. Ha! He'd tell that story at dinners with the *most sour* look on his face, and we'd all try not to laugh."

"Did you?"

"What, laugh?"

Genia nods, "Mmm, hmm."

Van der Beek stiffens with mock alarm. "Oh, God no! That man was like a samurai with a serving spoon."

Laughing filters in from off camera, and Van der Beek turns to them happily.

"Well, getting back to the *Europa*," Genia resumes, "who will be her captain?"

"Braemar Keller."

"Keller?" Genia repeats with surprise. "He's the administrator of your New Dresden colony, is he not?"

"He was, until recently."

"He's rather young I'm told."

"Thirty-two," Van der Beek answers.

"Not *too* young?"

"Not at all. As administrator of New Dresden, his record proves we can have absolute confidence. Besides, I think you have to be young to want to fly something that big out to the stars."

"I believe we have a photo, yes?" she says off camera again.

The panel switches from the *Europa* to the image of a handsome young man, hair blond from sun, teeth white and straight. He wears an orange flight suit with Soshiba Varicorp logos and poses boldly before a blue velvet curtain.

"That's our man," Van der Beek confirms.

"We have some other photos," Genia adds, and the panel switches to an outdoor scene among short, earthen dwellings. Keller stands in their midst, blond hair tossed, mouth wide open, snarling orders. The butt of an assault rifle is parked on his hip and he points with his free hand into the surrounding vegetation. At his feet slumps an azure-skinned creature, purple tongue lolling from its open mouth. The creature's skull is broken open from multiple shots.

Van der Beek's eyes bulge. His easy smile disappears.

"I've heard of Captain Keller," Genia adds, maintaining a polite and even tone. The panel shifts to an image of a wide trench filled with azure-skinned corpses. Keller supervises from the edge while a bulldozer shoves in another heap of reptilian bodies.

"You're right, Doctor, *nothing* equals a photograph," the woman says coldly.

Van der Beek begins unfastening the microphone on his lapel. Genia leans forward in her chair, her green eyes burning with intensity.

"*Why are we massacring an indigenous species, Doctor Van der Beek?*"

"They are predatory animals," he says dismissively, "with a penchant for sabotage. Nothing more."

"Since when do animals wear *clothes*, Doctor?"

The man rises from his chair, dumping the microphone in the cushioned seat. His finger wags at her and his mouth moves in inaudible speech.

"Threats aren't necessary," she spits, losing her composure. "With so many governments as partners, who would *possibly* stop you from committing any *atrocity* you want?"

Van der Beek faces the camera and waves a flat hand at his neck. His mouth deliberately forms the words, *We're done.*

The video ends.

Beckert blinks at the blank screen. His heart thuds in his chest, and he releases his grip on the console.

"Keller!" he says to himself, recalling the now elderly captain of the huge Colony Ship. "He was fighting the enemy...and winning!"

It was always a mystery to the young Geek how someone so feeble could have been entrusted with such a vast responsibility like the *Europa* and her crew. Moreover, that such a man would place value on frivolous ideas as free will, personal property, and individuality, proved he had the wrong priorities for leadership. But now, the Geek's mind spins at seeing Keller as a vigorous young man, slaying the enemy with zeal. While understanding little of what the man and woman on screen were discussing, Beckert hungers for more, ejecting the media record and dunking the next one in as fast as he can.

The counter beeps to zero and titles read, *DC News 2473, January 23rd, Financial Report*. When the video fades up, the same woman appears in a black suit coat without the gold-rimmed spectacles. She sits behind a round desk. Behind her, large windows look out over a sprawling cityscape.

"This is Genia Mendes with the Financial Report," she begins solemnly. "World markets fell sharply today on reports contact has been lost with New Dresden. North American, European, and African markets were particularly hard-hit due to their large-scale dependence on the colony's production. When reached for comment, Soshiba Varicorp spokesman Daniel Winston had this to say:"

A window opens beside the woman, where a thickly coiffed man in his sixties addresses a large indoor crowd.

"We are aware of concerns about an interruption in the flow of resources from New Dresden. Let us first remind everyone that this is most likely a hardware failure at their end, and there is *no cause for alarm*. However, to alleviate concerns over scarcity and price gouging, we will open our reserves to the world markets. At current consumption levels, our reserves can supply global demand for two years. If necessary, New Bangalore and New Beijing can be easily ramped up for increased output in that time. So, you see, there is truly no cause for concern."

Hands extend like roman salutes from the crowd, thrusting personal recording devices toward the spokesman. A barrage of questions flies from the group, which the silver coiffed man ignores.

"A team has already been dispatched to investigate. They will have a military escort as a precaution against terrorism, opportunism, or piracy. Be assured, we have devised solutions covering *every* contingency, and the regular supply of resources *will* be maintained. Thank you."

The window closes.

"Back to you, Todd," Genia says, and the video ends.

Beckert is disappointed by the brevity. He is about to eject the record when another video begins.

*DC News 2473, April 14th, Financial Report.* The counter beeps to zero.

"This is Genia Mendes with the Financial Report. Markets have been struggling to recover since the loss of communication with New Dresden. Today, they have *collapsed* on news of the colony's total destruction. Hang Seng, Nikkei, Dow Jones, Bombay Industrial, Eurofort, and AustralPac averages suffered crushing losses, all falling more than *twenty percent* by close of business. Swift intervention of government agencies and Soshiba Varicorp's increased output from New Beijing and New Bangalore helped prevent a more serious sell off."

A window opens beside the woman.

"When asked if the colony was attacked, Vice Admiral Welles had this to say:"

The window displays a man taking his place behind a narrow podium, dressed in a crisp white uniform with gold epaulets. Numerous rows of colored bars adorn his chest. He takes out a set of cards and scans the top card before speaking.

"I have personally toured the remains of New Dresden. After extensive investigation of the site, it is abundantly clear the colony suffered a catastrophic internal failure. The fusion reactor exploded, vaporizing most of the facility. There were no survivors."

"Admiral Welles," a voice calls from off screen, "was this an act of sabotage?"

The admiral scans the next card briefly.

"Because the colony reactors are equipped with multiple fail safes and redundant safety measures, we feel internal sabotage is the most likely factor."

"Do you have a suspect?" another voice blurts.

The admiral's jaw muscles flex.

"We are looking at several activist and fundamentalist groups suspected of infiltrating SoVar's colony program. We believe they successfully passed an agent through training and colonist selection, somehow. This is an insidious and patient kind of evil, which *must* be rooted out. Justice will be severe, I can assure you."

The window closes, slides over, and reopens over Genia's opposite shoulder, showing a sleek air car descending onto the roof of a high-rise hotel. The view zooms in as elegantly dressed men and women file from the limousine. Armed soldiers in gray body armor guard their path into the hotel's roof entrance, menacing the pressing crowds with fierce glances. Overhead, military gunships patrol in slow circles, shining bright lamps into the crowd. Cameras flash continuously.

"The World Reserve Board has called a meeting of the G-5 nations here in Washington, DC," the dark-haired reporter narrates.

"We are told the delegates have been endowed with unprecedented powers to negotiate a solution to this economic crisis. The summit begins tomorrow at 12:00pm GMT, and will not conclude until all delegates are in agreement on a plan of action. The entirety of the summit will be streamed live, and I will be there to report new developments as they occur. Back to you, Todd."

The video ends. Beckert waits to see if another starts. When one does not, he ejects the record and slaps in the next one.

*DC News 2473, November 2nd, Financial Report*

"This is Genia Mendes with the Financial Report."

The woman wears a pleased expression, despite the hollowness of her cheeks. Beckert studies her, seeing clearly she has lost weight.

"World markets breathed a sigh of relief for the first time in nearly a year after President MacFarlane's speech before the World Reserve today."

A window opens beside her, and a tan, late-middle-aged man steps behind a podium. He is flanked by dozens of aides and bodyguards.

"Ladies and Gentlemen," the President says with mid-western flair, "we can at last lay to rest the tragedy of New Dresden. It has been determined once and for all the colony was destroyed by suicide agents from the radical activist group, 'Terra Est Satis.' This group was well known for its highly publicized destructive pranks and Baader-Meinhof style ambushes. Now it will be known for the totality of its *elimination*. For the last two months, the Secret Service has been in concert with *all* other foreign intelligence branches in a *massive* sting operation. This operation resulted in 432 arrests and 267 confessions. The Republic of Haiti has volunteered to host the executions."

An aide leans over to the President and whispers in his ear.

"As a tribute to those lost at New Dresden," MacFarlane continues, "all assets of the criminals, their families, and their supporters have been confiscated. Proceeds from the liquidation will form the bulk of the New Dresden Relief Fund. The remainder will come from generous nations and from Soshiba Varicorp."

He closes his eyes in a pantomime of sympathy.

"Let us pray that such a tragedy never recurs, and that our example of justice will discourage *anyone* from ever again considering it."

His eyes flick open with stern resolve.

"But praying alone won't keep us safe. We are increasing our defense budgets across the board. The loss of one colony painfully illustrates how *vital* they are. To the loyal colonists who risk so much to give us our comfort, we owe you the finest protection we can provide. Yet even with a powerful military, only our *continuous vigilance* can guarantee safety. This is a burden we all must share. If any of us suspects another of terrorist affiliation, it is our *moral duty* to report that person to the authorities. If we do not, further tragedies await, possibly *right here on Earth*."

The window shrinks out of sight and the thin reporter addresses the camera.

"President MacFarlane went on to congratulate the G-5 delegates on the skillful execution of fiscal and monetary policies which formed the bulk of their Grand Economic Action Plan. But he saved the best for last:"

The window opens again. MacFarlane's forehead is damp with sweat, his mouth and eyes smiling.

"In light of these amazing accomplishments, I believe our crowning moment was the successful launch of Soshiba Varicorp's fourth colony mission yesterday. Though the *Europa* will arrive decades from now, her departure proves the Human will to explore and expand *cannot* be staunched. It proves we will carry on our grand traditions, no matter what group tries to stand in our way. Thank you all."

Great peals of applause rise around the President and the camera pulls back over the audience. All two thousand in attendance stand and clap. The window shrinks and disappears.

"With President MacFarlane's speech," Genia reports, "and the decisive action against the perpetrators, the promise of stability reversed markets' downward trend. All indexes felt a sharp increase in volume with solid gains in all sectors. What could have been the greatest depression of all time seems to have been averted. Back to you, Todd."

The wallscreen remains blank, telling Beckert the record is finished. He ejects it and spins it dexterously through his fingers.

*This is incredible*, he thinks, holding the plastic against his lips. It is warm from the reader, and smells vaguely melted. He holds it out and flips it over, looking at the date stamp on the back.

"Jenn-ya Men-dezz," he says to the air. "Hmmm."

The Geek sets the warm record down and picks up the next in line. It has a handwritten label and date.

"Integrity," Beckert reads aloud. He dunks it into the media slot.

The video begins in what appears to be a living space. Detailed and varied works of art hang on the crème-colored walls. A bookcase on the right holds rows and rows of awards for journalistic excellence. Centered in the video is a pillowed couch with carved and varnished mahogany accents.

The entire view jostles as a delicate hand pulls away from the screen. A thin woman steps in front of the camera and plunks herself down into the soft couch, exhaling deliberately. Her hair is pulled back into a ponytail, revealing large ears. Maroon silk pajamas drape loosely on her frame as though intended for someone more curvy. Her face is plain, absent any coloring of the eyes or lips.

Beckert thinks he is seeing someone new until the woman places gold-rimmed spectacles on her nose.

"I can't sleep," Genia says, clutching her temples. When she leans forward, there are lines in her brow and streaks of gray in her hair.

"I just don't buy it...*Terrorists*?" She drops her hands into her lap. "I keep thinking back to the Van der Beek interview..." she trails off, lost in thought.

"Everyone knew the risks of letting a company grow as large

as SoVar. We *all* knew. But their social programs *worked*. They really *worked*! And when an international government seemed impossible, here's this growing transnational company employing people in almost every country, alleviating some of the *worst* places of human misery ever known. There, *at last*, was something the whole world could unite behind, something we all felt in common."

Genia lays her arms across her knees.

"It wasn't overnight, but gradually, it came…*lasting peace*. The only corporation ever to win the Peace Prize…" She gets a satisfied grin. Another thought crosses her mind like a dark wave and the smile drains.

"But the Van der Beek interview…"

Her eyes focus suddenly on the camera.

"I didn't know what I was looking at when I got those anonymous photos. I saw a bunch of blue reptiles in a hole, and aside from the gore of their carcasses, I wasn't sure what I was supposed to think. But when Fred pointed out the mesh vests and belts on the bodies…"

She covers her mouth with her hand, her expression deeply troubled. She shakes her head and lowers her hand.

"*Are we killing off an indigenous culture?*" The question hangs in the air, unanswered.

"As a journalist, I get so much *bullshit* mailed to me, it's hard to tell real from fake sometimes. I've been fooled before, so when I saw dead aliens in a pit, *yeah*, I was skeptical. I took the photos to my cameraman, Fred, and he took them to his labs for verification."

She bats one of the cushions beside her as if it were to blame.

"They couldn't find any marks of forgery or alteration. They couldn't say for sure if it was fake, so I sat on it."

She looks away and purses her lips.

"I knew it was a bad idea to pull them out on Van der Beek like that, but…" Her eyes turn to the camera as if seeking sympathy. "I *had* to know. I wanted to believe they were fake. Still, I had to see his reaction, I had to hear his response. I had no idea he'd actually *confirm* them."

She looks down into her lap. When her head lifts there is indignant green fire in her eyes.

"He took off his microphone and said, 'If you even *think* about airing those photos, Soshiba Varicorp will assume you're the author and the lawsuit will burn down the entire news station.' He said, 'I'll be sure the journalist community knows you single-handedly ruined a respected news agency and *no one* will hire you again.'"

She looks at her feet then glances around the living space.

"A million a year and a condo in DC filled with beautiful *shit*." She grabs the cushion beside her and hurls it out of view. Something fragile hits the floor and shatters.

"He was so goddamned *guilty*! And I just *dropped* it. Because I was scared…"

Her face flops into her hands, the heels of her palms driving the water from her reddened eyes. She looks up.

"I was scared of losing all *this*, of losing my career, the access, the special parties, the status, the…" She trails off again.

"*I swore an oath*," she says, nearly roaring, "to serve the *truth*! To be the watchdog of the powerful, to report abuses to the people. And I *cowed* because some powerful *prick* can take all this away with a *word*."

She sniffs hard, wiping the tears away.

"I can't eat. I can't sleep. There's something awful happening and I can't let it go."

She lets out a long exhale, and her shoulders droop.

"Bob wasn't any help."

Her spine straightens and she crooks quotation fingers in the air.

"While we respect your position, we can neither assist, nor encourage you in your investigation of Soshiba Varicorp."

She relaxes her posture.

"*Jellyfish*. It sounded so rehearsed, it made me wonder how many times he'd given that speech."

She wipes her eyes dry with determination.

"I'm not gonna throw it all away on a set of photos, but as of *now*, I'm starting a file. Everything hincky with SoVar I'm going to keep with me, every interview, every newscast, every snapshot, every accounting spreadsheet, including this video. That way, if I start to chicken out again, I can watch this and shame myself back to some integrity."

Her face is flush with color.

"Terrorism? *No fucking way.*"

She reaches aggressively toward the screen, and the video ends.

Beckert can hardly sit still, energized by the woman's passionate determination. He still has no idea what any of it means, however, as the colorful vocabulary is lost on him.

He struggles to draw sense from the strange words and concepts, whirring images cascading one after another of splendid city and lavish lifestyles. The variety overflows his rational senses into a greater, subliminal awareness, and he suspects within the scenes of power and privilege are clues to the great mystery of humanity's fall.

The next two media records are filled to capacity with financial data, stock manipulations, suspect banking transactions, and Beckert surmises these are the troves of data the reporter swore to collect. Many interesting and chaotic patterns emerge from the data sets, which tangentially appeal to the young Geek, but they have little meaning otherwise.

He expects more data on the next record. Instead, he finds more video.

*DC News 2481, March 15th, Financial Report.* The counter beeps to zero.

"This is Genia Mendes with the Financial Report."

Her hair color is too uniform to be natural and appears dry under the intense studio lights. Heavy make-up tries to hide deep lines in her brow. A sharp gray and black suit fits snugly against her thinned frame. Sunken eyes carry a dire expression, and she takes a deep breath before speaking.

"World markets suffered their deepest collapse in history today on news New Bangalore *and* New Beijing have been lost."

She clasps her hands together to keep them from trembling but her face is stony.

"Unlike the loss of New Dresden, which was attributed to terrorism, New Bangalore and New Beijing were destroyed in a coordinated strike by an unknown enemy. President MacFarlane has recommended a formal declaration of war to the World Reserve, and has nominated our own General Westphal to command United Forces. While the World Reserve has declined a formal declaration of war, they have shown willingness to *prepare* for war by elevating Westphal to five stars. We tried to reach the President for comment, and were deferred to Westphal himself, due to the fact the general will be taking point on all activities surrounding the destroyed colonies."

A window opens beside the reporter, displaying a short man in crisp charcoal uniform. Medals and awards are stacked in rows on his left breast. Piercing eyes flash with fearsome cunning. Beckert's eyes bulge with recognition.

*That's the general from the tower office!*

The man appears much taller on screen as he steps up to a podium and speaks.

"We are facing a cowardly enemy, one who strikes against unarmed civilians. They spared no one."

Westphal's lips curl into a sneer.

"The military spending of the last four years has not been in vain! We will *hunt* this enemy. There will be *no* legal process. We will find *everyone* responsible, and we will *destroy* them. No matter where they hide, no matter where they run, we will find them."

His fist crashes onto the podium.

"And we will *wipe them out!*"

Hands fly up from the crowd, reporters begging for the general's attention. Westphal's strong arm points out at one of the reporters, who stands.

"General, what of the ships and soldiers defending the colonies? Has anything been heard from them?"

Westphal narrows his eyes. "I'd like to know myself. We found wreckage, but not nearly enough to account for the full defense force. That means many of the ships stationed at New Bangalore and at New Beijing are missing. I don't like the thought of it, but it's possible they were involved in the attack. One more question, I have work to do."

The hands fly up again, fervently. The General selects a slim, dark-haired woman with gold spectacles.

"General, is it possible this was an alien attack?"

Westphal scoffs derisively. Heckling laughter spreads through the group of reporters.

"Madam, I'm sorry you wasted your time coming here today. Now that's all."

The general steps away from the podium, an entourage of aides and advisors in tow. The window closes.

A new window opens on Genia's opposite side. The view is from a mountainside, looking down into a wide valley at a distant military installation. Long lines of vehicles crowd at the gates to get in. Within the gates, long fields of tarmac are occupied by large, squat transports. Soldiers and small craft load into the back of each transport. One at a time, the large vessels rise from the tarmac and new arrivals land in their place.

"The largest military mobilization since World War Two has begun, with all active duty, reserve, and off-duty personnel ordered to report for deployment. Retired officers under the age of seventy are being recalled to service as are honorably discharged servicemen under the age of forty-five. Such a large mobilization must have taken a long time to organize, and there is wide speculation the World Reserve was aware of the colony attacks well before today. With that in mind, it raises a question. What *else* are they hiding from us?"

"*Cut!*" shouts a voice from off camera. Genia bristles, staring daggers through the off stage voice.

"These editorials of yours are getting old, Gen. Just read the damn copy!"

"This *is* news, Bob," she spits back. "Our government is covering up something big, here. If we don't report it, we're complicit in the crime!"

"Jesus *Christ*, what *crime*? Our colonies are gone, and the government wants to show a strong response. People are scared *shitless* right now, Genia, and they're rioting! So maybe they waited a week or two to tell us so they could get the National Guards prepped. If it helps keep people from hurting themselves or each other, that's just good sense! I'm sorry if that damages your precious *integrity*."

"They're *lying* to us, Bob, and you know it."

"I don't give a FUCK! There *is* no free press while lawsuits abound. If by now, you can't accept that information *isn't* free, never *has* been, and never *will* be, I suggest you pack up your pompous naïveté and choose new work. And if *that's* not clear enough, let me boil it down: *Read* the copy, or you're *fired*."

Genia stares calmly at the off-stage voice. She turns her palm up and extends her arm toward the man as if she were offering a tray.

"Ladies and Gentleman," she says with mock respect, "my producer, Robert Tatascori."

She lowers her hand to the desk, her face rebuilt into a practiced mask.

"All right, Bob, just the news."

"All right," the producer cools. "We resume in five, four, three…"

Genia readies herself and looks into the camera. A window opens beside her showing a view from a hovering vehicle. Centered in the window is a large supermarket, burning and under siege by rioting mobs.

"Banks across the globe closed their doors to prevent depositors from draining their accounts. Automated Teller Machines suffered the brunt of the frustration with over twenty million reported destroyed or vandalized beyond repair. Without access to cash, and driven by fears of scarcity, many communities saw scenes like this one in Guadalajara, Mexico. Rioters stormed local supermarkets and looted whatever they could carry. To disperse the crowds, National Guard soldiers used tear gas, stun weapons, and, when confronting armed civilians, deadly force. Police and SWAT performed crowd control, allowing Fire and Rescue teams to get into the worst areas. Many neighborhoods were spared devastation thanks to the heroic acts of the uniformed services."

The window switches to a close-up of officers in thick vests batoning crouched looters before shooting them with shotguns, point blank.

"Several nations declared Martial Law today in efforts to pacify their populations. When asked if the United States would do the same, President MacFarlane had this to say:"

The window grows to full screen, displaying a still photograph of the President at a dark wood desk. Three tall windows stand behind him, framed with gold curtains. Between the windows, colorful flags hang on poles topped with gold eagles.

"Americans are too sensible to turn wild," says MacFarlane's pre-recorded voice, "because they see what happens in the world when lawlessness reigns. Americans don't want to see their loved ones taken down by well-trained soldiers, so naturally, there will be no need for such measures. Above all, we want to see Americans go on with their normal lives and have faith that we will prevail."

The window shrinks and disappears, leaving Genia centered on camera.

"Back to you, Todd."

The video goes blank. Entranced, Beckert cycles the media records.

The next video opens with Genia's face close to the screen without make-up. Her hair is tied back, and she wears a black tank top. The light from her computer monitor makes her pale face glow against the dark background of her unlit condo.

"Things are bad," she says, typing hurriedly. Her eyes dart back and forth over the screen. "*Really* bad. With governments and military so fully occupied, people are trying to get *in* to SoVar's production facilities to escape the violence."

Her fingers fly over the keyboard, tapping a frantic rhythm.

"Government bureaus are losing their hold on information… There've been leaks all over the place."

She pauses, her eyes bouncing back and forth between two points on the screen.

"Our ships are disappearing, presumed lost. One of my sources hacked a military archive and found an image of a strange vessel, unlike anything we've ever produced, almost as big as the *Europa*."

Her finger sweeps over a small pad beside the keyboard.

"Admiral Welles denies it, calls it fake, then can't explain why it has a verified archive tag. He was more interested in knowing who provided the photo, *of course*."

She shakes her head, her eyes still focusing on the monitor screen.

"I got a ton of data on New Dresden and the slaughter of the reptile people."

Her jaw flexes.

"It *was* a genocide. We had no idea the scale…burned them out of their homes, butchered them for the dirt they were living on. God, Keller must have thought they were primitives, but what if it was some kind of vacation spot for them, like Tahiti or the Bahamas?"

Her finger taps the pad.

"Maybe it was a commune like Tasmania. Maybe they *wanted* to live simply, I don't know. But I can tell you for sure if Indonesian pirates butchered every man, woman, and child in Tasmania, Australia wouldn't just *sit* by and *watch*."

A loud crash outside startles her and she looks toward the noise. Angry voices shout in the distance. Genia gets up from her seat and walks out of sight. The voices rise in fury, and metal clangs against metal. Three explosive *pops* echo and angry voices are replaced by terrified screams.

Genia walks back and sits into her chair. She shakes her head sadly.

"It's bad enough we slaughtered a peaceful species, now we're killing *ourselves* off."

She draws a stuttering breath.

"I don't see how we can last..."

The corners of her mouth turn down into a despairing frown. She brings a hand up and squeezes her jaw.

"No," she growls. "No time for that!"

Her fingers reach for the keyboard and resume their frantic pace.

"I don't think an apology will end the fighting, but we have to do *something*."

She sighs.

"There must be *someone* who isn't completely corrupt, *someone* in power who has some sense. I'm sending this out to everyone I know in hopes at least one person will try and *end* this... even if it means our surrender."

She taps the pad and slumps back in her seat. A loud knock on the door startles her again.

"Ms. Mendes," a muffled voice calls, "come quick! Your friend Marcos has been shot!"

"*What? Oh, God, NO!*"

Genia taps a key and the video ends.

Beckert turns away and grits his teeth, troubled, but fascination lures him back to the console. After the video, the media record is stuffed with images of New Dresden. Photographs taken high above the colony show black and gray fingers radiating from the complex into the surrounding environment. Thick haze billows from the main vent and shades thousands of square miles down wind.

The images progress to scenes of deep pit mines, soured rivers, clear cutting, and mountains of ore tailings. Machines rust where they failed, oozing thick fluids into the soil. Trash and broken tools lie haphazardly around them.

Destroyed communities form the bulk of the remaining images: heaps of burnt or buried reptilians, simple yet beautiful mud and wood homes leveled then scraped aside. The blighting is total, and it takes Beckert a long time to reach the end. He sits in the aftermath, stunned. Bewilderment and disorientation form oppressive clouds in his mind. The answer is right in front of him but he cannot grasp it.

Incomprehensible. Elusive.

*There's one more*, he remembers, thinking about the record still wedged into the broken camera. The Geek leans forward and removes the compartment from his rack. Opening it slowly, he looks down at the palm-sized device Argo gave him. His fingertips trace the edges as he contemplates what it might contain, then, resolved, he ejects the unlabeled record from the camera and slaps it into the console.

There is no countdown this time, just a shaky view running down an office hallway. Genia's voice calls from off screen.

"*There* you are! Did you get it?"

The camera turns right, showing Genia standing at floor-to-ceiling windows. The camera lifts toward the ceiling twice.

"Yeah, right here," a man's voice says. The camera lowers on Genia again as she looks through the glass over a massive city at twilight. She gestures with a hand, and the cameraman approaches her.

"Is it recording?" she asks, still looking out at the city.

"Yeah, yeah, we're rolling."

Genia points out, her fingertip bending against the glass.

"Can you get that?"

The camera turns and looks through the glass. It focuses on a raging fire, covering several city blocks. Above the flames, a black cloud rises and drifts with the wind. Emergency vehicles, stuck in gridlocked traffic, are unable to get near it.

"What happened?" the cameraman asks, and the camera swings to Genia.

"It fell from the sky," she mutters, looking up at early evening stars. The camera follows her gaze to bright red streaks cutting the heavens. One comes straight down, rolling and throwing off hot fragments.

"*Jesus*, Fred, *here comes another one!*"

Fred zooms in on the glowing object, tracking it all the way down to a distant suburb, and a tremendous fireball balloons from impact. Seconds later, the floor and windows rattle savagely.

"Whoa," Genia says, steadying herself. The camera sways a moment then looks to the sky again. More of the red streamers head toward them, growing larger. Fred zooms in on a dense cluster, and though shaky, the plummeting fragments resemble parts of a wheel.

"Oh, *shit*, Gen, it's the orbital hub!" The fragments rip apart into smaller, glowing pieces. "I think it's gonna miss us…hit the bay, maybe."

The camera turns back to Genia.

"Did the uplink ever come back?" Fred asks.

Genia shakes her head. "Satellites are gone. Airwaves are empty…it's so strange."

Building lights go dark. Across the city, whole blocks darken in a successive pattern until emergency lights activate. Genia presses her hands against the glass, her head bowed.

"I thought the end would be different."

"C'mon, Gen, let's get outta here."

Genia swings around, her arms rubbery, her eyelids heavy.

"Sure thing, Fred! Where to?" She gestures grandly toward the city streets, packed tight with unmoving vehicles. "Maybe we could hitch a ride with one of them!"

Genia faces the window. Without the city glow, the sky is bright with stars and falling debris.

"Lotta people dyin' up there today." She leans her forehead against the glass. "You know, I finally got that meeting with Senator Billings-s-s." The woman pats the brown canvas bag looped over her shoulder. "Yup, got everything right here, s-so he can know everything I know. Guess he got stuck in traffic."

She throws her head back and laughs in a bizarrely inappropriate way. The camera lowers slightly, filming her chest and shoulder.

"What's wrong with you?" Fred hisses. "You high?"

"Y-y-yup!" she answers, giddy, and produces a prescription bottle from her bag. She turns from the window and rattles the bottle at him. "Want some?"

A flash behind her whites out the screen.

"*AAAAH*," Fred yells. The camera falls and clatters against the floor, coming to rest on its side. Bright light sears the walls and flooring, blistering the paint. The camera tries to adjust to the intensity, focusing on an interior office window. Reflected there, a blue fireball mushrooms like a furious god.

Genia snatches the camera and aims it at her wobbly self. Her singeing hair and clothes throw off a smoky aura in the brilliant light.

"Isss all my fault..." she slurs.

"*C'mon*, Gen, we gotta go!" Fred grabs her by the jacket and hauls her over his shoulder. Genia's arms drape with the camera still in her grip, swaying and filming Fred's running legs.

Violent tremors shake the floor, and Fred's feet stagger across the hallway. Glass explodes and the camera swings wildly. A grating noise like tearing metal fabric is all the camera's overwhelmed microphone can convey.

Many seconds pass and noise dies down. Genia's groans mingle with the sounds of falling glass and distant sirens. The camera rises from the debris strewn floor and once again sways, filming Fred's gashed legs. He weaves between wrecked desks and office machines. Burning paper blows by.

"Wurr err we goin'?" Genia drones. A long line of saliva trails past the camera and soaks into the slashed fabric of Fred's jeans.

"Just hang on, Gen, 'K?"

Limping badly, Fred steps through the empty frame of a glass office wall. He pauses at a black metal door and lays Genia against an overturned desk.

The camera lifts, watching Fred work on the heavy door. His face and ears are scorched deep red with flecks of black on his nose, cheeks, and forehead. His right hand seeps blood though cracked and peeling skin.

"Whoa, Fred, heard o' sunblock?" She sniggers.

Fred turns in disbelief. One eye is seared shut with dark tears draining from it. The other has a halo of unmarked skin the size of the camera's viewfinder. He turns back to the door and jams a card into a slot with his left hand. The door dings once and Fred shoves it open with his good arm. The words "Media Archive" are painted in bold white letters upon the metal facing.

"S-s-so, Fred, mankind kicked over the *baddes-s-st* anthill in the universe like a bratty kid, and got isself killed. *How does this make you feel?*"

Another brilliant flash washes out the screen.

Fred's heavy grunts and scraping shoes are the only clues to what is happening until the screen dims. The camera looks up into Fred's face as he drags Genia by the wrists into a small room with no windows, just cabinets and racks filled with small plastic cards. He pivots, searching about the small space when an omnipresent rumbling begins. Media records dance and vibrate until an incredible shock launches them from their cradles. Fred pitches forward, scrambling over the loose piles of plastic, and hauls the door shut. The screen goes completely dark.

"Fred? *Fred?*"

"I'm here, Gen." Media records snap and crack under foot. His voice sounds closer when he confirms again, "I'm here."

Her breaths are short then gradually deepen. She sniffs.

"C'mon, Gen, don't give up."

The rumbling rises again, and Genia's breathing quickens.

"No, no, *no*…" Her voice is suddenly muffled.

"I've gotcha. It's all ri—"

A shock more powerful than the last slams the chamber. A shower of plastic rains around the camera. The building groans desperately around them, disintegrating. Rumbling overwhelms the audio in noisy distortion. The room is slammed again and again. Genia screams. The video ends.

Beckert twitches with surprise to see Argo standing beside

him.

"The download is complete?" the Brick asks, more assumptive than questioning.

Beckert gathers his wits, checking the display on Noromi's terminal.

"Uh…yes, sir. Download complete." The Geek hurries to disconnect and store the smaller memory core.

"Did you see?" Beckert asks.

"*This* one, I did. The others I heard from the corridor. Now, if you're finished, go search the back rooms. See if there's anything we can salvage."

Beckert looks up, disappointed by Argo's answer. He searches the big man's face for a sign of sympathy, but finds only the familiar stoicism.

"Lieutenant, we started the war…"

"*And*?" Argo replies, already impatient.

Beckert searches himself for words, coming up light.

"It changes everything!"

"*Does it*?" Argo leans in for emphasis. "Now that *you* know this, do you think the enemy won't kill you on sight? Seeing how they destroyed our people, you think they won't *finish* the job if they find Cadre One?"

Argo stares harshly at the silent Geek.

"Tell me, Sergeant, *how does this change anything at all*?"

Beckert grimaces, stymied for a response.

"This is the *second* time you've hesitated when ordered to action," Argo continues. "I think I'm more interested in knowing why you're still sitting there."

Beckert flies from the chair but Argo catches him by the arm and pulls him in close. The Brick glares severely.

"I wonder if you're able to maintain the Operator standard. Perhaps a more *analytical* role would suit you."

Beckert's eyes stretch at the only things he truly fears: being unworthy of the charcoal grays, losing the faith of his peers, disappointing those who depend on him.

"Sir, NO, SIR!" he roars in a deeper voice than he has ever dared. His eyes are shiny and hard like brown diamonds. Argo eases his glare and releases his captive.

"Prove it."

Beckert salutes rigidly and runs for the back rooms. The Brick watches him disappear down the long corridor of rooms before turning his attention to the console. Eight clean media records are lined up in a row, the last still in the reader. He takes them all into his large hands and shakes his head.

*This is bad.*

Argo closes his fists with the intention of crushing them but frowns instead and opens his hands. With a grunt, he stores the records in his rack, and strides back to the corridor.

# SAVAGE GRANDEUR

Thompson climbs out of the exploded complex and slides
like an ominous thought over twilight landscape. He follows rising
terrain west through sparse forest, looking for a high point, and
spies a ridge of upthrust granite slabs. Leaning behind a gnarled
tree trunk, he raises his rifle and peers through its scope. Coarse
gray bedrock has folded from some seismic event and pierced the
overlying strata. Its edges are still sharp, suggesting it is relatively
recent in geological terms, but numerous fractures in the upthrust
stone have spread into well-weathered hollows. Recognizing a
prime vantage, he checks the sky for aircraft then runs straight for
it.

The Gun skirts random boulders, vaults uprooted timber, then
slows to a halt beneath a sheltered overhang. Small furred creatures
flee from his sudden arrival, escaping to the low scrub brush with
squeaks of protest, but a violent hiss to his left makes the Gun
backstep. The sharp hiss becomes a low growl as a buff colored
feline with sky blue eyes pads out from a cleft in the rock. Its ears
flatten against its round head, it bares tremendous pointed teeth, and
screams, *rrrrrrrrrrROW-OW*.

Thompson watches the tension of muscle beneath its coat,
the twitch of its thick tail, and especially the curved claws jutting
from wide, tufted paws as it hisses and howls in threat. He stares at
the beast through inscrutable dark lenses, extends his bayonet, and
throws up arms in his own threat display.

The feline swipes a lightning fast paw at his face mask,

turning his head with the force of the blow. The Gun steps in, flat hands the creature's chest, and sends it tumbling out of the grotto downhill. It gets to its feet in an instant and looks up at him in pure hatred, hissing and growling, then it turns and stalks off into the underbrush.

Impressed by the huge cat's quickness, he shivers with the touch of adrenaline in his blood then nestles into the sheltered overhang and faces east.

Steam from the Arlington command center billows thicker in the cooling air and drifts over the DC ruins, pushed out to sea by prevailing breezes. Beyond the steam, hundreds of airborne searchlights pore over the blasted city. The Gun props his rifle on a notched stone and peers through his scope.

Heavy machines on wide tracks pull at the collapsed tower with robotic arms, lifting fragments away. Companion aircraft, hovering above each machine, run pink beams over every piece of debris. Progress is plodding and meticulous.

*Keep digging, you blue-skinned trash.*

Lifting his gaze from the scope, Thompson contemplates the greater scene. Tiny lights skim over treetops and rubble from city center to a thirty-kilometer radius like spokes in a rimless wheel. As Beckert mentioned, however, they are giving the still-hot craters and the steaming command center a wide berth.

He swings his rifle south and looks over a wide plain as white as the complex's interior. Cone-shaped vents cough their own clouds of steam, surrounded by pools glowing with heat. Twisted trunks of long-dead trees stand amid the calcified landscape like an orchard of skeletons.

A distant rumble perks him up, and he tracks the sound to the opposite side of his rocky outcropping. Kilometers to the south-southwest another column of steam rises toward the heavens, though far more compact and coherent, with brilliant jets of blue flame riding the pinnacle.

Moving fast, Thompson aims his rifle and zooms in with his scope. The craft is high in its climb and has leveled off, hidden behind its own exhaust plume, but the Gun smirks at the telltale launch signature of a trans-orbital shuttle.

*That's how we'll get Beckert off planet...*

Thompson zooms out, hunting for the shuttle's destination, and spots a cluster of bright reflections in orbit high above. Most appear like pinpoints of light, save an oblong reflection at the center. He zooms in on it and studies a tremendous vessel with smooth, muscular curves.

*I remember you*, he thinks. *Saw you on arrival... Might get a closer look, after all.*

He takes his eye from the scope and runs his gaze down the long vapor trail, looking for its origin. Strong breezes have blown the base of the trail out to sea, and tree-covered hills block his view to the coast, making further search impossible, so he waits.

*There'll be another.*

Early stars pierce the darkening sky, providing a gem-like backdrop for ribbons of shimmering aurora. The last rays of setting sunlight catch high altitude clouds painting the wisps a fiery orange. Thompson leans back in his shelter of stone, enjoying the beautiful display, when something bright rises from the horizon. He locks onto it immediately, recognizing the blue jets of another launch vehicle, and zooms in with his scope. Weapon optics plot precise direction and distance.

"Gotcha," he says with a gleam.

The craft thrusts east over open ocean then reclines sharply and powers skyward. Great clouds of vapor pile up behind the craft as it steadily accelerates. Many seconds later, roaring crackles roll over the tree-covered hills.

The ground vibrates lightly, and Thompson shakes his head in awe of such incredible output from such a small craft. As the craft ascends, the vibration grows into an omnipresent rumble. Awe turns to disbelief, and the Gun looks around himself. The calcified plain to the south is awash in geyser fountains thirty meters high. To the east, all search craft are retreating from the area as the command center is completely hidden within a colossal disgorging of vapor.

Rumbling becomes seismic. Loose stones tremble in his grotto. Thompson stares in alarm at the fuming complex.

"Argo, Beckert, *what have you done?*"

He zooms in on the command center. Between eddies of furious vapor he spies water frothing and boiling near the broken dome of the complex. Thompson shrinks back into his shallow cave, pressing hard against the naked rock, trying to comprehend how the great basin of the blasted facility could so suddenly have filled, when a shocking *thump* telegraphs through bedrock; and the churning cauldron erupts superheated water into a pillar hundreds of meters high. A devastating thunderclap batters him against the back of his grotto. Vaulted water spreads and falls, dousing the area in fat drops. Thick mists rise everywhere water lands, and the landscape becomes instantly dreamlike, surreal.

Rumbling fades abruptly, ending the magnificent fountain, leaving Thompson dazed by the spectacle. Then thought of his team strikes like a bullet between the eyes.

Gripping his rifle in both hands, the Gun dashes from his shelter into the mists. Droplets condense on his visor and he has to repeatedly swipe a hand to clear them. Trees and embedded boulders appear from the fog fractions of meters before he collides with them. He bounces off obstacles he cannot avoid, using his arms to push away and continue his pace.

He sprints from trees and high-steps over a softened field of tall grasses, feet plunging into channels of draining water, splashing himself up to the waist. Then the ground drops away and he pitches face first into a fast moving stream. He presses himself up one-handed, the other arm raised to spare his rifle from immersion, and he dashes onward.

Terrain takes a gentle turn upward, and the ground, though muddy, is firmer with each step. His vision is a total washout of hot mist, but a sound like a labored exhale draws him up the slope. Thompson follows it to the edge of a deep crater. Peering over, he finds the entire command complex is filled with impenetrable, roiling fog.

*Could this thing erupt again?*

The Gun stands gazing into the hellish maw, wondering what chance there could be his team was not drowned, boiled, or crushed.

*Doesn't matter. I have to find out, because this mission is over without them.*

Thompson rushes down the crater slope. Rivulets of water race him to the broken concrete dome and he splashes into a pond of hot water at its edge. Shifting stones roll underfoot, making him stumble and stagger through the chest-deep pool. He lifts his rifle high overhead.

Boots scrape the gritty, worn surface of concrete, and he climbs up from the steaming pond. Water stands to the very edge of the facility's broken dome, overflowing and pouring into interior levels. The Gun crouches at the precipice and leans, gazing into total whiteout.

Disregarding safety, he takes his rifle in both hands and hops off the edge. His boots smash into a withered railing, flipping him onto his back. He crashes through a section of flooring to the next level, and bounces off a weakened wall toward the upturned floor plates. He clutches blindly for a handhold, glancing off a floor joist, and slides over the edge then slams chest first onto a protruding joist below. Flowing water makes the joist slick and his hand slips right across it.

Falling upright, he bends his knees and lands astride a dilapidated partition. The wall folds beneath him, slowing his fall, and his feet crash onto sturdy plating. Thompson stays crouched a moment with arms out, waiting to see if the floor drops from beneath him. Having finally caught his breath, he feels his way down the remaining levels until he splashes down onto the solid foundation.

Draining water, concentrated by the funneling of the complex's structure, pushes his feet out from under him and washes him toward the fuming pit. He falls into a tripod with one hand forward, flailing his rifle with the other hand. The weapon smacks into an encased cluster of wires, knocking calcified deposits free, and catches between individual cables.

Thompson hangs onto the rifle and feels with his other hand for any lip, or raised surface. Finding one directly below his shoulder, he pulls himself up enough to hook his toe on it. Wiggling his foot, he plants his toehold and steps away from the pit like a horizontal mountain climber. Still bracing against the flow, the Gun carefully disentangles his rifle then extends bayonet and stabs it into the floor. The razor sharp point bites through layers of white mineral, giving a better purchase. Thompson ambles toward the foundation's outer wall, ducks beneath a curtain of cascading water, then crouches behind it, sheltered by remains of the floor above.

Still blinded by steaming whiteout, he feels his way along the perimeter and finds the toppled remains of a vault door. At the threshold, he yells down a long dark corridor, "REDLINE!"

There is no reply.

"*REDLINE!*" Thompson shouts, again without reply. He looks over his shoulder at the roaring pit, wondering if he can be heard over it.

*It'd be perfect if I start down this hallway and Argo blasts me in half. Yeah. That'd be great.*

The Gun dials his rifle output down to "signal" and points the barrel into the hallway, tapping the codeword in flashing light. He leans in and yells again for good measure then runs down the corridor.

Roaring from the pit and cascading water echo off the close walls. In moments he is at the command refuge bulkhead and he beats it with an armored fist.

"REDLINE!"

The Gun takes the bulkhead wheel, but it will not budge. He glances around the doorway, noting how the wetness extends to the ceiling.

*Did the refuge flood?*

The bulkhead wheel spins on its own and the door releases.

"*Blueshift,*" Beckert calls through the gap.

Thompson steps through into pitch-blackness. "You all right?"

He clicks his helmet lights on and scans the room.

"We're fine, but we lost power," Argo answers from the far side of the chamber. He hikes a thumb at the mechanical room. "Permission to keep working on the generator?"

"Sure, go ahead," Thompson affirms, lifting his faceplate. "Geek, show yourself."

Beckert steps from the shadows and clicks on his own lights. "Sir?"

"*What did you do?*"

"Nothing that could have caused that, Major! Lieutenant thinks it may have something to do with the reactor meltdown... That maybe the core did hit a big pocket of ground water. Or maybe it kept going and melted a shaft down to magma. Either way, all this water heats 'til it boils, and *BOOM*. Then ground water pours back in and it starts all over..." The Geek breaks off mid-sentence, staring at Thompson's shoulder. "What's that on you?"

"Hmm?" The Gun tries to see the spot where Beckert points, but his stiff neck armor will not permit it.

"There's some kind of haze on your armor," Beckert explains.

Thompson shrugs, paying it no mind.

"What were you working on before..." The Gun rotates a hand in the air as he tries to come up with the words. "...before *this* happened."

"Policing up supplies and organizing them in the General's quarters. Shall I resume?"

"Go ahead."

The Geek about-faces and disappears into the long hallway of rooms.

Thompson shoulders the bulkhead closed and locks it. He shines his lights over the ceiling, finding neither cracks nor leaks. Walls and flooring appear in equally good condition.

*Remarkable. Must be isolation bearings around this refuge... because this whole place should've been shaken to pieces.*

The Gun slings his rifle and skirts workstations on his way to the mechanical room. Argo is easy to find by his helmet lamps. His labset is linked to the generator and the Brick reads data from it.

"Hmm. Thermal protect circuit tripped," the big man announces.

"Can you reset it?"

"Don't see why not." Argo thumbs his labset and sets it down. He glances at Thompson with a raised eyebrow then grips the manual breaker for the generator and cycles the switch. Starter gears engage cleaner than before, and the machine hums with life.

The big man steps past Thompson on his way to the power console. With a couple of taps, Argo selects which breakers to close, and the room brightens with restored light.

"Well done, Brick."

Argo nods on his way back to the generator, monitoring function with his labset. Thompson follows him.

"Everything check out?" Thompson asks.

"Fine so far." Argo notices the Gun standing closer than usual. His brow furrows. "Something wrong?"

Thompson backs up, aware of his proximity. "No, but…what I saw up there…thought I'd lost you both."

Argo grins with curiosity. "What did you see?"

"I was over a kilometer away and the ground was shaking. Sky to the east was nothing but steam—couldn't see anything of the complex at all. Then a jet of water over a hundred meters high…"

Argo grips his chin in thought. "Would take gigajoules of energy to make a water jet like that. A *terajoule*, maybe. But what about the enemy?"

"Crowded out there. Tight search patterns in all directions, except here. Beckert was right. They're avoiding this place."

"I can see why. All this steam and water is *highly* radioactive. In fact…" Argo taps a new setting into his labset and holds it near the haze on Thompson's shoulder. The device *ticks* furiously.

"Gun, you're *glowing*. Follow me, right now."

Thompson looks down at his arms. Warm dry air of the refuge has almost completely dried his armor, leaving a wispy white residue. He hastens after his comrade.

The Brick leads him out of the mechanical room and makes the first left into the head. White tile extends across the floors up to waist height along the walls. A white marble counter with four sinks extends from the wall opposite and a laminated metal mirror runs the counter's full length. Fluted-glass light fixtures aim down from above the mirror, shining on each sink with diffuse light. As Thompson strides past his reflection, he sees his dark armor is pale with white mineral deposits.

"Over here," Argo directs, pointing at a dual shower stall. He takes hold of the stainless steel divider and rips it from the wall like cardboard, creating a wider stall with dual shower nozzles, then aims both nozzles at center and runs water.

"Hurry!"

Thompson lowers his faceplate, takes a step toward the nozzles, then pauses. "Is the shelter's water radioactive, as well?"

"No, it's an isolated system. Now c'mon, *let's go*!"

Thompson steps under the brisk jets and turns so the water can coat his armor evenly.

"I'm going to find something to scrub with. Use your hands for now, and keep the water hot."

Thompson nods, rubbing his rubberized palms over helmet, torso, and limbs.

Argo strides over to the marble counter top, throws open the cabinets below, and rummages past stacks of folded white towels, crates of dried out soap gel, bins of toothpaste tubes and toothbrushes, razors, combs, bottles of solidified shampoo, hand towels and face cloths, trimmers and clippers, evaporated disinfectant, and lotions. The last cabinet he checks contains a wheeled plastic bucket, sealed in transparent plastic. He pulls it from the cabinet, fingers gouging through the plastic wrapper.

Inside the bucket, Argo finds an empty spray bottle, a mop with a telescoping handle, a stiff bristled brush, and a large sealed jar. He hefts the jar and turns it in his hands to read the generic label.

*Cleanser, General Purpose, Bathroom, G-19-8X. For removal of soap scum, mineral stains, and mildew. Safe on all non-porous ceramic and metallic surfaces. Do not combine with chlorine bleach, as toxic fumes may result. For regular cleaning, mix two parts cleanser with full mop bucket. For heavy cleaning, add two parts cleanser to full spray bottle and allow to soak for several minutes.*

Argo rips the lid off the jar and twists open the spray bottle. He jams the open bottleneck into the cleanser powder and tilts it upright quickly, trapping a generous portion inside and wafting a cloud of stinging, lemon-scented dust.

He props the bottle under a faucet and opens the tap. Hot water fills the angled bottle until it spits out of the neck. Argo lifts the bottle. It is less than half full.

"Will be a little strong," he grumbles. Armed with his astringent chemical and the stiff brush, the Brick strides back and assaults his teammate. Thompson braces himself against the tiled wall to keep from being knocked over by Argo's aggressive scouring.

Multiple rounds of spraying, scuffing, and rinsing ensue until the labset confirms the Gun's sanitation with unhurried *ticks*. Most of the armor's light absorbing glaze is gone, exposing mottled patches of native gray. Thompson scowls at the loss of camouflage.

"Did your weapon optics get wet?" Argo asks.

Thompson hefts his rifle and peers through the scope. A hazy ring encircles the view, and a small dot loiters off center. He lowers the weapon, thinking about the spare optics he had in his rack—a rack that is either buried in muck at the bottom of a drowned tunnel or in the gullet of a scaly, dead animal…

Argo reads his comrade's expression easily. "Let me have it, I'll see what I can do."

Thompson passes the rifle over. Argo props the weapon beside him and grips his friend by the shoulder.

"You're going to get very sick."

"What do you mean?"

Argo leans closer. "Nausea, vomiting, and diarrhea. Then organ failures. You may feel okay for a few days, but after that…"

"All I need is a few days, Argo. Maybe less."

Argo cocks his head in confusion.

"There's a way off planet," Thompson finishes.

Argo's stone face lifts. When Thompson fails to mirror the sentiment, the big man suddenly understands they are approaching their end of the mission. Understanding yields to acceptance and, ultimately, to determination.

"We'll get the kid home safe," the big man says.

Thompson nods sternly. "That's the idea."

"Doesn't mean we have to go easy," Argo concludes.

"*That's right, brother.*" Thompson extends his hand. Argo clasps it firmly.

"Okay," the Brick says, releasing the Gun's hand, "when do we leave?"

"ASAP. Enemy's scattered right now and we have cover of darkness. Does Beckert have all the data from the memory core?"

"He has all of the *battle* data. There was no way to squeeze anything else."

"Find anything on Cadre One or Two?"

Argo shakes his head. "Nothing. And Geek searched *thoroughly*. If it was here, they did a good job covering it up."

Thompson drops his head in disappointment.

"Actually, there was something," Argo adds. Thompson looks up in rapt attention.

"Not data," the Brick explains, "but a clue. He said he found it at the tower and stored it in his HDI."

"Even better!" Excitement turns to concern when he recalls methodical machines excavating the collapsed tower. "Did he leave it behind?"

"No, he said he pulverized it after image capture."

Thompson bobs his head. "Good, good. Cadre *Two*…"

Snapping back to the present, he reaches for his rifle.

"Let me take this back. I can deal with it." He looks the Brick over and finds him missing something.

"Where's your weapon?"

"Mechanical room, charging." Argo pivots a half turn, presenting his back rack. "Here, take a fresh cell and leave me yours."

Thompson opens a compartment on Argo's rack and removes a heavy module. Inside are rows of spare cells. He plucks out a fresh cell and exchanges it with the one in his rifle.

"Thanks," he says, returning the module to Argo's rack. "Tell Beckert to wipe everything in memory. Then gear up and shut the power down, *permanently*. We leave via escape tunnel once you're done, got it?"

"Got it." The Brick hustles out of the restroom.

Thompson opens latches on his rifle and inspects the internal optics. Expecting them to be as hazed as his scope, he is surprised to find the platinum surfaces bright and unmarred. Relieved he took such care to keep it dry, he closes the rifle body and strides out into the main chamber.

As his eyes roam the protective walls a profound feeling overtakes him. This shelter, with its familiar machinery and ancient bones, is a link to a lost history. It is further proof of mankind's accomplishment, proof that humanity once thrived...and is a reminder this planet was stolen by a relentless, genocidal enemy. Desperately, he wants to remain and explore this gathering of generals and colonels, to benefit from their combined wisdom, to understand them in how they lived, struggled, and died. But the same enemy who murdered an entire civilization now hounds them in the ashes of their home world. Not only must he leave this treasure behind, he must obliterate it to ensure nothing remains for the remorseless foe. There are no words in an Operator's vocabulary to describe such a feeling and it lodges in his chest with cold, malevolent intent.

*To my last breath, I will balance this equation...with bare hands and teeth, if I have to...*

Suppressing such uncharacteristic rage, Thompson climbs up to General Noromi's station and lifts the top of the console. Constellations of orange and green lights wink at him.

"Geek, is the memory core wiped?"

"Aye, Major. All nodes wiped and corrupted after data transfer."

With a sigh, the Gun spins his rifle butt forward and smashes it repeatedly through the circuit boards. Smoke and ozone waft from the obliterated innards.

Twin sacks of media records remain beside the general's terminal, and Thompson collects them. As he slips the harness over his head, a tremendous *clang* from the mechanical room is followed by a shudder and fading screech. Chamber lighting and all terminals go dark. Ventilators and water pumps wind down, leaving the room eerily still.

A faint whirring sound carries through the sudden quiet. The Gun turns a circle, trying to figure out its direction. Cinching media sacks tight across his chest, he marches to the bulkhead and swings it open. Hovering whisper-quiet in front of him is a compact object with rows of lenses embedded in its disc-shaped body. It sweeps a pink beam over him.

The Gun leaps at the hovering thing and clubs it out of the air. The machine bounces off the metallic floor plates and splits open with a mild spark. He jumps on top of it, trampling it to bits.

"ENEMY CONTACT," he shouts. Adrenaline courses through him, igniting cold fury. Sealing his faceplate, he strides over the flattened drone and kneels at the intersection. Pink beams, scattered by steam, shine down the corridor from the far end.

Thompson links his visor wirelessly to the scope of his rifle and holds his weapon out past the corner. Haze on the scope lens and steam obscure any useful detail.

Heavy footfalls approach, and Argo crouches behind Thompson. The big man's eyes are wide, nostrils flaring. Beckert pads silently next to him and waits, pistols raised. Both men seal faceplates and await further instruction.

"Smoke," Thompson whispers.

Argo palms a grenade from his waist, activates it, and flings it down the corridor. Pink beams switch off abruptly, and sounds of heavy motors in retreat echo down the hallway.

The grenade bounces, skids to a halt, then *pops* and *hisses*, belching dense clouds.

"Geek, get to the escape tunnel," Thompson orders. "Brick, trap this bulkhead, high yield."

Operators reply with a staccato, "*Sir!*" and act on their assignments.

Thompson peers past the corner again. Pink beams diffuse in the steam and smoke, silhouetting spindly robotic arms at the far end of the hallway. They reach tentatively around the threshold and extend toward the hissing, spinning device.

Beckert unbars the escape hatch with a subdued *clunk*, guides it softly to its open extent, and jabs pistols into the room beyond, sweeping for the enemy. Facing Thompson, he hand signals, *clear*.

Argo sets a cylindrical device to *motion sense*, tucks it just inside the command center bulkhead, then pulls the heavy door shut, and turns the wheel as quietly as possible.

"Brick, *move*," Thompson orders.

Argo hefts his cannon and dashes across the intersection.

At the corridor's far end, Thompson watches articulated arms stretch to full extension, followed by a squat body on treads. Cautious in approach, the vehicle sweeps pink beams rapidly on the source of smoke.

Thompson hops across the intersection and crouches at the opposite corner, still watching the intruding machine. Another arm of the vehicle lowers toward the grenade and delicately picks it up then hurls the grenade back into the complex's central pit.

Thompson slides away from the corner, steps through the escape hatch, and swings the portal into place.

"Brick, give me another trap on this door, high yield. Geek, get going."

"Aye, sir," Beckert pipes and he sprints down the tubular

tunnel.

Argo places a device in the corner closest to the hatch and sets the detonator to *motion sense*.

"What're we up against, Gun? *Gun?*"

Argo looks toward the tunnel. Thompson is already gone. The Brick taps the detonator, collects his cannon, and sprints after his team.

# MOUNT VERNON

Argo's legs pound the floor in a frantic dash, every step booming off the close walls. He grimaces at the racket, but, with pursuers so close, reaching safe distance from the deadly trap he set is his only concern.

One minute stretches to two, and he mulls Thompson's radiation exposure, Beckert's discoveries, the surrounding crush of enemy forces. More than anything else, he thinks about the slender news reporter and her revelations...the image of Keller, standing at a pit of heaped blue corpses.

*We really did start it all...*

A violent shudder rips through the tunnel, and a shock of air catapults the Brick onto his chest. He skids for several meters then picks himself up and resumes his thunderous pace.

*The trap is sprung. Nothing between us and them now.*

Ahead, standing water ripples at his approach, and reflections of his helmet lamps bathe the round walls in shifting web-like patterns. He slows and searches for signs of his team. On the floor, two sets of dusty boot prints lead straight into the flood, and walls to either side are wet from recent splashes.

*Yep, this is the way.*

Argo charges ahead, first high stepping then slogging through deepening water. His bulk fills most of the tunnel, and a short wave builds up in front of his torso, resisting his progress. He turns his broad shoulders sideways, but a thick back rack and cannon negate any advantage in profile, so the Brick uses brute strength to carry on.

Soon, he is completely submerged, pressing through the tunnel like the plunger in a giant syringe. Unable to keep up his pace while upright, Argo drops to all fours and crawls.

After a tedious hour through flooded darkness, faint light registers in Argo's visor. He switches off his helmet lamps and creeps toward it.

Near the roof of the tunnel, milky blue radiance undulates. It grows brighter at his approach, seemingly activated by the currents of his movement, with individual grains winking on and off.

*It's like electric dust*, he thinks.

The big man reaches his large hand up to the haze and stirs it. Eddies of light swirl in the wake, fascinating him, when Thompson's warning echoes in his mind,

*There're plenty of things here that'll distract us...*

With a jolt, Argo remembers the enemy in pursuit and he whirls about. The tunnel behind dissolves to a deep, empty blackness. Chiding himself, he faces front and surges onward.

For the most part, the tunnel remains consistent in its slope and direction with minor curves. Then Argo spots a kink that diverts sharply up and to the left. Pleased for something to break the monotony, he crawls a little faster toward it.

Once at the tunnel bend, he stands upright for a better look. The ceiling is crumpled and cracked where tunnel segments jammed together. At his feet, where joints of the tunnel section have spread, strings of minute bubbles rise, lofting a thin cloud of brown sediment.

*I'm still underground, then.*

Putting clues together, he guesses the surrounding earth must have shifted—possibly a natural geological fault, or a sudden displacement from extended bombardment. Such a severe bend in the tunnel would have been catastrophic to any escape vehicle flying through. If the tunnel was not flooded, Thompson would surely have been tempted to try the cart for swiftest escape, and it occurs to the Brick that all the water he has fought against in his trudge might have saved their lives. But interest in that line of thought vanishes when he notices smeared boot prints leading up the slope.

Delighted to find a sign of his team after so many hours, Argo looks up the ramp and finds the water's surface only a few meters away.

*Ah, at last.*

Argo's first step up the greasy slope slides out from under him, and his thick arms fly out to brace the fall. Pressing against the tunnel walls, he gets his feet beneath him and staggers his way up. Once clear of the standing water, slippery sediments thin to a trail down the middle of the floor, which suggest an easier climb. But as much as the water slowed his movement, he misses its buoyant effect now—with no rope and no handholds on the smooth walls it is a battle to drag his bulk all the way up without slipping.

After much groaning, Argo crests the slope. Hope of easier progress ahead is dashed when his lights shine down into another flooded section of tunnel. A long stripe of greasy sediment, marked with skidding boot prints, runs straight into murky water. So he shakes his head, takes a wide stance, and skates down the grade to a dramatic splash.

Just as he expects another extended slog, the Brick emerges into a flooded escape chamber identical to the one at the command complex. Walls here are severely corroded, however, and what remains of stored carts overhead have crumbled into piles of rust at his feet.

Directly opposite is an open doorway. The big man heads for it and sidesteps through, discovering what remained of its hatch has been forced aside, hinges broken off at knobs of rust.

*Must be getting close to Thompson and Beckert...*

The Brick works his way down a slim passageway that opens into a wider, taller space. A disintegrated terminal is recessed into the left wall, which Argo assumes must have controlled access at one time, and a plastic red exit sign dangles from a bundle of wires overhead. Beyond is dark, watery stillness.

*Where are they?*

Argo shines his lamps out into the space and discovers it is much larger than suspected. Reinforced concrete walls and buttresses rise fifteen meters to an arched ceiling that extends well-beyond range of his lamps. Dozens of rusty heaps, jutting corroded alloy plates and composite parts, stand in regular intervals across a floor of sandy muck. At his feet, a severely corroded vault door lies flat on the deck. Sediments are blasted away from its edges, telling the Brick it recently fell.

*Okay, I'm definitely on their trail...*

With a reassuring squeeze of his cannon grips, Argo ventures into the open. A large-mouthed eel juts its head from a burrow, watching with round eyes and gulping continuously. Curious fish, lured by his light, emerge from nooks in rusted piles and hover at a safe distance. They startle at his movements then return a bit closer.

Radiant colors and myriad shapes mingle in his lamp beams, crisscrossing, mesmerizing. He forces himself to look past the startling variety, suppressing a deep urge to study. But when the crowd swims close enough to block his line of sight, he throws up his arms. Flashes of color streak away to safe nooks and loiter at the entrances.

Freed of the obscuring huddle, Argo spots boot prints in deeper sediment. Tiny crustaceans flit and scamper through them, feasting on newly revealed nutrients in deeper layers. The tracks lead farther into the enormous manmade cavern, which the Brick follows to a decrepit fuselage. Still propped on triple landing struts, the airframe is streamlined from a rounded nose to a long, tapered tail. Slender rotor blades slump from a central hub on top and rest against the airframe. Along the body, random patches of green and white paint still cling to ceramic armor plating several centimeters thick.

The Brick shines his lights in through a porthole. The ceiling of the craft has fallen in with a dense heap of oxidized engine components beneath. White ceramic cladding juts from the pile, one bearing a rectangular emblem: the upper left quadrant is a blue field with sixty-one stars and the rest is comprised of thirteen alternating red and white horizontal stripes. Argo steps back, trying to figure out how all of the eroded parts fit together.

*Some kind of armored transport? But the means of locomotion is a complete mystery...*

He turns to the dozens of corroded heaps around him, recognizing many of the same composite and ceramic parts, but none of the surrounding wrecks are so well-preserved. The Brick returns his attention to the green- and white-flecked airframe.

*This one was built tougher than the others. Made for someone special?*

He steps around the rotted airframe, picks up his comrades' trail, and follows it deeper into the cavern. Far ahead, a light winks on and off twice.

Argo saves the location in his visor and clicks off his own lamps. Guided by his visor and sense of touch, he trudges down a lane between decayed aircraft to a low hill of sand at the far wall. A light atop the hill blinks once. In that momentary glance Argo recognizes Thompson's crouched outline against a concrete backdrop.

The Brick crawls up shifting sand, finding hard fragments just beneath the surface, and kneels beside his leader. The Gun takes Argo by the helmet, presses his visor hard against Argo's visor, and yells for sound conduction.

*"We're in another bunker, but it's breached. We'll get out, easy."* The Gun turns Argo's head up and the Brick can just discern a gap in the wall. Their helmets *thunk* together again.

*"The space port should be due west of us. Keep lights off and stay close."*

Argo nods in acknowledgement.

Beckert emerges from darkness and climbs the hill, dragging a long composite rotor blade. He guides one end into the wall gap and plants the other into the sand. Thompson pats the Geek, slings his rifle, and shimmies up the blade.

Beckert gestures for Argo to go ahead, but the Brick shakes his head. Beckert shrugs and follows the Gun up through the wall breach. Argo looks back at the expansive hangar bay one last time and climbs after his comrades.

Atop the improvised ladder Argo looks over a broken wall seven meters thick. Where he stands is filled in by sand and silt, but overhead he finds alternating layers of reinforced concrete, crumple zones, and seismic isolators. Despite heavy colonization by invertebrate life forms, the basic architecture is readily apparent in cross-section with systems of blast deflection, energy absorption, and self-sealing that could shrug off all but repeated direct hits.

*The fact this structure still stands...and underwater, at that... even Colonel Munro would be impressed.*

Thompson and Beckert perch at the outer edge of the breached wall. Argo strides over and squats beside his teammates, looking out into open water. A blush of light from the east tints the shallows a deep blue. At his feet, a manmade cliff drops into a dark forest of rope-like plants that undulate in the currents.

Thompson turns back toward the bunker and looks up toward the roofline. He points, climbs the wall breach's rugged edge, and hauls himself over the top. Beckert and Argo follow.

Together, they survey a concrete dome with long, conical spars extending from the arch. Some are straight but most lean at bizarre angles like fat quills of a matted porcupine. Where the team stands the spars are broken away completely, so Argo kneels beside one and inspects the circular base. Its foundation is hollow with an interior encircled by a rusty lattice, suggesting it might crush readily. Compared with the supple fortitude of the dome itself, such a fragile construct seems counterintuitive.

*Unless being easily compacted is the point... Another layer of shock absorption?*

Beckert taps Argo's shoulder then points. Argo follows Beckert's point and sees Thompson is already walking away. The Brick nods and follows.

The Gun weaves through leaning spars, leading the team toward shallower water. As they near the beach sand, rocks, and rubble fills in between the spars, allowing a diverse ecosystem to take root. Some plants are mere tufts of corkscrewed grass or patches of green fuzz; others have long leaves and buoyant air-filled bladders that sway with passing waves overhead.

Spiny, hard-shelled creatures proliferate the vegetation, clinging with segmented legs, watching with eyes on stalks, and flaring pincers menacingly as the Operators pass.

Translucent globes drift by, trailing fine tentacles. Beckert momentarily loses himself in the rhythmic pulsing and cups one in his hand. It seems insubstantial, merely sliding around his grip without sensation. Then, feeling the weight of Argo's stare on him, he releases the delicate beauty and resumes his underwater march.

Dawn breaks, brightening the oscillating shallows. Thompson looks back at his comrades and frowns at what a stark contrast they cut against bleached sand and cement. He looks ahead to the surf zone, to the empty sandbars, to the lack of cover.

*This won't do.*

The Gun turns parallel to the beach and follows the downward arch of the bunker to its edge. Peering over, he finds another dark forest of swaying vines. This close to shore, however, the drop off is not nearly as far. He turns toward his team, points down, and steps off the edge. Twin media sacks billow behind him like balloons, slowing his descent, and his boots sink into loose sand at the base. With effort, Thompson pulls his mired feet free and plods into the swaying weeds.

Beckert raises his arms, points his toes, and dives off the edge, streaking toward the bottom. At the last moment, he curves his back and legs, swooping upright to gently land on his feet beside Thompson.

Argo steps off the edge and drops like a bomb, disappearing in a cloud of sediment on impact, then emerges from swirling murk with the determination of a steamroller.

Thompson forges ahead, ignoring the crunch of urchins and starfish underfoot. Air in his helmet is beyond stale from his own foul breath, and a metallic taste coats his tongue. For hours, his stomach has tried to escape through his mouth, and he has bested its attempts with forceful swallows. Now it seems to be trying the other end, gut cramping with sharp pressure as if being stirred by a knife.

*Probably the lining of my intestine dying.*

A leisurely shadow slips across Thompson's path. In a flash, he pulls his rifle from his shoulder, extends the bayonet, and crouches in the weeds.

Graceful and elegant, an elongated creature circles back and swims over the team. Flat lobes protrude on each side of the creature's head, dark eyes embedded at the tips. A frowning parabolic mouth, brimming with triangular teeth, gulps mouthfuls of water and squirts them through five vertical slits behind its head. Pointed, backswept fins jut from the creature's spindle-like body, and a vertical tail fin propels the seven-meter creature with effortless strokes.

The tremendous fish orbits twice then departs. Thompson fixates on its pointed teeth.

*Does everything on this planet eat the other?*

A yellow icon flashes in his visor, and Thompson scowls at it. The alert is no surprise, as he has been operating on rebreather for better part of a day and his carbon traps are nearly saturated. With the sun high overhead, however, leaving the fields of seaweed would make his team far too visible.

*May not have a choice soon...*

The Gun halts in place, sucks his teeth, then turns about. Beckert is right behind him, and waits for orders. Argo tromps up through the weeds, finds his team halted, then shrugs with a palm raised. Thompson grabs both of them by the helmet and *thunks* visors together.

"*Getting a CO2 warning,*" he yells. "*Are you?*"

Argo and Beckert both nod.

*"Then I need to find a place we can surface. Brick, take a knee."*

The men pull apart and Argo kneels. Thompson climbs up the Brick and stands atop his shoulders. Argo takes hold of Thompson's ankles and stands, allowing the Gun to peer over the swaying vines.

Thompson taps a foot on Argo's shoulder and the Brick turns like a periscope until the Gun double taps. Argo plants his feet, rocking ever so slightly in the gentle currents, until Thompson crouches down and pats the top of his helmet. The Brick releases his grip and Thompson gathers all three together again.

*"Something in the water ahead. Looks like a structure. Gonna check it out."*

*"We have enough air?"* Argo yells back.

*"It's close. We'll make it."*

The team sets off again, this time veering away from shore toward deeper water. Argo raises an eyebrow at his CO2 warning, now flashing red, uneasy about putting more space between himself and the surface. He looks up to gauge the distance—should he have to swim for it—and sees distorted aircraft skimming above the waves, gouging circles of foam into the water with bright blue jets.

Just as the Brick is resigning himself to the gasping death of asphyxiation, clouds part in sky above. Sunlight streams into deeper water and reflects off something dead ahead. Argo lifts a hand to shade his eyes, squints, then marvels at the faint curve of an enormous underwater dome. At its apex, the dome is only a few meters beneath the waves with a conical stack that projects skyward for ventilation. But tracing its curve into darker, deeper water, he guesses the foundation would have to be a kilometer or more in diameter.

Argo grins, grabs Thompson's shoulder, and presses helmets together, visor to visor.

*"Launch facility?"* the Brick shouts.

Thompson nods and shouts back, *"We're right on top of it."*

Using his rifle like a needle, Thompson threads his way through shifting vegetation toward the bright glint of the dome.

Angled sunlight dances through the shallows in parallel shafts, shining across his mottled gray shoulders, soaking into the dark plants around him.

Encouraged to have their destination in sight, and spurred by flashing red $CO_2$ warnings, the team hustles through deeper water until Thompson's bayonet *tinks* into something solid. He sweeps the dark plants aside and looks at a dark gray material, rock-like and monolithic, barring his progress. The wall stands several meters above the swaying vegetation, and runs out of sight to each side. At first, it appears flat, but as the Gun follows the tops to the left and right he sees a subtle curvature, and he knows he is standing at the dome's foundation.

Thompson spins and points at Argo. When the Brick steps up, Thompson gestures to the base of the gray monolith. Argo squats where directed.

Thompson climbs onto his teammate's shoulders and crouches. With a tap of the foot, Argo thrusts up. Thompson pushes off and flies up to the top of the wall, settling onto a narrow, curved ledge. Atop the foundation are enormous panes of triangular glass, anchored in hexagonal sections, assembled into a colossal geodesic pattern. The Gun leans close to one of the panes, cups his hands and peers through. Inside are tall buildings, paved roads, and cultivated fields. Mobs of azure-skinned creatures fill the streets between buildings, most clutching a personal belonging, case, or young one. Thousands of saffron eyes dart back and forth among the crowds, tails swishing anxiously as the mobs shuffle toward the city center.

The Gun glares with malice at the permanent structures and the shuffling crowds.

*So, you've come to stay? We'll fix that.*

Thompson turns from the thick glass, leans over the ledge, and waves at Beckert. As the Geek crouches, Thompson grips his rifle by the barrel and lowers it over the side.

Beckert launches, flaps his arms once, catches the edge of the ledge, and pulls himself up, not needing the lowered rifle. He kneels, awaiting instruction.

Thompson hooks a hand behind the Geek's head and presses their helmets together.

*"It's a long drop to the floor inside. Have your rope ready. First, let's get Argo up here."*

Beckert nods, takes the coils from his shoulder, and spools out a line to his waiting comrade. Argo takes hold and nearly tugs the Geek off the ledge before Thompson catches him. Together, Gun and Geek reel in the line as Brick climbs hand over hand. At the edge, Thompson takes Argo under a shoulder and hauls him up. All three crouch on the gray foundation and knock visors together.

The Gun yells, *"Argo, can you take out this window?"*

Argo glances at the triangular pane, snorts at lack of challenge, and nods. He pulls a compartment from his rack, opens it, and removes what he needs.

While Argo fashions a charge, Thompson spies through an adjacent pane. The enclosed city is bright with natural and supplemental lighting. Orderly fields of agriculture, wide pools fed by terraced waterfalls, and recreational parks shaded by sculpted trees intersperse buildings that blend with the environment as if they grew naturally from native rock. The place would be beautiful, if not for the creatures who built it.

The Gun looks down at the interior floor. Through the angle of thick glass, it is difficult to be certain, but to guess he figures it is at least twelve meters below the foundation.

*Quite a drop. Gonna be tricky rappelling down with all the water pouring through... Maybe we let it flood a bit, first. Then we'll have a cushion to land...*

Thompson looks across the alien city again, only now the masses of blueskins are surging away in panic. At the edges of the herd, uniformed aliens with slim rifles fight their way against the fleeing current. They point directly at Thompson, mouths wide open and shouting.

Thompson shrinks from the glass as an energy bolt crosses the thick pane and explodes the water in front of him, jolting him backward over the ledge. Beckert's hand flies out, catches the Gun by his media sacks, and hauls him back to the ledge.

More bolts cross the glass, vaporizing seawater in concussive shocks, as Thompson and Beckert slide along the ledge toward Argo. Frantically, Thompson signals Argo to set the explosive.

Argo slaps a conical wad at the center of a hexagonal brace. He mashes the timer and snatches his teammates by the arm, dragging them off the ledge to deeper water.

The charge detonates with teeth cracking force, stunning all three Operators.

When Thompson comes to, he feels his hands flop against the dark gray foundation, but gravity seems reversed—he is being pulled up the monolith. Sand streaks by. Ropes of seaweed catch under his arms and groin. Turning his gaze upward, he watches the limp forms of Argo and Beckert slurped over the top of the foundation.

The Gun clambers for a handhold, scraping his gauntlets over smooth stone. There is nothing to grip but his rifle. With grim acceptance, he curls into a ball and submits to the overwhelming draw.

Current pulls him faster up the foundation. It rips him over the ledge and spits him through the gaping hole like a cannon ball. He is weightless, careening through air, surrounded by tumbling blobs of water, glances off something solid, spins wildly, and slams onto a flat surface. Torrents of seawater blast over him, shoving him toward a metal railing. He folds at the waist around a vertical pole, instinctively clutching the bar, as a frothing river washes by. Bitter fluid of nausea rise to his throat, but he chokes it back and gasps for air.

Using the railing for support, he drags himself out of the gushing seawater, gets to his feet, opens his visor, and vomits.

"Brick, Geek..." Thompson spits bile and blood then reseals his faceplate. "...transmit position."

Two dots illuminate in his visor, one to left and one to right, several meters below him. Thompson runs left and looks over the railing down a three-story drop. Seawater flows over the roof edges in long curtains.

The Gun unlatches his weapon, bangs the water out of it, and slaps it together. Unsure if it will short out, he primes it. First there is a spark and a burst of steam, then the weapon sings. He tucks the stock into his shoulder and raises the water-flecked scope to his eye. With aid of the illuminated dot, he finds Argo hobbling through knee-deep water in the street, limping badly.

The Brick radios, "*Enemy sighted. Permission to engage?*"

"Weapons free," Thompson replies.

The Brick's cannon lances a channel through the panicked mob, vaporizing flesh and bone with a deep *Bah-ROOM*. In fading echoes of the blast, braying yelps and terrified screams reflect off building facades.

Thompson scans ahead of his comrade and spies a group of enemy soldiers huddled at the corner of a building. Each holds a rifle in one hand and a small orb in the other.

"Brick, *hold*, ambush ahead, one hundred meters, *left*. Painting target." Thompson dials his weapon down and triggers a continuous beam at the ambush.

"*Target acquired.*" Argo halts, thumbs up his cannon output, and leans forward. A violet glow coalesces around him then leaps away, exploding through the building and ambush on the far side. Clouds of dust and smoke billow from the detonation.

"Targets destroyed," Thompson confirms.

Argo trots into the dust cloud.

Beckert's roaring machine pistols call Thompson to the opposite side of the roof. The Gun zeroes in on the illuminated dot in his visor, and he finds Beckert pinned down behind the body of a large animal. The animal lifts its horned head from the ground and bellows as energy bolts repeatedly plunge into it. Beckert slides and rolls behind the animal, blindly returning fire.

Thompson tracks the flashes of enemy weapons with his visor, plots their positions, and triggers clean headshots in swift succession.

"Geek, you're clear," Thompson radios. "Move up and support

Brick."

"*Received, moving now*." Beckert stands from behind the slumped beast and sprints after Argo.

Before he leaves his perch, Thompson peers through his scope to the center of the city. Thousands of individual aliens blend into a sea of blue, crowding up a ramp toward shore. Tall buildings block most of the ramp from view; but in the gaps, Thompson sees uniformed aliens, mouths wide and shouting, being shoved aside by a heedless mob.

Vicious, short *thumps* draw the Gun's attention. He swings his scope left, where fresh clouds billow in the street. The scope compensates in infrared and in the cloud he sees two dark shapes running parallel. One sprouts flashes of flame at the end of each arm. The other, much thicker, limps quickly and lobs objects ahead. The pair disappears behind a building.

Thompson vaults over the roof railing, splashes down in waist deep seawater, and charges through the rising flood after his teammates. Smoke fills the air.

Noise of combat pulls him forward as if he were on a line. Chemical triggers sharpen his awareness and reflex, amplifying aggression. There is no longer nausea or pain in him, only the intent of swift death to the enemy. His legs power through eddied currents, treading over submerged blue bodies, until he reaches water low enough that he can run. His boots fly over the surface, plunging with great splashes and propelling him onto drier ground. All around him the enemy lay dead or dying. Some are whole. Most are in pieces.

"Brick, Geek, approaching from rear."

"*You close?*" Argo grunts via radio, "*Takin' a lotta heat.*"

"Understood, will support."

As Thompson races through smog, hot tracers zip through the air ahead. His visor saves the angles, pinpointing sources of fire. With smooth automation, he snaps shot after shot, exploding reptilian skulls and torsos with tight beams of directed energy.

A great wail rises from the streets, seemingly everywhere

at once. Random fires glow in infrared. Bodies litter the ground, marking an easy trail to follow.

Ahead, smoky air strobes with machine pistol fire. A violet glow silhouettes Argo as his cannon builds to maximum, and the beam smashes through a barricade. Shots rain down on the pair. Beckert staggers in his dash, yet keeps his feet, and returns fire with deadly accuracy. Argo shrugs at the hits and swings his cannon where resistance is fiercest.

"Twenty meters behind you," Thompson radios. "Get up that—"

A rocket streaks into the ground and explodes, tossing the Gun end over end. All sounds are gone but a single, high-pitched tone, and he lands flat on his back. In disorientation, he imagines a circle of people around him randomly striking his armor with heavy mallets.

The air strobes with bright flashes, and the circle lurches away as if taken by a strong gust. A dark figure approaches, kneels, and takes his arm. The figure stumbles, repeatedly knocked down, and drags Thompson past a pair of legs like tree trunks. A violet glow gathers in the haze and leaps away. The ground shudders savagely.

At last, Thompson's eyes converge. Sounds of raging battle filter in as the high-pitched ringing fades. Strength returns to his limbs and he feels for his rifle. Finding it beside him, he snatches it from dusty gravel and props himself into a crouch.

The Gun looks around at high walls of a narrow alley. Beckert kneels at the entrance, pistols raised at the buildings across the street. One pistol fires dry, and the Geek drops the spent clip, slaps the emptied grip over one of the thick bristles on his thigh, and lifts. Reloaded, the pistol action slides home, and Beckert sprays an open window across the street.

Outside the alley, Argo sidesteps, triggering cannon shots like a slow-rolling tank.

Thompson shakes his head to clear the last of the cobwebs then duck walks under an open window and stands, coming face to face with a surprised blueskin soldier. The reptilian barks and mashes the button on a small orb. Thompson bashes the creature with his rifle butt and runs, grabbing Beckert by his back rack.

The alley corner explodes with a sharp *crack*, pummeling the team with chunky debris. The destabilized building groans then leans.

"Move, *MOVE!*" Thompson yells at Argo.

The building pitches forward and collapses into the street with a resounding *thud*, choking the air with thick dust. Immediately, weapon fire ceases, and the echoes of combat fade.

Completely obscured, the Operators hustle toward the ramp, using coughs and terrified braying to guide them. A singular glow of heat emerges in Thompson's visor—a collective press of azure reptilians stalled on the ramp. He leads his team headlong into it, pushing his way through and over the dust-blinded, confused creatures. Some attempt to scream and draw dirty air deep into their lungs, gagging. Those who have pulled a piece of cloth over their faces get deeper breaths. Their screams are deafening.

The three keep a tight line as Thompson barges through the pressed crowd. With nowhere to move, reptilians fall into one another like dominoes. Beckert aims his pistols over Thompson's shoulders, watching for uniformed soldiers and dispatching them with quick shots, as Argo back steps in rear guard.

Through settling dust, Thompson spots a large, round exit portal at the top of the ramp. Its entire aperture is jammed with desperate, wriggling figures.

"*One side, Gun.*"

Argo shoulders past his leader and sets a wide beam. Leveling his weapon at the wriggling jam, he triggers.

Particles streak through the crowd and plunge into the frenzied clog. The center of the jam instantly vaporizes and explodes, compacting the rest around the rim of the portal, showering the ramp in blood and charred flesh.

"*Exit clear,*" Argo announces. Operators surge over the stunned crowd, fragile bones snapping beneath their strides. Rags of oily skin flop onto their shoulders as they pass the ring-shaped exit into a spacious area, with high roof and open floor. Furniture, cordons, and moveable partitions have scooted meters away from the blast, some burning or smoldering. Thompson takes the lead, skating across greasy tiles until he reaches clean floor beyond Argo's blast.

The far wall is made entirely of glass, and its sliding doors are stuck with prone reptilians. Some of them stir, rising groggily. Thompson puts them down with precise shots and runs to the glass. Argo and Beckert take position beside their leader, keeping watch.

Outside, bright sunlight streams onto a wide landing pad strewn with discarded bags and cases. Twin control towers stand at the far corners. At center, chaotic swarms of blueskins clamber over one another, hanging onto a hopelessly overloaded transport. The transport's jets whine, yet it cannot rise from the hundreds clinging to it.

Just above the transport, two platform-like skiffs hover. Soldiers lean over the skiff rails, gesturing wildly, yelling as loud as they can at the crowd.

"Brick, on my command, you and I'll take down those skiffs."

"*Aye, sir,*" Argo confirms.

"Geek, get on that transport and take control. We'll cover for you and pick off the extra riders."

"*Aye, sir.*" Beckert leans forward, pistols close beside his head, perched on his toes like a professional sprinter. Thompson and Argo dial up their weapon outputs.

"Now!" Thompson commands.

Beckert dashes past the parted glass doors. Thompson and Argo step out and trigger. The skiffs puff with blasted parts then dip and spin, tossing soldiers like toys before slamming down into the crowd. Blue mist launches through whirring hover fans.

The crowd's attention pivots to Beckert sprinting at them. Reptilians flee en masse, bowling over soldiers rushing in to defend them.

Like a shark through a school of fish, Beckert streaks up the middle. The shuttle's lowered ramp is overstuffed with passengers trying to board, but the holdouts scatter when staring down Beckert's machine pistols.

Thompson dials down his weapon and shoots into the clinging blueskins. His shots create a chain reaction, riders sliding off the transport like thawing ice. Less burdened, the transport rises from the pad.

With magnificent grace, Beckert clips a pistol to his back and leaps for the closing ramp. He snags it one handed, swings once, flips himself onto the ramp, and dashes inside.

While keeping a wary eye for the enemy, Argo watches the transport. In the shaded cockpit, he sees two quick flashes and the rising craft veers backward toward one of the towers. It wobbles, grazes the tower, then rights itself before smoothly descending back to the pad.

Thompson's eyes are elsewhere, searching for fast-moving aircraft that swept the hills and valleys on arrival and harried his team ever since. In the gap between control towers, he spots one far off. It loiters, hovering in place. The Gun peers through his riflescope at it. In magnified view, the nose of the plane is pointed straight at him, weapon clusters jutting from stubby wings, but it does not move.

Noticing Thompson's concern, Argo asks via radio, "*Gun, what do you see?*"

"*Aircraft, armed, but holding position. Geek!*"

"*Sir?*" comes Beckert's radioed reply.

"*Bogey spotted, three kilometers to your six.*"

"*I see him, Major, plus twenty-two more, surrounding the complex.*"

The transport touches down, and Beckert is seated behind the windshield, faceplate raised. He lowers the ramp. Thompson and Argo run for it.

"*Why aren't they attacking?*" Thompson demands.

"*Don't know, sir, but comms are hot with chatter. Sounds like a colonist meeting.*"

Argo yells, "*Gun! Behind us!*"

Thompson whirls around and looks into a row of soldiers sprinting from the underwater complex, weapons blazing. Shots batter the Operators to the ground.

Argo snarls with focused rage and rises, triggering his cannon through a storm of bullets and energy. His shoulders twist, his legs twitch with impacts, yet he stands.

Thompson stays on his back and triggers from the ground, picking off the leftovers from Argo's wholesale destruction, clicking from kill to kill.

A terrible shudder shakes the deck, and within the billowing smoke of Argo's blasts, the ring-shaped portal collapses upon itself. Support structures shattered, the tunnel caves in with sharp cracks and groans. Seawater roars through in a deluge.

Climbing to his feet, Thompson orders, "*Brick, go!*"

"*Moving!*" Argo shouts, and the big man hobbles up the transport ramp. Thompson shuffles backward, covering his own retreat, and he steps onto the ramp.

"*Geek, lift off, we're clear!*"

Hover jets whine with higher pitch and the transport powers smoothly into the air. Thompson climbs the short ramp into the body of the craft and confronts a shivering huddle of blueskins. Saffron eyes watch him in mortal terror.

The crowd presses together and scoots against the far wall, keeping as much distance as possible. Delicate arms embrace one another, pulling close. Some wheeze with short, choking breaths.

Lifting his faceplate, Argo announces, "I got 'em, Gun."

Thompson glances to his side and sees Argo staring fiercely into the huddle. The Gun nods to his comrade and strides up the center aisle toward the flight deck. A flight-suited alien slumps on the floor just outside, a single high-caliber hole perforating its helmet.

Beckert occupies the pilot's seat, faceplate raised, holding the controls with comfortable ease. Another flight-suited alien slumps in the co-pilot's chair, bearing an identical hole through its helmet.

Thompson hefts the dead co-pilot from the chair and heaves

it out with its counterpart, drawing a collective gasp from the back of the craft, then he squats for a look through the windshield. Ventilation towers rise up through the waves from the submerged dome, and at the water's edge are rigid structures for channeling and focusing wave energy. Between them is a swirling vortex where the ring-shaped portal once stood, draining vast quantities of seawater into the dome.

"*Status*," the Gun demands.

"Six hundred meters and rising," Beckert reports. "Currently tracking one hundred twenty-eight enemy contacts in our vicinity, including the twenty-three surrounding us. They are *locked on*."

Thompson lifts his faceplate, letting fresh air cool his grimy, sweaty skin. He spits a foul taste from his mouth then squints at the distant aircraft. They keep exact distance and ascend with the transport.

Thinking out loud, the Gun asks, "What are you waiting for?"

"Maybe *they* have something to do with it." Beckert tosses his head toward the huddle of blueskins behind him.

Thompson follows the Geek's gesture and drives a hard stare into the quivering group. All of them avert their eyes.

"Major," Argo calls. "We've got a lot of extra weight here. Shall I take out the trash?"

"Not yet," Thompson answers.

"Whoa," Beckert says, flinching back in his seat.

"What is it, Geek?"

"Radio traffic just dropped from seventy-eight conversations to *four*."

Argo scowls. "Guess the argument's over."

"Stay alert, brace for attack," Thompson orders. "Geek, does this vessel have any weapons?"

"No, sir, totally unarmed."

Argo grunts and hefts his cannon, "Not *totally*."

"Contacts closing!" Beckert shouts. "Two planes advancing behind us."

Thompson runs from the cockpit, dialing his weapon up to

maximum. He halts at the crying huddle and rips one up by the elbow.

"Brick, take one and follow."

The group howls as Thompson drags his captive away then recoils at Argo's approach. The Brick snares a blueskin with a thick mid-section when something *clangs* off of his helmet.

Argo's furious eyes bore into a more masculine creature full of anguish and rage. It stands and clutches a metal tube with both hands, bent in the shape of Argo's head. With speed belying his great size, Argo releases his heavy set captive and knife-hands the standing blueskin in the throat.

The masculine blueskin crumples, dropping its pathetic weapon and clutching its neck. As it gasps for breath, Argo takes the wheezing creature by the nape and drags it from the sobbing crowd.

Thompson lowers the ramp, sending torrents of wind through the cabin. The Operators march their captives to the end and, gripping with one hand, lean them over the edge.

Tiny feet, clad in smooth-soled shoes, scrape and dig at the edge of the ramp. Manicured azure hands clutch at the air, grasping vainly for a handhold. Tails curl around the Operators' legs.

With their free hands, Argo and Thompson aim their fully-charged weapons at the advancing threats.

The planes' noses lift suddenly, slowing approach, then level off so near that Thompson can see every fine detail: the high caliber gun barrels, the polished rivets in armor plating, the whirring fanjets, and blueskin pilots perched high in their bubbled canopies. Brick and Gun stare at the pilots. The pilots stare back.

"What are we doing, Gun?"

"Don't move," Thompson says coolly. "Wait for my command."

The hostages shiver in their captors' grasp, perched at the precipice of a very long fall, toes shifting and seeking for a foothold.

"Geek," Thompson radios, "status."

"*Two kilometers and rising. Now monitoring twenty-eight conversations.*"

"What do they sound like?"

"*Anxious, sir. Most of the comm-traffic seems to be going through the aircraft in front of you.*"

Thompson mulls the information, unsure of its usefulness, but his gut raises an alarm. He props his rifle on his captive's shoulder and zooms in on the pilot. The buffeting of wind and the vibration of the thrusting transport make it a shaky view, yet he can just see the pilot's saffron eyes above its ventilation mask. The eyes are intensely focused and narrow. The pilot's head dips, attending to some interior feature of its cockpit and lifts. The alarm in Thompson's gut grows stronger.

"*Dialogues have stopped,*" Beckert warns.

The Gun's sinews involuntarily tighten. He zooms closer on the pilot's eyes, and they are drawn up at the corners. Hair on his neck stands.

"*FIRE!*" Thompson bellows.

Gun and Brick trigger as dazzling light radiates from the aircraft. They crush their eyes shut against blinding beams while sounds of grinding, shattering metal fill the sky. One aircraft spirals out of earshot with disintegrating engines. The other hovers briefly, tilts over, and slowly falls away in an uncontrolled dive.

"*Sirs! Sirs!*" Beckert calls, "*Are you okay?*"

"Gah!" Thompson grunts. He slumps back on the ramp, still keeping hold of his captive; and he blinks over and over, trying to clear the blots in his vision. "Brick, can you see?"

"Barely," Argo says, squinting.

"*Four more aircraft incoming!*" Beckert radios.

Thompson drops his faceplate with the back of his gauntlet. It seals with a *hiss*.

"*Dump 'em.*"

Argo and Thompson roughly shove their captives. Curled tails slip from around their legs and braying instantly fades in the rushing air. Thompson feels his way up the ramp with Argo's guidance. The huddle screams and sobs at the Operators' return.

"Get two more," Thompson orders.

Argo slings his cannon and steps into the crowd, grabbing the two closest.

Barks and pleading yelps assault him. The others cling and clutch at the two being torn from their midst, yet even their combined effort is insufficient. The Brick kicks the treads of his boot into any still holding on and marches his new captives down the ramp.

Thompson moves halfway up the center aisle and turns back. He cracks open one eye, peering through electric blue spots. Only his peripheral vision is unfazed, and he cocks his head to see the crowd.

Many in the crowd get to their feet, starting after Argo and their companions. Thompson menaces them with his rifle. Frustrated, enraged faces sink back to their huddle. Loathing etches deep lines into their flushed, alien expressions.

"Brick, what's happening?"

"*Line of four craft, five hundred meters apart, closing slowly,*" Argo radios.

"Hold 'em out. Let 'em see."

Argo dangles his victims beyond the ramp like large, flailing marionettes.

"Geek," Thompson calls, "anything happening?"

"Uh, yes, sir. They're slowing, halting approach. Sounds like they're arguing again."

"Good. Brick, bring 'em back, close the ramp."

"*Understood.*" Argo retracts his living puppets and marches the wobbly creatures up the ramp. A huddle reaches out for them, cooing and blubbering in relief. Argo shoves the two into the outstretched arms. The arms take them, embrace them, and with soothing sounds, caress them.

Argo steps up to Thompson, looking him in the face.

"How's your vision? Any better?"

"Still full of spots. I—"

One in the huddle is on its feet, mouth open wide with words of outrage. The creature berates them accusingly, hatefully, sobbing between unintelligible sentences of a vilifying monologue. Glistening tears fall from wild saffron eyes tinged with green. Its arms gesture forcefully at the Operators, at its companions, and at the floor. The delicate hands smack together, emphasizing syllables. The diatribe is passionate, hypnotic with fervor. When it ends, the creature remains on its small feet, standing and staring defiantly.

Thompson returns the baleful glare. In the silence, all hear the *shick* of his bayonet sliding into useful position.

The creature tries not to look at the sharp and serrated blade, but the cruel weapon has an irresistible gravity. Hands from the seated huddle reach up for the splendid orator, urgently pulling with hushed whispers.

"…I'm starting to see through the spots," Thompson finishes, still staring at the orator. When the creature sits and drops its head, averting its eyes, Thompson retracts the bayonet with another *shick*.

"Where are we, Geek?"

"Five kilometers and rising. Do we have a destination?"

Thompson thinks then says, "Those transports I saw earlier must've gone somewhere." He faces Argo and taps him with the back of his hand. "Geek, is that huge ship still in orbit?"

"Affirmative. Plus forty-eight other contacts in low orbit."

Argo nods at Thompson approvingly.

"Take us there," the Gun orders.

"Aye, sir. Hold on to something, I'm switching to boosters."

"Hang on a sec," Thompson counters then turns to face Argo. Flicking his head at the huddle, he says, "Keep an eye on them while I clear your carbon trap."

The Brick wedges himself into a row of empty seats and glares at the sniffling hostages. Thompson releases the catch on the small of Argo's back, pulls the trap, bangs it against the wall, then replaces it, and strides to the cockpit.

Taking hold of the too-small co-pilot's chair, Thompson rips it from the deck plates and parks it outside the doorway. Settling into the cleared space, he looks out through the windshield and clears his own carbon trap. Through fading electric blue spots in his eyes, Thompson can just make out the distant shape of an enormous vessel. Several smaller vessels, still giants on their own, have dropped below the great ship in defense.

"All right, Geek, let's do it."

"Hang on," Beckert announces, "starting main boosters."

The craft rocks smoothly back, and a surge of vibration issues from the stern. Thrust plants Thompson against the back wall of the cockpit.

In the passenger cabin, an entire row of seats flexes under Argo's mass. He reaches up with one hand and presses against the ceiling, bracing himself.

"Transmit data to the orbital relay," Thompson orders. "If you have time, add stats on these ship configurations."

"Aye, sir." Beckert's goggles stream with code.

With each blink Thompson's vision improves, and he studies a hemispherical display, projected holographically, on the center console. All of the shining vessels loitering outside the windshield correspond to dots in the display. Alien script is captioned beside each projected dot.

Thompson focuses on the waist of the large, curvaceous vessel, noticing a string of identical dots in a linear queue. The Gun points at them.

"Geek, what are these, here?"

Beckert follows Thompson's finger to the line and he smiles with recognition.

"Those are transports like this one, waiting to dock." Still grinning, Beckert banks the transport toward the queue. "Got an idea. You'll like this, Major."

Intercepting warships hasten to block Beckert's approach, but the young pilot jinks and swerves around the larger and less maneuverable ships. Grappling lines slither vainly after them, which Beckert easily evades as he runs the blockade.

Thompson presses against the side of the wraparound

cockpit glass. Outside, weapon batteries bristle from the massive interceptors, all of which track with the transport yet do not fire.

"Almost there," Beckert narrates.

Thompson turns from the glass. "What's the plan, Geek?"

Beckert points to the hemispherical display. "Watch here," he says cryptically.

Thompson's eyes fall to the display. At Beckert's approach, the orderly row of transports becomes loose and chaotic in attempts to flee.

"No, no, you're not going anywhere…" Beckert's goggles race with code, and all fleeing transports halt their retreat. In the holoprojection, ID tags of each transport are cleared then replaced with tags identical to their own.

"I have control," Beckert reports, "and we all look just alike." The commandeered shuttles swing about, approach en masse, and swarm around the Operators' transport, changing positions randomly. Beckert folds into the shuffling crowd, mimicking the random movements and blending with them. Occasionally another transport rolls so close, Thompson can see its pilots behind the windshield, frantic to regain control.

"*Oof*," Beckert winces.

"What is it?"

"They're trying to jam wireless…break my grip." Beckert grits his teeth, concentrating hard. He draws the milling vessels closer together, using their hulls as shelter against the waves of broadcasted noise, and shifts frequencies over a wide band in his mesh network. In so doing, the Geek keeps just ahead of the interference and maintains a tenuous hold.

"How are you doing this?" Thompson asks in awe, bracing himself against Beckert's sudden maneuvers.

"That big ship…" The Geek breaks off in a moment of intense focus. "…was remotely piloting the transports into dock." He cranks the stick to the limit of travel, goggles blazing with data. "I hacked that system…routed control through this transport. So now…*I'm* the Auto-Dock." He hauls the stick to its opposite extent.

A collective gasp rolls forward from jostled passengers.

The nose of an intercept ship glides in front of the huge vessel's docking bay, attempting to block Beckert's path into it. Long, forward-angled struts jut from its bow like hundred meter whiskers.

"Yeah?" the Geek snarls, "How 'bout *this*?"

Five transports peel from the jumble and bloom with thrust, streaking down toward the planet. Once the five are sufficiently distant, Beckert halts his violent maneuvering and releases control of the surrounding transports, allowing them to drift. ID tags in the display clear and restore their original configurations with an exception: the ID tag originally marking the Operators' shuttle is now streaking toward the planet below.

The intercept ship dives away in pursuit.

Thompson smiles in admiration. "*Brilliant.*"

Beckert and Thompson watch the nearby crowd of transports right themselves then steer toward the gaping docking bay. Rather than form an orderly queue again, pilots race competitively for the dock, crowding one another off course to be first. Beckert keeps close to the fray but hangs back, knowing the remote docking program will resume to prevent a massive pile up. Confirming his assumption, the transports ahead slow drastically then fall into line like a zipper closing. The Geek takes his hands from the controls and lets the shuttle steer itself into line.

"It really is *too* easy sometimes," he quips.

Thompson casts a side-glance at Beckert in genuine amazement. With an appreciative nod, he returns his gaze to the ship they glide toward. It looms like a mountain range, impossibly large for a space going vessel.

*To lift every molecule from a planetary surface? The energy required... Might as well chisel it out of a small moon...*

*Huh. Maybe that's what they did...*

While little more than a pore in the vessel's great body, the landing bay fills their windshield. Lead transports in the queue pass a transparent membrane and steer to vacant pads, marked by flashing lights embedded in the deck. As soon as landing skids touch down, ramps lower and the craft vomit skittish passengers, enlarging an already dense mob in the bay.

"So *many*," Thompson mutters in disgust.

Beckert's eyes are glued to the hemispherical display. At the lower edge, all five blips he sent speeding toward the planet have been snared.

"That was fast…"

Thompson turns from the windshield. "What was fast?"

The smug look Beckert's face straightens. "They'll know we're not among the five." He grabs the controls, and his goggles flare brightly. Once again, all shuttle ID tags blend in the holographic display.

Speakers at the upper corners of the cockpit blare with a gruff alien voice, and floodlights sweep over transports ahead. The gruff voice repeats its challenge.

"Hang on!" Beckert's goggles flash.

The line of transports jumbles up and the Geek flies into its midst. Sheltered on all sides, he thrusts the entire formation at the bay, top speed.

Thick shutters at the top and bottom of the bay roll toward each other. From behind the closing shutters, thousands of horrified yellow eyes stare at the formation barreling toward them. The terrified mob turns and runs for the back of the bay.

A bright flash to the left precedes a jolt and the clanging of metal parts against the hull. Beckert glances through the wraparound glass on his left at the stern of a transport beside him. One of its two main boosters has exploded, and the vessel yaws away with unbalanced thrust. Exhaust gases wash across the glass, scorching a black streak, as the craft spins out of formation.

"Get us in there, Geek!" Thompson yells, dropping his faceplate. "Brick, seal up!"

"Aye, Sir!" Beckert answers, eyes wide and alert. With a brusque slap, the Geek drops his faceplate into place.

The transport directly ahead erupts in flame as a knife of

energy burns through it. Venting plasma pitches the craft into one beneath. Both crumple then explode.

Heavy fragments strike Beckert's windshield, cracking it. The shuttle lurches, slamming Thompson against the ceiling. Blood chilling screams fill the passenger cabin.

Beckert squints through the broken windshield at the slim line between closing bay doors. Another transport to the right detonates with a flash, a brutal jolt, and pummeling of fragments against the hull.

"*So close*," Beckert advises, his face a mask of total concentration. Then he glances at the console display, bares his teeth at a warship sliding up behind, and shouts, "*BRACE!*"

A deafening electric sizzle carves through the rear of the cabin. The transport shudders. Shattering metal drowns out emergency alarms from a console turned bright red, and both boosters detonate.

# MAIELLA WAS RIGHT

*\<Subject unconscious…initialize neural stimulus\>*

*\<Pulse…\>*

*\<Pulse…\>*

*\<Pulse…\>*

*\<Subject conscious\>*

Beckert's eyes open to painful smears of light. His ears ring, and his head *thuds* like a drum. As vision clears, he looks out at a smashed cockpit, the confines of which are much closer than before. A darkened console presses hard against him, pinning him in his chair. The windshield is gone, its frame kinked inward. Beyond the kinked frame, the world is a sooty gray tangle of wreckage.

He feels a pressure in his face, a bulging, and his tongue seems too large for his mouth. He clucks a few times in confusion until the space's only light source grabs his attention—on the center console, where the hemispherical display used to be, a lone finger of flame licks upside down into the circuitry.

The Geek focuses on the flame, watching it devour the wire insulation and throw off strings of black smoke. As the flame burrows deeper into the console Beckert finally realizes he is upside-down, held aloft by the smashed console.

Throbbing behind his eyes takes a sudden turn to astounding pain. Salty saliva runs from his open mouth up the side of his face. He grips the sides of his helmet, panting in short, controlled breaths, and coos to himself. In time, spikes of pain in his head ease, his wandering vision converges, and his churning gut settles.

Twitches to his right draw the Geek's attention. Thompson, heaped in a ball against the ceiling of the cockpit, spasms in one-second pulses then awakens with a start. He scrambles to his feet, crazed like a cornered animal. Frantic hands and eyes search for his weapon. When he finds it, he pulls it tight to his shoulder and primes it.

"Major," Beckert greets then coughs.

Thompson flinches back and sees Beckert suspended upside down, pinched at the midsection between the pilot's chair and the console.

"Beckert!"

Before he can lay hands on the console Thompson convulses with a fit of violent coughs then doubles over, one arm across his stomach. Propping himself against the crushed cockpit framing with one hand, he groans then looks at his inverted teammate.

"You okay, Geek?"

Beckert shrugs. "Still breathing. Can you get me outta here?"

Thompson slings his rifle and plants a boot on the intruding console. He strains but cannot free his comrade.

"Hang on," the Gun says and ducks through the twisted doorway.

At the front of the passenger cabin, Argo pushes out of a pile of broken and entangled blue bodies. Rows of seats hang from above.

"How long were we out?" the big man asks.

"Over a minute." Thompson stares at the wall of the transport, imagining how many enemy troops could have amassed in that time. He extends a hand to the Brick and helps him up.

"See to Geek, he's pinned."

Argo nods and limps past Thompson into the cockpit. He

blinks at the inverted Geek then puts his back to the cockpit wall and puts both boots against the console. Growling, the Brick strains. Centimeter by centimeter the console yields until Beckert slips through the gap.

With Beckert freed, Thompson moves to the back of the cabin and looks up. Where the entry ramp used to be, the transport is ripped wide open. Thick smoke hangs in the air outside.

Double blinking at an icon in his visor, he links wirelessly to his riflescope and holds the weapon up through the transport's torn belly. The scope automatically compensates to infrared, revealing a scene of wreckage, flames, and charred bodies.

Figures in thick suits shuffle around a distant blaze, hosing it with suppressants. Thompson zooms in on them. Through hard-water spots on the scope optics, he sees fire fighters in full-face masks with self-contained respirators. As far as he can tell, the hoses and extinguishers are their only weapons.

Above, a dense layer of smoke loiters at the ceiling, growing thicker and lower from numerous sooty fires.

*Good. We'll have some cover…*

He pulls himself up through the open hull, perches at its edge, and surveys a hangar bay that is vast by any definition or comparison. Between him and the sealed shutters is open flooring with a long gouge in the deck plates, as if struck by a meteor at shallow angle. Any paint or lamps dividing pads are obscured beneath layers of sooty scorches. Parked transports that recently filled that space are swept to either side in a wide ring, many still burning; and unlucky ones in the path of Beckert's crash are fused into a mangled heap against the rear bay wall, nearly reaching the high ceiling.

Thompson looks down at what remains of his own transport. The stern is entirely gone, boosters and all, with mounts and bracing curling away in discolored stumps. Bent landing struts stick up like the limbs of a dead insect. And the nose of the craft is stuffed deep into a jam of other wrecked transports. Only the sturdy passenger cabin seems intact. He pats his armor, knowing it has saved his life yet again.

"Gun."

Thompson looks down and sees Argo peering up at him. The Brick waves him inside the transport, and the Gun drops quietly from his perch.

"What's up?"

"Geek's in bad shape. Just had a grand mal…"

Thompson peers past Argo's wide shoulders. Beckert leans against the wall of the cockpit, faceplate raised. His eyes seek with the perplexed wonder of an infant.

"He's seeping cerebrospinal fluid," Argo continues. "Had to drill a shunt to ease the pressure. Don't know how long neurostims'll keep him operating."

Thompson easily reads the meaning in the Brick's insisting eyes. "You want to take him off-line."

"This is his second head trauma in *days*. He's in mortal peril, and I'm concerned—"

"We can't," Thompson counters.

Argo glares back. "And our promise to O'Kai?"

"I KNOW," Thompson thunders, hands curled into fists. "I *know*." The Gun exhales through his nose, suppressing a cough. "There are over a million variables in a jump plot home. *I* can't calculate them, Argo. Can *you*?"

Argo lowers his eyes submissively, assumes the appropriate Cadre stoicism, and stands straight.

"What are your orders?"

"Do what you can for him, but keep him *alert*. Until we get outta here, we need an extra shooter more than anything."

Argo nods then frets at the hugely difficult task of controlling Beckert's seizures without dulling his nervous system. As the Brick steps toward his groggy patient, he takes labset in hand and builds a neurochemical concoction. Captioned molecules scroll by on the labset's display: sodium and calcium channel blockers, L-Dopa, dopa decarboxylase and catechol-o-methyl transferase inhibitors. His thumbs trigger the keys again and again, seeking the right ratios.

Thompson leaps up to his perch.

Argo asks, "Where are you going?"

Thompson hunches to look his comrade in the eye. "Gotta find an exit." He faces front and drops off the side of the crumpled transport.

The Gun's boots sink into a rough terrain of conduits, ducting, machine parts, and luggage. Something crunches under his first step forward. He stoops for a closer view and sees a brittle, carbonized arm. The hand is flexed so hard, its claws stab through the charred palm.

Moving on, Thompson picks his way toward the nearest wall and contemplates the frozen wave of wreckage washed against it.

*Any clear passageway will be crawling with the enemy...but maybe behind this wreckage is a wall fracture we can slip through.*

The slope of sharp, brittle debris shifts as he climbs, making the summit seem farther than it is. When he reaches the top, he presses against the bay wall. Despite the tonnage slammed against it, the wall is straight and unyielding.

A shout near center of the bay startles him, and Thompson whirls about. He looks out past smoldering, oxygen-deprived fires, and spies a cluster of lamps sweeping and pivoting between tossed transports.

Rifle raised, he peers through his scope. In water-spotted optics, Thompson watches the beams converge at a spot on the floor, crowd together, and stoop down, bathing a shadowy figure in artificial light. Heavily clothed arms reach into the light and take hold of the prone figure. The figure rises limply from the floor and is carried off toward the bay's far side. Lamps spread out and resume their sweeps.

Thompson steps down from the mound of debris, unable to silence the jangling of loose fragments. He glides away from the wall, rifle aimed at the lights, and takes a knee, again studying through his scope. A hand taps him on the shoulder.

The Gun looks up, expecting Argo. Instead, he sees a grungy

blueskin deckhand wearing a transparent respirator mask. Its saffron yellow eyes swell from dazed relief to wide-open terror. Mouth stretches, baring teeth, and its purple tongue arches.

Thompson strikes with his rifle butt. The fragile respirator mask shatters, and the creature's head snaps backward. Tripping over debris, the deckhand collapses and clutches at its throat, gagging on the fouled air. Thompson follows with a vicious stomp to the neck, silencing it for good.

Headlamps pivot as one and shine in Thompson's direction. Dark, angular figures streak in from behind the lamps, slide between them, then split up, weaving through the wreckage into smoky shadows. All clutch fat barreled weapons with dual grips.

Screech of metal startles the Gun, and he spins to face it, finger on trigger. Only a few meters from his crashed transport, long spikes of light filter through the slope of debris like glowing spines of a sea urchin. With each screech the light gets brighter, and he understands a portal behind the wreckage is being forced open.

"*Brick*," he radios, "d*emolition required, painting target*."

Argo climbs out of the cabin and perches on the edge like something half boulder, half spider.

"*Target painted*," Thompson radios.

The Brick palms a canister from his waist and arms it. "*Cover*," he radios. With the flick of an arm he lobs the canister precisely where indicated and drops into the transport.

Thompson sprints then slides on his knees behind the transport's twisted hull as a mighty *POOMP* bounces the deck plates. A blast wave shoves the wrecked hull several meters, knocking Thompson over, and lofted debris rains over him.

Thompson scrambles to his feet and peeks around the transport. Wreckage is cleared and the doorway is open, blue sparks sizzling at its doorjamb.

"*Exit clear*," he radios. "*Move out!*"

Beckert launches from the cabin and lands unsteadily as if tossed. His hands hang at his side, eyes roaming behind his goggles.

Argo climbs out beside him, media sacks slung over one

shoulder. Taking Beckert around the waist, he jumps down and sets the Geek onto his feet.

Thompson runs to his comrades, looking Beckert over with alarm. He shoves the Brick angrily.

"I said *alert*, Argo!"

Argo takes the sacks from his shoulder and shoves them into Thompson. "He *WILL* be!"

The Gun snarls behind his faceplate. *No time to argue*. Hefting the sacks and slipping his arms through the harness, he orders, "On me. *MOVE!*"

Thompson plants his rifle against his shoulder and dashes for the exit. Argo takes Beckert by the waist again and, one handed, hefts him as though he were tossing a duffel of laundry over his shoulder. Beckert's head lolls as the big man shrugs him into a manageable position.

Thompson pauses at the doorway. Dense smoke courses through the open doorway, smothering light from the corridor beyond. The floor is slick with seeping blue and purple flesh. Seeing no sign of ambush, he dashes past the smoke into full illumination. Another few meters and the corridor bends to the right. Thompson pads up to the corner and crouches. Argo takes position behind.

"Put me down," Beckert says.

Argo lowers his comrade to the floor. The Geek raises his gauntleted hands before his face and wiggles his fingers.

"This is *really* weird."

"I know," Argo explains, holding the Geek's chin to look in his eyes. "Your brain chemistry is highly modified. You may experience some sensory cross-over."

Beckert reaches for his pistols, missing the first time. Annoyed, he stiffens and concentrates, snatching them cleanly. He checks the actions.

"Well, you got rid of my headache," he says appreciatively.

Thompson asks, "Are you good?"

Beckert looks past Argo at his leader. "Yeah…I mean, yes, sir!" The Geek shakes his head sternly. "Just have to focus."

"Argo, cover our rear. Geek, you—"

Beckert's pistol flicks out beside Thompson, and the Geek triggers. Muzzle flashes *thump* against the Gun's armor like a drum roll of heavy rubber mallets. Thompson spins, training his rifle on a perforated reptilian soldier. The soldier snorts, falls face first, and lies still.

Beckert drops the spent clip and slips his pistol grip over a fresh magazine on his thigh. Releasing the pistol's action, he looks at Thompson patiently.

"Thanks," Thompson says then peeks around the corner. "Corridor's clear. Follow me."

The team tears off in unison, delving through the vessel's unknown interior. Thompson triggers methodically at anything that moves. Beckert covers the side passageways and open rooms with his peripheral vision. Argo runs backwards, aiming his cannon into their wake.

Long, egg-shaped corridors fade one into another. Identical spacing between regular intersections, identical spacing between identical red doors, identical rows of low-mounted light fixtures— the features all tick compulsively in Thompson's mind. The farther he goes, the less sure he is of his course.

As if channeling that uncertainty, Argo asks, "Where are we going, Gun?"

"A ship this big must have more than one flight deck," Thompson replies. "We might even…"

A chill claws into the nape of Thompson's neck. Far ahead, past multiple intersections, a corridor on the right is slightly dimmer than the rest. His fist flies up, and the team pads to a halt. Rising to his toes, the Gun glides silently ahead and signals his team to do the same.

As close to the suspect corridor as he dares, Thompson throws his fist up again and takes a knee. Beckert and Argo hunker down behind him without a sound. The Gun duck walks toward the intersection with deliberate steps, every sinew taut. His mind focuses to a needle point, and he listens: a shoed foot shifts over metal floor plates, something hinged squeaks as it is turned, whispers pass and are urgently hushed.

Thompson hand-signals Argo for a grenade. The Brick palms an appropriate charge from his waist and underhands it to his leader. In one fluid motion, Thompson cups it silently from the air, activates it, and hurls it into the dimmer corridor.

Barks and shouts roll from the corridor before a deep *POOMP* silences them. Lights fail and flicker before relighting.

Looking down the sights of his weapon, Thompson rounds the corner, leaps over a hastily erected barricade, and triggers kill shots into all four prone heat sources.

"Clear!" Thompson shouts. Argo and Beckert round the corner and vault over the barricade. While Thompson dashes ahead, Beckert and Argo quick-search the bodies.

Beckert rolls a soldier over and rips a bandolier from its chest with four apple-sized spheres. He throws the bandolier over his head.

Argo picks up a tripod-mounted weapon, knocked over by the blast. Just below the gun mount, there is a hinge that allows the weapon to pitch and yaw. It squeaks with the motion.

"Lieutenant."

Argo turns to see Beckert holding another strap of spherical devices.

"You'll like these," the Geek says, offering the bandolier. "*Big boom.*"

Argo takes the strap and dons it, barely able to get his arm and head through the loop.

"*Enemy sighted*," Thompson radios from out of sight. "*Committing.*" His rifle *pangs* and return fire reverberates down the long hall.

"Go!" Argo orders, and Beckert sprints toward the sounds of combat. Argo rips the battery pack from the tripod-mounted weapon, hurls it back the way they came, and chases after Beckert.

The Geek pauses at the next intersection. Holes are scorched into the white walls on the left with small wisps of flame. Large notches are burned out of the corner on the right.

Argo storms up behind Beckert. "Gun, what's your position?"

The radio blares with crackling hisses, weapon fire, and labored breath. "*Eighty meters ahead, then right. Stay low, and watch our line of retreat.*"

Argo pops his head past the corner. Soldiers in angular armor lie flat on their backs, tails sprawled to one side. He slaps Beckert on the back, and the Geek runs behind his pistols to the next intersection. Checking over his shoulder, the Brick jogs after his comrade.

Beckert kneels at the corner. Smoke rolls in from the right hallway like a demon's exhalation. Bullets and beams spray across the intersection, ricocheting and scoring the once-polished walls. A sizzling *hiss* zips through the smoke, followed by another, and delayed explosions rumble in the distance. Nearby, a weapon chugs with high-output shots.

Argo peeks around the corner and sees Thompson squatting behind a smoking barricade, hands gripping a tripod-mounted weapon, triggering continuously into a vast and smoky bay. Small rockets, bullets, and beams plunge into the barricade, scooting it backwards with each hit.

A bullet *tangs* against the Brick's helmet, jolting him back, and an instant later the corner burns with multiple impacts. A rocket streaks through the new notch, missing Argo by centimeters, and ricochets off the wall behind him. It spirals down the hallway, *ticking* loudly with each bounce before exploding at the next intersection.

"Coming to you, Gun," Argo states. A bright flash, a sharp crack, and a burst of sparks explode from Thompson's position. The chugging shots cease.

Dense smoke billows through the intersection, and sounds of combat fade.

"*Gun!*" Argo calls. He leans forward, starting a dash.

Thompson groans, "Brick, continue through intersection, take point."

The Brick stops short and straightens, relieved to hear Thompson's voice.

"Aye, si…"

"Brick!" Beckert yells.

Shots from across the intersection batter Argo, knocking him off balance. Beckert aims his pistols and strafes.

Argo rights himself, following Beckert's muzzle flashes to a pair of falling soldiers. Thin blue arms reach out from an open door and haul the fallen soldiers out of the hallway.

Argo's teeth clench as he leaps across the intersection. Energy beams pour from the closing doorway, sizzling into his thick armor. He brings his cannon to bear and triggers a devastating blast. The door crumples like foil, and the room belches a great thunderclap of superheated air. Smoke and fragments burst through the ragged doorway.

Glowing orange spots on Argo's armor fade to red and dissipate across the surface. The Brick leans forward, daring anything else to present itself.

"Gun, the way is clear. Geek, provide cover."

"Aye, sir," Beckert says. Keeping one pistol trained down Thompson's corridor, he crosses the intersection and snatches a sphere from Argo's bandolier. Holding the sphere in his palm, he taps the top with his thumb and traces a quarter circle counter clockwise.

Thompson's rifle *pangs* twice in his retreat. Random shots zip and dart through the smoke, passing over his head.

When Thompson rounds the corner, Beckert taps the top of the sphere twice. It whirs and buzzes like a furious insect. Standing up, the Geek hurls the device into the smoky bay and runs for his life.

Beckert's feet roll swiftly over the polished deck plates in an urgent rhythm. Thompson's hunched shoulders sway ahead of him, the Gun's helmet almost scraping the curved ceiling. Beckert spins mid-stride and runs backwards, pistols aimed toward the pocked and scorched intersection.

*Should have gone off by now… How long did I set the timer?*

The corridor lurches violently, polished plating and fixtures bursting from their mounts. Light sconces go dark and do not re-light.

"Geek," Thompson calls, "what's on the wireless?"

Beckert glances at a list of active frequencies in his goggles. "High message density, Major. They're *very* excited."

"Any networks you can access?"

"Been trying, sir," the Geek adds apologetically. "I'm having trouble concentrating…hard to think…"

"Contact ahead," Argo says in low voice. The team slows to a glide step, and sneaks to a darkened intersection. Stray beams of light spill in from the right. Urgent voices pass back and forth, and there is a faint electric beep.

Argo pads ahead, taking a bulb from his waist. He mashes the stem button three times and bounces it around the corner.

Horrified shouts and screams are crushed to silence by fierce detonation.

The Brick steps into the broad intersection like a wall, covering his teammates as they sprint by. Through the smoke and settling debris, he sees lines of bodies stretched out beneath blotchy white sheets, lining each side of the wide corridor. At the end, heavy doors hang loosely on their hinges, partially open. Beyond are the smoldering hulks of crashed transports.

*We must be moving parallel to the landing bay... It's bigger than it looked.*

There is a flash from the bay and a large caliber bullet slams dead center of his breastplate. The Brick staggers back from the impact, just keeping his feet, and dashes after his team. Behind him, weapon fire pours from the bay like onset of a hailstorm.

"*Geek,*" Thompson radios, "*find us a diagram, map, directory, anything that'll show us where to go.*"

"Understood, Major." Beckert pushes through the hammers and gongs in his disjointed mind. Random thoughts scatter across his frontal lobe, mixing with memories of unrelated events as if a thousand movies were cut and spliced together then run simultaneously.

Confused by the Geek's misfiring neurons, Beckert's HDI remains idle, stubbornly displaying a command prompt. The young man, sheltered on each side by Thompson and Argo, labors to blank his mind of the cluttered thoughts.

*HDI initialize*, he thinks as clearly as he can. His goggles flash once. Boot commands scroll in a blur.

*Calibrate neural interface.*

His goggles flash myriad patterns, shapes, and colors. The HDI reads feedback from his eyes and synaptic responses.

*<Analysis complete>*

*<53% signal to noise>*

*<Cause: chemical imbalance and/or traumatic brain injury>*

*<Compensating...>*

*<Synaptic bridge sensitivity decreased 42%>*

*<Re-calibrating...>*

*<Ready>*

With sensitivity reduced, Beckert finds the HDI is no longer overwhelmed by interference from his chaotic, fluttering mind, but he has to mentally shout his thoughts to operate.

*DISCOVER NETWORKS*, he thinks, and two hundred distinct access points list in his goggles. Hack tools pry open a gateway and lock out other users. With effort, a piece of his consciousness barges into the system, discovering, mapping, and searching the greater structures. Most nodes are in high alert, with formidable security hampering access to vital areas. A general information node is unlocked, however, and Beckert unfurls a three dimensional map in his mind. The team's location highlights in blue.

"I have a map, Major."

"Find us the nearest flight deck."

Faster than Thompson ordered it, Beckert has the closest flight deck selected. The route auto-plots, and he transmits data to his teammates.

In Thompson's visor, the map overlays his visual sightlines perfectly, adding light blue edges to the corridors' contours. A red line forms on the floor, indicating path.

"Good work, Geek. On me." Rifle level and ready, Thompson's strides become longer, more confident, and he leads his team at a blistering pace through darkened halls. Always, he watches the angles and corners, vigilant for the slightest threat. At first, absence of resistance seems a blessing, but it makes him wonder where they might be massing instead.

His route turns down a long, straight corridor with no doors along the sides. The Gun halts his manic sprint and he backs his team up, wary of such a long tunnel without exit.

"Geek, any other way?"

"Uh, not to this flight deck. There's another one on the far side of the ship, but that's a lot of ground to—"

"Forget it. Let's go."

Thompson levels his weapon and races for the far end of the corridor, team close behind, when a dark gray door drops from the ceiling and seals the passage. He spins about only to watch the end of the corridor behind them seal with an identical door.

"I knew it! STUPID, STUPID!"

Argo puts a hand on Thompson's shoulder and moves past him.

"You two, stand back, get down," the Brick warns, thumbing his cannon's output to maximum. He jogs ahead and plants the weapon at the center of the corridor, aimed at the gray barrier. He sets a switch, squeezes the trigger, and runs back toward his comrades at top speed. At the last moment, he dives to the floor. Sliding on his chest, he drags a hand, spins around, and waits for oscillator whine to peak. At the last moment, the team looks down at the floor and wraps their arms around their heads.

The cannon glows with an eerie violet aura and discharges a devastating stream. Superheated air explodes in a tremendous thunderclap, rattling the Operators against the deck and washing them in a punishing shockwave.

Argo lifts his head and studies the end of the corridor. Dense webs of frayed cords slump from walls and ceiling. Hissing jets of vapor gush from shattered air and liquid ducts. Yet amid the haze and arcing sparks, the barrier remains defiant. Its only injury is a half-meter spot near the floor blushing dull red and fading back to gray.

"Huh," he says, propping himself on his elbows. "That's a good door." He sucks his teeth as he considers other options.

"Maybe the walls aren't as strong," Beckert suggests.

Argo turns to the Gun, his gloomy expression brightening. They both rise in unison and hurry toward the fuming end of the corridor, Argo snatching up his cannon on the way. Together, Argo and Thompson dig into the blasted walls, ripping out layers of insulation, wire bundles, bracing, and piping.

While the larger Operators attack the wall, Beckert kneels in contemplation. In stillness, a subtle tone reaches his ringing ears, high-pitched, almost inaudible. The more he focuses on it, the easier it is to distinguish; and Beckert realizes he is not hearing the tone as much as he is detecting it with his implanted hardware: high-frequency switching, electromagnetism, and flows of immense power.

"Major! Lieutenant!" The Geek calls rising to his feet. He turns to the left and presses his hands against the smooth, polished wall.

Thompson and Argo halt their demolition.

"Whatcha got?" Thompson yells down the hall.

Beckert looks up and down the unremarkable wall, sensing the treasure behind it. "Processing node, I think."

Argo jogs toward the Geek, intrigued. "Certain?"

Beckert nods emphatically, tuned to the ultrasonic orchestra.

"All RIGHT!" Argo growls. He sets his cannon down and slams a huge fist into the white metallic tiles, splitting them at the seams, then pries the wall open. Beckert steps back, careful to stay clear of Argo's massive swings and rips.

Thompson jogs up to the new site of destruction, eyes darting between gray barriers anxiously. Every second they are stalled in the corridor means more time for the enemy to reinforce the exits, more time to surround, to trap, to overwhelm.

Argo digs through the wall like a bear through a rotten log, his massive paws scraping deeper until they strike solid framing. His hands curl to battering rams and pound the frame, nudging it, denting it with each hit.

Thompson shifts from one foot to another, expecting the barriers to rise at any moment with an army behind each one. He raises his rifle at the torn open wall.

"Brick, stand back."

Argo steps away, surprised to see Thompson ready to fire. He ducks aside as the rifle flashes repeatedly, melting into the rigid structures.

"Careful, Major," Beckert warns meekly. He cringes with each rifle flash, knowing the node is taking the hits.

Thompson burns a dashed archway into the interior framing and lowers his weapon. Taking the cue, Argo steps up to the arch and peers through one of the holes.

"I see dim light." Swinging his arms, the Brick retreats to the opposite side of the corridor and breathes heavily, stoking the furnace within. He bellows with channeled rage and lunges at the arch. Dropping his shoulder, he slams into the wall, ripping a small section apart. He backs away, roars, and rams again.

The metallic inner wall unzips, retreating into a darkened room beyond. Argo's momentum carries him into a low beam face first, and he drops flat onto his back.

Beckert darts through the gap, pistols raised, and scans the ten-meter-high room. Symmetrical floor, walls, and ceiling are planted with cube shaped processors. The cubes stand to Beckert's chest, each sparkling from thousands of illuminated pinpoints. He moves between them gracefully, bathing in the hum and flow of data all around him. After a quick sweep, he finds the room unoccupied.

"Clear!" he shouts.

Argo shakes his head and picks himself up from the deck. All around, warm cubes glow in his visor. Two of them sizzle, leaking hot, runny oil from pencil-thin holes.

Thompson slides into the ragged archway, keeping watch on the gray barriers, and he asks, "You okay, Brick?"

"Yeah, yeah, fine." Argo retrieves his cannon from the corridor then wedges his way toward Beckert at the center of the room. The Geek hunches over a shuttered terminal, trying to open it. Argo takes the shutter by the locked handle and rips it open like he was pulling a shade.

"Thanks," Beckert says.

"Brick," Thompson calls, "find us an exit. We're not staying."

"Aye, sir." The big man makes his way between hot, twinkling nodes and feels his way around the outer wall.

Beckert activates a flip-out data panel from the terminal and the display illuminates. "Gimme a few secs, Major. This is worth it, I assure you."

Thompson nods coarsely. "Make it quick."

Beckert extends the lanyard of his HDI and jacks into a data port. The moment he connects, his goggles fill with streams of overlapping code. His head twitches and he drifts to his knees as consciousness projects into the pathways of the machine.

Streams of chaotic light, fractal patterns, and code swirl before his eyes then assemble into coherent structures. At his command, they obediently shift and adapt to his preferences. In moments, a seemingly infinite landscape assembles in three virtual dimensions, tantalizing in its vulnerability.

Before the Geek can fully merge, virtual barricades assemble around him. He smirks, and his goggles blaze with code, keeping just ahead of system countermeasures.

*<Alter display setting,>* he commands, *<3D to 4D>.*

Immediately, the landscape folds in on itself, collapsing into the new configuration. The way one can look at a square, seeing all sides and the inside simultaneously, Beckert's perspective becomes omnipresent, seeing all sides and inside of virtual structures at once.

"Interface achieved," he monotones.

Thompson flexes his jaw impatiently. "Keep those gray barriers in the corridor sealed, Geek. Then find us a transport and a clear path to it."

"Understood."

The system resists Beckert's intrusion at every turn and data gate, but Beckert has already multiplied his presence exponentially. Millions, then billions of digital instances assault the system, flooding resources, overflowing buffers, overwhelming defenses, while keeping compromised nodes available to his whims.

"Corridor barriers sealed and isolated from external control," he monotones. "Fourteen transport candidates available."

Thompson steals a glance at his young comrade, hanging on his words.

"Exit!" Argo announces on the opposite side of the room.

Thompson rushes across the room and finds Argo forcing open a small hatchway, barely big enough for the Brick to squeeze through. He aims his rifle into the dimly lit crawlspace, expecting soldiers to pour through at any moment.

"Three of fourteen transports deep space capable," Beckert drones. "In pre-flight, and taking fuel."

"Show us the way, Geek."

"Acknowledged...*Gah*!"

Thompson rises from his crouch, hurrying to the sounds of Beckert's distress. Beckert's face is scrunched, eyes squinted, and a single drop of sweat rolls down his forehead. The goggles flare with intensity.

"*Geek.*"

The young Operator's face twitches randomly, and a subsonic throb rolls through the deck plates. The ship is moving.

"*Sergeant!*"

Beckert's goggles lose their radiant intensity. The Geek gasps suddenly and exhales with relief.

"Sorry, sir. Had to concentra..." He sways, blinking hard, and leans onto his fists. His stomach heaves.

"Brick! Get over here!"

Beckert raises a hand. "I'm okay, sir." The Geek gets to his knees, hiccoughs, then looks down at the terminal, admiring his handiwork. "They'll be *very* busy."

Argo tromps over and takes Beckert by the face. He lifts the Geek's faceplate, stretching a long trail of drool over Beckert's head. Labset in hand, Argo takes a spare lanyard from Beckert's HDI and plugs in. The device scrolls with diagnostics, halting suddenly and displaying, *intracranial pressure above normal*. The big man grits his teeth.

"They'll be *very* busy," Beckert repeats.

Argo's eyes flick up from the labset and study the Geek's face.

"They'll be *very* busy," he says again.

Thompson peers over the warm cubes. "What's going on?"

"I'm on it, Gun," Argo answers.

"They'll be *very* busy," Beckert perseverates.

Argo programs a serum into his labset. When complete, an attached phial fills and the Brick plugs it into Beckert's neck.

"He's gonna be a little dopey for a few minutes," the Brick explains.

Thompson stifles a remark, grunting instead.

"Geek," Argo asks, looking directly into Beckert's face, "do we have transport?"

"Uh, yes sir." His eyes blink hard. He looks down at the lanyard connecting him to the terminal, confused. "I lost the connection?"

"It's all right. Do we have a path?"

Beckert disconnects the lanyard and allows it to retract. His eyes lose some of their dreaminess. "Yes, sir. We make for the flight deck, just as before." With each blink, his expression sharpens. "There are two vessels there that can serve us."

"Send us the path, Geek," Thompson orders.

Beckert nods and transmits the map. Argo's and Thompson's visors update with the information.

"All portals have been opened along the way, and I locked out the system," Beckert explains. "They shouldn't be able to trap us again."

Thompson looks through the ragged archway to the bright

white corridor beyond. "Re-connect and kill the ship lighting. All of it if you can."

"Aye, sir," Beckert replies crisply.

Argo peers sternly at his patient and gives a tacit nod. He disconnects the lanyard from his labset and allows the Geek to work.

Beckert plugs in as before, goggles streaming with copious data. In scant moments, he reconquers the digital domain and reroutes power from all illumination. The bright corridor and the dim hatchway lights fade to darkness.

From far beyond the hatchway, Thompson hears muffled shouts. His lips twist with conditioned rage.

*"Gimme a grenade."*

Argo palms a bulb from his waist and lobs it to the Gun. Thompson snatches it, arms it, and hurls it past the hatchcoaming.

*"Cover!"*

Beckert and Argo crouch behind cubic processors. The hatchway flashes and thumps violently. Hot smoke gusts into the room.

"On me!" Thompson commands. *"Move!"* He ducks into the low crawlspace, rifle level and ready.

Argo stows his labset, collects his cannon, and hustles through the hatchway.

Beckert relocks the system and disconnects. Pulling his pistols, he dashes to the hatch and follows his team, keeping a watchful eye to their rear.

Thompson speeds through the smoke-filled crawlspace. Traces of heat shine in his visor, marking the edges of a spherical detonation where the crawlspace is forcibly expanded. His eyes search hungrily for the enemy, flow of combat stims stoking eagerness to kill.

The crawlspace turns left at the blast site, and the Gun pauses at the corner. He holds his rifle past the edge, streaming video from the scope. Nearby, two scorched bodies slump together. Residual warmth glows faintly.

Thompson duck walks onto the blasted flooring, and it gives way beneath him. He crashes down into a wide corridor, lit only by headlamps from seven blueskin soldiers surrounding him. The soldiers shout and stumble backward.

Thompson's bayonet *shicks* into place and the Gun slashes it across the throats of the closest two as enemy shots *piff* into media sacks on his back. In the same motion, Thompson swings behind his gargling victims, snatching one of them around the chest. Holding his dying shield close to him, he slides backwards and raises his rifle. Two soldiers turn and flee. The other three shout savagely and aim their weapons but will not fire through their dying comrade. Thompson clicks killing shots into the three then drops his shield, aims with both hands, and snipes the last two in the back.

The Gun pivots, rifle level, checking behind him. There is no other movement, only beams of headlamps cast haphazardly at the corridor's walls. He retracts the blue-smeared bayonet and turns another circle, metalized bits of media records crunching underfoot.

"Clear," Thompson states.

"Coming down," Argo announces, and Thompson steps away from the ceiling hole. The Brick punches a much wider opening and slams down onto his boots. Beckert drops through and lands with the poise of a cat. His goggles strobe momentarily.

"I've updated our path," he explains. "Sending now."

Thompson's and Argo's visors overlay the virtual map onto the corridor walls around them. A red line paints on the floor and extends into the darkness.

"Tight formation," Thompson orders. "On me."

The team races through hallways, following the augmented view in their visors, no longer pausing at intersections. Sounds of their exertion, hushed footfalls, and rustle of media records seem excessively loud. But in total darkness they are invisible.

Subsonic throb in the deck plates rises in pitch. Air takes on an electrical charge, raising hairs on their arms and necks. The team staggers in their gait, momentarily insubstantial. Just as suddenly, the air discharges, the subsonic throb resumes, and the team feels the full weight of body and kit once more.

"What was *that*?" Argo hisses.

"I programmed the ship to make random short jumps," Beckert explains. "If we're to get away, we need some distance from those armed escorts."

"Not through the planet or moon, I expect," the Brick grouses.

"No, sir! Unobstructed jumps only. But the ship knows to ram through any blockade before engaging DSDs."

Thompson thinks about Beckert's claim and the phenomenal amount of computation required. *He was only plugged in for a minute…less than a minute.*

*Maiella was right. You ARE good.*

# Judicium Dei

Thompson turns down a long corridor that bends out of sight. Intermittent rays of light spill from around the corner, as of someone moving in front of bright lamps. The Gun slows his pace and glides silently to the bend. Argo and Beckert take their cue, coasting to glide step.

"Flight deck's close," the Gun whispers.

Thompson nudges his weapon around the corner, looking wirelessly through the scope. Silhouetted in dim light is a barricade, a meter and a half high. Random gaps betray a hasty construction. Twin box-like devices stand above the barricade, supported by stout poles.

Keeping his rifle aimed, Thompson whispers, "Enemy sighted, barricade, ten plus combatants, unknown weapons." He watches a moment longer, retreats from the corner, and reaches into the blackness, finding his invisible comrades by touch and pulling them close.

"Geek, take a grenade and stealth approach that barricade. Brick, when Geek gets there, we'll draw fire. Geek, when enemy commits to action, lob grenade and cover. Understood?"

"Understood."

"Understood, Major."

Thompson pats Beckert. "Go now."

Thompson resumes his crouch at the corner and leans his rifle around it, peering through his scope at the distant barricade. Argo cycles his breath, preparing for an intense firefight. He pulls a bulb from his waist and clips it to Beckert's waist. Pistols in hand, the young Operator slips around the corner and hunches in a silent run.

In stray reflections of light coming from beyond the barricade, Thompson can just see the Geek's silhouette, a shadow among shadows. But Beckert is only half-way to the barricade when the rectangular devices *click* and bloom with stellar luminance. Thompson's dark-adapted eyes wash out from the glare, and he recoils from the painful brilliance.

Terrified shouts and barks fill the hallway. Beckert's pistols roar. Enemy fire answers back.

Argo darts past Thompson into the blinding light. As his lenses compensate, he sees Beckert twisting and staggering under a coordinated barrage.

Bellowing madly, the Brick triggers brutal streams into the barricade, smashing it back and exploding through it. Mixed ordinance batters him from high and far beyond the barricade, scorching deep pockmarks into his armor and knocking him back against the wall behind him.

Thompson's rifle *pangs*, connecting with the rectangular lamps and exploding them in a dazzling shower of sparks. Shrill cries intersperse the weapon fire as the exploded lamps fade. Without light, enemy fire turns random and sporadic.

The barricade ahead seethes with heat, a shining bonfire in infrared, yet stands defiantly. Argo shoves off the wall, thumbs up his weapon's output to full, and leans forward. A violet aura coalesces around him, compacts into his anvil-like cannon, then leaps through the barricade, blasting it backward over a pack of retreating soldiers.

Through the thunderclap's fading echoes, Argo races ahead and shouts, "Beckert! Respond!"

Along the right side of the corridor, copious dents and perforations mar a section of wall. Below it, Beckert slumps face down.

Argo tromps to his fallen comrade, takes the Geek by the arm, and rolls him over. "Sergeant, look at me."

Beckert looks up in confusion at the big man, eyes dazed and rolling.

Thompson hustles over and kneels, rifle aimed down the hallway. "How is he?"

"Took the wind outta me, Major." Beckert slurs, blinking hard, then climbing up to a crouch. "But I'm okay." The Geek deftly spins his pistols around his fingers.

"Good, we're almost there," Thompson states, already striding forward.

Argo and Beckert take formation behind their leader.

"They must know where we're headed," Argo states gravely.

Thompson pauses, looks over his shoulder at Argo, and nods. He faces front and resumes his stride.

"Sound off, ammunition status."

"Current module's near empty," Argo reports. "Got one in reserve."

"Change it out. If there's an undrained cell in your current module, give it to me."

Beckert drops spent clips from his pistols and looks down at his thighs. Many of the clips are shot away, leaving three. His head spins back and forth, searching the floor around him.

"No, no, *no*!"

"What's wrong?" Thompson asks.

Beckert slides the pistol grips over two of the remaining magazines. "Current load plus one clip reserve," he replies dejectedly.

Argo pulls the module from his cannon and offers it to Thompson. Inside it, a row of dark gray cells ends at one glowing a mild green. He plucks the green cell and exchanges it with the one in his rifle.

Argo jams a fresh battery module into his cannon, takes the old module from Thompson's outstretched hand, and stows it in his rack.

Thompson looks at the corridor ahead. "We're in for a bad fight," he says. "Best get it over with."

Thompson passes the blasted remains of the barricade and breaks into a run. The corridor beyond continues without doorway or intersection until it turns sharply to the left. He reaches the corner and kneels, sighting with his rifle again. Argo steals up behind him. As the big man waits for orders, he sees Thompson's raised leg bouncing on its toes.

Thompson turns to address the Brick and notices the big man staring at his anxious leg. He grabs his knee and shifts weight onto it. The bouncing stops.

"Corridor is empty," Thompson reports, "wide intersection sixty meters ahead, entrance to flight deck on right." The Gun leans out for another peek. Brilliant light shines from the entrance. Industrious shadows play across the intersection floor.

Two thin figures run across the intersection toward the light with diaphanous gowns flowing behind them. An entourage of porters and aides, burdened with luggage, hurries after them.

Another group, armed and armored, hustles into the intersection. They halt, forming a line. With a staccato bark from the lead soldier, they take a knee and aim weapons down the hall.

Thompson is about to signal Argo for a grenade when three burly figures enter the intersection from the left. Each of them is larger than the kneeling soldiers in their armor. All three carry a bulky pistol, raised in one hand beside their head, and a shimmering half-meter blade in their opposite hand. The leader shouts in a demanding tone and the trio halts their march, taking position behind the row of kneeling soldiers. Unlike the undulating tails of the armored soldiers, these three stand perfectly still and stare without fear into the darkness.

Thompson dials in on the leader, studying him closely. Heavily muscled arms jut from a barrel-like torso. A thin vest drapes from broad shoulders and attaches to a similar pelvic garment. Multiple nicks and scars interrupt rough, pale blue skin. Fierce orange eyes burn within a broad, angular face.

A tall and elegant creature enters the intersection without hurry or anxiety. An intricate headdress rides on its brow. Silken veils enshroud it, deceptively simple in cut, yet remarkably accentuating in the curves of the midriff, chest, and leg. The eyes are half-open with detachment, and its graceful strides carry it out of sight into the light. Entranced by alien majesty, Thompson lowers his rifle.

The three large bodyguards peel away from the line of kneeling soldiers, following the elegant one into the lights. There is a loud bark, and the kneeling soldiers rise as one unit. Keeping their weapons aimed in Thompson's direction, they march into the bright lights of the bay.

With a hand gesture, Thompson orders his team around the corner. His breath is heavy, his sinews twitchy, as he runs on toes, anxious to close the distance in the long approach. The closer they get, the louder the screeches and bangs emanating from the bay entrance.

Tromping boots approach from the left, and another row of soldiers forms a line across the intersection. They blink repeatedly, dazzled by powerful light coming from the bay.

"FIRE!" Thompson yells.

Brick, Gun, and Geek trigger a withering barrage. Armored soldiers stumble back from the onslaught, colliding with a large group of plainly dressed blueskins running by behind them. Shrieks and yelps pierce the air.

The mass tangles and collapses in the middle of the intersection. Wide mouths shout their terror. Glassy eyes hunt and search for help or escape.

From far beyond the braying, struggling pile, a massive slug bashes Thompson's shoulder, twisting him completely around. Repeat hits to his back rip through the sacks of media records, exploding them into glittering shards as the Gun is hammered to the deck.

Argo and Beckert trace lines of fire to another barricade far beyond the intersection. Weapon flashes reveal the structure like a series of photographs. Brick and Geek trigger return shots, hits sparking against sturdy plating.

Rectangular lamps illuminate above the distant barricade with blinding intensity. Argo's and Beckert's vision wash out completely and they dive behind the struggling pile of blueskins.

"Gun," Argo calls, "are you injured?"

Thompson answers with a groan. He rolls himself onto his belly, favoring his impacted shoulder, lays his rifle over the thrashing heap, and triggers at the dazzling lights. Lamps burst with a spray of orange sparks

From his position on the floor, Argo looks back at his leader and sees a deep gouge in the Gun's shoulder armor. Spidery cracks radiate from it.

"*Gun,*" Argo repeats.

Thompson crawls stiffly toward the intersection.

"Take out that barricade," Thompson wheezes.

A panicked blueskin wriggles free of the heap. Beckert puts a round into its leg and it drops onto the pile again.

"Lieutenant," Beckert calls, pointing at the Brick's bandolier. "Use the big boom."

Argo takes one of the apple-sized spheres from his bandolier. He looks at it, unsure how to use it.

"Like this," Beckert instructs, pulling a device from his own bandolier. Cradling it in his palm, he taps the top with his thumb, and traces a half circle counter clockwise. A semicircle glows from the trail of his thumb.

"That's the timer."

He waits for Argo to mimic the action.

"Now tap twice, and throw."

Argo and Beckert double tap the tops and fling the buzzing devices down the long, dark hallway.

Rapid fire opens from the distant barricade. Amazingly, one of the shots connects with a sphere and it splits without detonating. The other bounces twice and skates all the way to the base of the barricade. Angered shouts echo down the hall as defenders retreat from the imminent blast.

The hallway flares with a light more brilliant than the lamps, compacting ceiling, walls, and deck plates into adjacent levels. A terrible shudder passes the floor's length, tossing blueskins and Operators into the air; and a gale force wind blows them all back several meters.

Argo sits up, astonished, then climbs to his feet.

Thompson pulls himself from beneath a limp soldier. He shakes his head, trying to clear his blurry vision, and lays his rifle over a mound of blueskin flesh. He leans on the pile, searching the distance for hint of the enemy.

"Grenades, left and right corridor," he orders.

Argo takes two bulbs in each hand, passing a pair to Beckert.

"I have left, you have right," the Brick commands. Beckert and Argo activate the bulbs and chuck them around the corners.

"*Cover!*" Argo snarls.

Blasts shudder left and right corridors a fraction of a second apart. Thick smoke billows into the intersection with a rain of fragments.

Thompson jumps to his feet and slides his rifle around the corner to his right. A parabola of intense lamps shines at him from inside the bay. Between him and the lamps is a staggered set of blockades.

He triggers at one of the lamps, exploding it spectacularly. Before he can trigger again, withering small arms fire pours onto him. Then a hole burns through the corner and carves a divot out of his left arm. His legs spring reactively, propelling him away from the corner as chugging shots burn hole after hole through the wall.

Once the shots subside, Thompson glances at his arm. Armor above his elbow is cut away in a cylindrical notch four centimeters wide. The notch curves through cauterized flesh, which cracks and seeps blood.

Argo and Beckert cautiously approach, and the Geek points at how light from the bay streams through the perforations in long, glowing shafts.

Argo studies the angles of smoky light, realizing they point toward their origin. As his visor traces the lines of light and plots a location, the Brick thumbs up his cannon's output, plugs the muzzle of his weapon into one of the holes, and triggers a full output stream.

Crackle of thunder *booms* from the bay, and the intense light dims considerably.

Argo's eyes burn with murderous intent as he rounds the corner, triggering stream after stream into the staggered blockades.

Thompson moves into the intersection behind Argo, aiming toward the blasted barricade, rifle blazing at any moving heat source. Shards of media records snap and crunch underfoot.

Beckert looks down at the litter of shattered media records. Thousands of hours of human history, memory, and experience are strewn the floor, irretrievably lost.

"*Keep pressure on*!" Thompson yells.

Beckert hurtles back from distraction, chases after his teammates, and triggers at the slightest hint of enemy movement. One pistol fires dry. He drops the clip and reloads.

"Last mag!" he shouts.

"Find a replacement!" Thompson yells back between grunts.

Argo and Thompson duck behind the switchback obstacles, alternately shooting and moving as withering fire hammers the barricades.

Beckert clips a pistol to his back and searches the floor. At his feet, two soldiers overlap, weapons still slung over their shredded torsos. The Geek takes both weapons and throws the straps over his head then walks backwards after his team, aiming both pistols to the rear.

Uneven terrain of corpses trips him, and he stumbles back onto the spongy bodies. Tracers and energy beams rip the air above, hissing and crackling through space he occupied a split second ago.

"*Cover*!" Argo's deep voice bellows.

Beckert scuttles to the blockades in a combination back crawl, backstroke. The sturdy barrier thumps violently, jolting him away as though in rejection. Fragments rain over him.

"Geek! Move up!" Thompson orders.

Beckert sits up from his supine pose. "Aye, sir!" With his feet beneath him, he springs up into the dense smoke, lighting atop the blockade wall. Entrance to the flight deck is only ten meters away, its doors battered, perforated, and jammed half open.

Thompson and Argo continue their blazing advance, helmets and chests glowing with absorbed energy.

Beckert leaps from blockade to blockade, skipping across the tops and jumping down on the right side of the entryway. He slides on his knees behind the twisted door.

"In position," Beckert radios. He crosses his arms at the wrist, pistols pointing left and right, pokes them past the bent doorway, triggering to the sides full-auto and clearing unseen defenders. The *tick-tick-tick* from the pistols announces the end of his ammunition, and he clips them onto his back. Raising a knee, the Geek takes one of the enemy rifles from around his neck and aims it into the smoldering bay.

"Committing."

"*Clear above, Geek*! *CLEAR ABOVE*," Thompson shouts, vaulting over the last blockade.

As Beckert pulls the weapon to his shoulder, something drops straight down between his knees and sticks like a lump of wet clay.

"GEEK!" Thompson yells.

The lump detonates, launching Beckert into the ceiling and smashing Thompson flat. The Gun's vision doubles. Dazed, deafened, he sits up amid the smoke and gawks through his cracked and functionless visor. Air in his helmet grows instantly stale, smothering him. He lifts the seal of his broken faceplate, taking a lungful of acrid smoke, and searches for his rifle. Instead, he finds Beckert's ankle. He gives his comrade a shake to rouse him. There is less resistance than there should be. He tugs on the leg as his vision merges, and the whole leg slides toward him like a gory mop.

A burly figure drops down from above the entrance, silhouetted by light from the bay, with a heavy pistol in one hand and a crackling blade in the other. It spots Thompson and aims.

Argo howls from the blockade, hurling his spent cannon at the creature. The orange-eyed warrior staggers back from the hit, recovers quickly, and triggers at the charging Brick.

Argo's agile feint diverts the killing shot from the center of his head to his ear, burning completely through his helmet and charring his face. The Brick lowers his shoulders and spreads his arms for a tackling clinch. Unable to side step the Brick's wide reach, the bodyguard is snared and Argo slams it to the deck.

The creature grunts with the weight driven into its gut, but its eyes focus with zeal. It curls its wrist, hooking the pistol toward Argo's head again. The Brick leans toward it and backhands the pistol away. With the big man's weight off balance, the creature rotates and plunges its shimmering blade into Argo's side.

Argo shudders as the crackling blade sears flesh. He stiffens, hands wracked, head thrown back, screaming through his nose. The creature shoves Argo's stiffened bulk aside then sits astride him. It pulls the blade from the Operator's ribs and takes it two handed, pointing at Argo's face.

Still clutching Beckert's leg, Thompson hurls the limb at the alien, wet end slopping the creature's snout. The leg glances off, not harming it, but orange eyes lift with malice. Wary but confident the creature rises to meet its new challenger, Argo's blood boiling on the crackling blade.

Thompson fakes a jab, drawing a swift counter strike. The Gun slides just enough so the blade skitters across his torso and he steps in close, trapping the creature's knife arm in his left armpit. He opens his right hand and jams it under the creature's jaw, gripping the wide throat. Continuing forward, he lifts with the gripping hand, sweeps the feet, and slams his opponent's head to the deck.

The creature snarls from the jarring hit, yet does not flinch. It clutches at Thompson's unlatched faceplate with its free hand, getting a claw beneath it and lifting. Orange eyes spread wide with delight, as if appreciating a practical joke.

"*Da-oma Kachi-in? PAH!*"

With a flex of muscular tail, the bodyguard rolls over onto Thompson, breaks the Gun's grip of his throat, and pounds the Operator's face. Keeping the creature's knife arm trapped,

Thompson hooks his right hand behind his opponent's head, slides treads of his boots to his backside, and springs explosively, flipping the clinched fighters head over heels.

Thompson scrambles atop his flailing enemy and reinforces his hold on the trapped arm. He braces his left arm in the crook of his right, and lays his right hand on top of the creature's trapped arm. With a growl, he arches his back, hyper extending the elbow.

The fierce blueskin's mouth gapes, teeth bared, howling with pain and rage, blade clattering from its grip. It punches, thrashes, bucks, and strikes to be free. Hits glance off Thompson's helmet, claws rake the exposed skin of his face, but the Gun ignores the minor abuse, intent on the sizzling blade beside him. In a blur, he spins around, snatches the weapon from the floor, and stabs it to the hilt under the creature's chin. Crackling energy burns through its brain, launching powerful convulsions. Orange eyes cross, as though drawn to the intruding blade by magnetism. The knife ceases its crackling, and the convulsing bodyguard falls still.

Another bodyguard rushes into the doorway. Before Thompson can react, a flash from his right drops it dead. The Gun turns and sees Argo crouched with his long rifle.

The Brick heaves the weapon to his comrade and rises, one hand covering his leaking side, then stoops to pick up his cannon and throws the wide strap over his shoulder.

Thompson gets to his feet, checking his weapon and finding a few shots left. His eyes are vacant.

"Where's Geek?" Argo wheezes.

Thompson steps over and plucks grenades from Argo's belt. "Which part?" he says coldly.

Argo spins in place, searching among the spots of warmth around him. He finds the detached leg.

"Oh, no..."

Thompson strides toward the bay entrance. One by one, he arms his grenades and hurls them out into the smoky bay. Renewed shouts and weapon fire pour from the haze, abbreviated by sequential detonations.

Argo's search becomes frantic, following the gore until he finds his comrade. The Geek's left arm is a mess of broken bone and charred, ragged skin. Both legs are gone, one at the knee, the other mid thigh. Torso plating is smashed with multiple gaps down to the mesh underlayers. Only his right arm is intact, draping to one side, palm up like a beggar's.

Argo checks around for the enemy, crouches down, and lifts the Geek's shattered faceplate. Beckert's eyes are open with clouded corneas and bright red sclera. Blood rolls from his nose into and around his open mouth.

*"Oh, Beckert, no..."*

Beckert's eyes turn blindly toward the voice. His lips quiver over cracked teeth.

"A-Argo? Is that you?" He swallows with effort. "I can't see..."

Argo blinks in amazement.

"Don't move! Gun!" he radios, "I found him, he's alive! Beginning surgery...Gun?" Argo looks for his comrade and no longer finds him in the entryway. Fresh explosions reverberate from inside the bay, weapons discharging in all directions.

Thompson's distant voice shouts from the bay, *"Brick! Get out here!"*

Argo opens his mouth to decline when the sound of sprinting reinforcements spills in from behind the blockades. Palming a sphere from his bandolier, Argo scowls and traces a quarter circle on the top of it. Gauging their distance, he lobs the sphere into the intersection, scoops Beckert, and rushes into the bay.

A punishing blast gusts from the entryway, sending the battered doors careening across the deck and shoving the Brick to the floor. When he presses up, his visor glows with hot spots of flame, savaged metal, and bodies.

Weapon fire sparks and scorches the deck plates around him, zeroing in fast. Argo jumps up with his tattered comrade and skids behind a long baggage conveyor. Multiple soldiers lie on the deck, tongues hanging from open mouths, skulls burst open from

Thompson's rifle shots.

Bright lights from the high ceiling shine into the gray-white haze, creating a diffuse glow. Argo's head swivels, searching through the bright fog for his comrade and the enemy. Neither is in sight, but the thunder and crack of combat rolls close by.

*Where's our ride outta here?*

Transports form orderly rows along extensive lanes. Gleaming in their midst, and standing much taller, are two polished vessels. Angular, stylish lines suggest performance and refinement. Nacelles at the ends of thick wings waver with heat and energy. The ramp is down on the nearer one, littered with prone figures.

*That must be it.*

The Brick pulls a compartment from his rack, draws three cinch straps from the box, and whips them around each of Beckert's dribbling stumps. He cinches the last tourniquet when a slug slams into his shoulder, twisting him to the deck.

"Gun!" he shouts.

High caliber shots clang and ricochet against the heavy conveyor, tracing a line toward Beckert. Argo, still clutching a cinch strap, yanks the Geek to him and lays over him. Slugs bash into the Brick's back, exploding compartments of his rack.

A black form rushes from the smoke with a short weapon, triggering into the haze, then leaps behind the conveyor, lands on a pile of shot-up luggage, and rolls to one side.

Argo stares at deep scorches in Thompson's armor and the notch in his left arm. His chest plate glows with absorbed heat. The Gun's rifle hangs from his shoulder by the strap, and the tall Operator cradles an alien weapon like a toy in his hands.

"Thanks," Argo says breathlessly. "I need cover for surgery—"

"*Negative*," Thompson interrupts, staring at the body-strewn ramp of the nearby vessel. As Thompson watches, blueskins tug and pull at bodies blocking the ramp. The Gun aims his captured weapon and snipes. Three figures collapse, the rest flee.

"That's Beckert's ride," Thompson says, "and it's trying to leave without him."

Argo peeks over the conveyor at the gleaming vessel. Two blueskin pilots are seated behind the wide windshield. One touches a button overhead and the ramp struggles to close. Bodies drape over the rising edges, sliding off and bouncing limply on the deck.

Thompson tosses a bulky pistol to his comrade.

"Take this. I'll cover you. Go now!"

Glancing at Beckert then at the pistol, Argo vaults over the conveyor. Thompson leaps over the conveyor in the opposite direction, triggering into the smoke and drawing fire while Argo trots to the closing ramp.

The Brick hunches and leans forward, pistol raised beside his head. Shots streak from the haze, smashing his legs, making him wobble and stagger. His visor tracks the incoming shots, highlighting where to aim, and he fires the pistol in answer. For such a small weapon, the output is devastating.

Suppressing pain of his many injuries, Argo catches the edge of the closing ramp, hauls his bulk onto it, and hobbles up into a luxurious passenger compartment appointed with plush couches, beverage taps, and misters in opulent hues. His boot treads sink deep into light-colored floor padding, staining it with soot and blood.

Slipping his cannon strap from his shoulder, he lets the spent weapon drop to the floor, and he follows a short corridor toward the front of the vessel. Flimsy doors attempt to block his advance, and he barrels straight through them to a closed bulkhead. Keeping momentum, he slams his fist into the bulkhead with all of his might. The sturdy door caves under his powerful fist, curling at one edge. He slides his fingers in the gap and rips the whole bulkhead aside.

Thin beam weapons flash at him from the cockpit, burning into his armor. Argo triggers his pistol twice, and the weapon explodes the pilots' torsos with sickening *pops*. Organs spill wetly to the floor.

Argo climbs up into the cramped cockpit. Both pilots drape over the side of their chairs, torsos gaping. Blue spray mars the windshield and controls. The Brick seizes the bodies one at a time and hurls them out then peers through the blood-spattered windshield at a smoke-filled bay. Small fires lick up from baggage and machines, filling the air with smutty fumes. Civilians and soldiers alike mill about like zombies, all sense hammered out of them by repeated explosions.

Another blast to the right buckles the front landing strut of a transport, dropping its nose to the metal deck. The back of it pivots up like a seesaw, ripping a connected fuel hose in half. Frosty clouds of vapor gush from the severed hose.

"Gun," Argo radios, "vessel is secure…"

There is no response, only the periodic *ping* and *crack* of gunfire. Argo searches through the windscreen for a trace of his comrade. Even with the aid of his visor, he finds none.

"Gun, *respond.*"

Nothing.

The Brick flies from the cockpit, down the stairs, through the plush cabin. He crouches at the top of the ramp, and presses the button to lower it. Wary of attack, he lowers himself flat and aims his pistol through the ramp's widening gap. Though he paid no mind to it on the way in, there is a dense group of bodies at the base of the ramp. One of them is wriggling, trying to pull free from beneath a heap of bodyguards.

There is still no reply from Thompson, and Beckert lies unguarded, mangled, helpless. An icy sensation grips his chest.

*The mission is over.*

"No!" he growls. "*NOT YET.*" He breathes as deeply as his knife wound allows and limps down the ramp.

A shape emerges from the haze. Argo turns on it, pistol aimed, almost triggering but for the mottled gray of its exterior.

"Brick!" Thompson croaks. The Gun lopes stiffly to a halt in front of Argo, cradling what remains of Beckert. Dark fluid is splashed across the tall Operator's hands, forearms, feet, and face. Deep holes perforate his armor. Plates at his thigh, shoulder, neck, and elbow are missing entirely. He passes the Geek over and snatches the last two grenades from Argo's waist.

"Get him interfaced," the Gun rasps, "we're leaving now."

"Interfaced?" Argo counters. "He's barely alive!"

A barrage of weapon fire opens up from the entryway, pounding into Thompson's back and slamming him face first into the ramp. Argo turns and races with Beckert into the ship, shots glancing and smashing the back of his legs.

Thompson presses up from the ramp, his back burning with searing pain. He tries to run, but his left leg accepts no weight. He looks down at it, finding a circular hole burned straight through the thigh.

He turns to the entryway, where fresh soldiers file through and fan out. All carry long, heavy rifles.

The Gun crushes his eyes shut and drags himself down to the pile of blueskins by the overturned luggage train. All are dead, except one, and he looks into the feminine eyes of the most regal blueskin he has ever seen—the one he saw stride without hurry across the hallway earlier. Her bodyguards lay atop her in a shredded pile, having shielded her from the blast. Now she is trapped beneath their massive frames.

She holds a wound at her shoulder with a delicate claw and holds his gaze with an expression of remorse, pity, and sadness. She shakes her head softly.

Thompson arms the grenades in his hands and flings them out at the advancing soldiers. Hoots and shouts precede ferocious detonations.

He grabs the elegant creature under the jaw and drags her from the pile. One handed, he lifts her in front of him and snakes an arm under her chin. Using his free hand, he locks the knee joint of his perforated leg armor and stands on it like a stilt.

Dozens of soldiers run from the smog, long rifles aimed, saffron eyes glaring malevolently. Thompson slides his rifle from his shoulder, and grips it by the barrel. The bayonet extends just above his fist, smothered in dark blood. He holds it to her throat in warning and backs his way up the ramp.

Soldiers slide closer, keeping weapons aimed, shouting in rage and fury. Dozens more pour through the entrances, wheeling in barricades and tripod-mounted weapons.

Once inside the plush interior, Thompson strikes a button with his elbow, and the ramp rises from the deck. He drags his captive into the luxurious passenger cabin and hurls her at the sofas. She staggers off balance, trips over a low table, and plows with her wounded shoulder into the cushions with a yelp. Her expressive eyes turn to the ceiling, and she pants in short breaths.

"You," Thompson rasps, pointing at her, "stay *here*." He drops his pointing finger to the floor.

She looks at him cautiously, conveys gentility with open hands, and presses herself into the soft couch.

Thompson follows Argo's tracks, dragging the butt of his rifle and marking his own trail in black, red, and blue. He shuffles through the corridor, pausing at the exploded pilots. Sounds of compressed air *hiss* from the cockpit.

"Brick…" Thompson looks up from the pilots to the cockpit and sways on his good leg. "S-s-status."

Argo perks up, peering over the short staircase. A tube plugged into his neck flows with bright red fluid.

"Geek is interfaced, stabilizing." Argo looks down at his patient and the hissing of compressed air continues.

"Why didn't you respond?" the Brick asks.

Thompson stiff legs his way over the corpses, tapping a blood-smeared fingertip against his smashed faceplate.

"Radio…knocked out," he rasps.

The Gun steps onto the short staircase. Beckert's charred left arm lies amputated before him. The Geek himself is reclined against the center console between pilot seats. One lanyard from his HDI connects to the console, another is plugged into Argo's labset. Hardening foam covers Beckert's leg stumps like the caps of giant mushrooms.

The tube at Argo's neck runs down to a small pump and continues on to Beckert's neck port. A counter on the pump ticks off cubic centimeters of transfused blood.

Argo holds a canister to the Geek's arm stump and applies a large quantity of expanding foam. The foam hisses out and bonds to the exposed flesh. Before the foam hardens, Argo slaps a square of metallic mesh over it. He bends the mesh corners up against the broken armor plating and tack welds them in place.

"Get 'im home, Argo." Thompson's eyes flutter, and he falls backwards off the stairs.

Argo rises suddenly, staring down at his collapsed comrade lying over the exploded pilots.

"Gun!"

Torn between two patients, Argo stops the pump and disconnects the tube at his neck. He leaps off the staircase, thudding beside Thompson. Tearing at the Gun's armor latches, he rips the ruined plating away. Thompson's face, chest, and abdomen look like they have been repeatedly impaled by a hot poker. He is not breathing. There is no pulse.

Argo slides Thompson onto his back, begins heart compressions, ventilates with firm breaths, and resumes compressions.

A rumble deep within the vessel rises in pitch and smoothes into a constant hum.

"Engines up to temperature," Beckert advises dreamily. "Nav calibrating." The Geek's blind eyes dart erratically. "Huh. All the wireless just shut down."

Argo continues his efforts without reply.

"They've restored ship-wide control," the Geek warns.

Argo still does not reply.

"Lieutenant, we have to go! Now!"

"*Then take us out!*" Argo snarls.

Beckert's lips peel back from broken teeth. "I can't see... You have to!"

In agony, Argo leaves his dying friend and re-enters the cockpit. He takes one look at the cramped pilot seat and rips it savagely from the mount. The big man swivels and hurls the seat down the corridor, well past Thompson.

Settling into the cleared space, he wraps his large hands around the control wheel; but he pulls too hard and the craft leaps up, smashing against the bay ceiling. Argo steadies himself after the jarring collision, relaxing his grip. He turns the wheel, and the craft smoothly pivots. Weapon fire raps against the windshield from all directions.

When the craft comes around, Argo at last understands Beckert's alarm. The large shutters of the bay are rolling toward each other. The Brick's jaw clenches and he thrusts the craft forward, shoving smaller parked transports aside. Between narrowing shutters, the planet's horizon looms larger than it should be, and a faint pinkish-orange aura frames the lower edge. Fiery debris streaks past the closing shutters, dashing up and to the right.

"*Why are we in atmosphere, Geek?*"

"Explain later! Go, *go!*"

Argo throttles full, inundating the bay in flame, and the ship hurtles between closing shutters.

Free of the hangar's gravity, Argo drifts up from the floor. Still gripping the controls, his movement pitches the craft down radically, flipping it end over end. The view rolls from planet to space like a slot machine.

"Geek! *Help!*"

Beckert battles through fatigue, sickness, his own dismemberment. Holding onto the console with his one hand, he presses his stuttering mind into the ship's basic instrumentation. Virtual gauges assemble as three-dimensional constructs, gimbals tumbling wildly. Beckert extends his consciousness, momentarily overriding the controls.

"Let go of the stick!" Beckert shouts.

Argo releases the controls, and reaches overhead to brace himself against the low ceiling. In moments, the craft ends its sickening flips and levels out. Argo feels his gut drop inside him as gravity enhancement comes on-line. Thompson and the dead pilots flop to the deck.

Beckert gasps with discomfort, belching blood over his lower lip. "Lieutenant, take over!"

Argo's big hands seize the controls again. He hauls smoothly and the planetary horizon drops out of sight. Innumerable pinpoints of light speckle the dark sky, majestic and serene.

An impact rattles the vessel, then another. Argo cuts the wheel and the ship responds nimbly, jinking and banking with every flick of the stick. In other circumstances, he would be lost in admiration of the craft's performance, but all of his concentration is pressed into keeping ahead of enemy fire.

"I need a heading!" Argo snarls. His beefy limbs snap the stick back and forth. Crackling bolts, tracers, and missiles streak by the windshield. One connects, shuddering the entire vessel.

Argo turns an anxious eye to the hemispherical Nav display. Below, the colossal ship is leveling out in the upper atmosphere. Long streaks of plasma and vaporized metal shine behind it. The giant ship's escorts, surprisingly distant, have formed a wide parabola and rush to intercept. Clouds of ordnance pour from them, trying to claw Argo's vessel from the sky.

"Geek?"

Beckert's head lolls with Argo's sudden banks and turns. "I can't keep up with your course changes!"

A formation of ships de-mask directly ahead. Long bow struts are fully extended, and a shimmering field undulates between warships like the surface of a black and bottomless ocean.

Argo dives toward the planet. Unmasked ships pursue, taking formation with others, and shimmering fields merge into a wide dome, shepherding the small craft toward the planet.

"*We don't have to get home*," Argo shouts desperately, "*JUST GET US OUT OF HERE!*"

A punishing hit triggers an internal explosion, and the ship skids to the right. Argo pins the wheel to the left just to keep the ship flying straight. He aims for a thin gap between the descending dome and the planet's atmosphere.

Shots connect more frequently, battering the sturdy vessel.

"Course free of obstructions," Beckert announces. Nacelles

at the wing tips flare brilliantly, and the ship jumps thousands of kilometers ahead in an instant.

"Hold steady," the Geek instructs. Argo holds the controls in a vice grip, maintaining a straight and level path. The planet is smaller behind them. The moon looms humongous and bright.

"Calculating jump," Beckert monotones.

Argo watches the Nav display anxiously as it resets. Earth shows as a distant sphere. The moon resolves in large detail.

Warships, bristling with weapons, jump into view with a flash. Struts extend from the bows and dark energy weaves between them.

"Jump set." Beckert announces.

Wing nacelles flare as the sleek craft turns robotically to a distant point and streaks into the void.

THEIR STORY CONTINUES IN

## *THE EXHAUSTED DEAD*

AVAILABLE IN SOFTCOVER AND KINDLE E-BOOK

LOG ON TO

WWW.CADREONEPUBLISHING.COM

FOR NEWS AND UPDATES

CADRE ONE

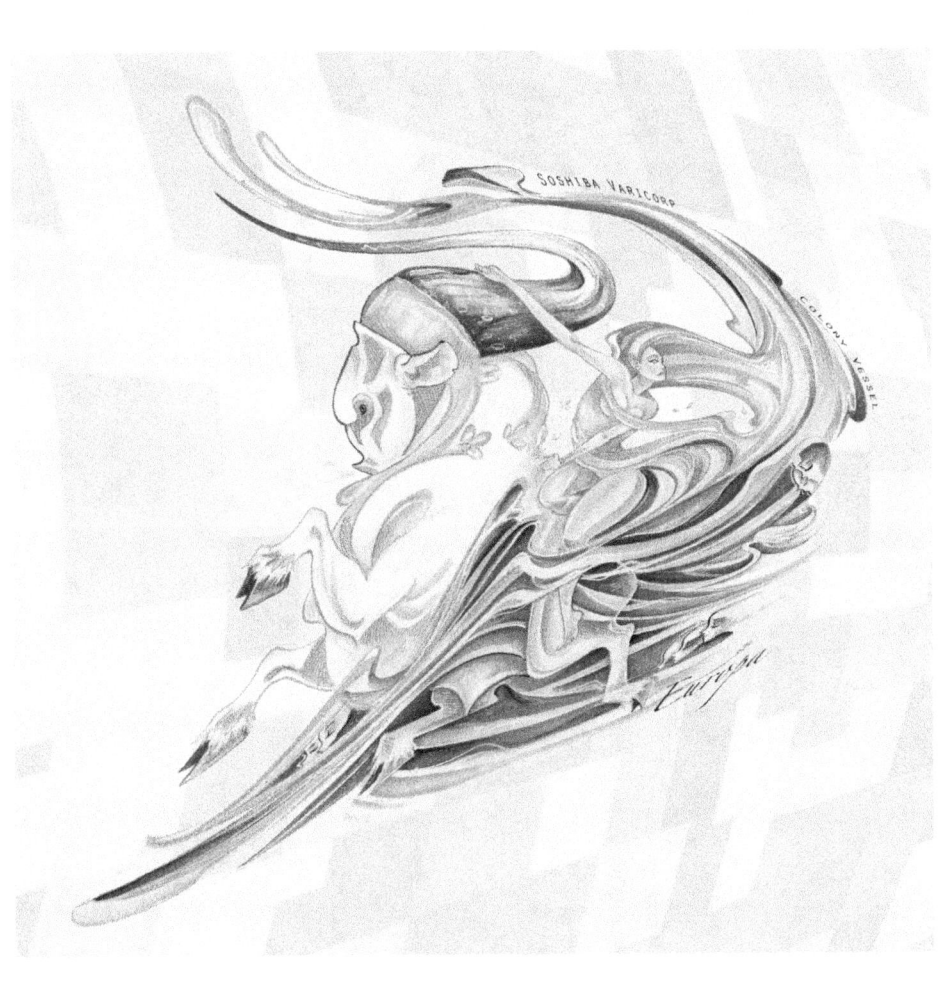

# ABOUT THE AUTHOR

A child of the Space Age, F. A. Farnham has always been passionate about high technology. Impatient to live in a futuristic world, he eagerly consumes any scientific article or Science Fiction novel that promises a glimpse. Herbert, Heinlein, and Huxley are three of his greatest influences.

*Angry Ghosts* (2009) is the first of a five book Science Fiction series, which includes *Black Hawks From a Blue Sun* (2010), *The Exhausted Dead* (2012), *Of Mortal Creatures* (2015), and *Plasma Rain* (2019).

Farnham's short story, *Tuckahoe Marble*, was selected by SciFi Saturday Night for their macabre anthology, *My Peculiar Family* (2016).

His latest work, *Panda, the Heart, and the Mirror* (2020) is an illustrated parable about love and redemption for children and adults.

When not working he loves to travel, enjoying the variety of people as much as the landscapes. Born in Newport, RI, Farnham now lives with his dog, Hamlet, in Pflugerville, TX.

www.ingramcontent.com/pod-product-compliance
Lightning Source LLC
Chambersburg PA
CBHW070808180626
46818CB00001B/152